I've Got This Brother

To Karen —
"Keep Writing!"
Marilyn DeMars
12/02/06

I'VE GOT THIS BROTHER

Marilyn DeMars

iUniverse, Inc.
New York Lincoln Shanghai

I've Got This Brother

All Rights Reserved © 2004 by Marilyn M. DeMars

No part of this book may be reproduced or transmitted in any form or by any means, graphic, electronic, or mechanical, including photocopying, recording, taping, or by any information storage retrieval system, without the written permission of the publisher.

iUniverse, Inc.

For information address:
iUniverse, Inc.
2021 Pine Lake Road, Suite 100
Lincoln, NE 68512
www.iuniverse.com

ISBN: 0-595-32561-0

Printed in the United States of America

For my brother, Ronny.
A brother beyond all brothers,
long passed into the afterlife.
I miss you dearly.

Acknowledgements

Again…thanks, Dick,
for putting your head and your heart
together with mine on the editing.

When I was a kid,
my dad had this wonderful, old, double-door
garage. It was full of character, charm,
yesteryear's simplicity, his car, his yard tools,
and his adored personality.
Thanks, Dad, for this picture.

Chapter 1

▼

Tracy stood looking at the diamond ring Mark had moments ago slipped onto her finger. She couldn't feel happy about his proposal. Something threatened it. There was an enduring problem in her life that she'd never told him about, but was going to have to now despite the probable outcome.

Outside of Martino's Restaurant, where they'd just had dinner, it was late, cold and snowing. The streets of New York City were abnormally quiet.

"Your non answer is beginning to sound like a no," Mark eventually said.

Tracy lifted her eyes to meet with his. This man, who looked so remarkably like a young Kevin Costner, and generally possessed the same charming manner as did the actor, was now sadly broken.

"I haven't said anything yet," she told him.

"Exactly."

"It's complicated."

"Yes or no, how complicated is that?"

"Because you don't understand."

"Want to give me a try?"

The wind rippled Tracy's dark hair trailing out from beneath her knit cap and sent icy chills down her neck. She turned up her coat collar. "Sure, yes, we need to talk, Mark. But not here. I'm freezing. Let's go home."

"Your place or mine?"

"Mine is closer."

"Right." Mark started in that direction.

Pulling on her gloves as she walked, Tracy had to work hard at keeping up with him. "Hey, come on, I can't walk this fast, Mark."

He was taking this hard and she didn't blame him. She'd wrecked his proposal, possibly their whole relationship.

They stopped at the red traffic light on the corner. The wind seemed to be coming from all directions, wildly swirling the falling snow. Cars moved slowly in the thickening accumulation.

"Tracy…" Mark began like the beginning of a difficult sentence.

The light changed to green and she started ahead of him into the intersection.

Now it was he who had to work at keeping up with her. He took her hand and matched his stride to hers. "You're scaring me here, you know that? You're really scaring me."

"I know. I'm sorry. I'm scared too."

"The ring, if you don't like it we can get you a different one."

"The ring is fine. I *love* the ring. This isn't about the ring."

She looked at Mark. He looked at her and hunched his shoulders up about his neck.

They walked fast against the wind. The Howell Hotel, where Tracy stayed when making her periodic visits to town as the hotel chain's traveling field manager, was three blocks from Martino's. The weather was decent when they'd started out from Mark's apartment earlier that evening, five blocks the other way from Martino's, but leaving the restaurant they found it colder and snowing.

When they got to the hotel they burst inside, brushing off their coats and stomping their feet.

The desk clerk welcomed them. "Good evening, Ms. Lawton, Mr. Rydell."

Both returned the man's familiar greeting as they crossed the posh lobby to the elevators. Tracy pulled off her cap, sending more carried-in snow flitting and dissolving into the warm air. Mark pressed the service button. They rode to ninth floor in silence.

When they entered her room, she switched on a light, stepped out of her wet shoes, drew the drapes shut, and turned on a second light.

Mark closed the door, saying, "I'm sorry about proposing to you on a cold street corner."

Tracy stopped doing things. "Sorry?"

"Not for proposing," he said, "for the location of it. I'd been trying to find the right moment all evening through dinner only there never seemed to be one."

"Your timing was nice. I loved being proposed to in the snow."

"Really? Huh, I didn't get that."

"It was *my* timing that was bad, not yours." Tracy took off her coat and laid it over the desk chair. Mark did the same with his jacket. She had a beautiful room.

A large sitting area as you came in, done in mauves and greens, and a cozy bedroom area just beyond. The Howell Hotel always put her up well.

Mark was wearing that wonderful heather-gray sweater of his. How Tracy loved that sweater on him. She wanted to snuggle against him right now and pretend everything was fine. But instead, she took off his ring and gave it back to him.

He stared at the symbol of undying love in his open hand. "Well, I'd say *this* is a definite no."

"We need to back up a little," she said.

Mark shoved the ring into his pants pocket, like one more coin to his loose change, and sat down on the couch.

Tracy sat beside him, tucking her cold, stocking feet beneath her.

"Don't tell me you didn't see the marriage bit coming," he said, as if he'd figured out where she was coming from but hoped it wasn't true.

"No. I mean yes. I mean—"

"Come on, Tracy, you live in Minnesota, I live in New York. The only time we see each other is when you're here on business. And then it's back and forth between my apartment and your hotel room. Don't you want more than that for us? I do. I want a life, a real life for us."

"A real life," she tested the sound of it.

They weren't kids. Tracy was thirty-four, Mark thirty-eight. They had a good relationship. Happy. Solid. Honest, except for what she'd been keeping from him. "I love you, Mark," she said.

"But?" he asked.

She should have told him about this problem of hers long before now. But their relationship had started off with such sweet simplicity six months ago that never, at any point since, had she wanted to risk hampering it. Tonight, with his proposal, risk gave way to necessity.

She thought about how they'd met. In Central Park. She'd been walking and he'd been sitting on a bench writing on a yellow legal pad. Just as she approached he ripped off the top page, scrunched it in frustration, and tossed it aimlessly. The yellow ball landed directly in her path. She stopped, picked it up, opened it, and read the entirety of it aloud. "Chapter one, page one." Then added wryly, "Ahhh...a writer."

This guy, who looked so amazingly like Kevin Costner, gave her a cute Costner sort of grin as he took the wrinkled paper she handed him.

"Nice beginning," she teased about the diminutive piece of work. "Stick with it and maybe it'll grown into something."

His blue eyes held with her brown ones as he stood up, saying, "My last book grew into something."

"Last book?" She felt pretty stupid.

He nodded, doing that winsome grin of his again. *Street Winder*. On the best-seller list a while back."

She knew her face was red. "Published. Best-seller. Wow. I'm sorry."

"For my success?"

"No, for my not knowing."

"That's okay. Sorry my paper landed in your way."

"There's a fine for littering, you know."

He pretended to be worried. "You're not a cop, are you?"

"No." She laughed.

"Good." He laughed too.

Tracy usually didn't go around striking up conversations with strangers, but she'd fallen head over heels into this one. "I'm a field manager for Howell Hotels," she said. "New York City is just one of the locations I travel to."

"Field manager?" he questioned.

"I check up on things, make periodic managerial reports to take back to Howard Howell in Minnesota, owner of nine Howell Hotels."

"Sounds like you're a busy person, yet here you are strolling in the park."

"And you're a writer, yet here you are hanging out on a park bench."

Somewhere amidst their exchange of easy smiles and eminent interest in one another, he asked her to go have coffee with him and she accepted. Thus their relationship began. Fast, effortlessly, out of the blue. After she'd left New York to go back home, they'd kept up with one another by way of long distance phone calls, letters and a second get together when her job brought her back in the fall.

Two days ago, amidst winter's fiercest month of January, Tracy's work once again returned her to the Big Apple and to Mark and to the exciting affirmation of just how much they'd come to mean to one another. Everything was enjoyable and perfect. Until the proposal. Which made her face the fact that she could no longer put off telling him about…

"What?" Mark urged from his waiting. "You going to tell me, or what?"

Tracy fingered the sleeve of his sweater and took a deep breath.

"What?" he asked again, as if he were already sure he wasn't going to like it.

"Mark, there's something about my life I haven't told you yet."

"I'm listening."

"It could make a big difference as to whether we can have any future together."

"Sounds serious."
She gave a serious nod.
"Go ahead," he said bravely, "I can take it."
"Mark, I…I've got this brother."

Chapter 2

▼

"My brother, Evan, he lives with me," Tracy told Mark in the tone of a confession.

He was relieved, as though he'd been expecting something far worse. "So you never told me you had a brother, I won't hold that against you."

"Not just any brother. Evan is different."

Mark cocked an eyebrow. "Different?"

"He doesn't go out."

"Out. You mean on dates?"

"Out. Of the house. Ever." There, it hadn't been easy but she'd said it.

Mark got up from the couch and walked around the room, trying to absorb what he'd heard. "A homebody. A quiet one. Nothing wrong with that. I'm kind of like that myself. How old is he?"

"Twenty-six. Evan hasn't been out of the house in five years. He has agoraphobia, a fear of open places, of leaving the house."

Mark stopped pacing, and Tracy stood up before him, concluding. "Guess you don't love me so much now, huh?"

His mouth dropped. A writer with no words.

"You probably never heard of anything like this, right?" she gathered. "And don't like hearing of it now. And for sure don't want to get mixed up with someone who has this sort of problem in her family, right?"

When Mark got around to speaking for himself, he was direct but calm. "Tracy, I'm sorry about your brother. I wish you'd have told me about him sooner. I can't believe that you didn't."

"I know," she said, sheepishly. "I should have. I'm sorry. And I'm giving you this chance now to back out if you want to."

Mark's eyes widened. "You think I'd retract my feelings for you because of your brother?"

She wrung her hands together. "Well, you did say you wished I'd told you about him sooner."

He held his head and moaned. "Because I love you, Tracy, and want to share everything that's going on with you, that's all."

Mark obviously wanted this to be simple and was trying to make it be, but Evan had never been a simple matter to Tracy. She bit her bottom lip and continued fidgeting with her hands.

"Come on," Mark said, "did you really think your telling me about your brother would change things for us?"

She went over to the window, held the drapes aside, and gazed out at the still-falling snow that was softly illuminating the dark. The wind had died down and the world outside stood beautifully serene.

Mark was soon beside her. "How could you think that?"

Turning to him, Tracy meekly asked, "You're not put off by it? Because my brother's problem, agoraphobia, it's pretty strange."

Mark gave her a trust-me look and wrapped his arms around her. "I'm not put off. Hey…he's your brother."

Suddenly Tracy's world simplified in her closeness to him. "I'm sorry for doubting you. It's just that all the other men I knew had attitude problems with this."

"All?" he asked, with his face nestled against her hair. "How many is all?"

"An occasional boyfriend here and there, until they found out about Evan's problem. Then they were gone."

Mark loosened his hold of her and leaned back to see her face. "Guys left you because of your brother?"

"They, uh…well, Evan was like this obstacle they just couldn't get past."

Mark's surprise turned to adornment. "So who needed them, huh? You deserve better, some nice guy like me."

Though Tracy smiled, she was not entirely free of skepticism. "My having a brother like Evan doesn't make you think that I, too, could be a little strange? Or that our children could turn out to be?"

"Children?" Mark's face took on a glow. "Is this a yes to my proposal?"

Tracy stopped his hand from going into his pocket for the ring. "Not yet. We have to resolve this problem first."

"Evan," Mark verified. "Okay, so what does his doctor say about his situation? I would think he'd need some counseling. Maybe some medication."

"Evan refuses to see a doctor, and I've given up trying to persuade him. Anyway, other than his agoraphobia Evan's not actually sick. He feels great and is amazingly acceptant of the way his life has become."

"Acceptant?" Mark shook his head. "I can't buy that. How can he be? That's not normal."

"Evan's normal," Tracy insisted, "he just doesn't—"

"Leave the house, right," Mark affirmed.

"He's content with that."

"He needs help."

Okay, here it was, the snag. Mark was already thinking he knew more about her brother and what to do about him than she did. It swayed her, since her initial fear had been that he'd be put off by Evan's problem and might only want to steer clear of it. Now, and not all that better, he was going the opposite way of evaluating, advising, seeking solution. It wasn't what she wanted or needed, from him or anybody.

She walked across the room, rubbing the tension in her forehead. This didn't make sense. Here was a guy showing more compassion than disgust for Evan's problem, and that ironically bothered her just as much.

She turned at the desk and looked back at him. "I've been dealing with this for a long time now, Mark."

"Yeah," he said, "so I'm finding out."

"I should have told you sooner, but I didn't."

Mark stood there listening, not yet seeing the problem.

"Evan is happy and content," she continued. "I don't want advice or criticism on that. What I need from you is for you to accept my brother's state of being. And I'm hoping that when you meet him you'll be able to do that."

"But he's in Minnesota, right?" Mark hitched his chin in the direction of the Midwest.

"Yes. At our old family home in Drendal, where Evan and I grew up."

"With his agoraphobia he's okay when you go off and leave him like this?"

"Yes."

Mark rolled his hand in the air. "But if he has—"

"It's okay, he's capable," Tracy said.

"Of?" Mark pushed.

"Everything."

"Except leaving the house," he affirmed.

Sometimes, like now, Tracy felt as if she were more afflicted by Evan's phobia than he himself was. Times when she had to explain, justify, endure his phobia. Times when she felt guilty for managing poorly, and strangely enough also for times when she'd managed well. "He does fine by himself. I do feel a little guilty for leaving him, but he does fine."

"So you're supporting him, right? I mean, financially as well as emotionally."

"Yes. Of course."

"And you really feel this is helping him?" Though Mark's voice was soft, it had a critical undertone.

Tracy crossed her arms and gave a nod.

Mark studied her. "I don't know, Tracy, I don't know."

"Don't know what?" she asked.

"If you're doing right by him."

She resented Mark's doubt toward what she was doing and had done for so long. "I'm looking out for him, that's what I'm doing."

"Maybe too much," Mark suggested.

"So what would you do if it were *your* brother?"

Mark didn't need any time to think about it. "I'd kick his butt out the door and tell him to get a job, a life."

Seeing Tracy's distress, Mark came toward her adding, "But then that's Jim I speak of, not Evan. I guess I shouldn't judge Evan without actually knowing him. The thing is, Tracy, you told me about the dark secret in your life and I still want to marry you."

"Arguments always happen when I tell someone about Evan."

"We're not arguing. And I'm not anyone," he said, poking himself in the chest. "I'm me, Mark. And in spite of your brother and his phobia, I still love you and want to marry you. Let's put the ring back on your finger."

She wasn't ready for that.

"Come on," he coaxed, "we'll get married and live here in my New York apartment. I've got a great apartment, haven't I?"

"I don't want to live in New York," she said.

"I thought you liked it here."

"Evan needs me."

"I need you."

"My home is Drendal."

"My home is here."

"Evan needs me," she repeated.

"You said he manages okay by himself, so let him."

Tears welled in Tracy's eyes. "You're not accepting his problem, Mark."

"Yes, Tracy, I am. *Sort of.*"

"Because right away you're thinking that something should be done to fix him. And that's not what I want from you."

"How can you accept this problem? How can he?"

"See what I mean?" She threw up her hands and gave a huff, wishing Evan was still but a guarded secret in the back of her mind. "I shouldn't have told you about him."

"Yes, of course you should have. It's okay, honey. We're going to be fine."

Tracy didn't move away when he closed in on her this time. But while she truly loved being in his warm embrace, and was starting to feel at least somewhat convinced that everything might be okay, she found it necessary to explain, "It's only been my brother and me for a long time. Just the two of us managing his problem. And we've done okay. I just…I don't want anyone coming into my life now that might disrupt that."

"Such as me," Mark gathered coolly.

"Things have to be right between us, all three of us, before I can accept your ring."

"Like marry you, marry your brother?"

She nodded, but rephrased it. "Like seeing Evan the way I see Evan or—"

"Or?" Mark asked.

Breaking away from him now, Tracy stated her rules, "I can't marry you until you meet Evan, take some time to get to know him, and show me that you can accept him for what he is rather than for what you think he should be. That's the deal." She lifted her purse off the desk, opened it and pulled out a snapshot of her brother.

Mark took it. Looking at the picture seemed to make Evan more real to him than any of Tracy's words had thus far. "So you want me to go to Minnesota to meet him."

Tracy turned up a feeling-better grin. "Well, he couldn't come here, could he?"

"Drendal," Mark said.

"Yes."

"A small town."

"Very small."

Though Mark was obviously trying to see this her way, he was still hopelessly skeptical. "I'm a long-time New Yorker. I'm not sure I could cope in a small town, would even be able to breathe in it."

"Breathing is much easier there, believe me," she assured him.
"I always felt that a small town had—"
"You'd be going there because of Evan, not the town."
"To get to know him," Mark mocked her earnestness.
"And accept him," she said.
"In order for you to accept me."
"Yes."

As Tracy watched, waited and hoped for the best, Mark struggled with the concept. Then finally, with his face mellowing into that wonderful Costner smile of his, he asked, "Okay, so when do we go? When will you be finished here?"

"Not we," she had to tell him now. "You."

He was perplexed all over again.

"I want you to go by yourself," she said.

"Oh, Tracy, I don't know about that, my going there alone."

To Tracy, his doing this would be proof of his love and trustworthiness. And proof, more than chance, was what she needed now. "I have a lot of work ahead of me here," she said, "plus I still have the New Jersey hotel to cover before going home."

"I'll wait for you and we'll go back together," he suggested.

"No, you go on ahead of me, Mark."

"You're kidding, right?"

She gave him a pretty-please look off the tops of her eyes.

He shook his head.

"Mark?" she pleaded in a pretty-please voice.

He rolled his eyes.

"My brother is a friendly person," she said, "yet he doesn't have one friend who comes to see him. Be his friend, Mark, and then we'll see about us." Close to him again, she caressed his sweatered chest like a wishful person rubbing a genie.

"Tracy, I'm going through a writer's block right now, and I'm not sure this would be a good time for me to distract myself even more from my writing."

"Drendal is a writer's dream for unlocking a writer's block."

Mark gave it additional thought. "So you've got a computer I can use, right?"

"No," Tracy had to tell him. "Neither Evan or I have one."

"I can't *believe* you guys don't have a computer in this day and age."

"I have one at work and I travel a lot. I don't need one at home. Evan hasn't become interested in computers. Don't you have a laptop?"

"No, I don't have a laptop. And no, I'm not hauling all the components of my regular setup out there."

"Take a couple legal pads and work in longhand."

"Yeah," he sneered.

"Sorry," she said.

Mark sighed. "Well, I've got an old portable typewriter in the closet I suppose I could dust off and take with…if I even remember how to use it anymore."

"Good. I'll tell Evan you're coming, it'll be okay."

"I just don't understand your hurry," Mark said. "I mean, whether I meet him in a few days or in a couple weeks when you and I could go together?"

"Because it would be good for the both of you, just the two of you alone, getting to know one another. Kind of like a test."

"Ask a girl to marry you and you get a test thrown at you," he complained in a giving-in sort of way.

She locked her arms around his neck. "But I'm worth it, right?"

"Mmm…well, let's see," he said ahead of kissing her.

Chapter 3

When Tracy woke up beside Mark in bed the next morning she found him holding and staring at the picture of Evan.

When she moved some, his look shifted to her and he took her under his arm. "Hey, sleepyhead."

"What time is it?" she asked, reluctantly remembering her job.

"Seven. You've got plenty of time for—"

"*Seven*? No, it can't be." When she tried to roll away from him and get out of bed, he tightened his hold and kept her. Which was all it took for her to relent to the here and now and a deep, sensual kiss with him. Last night's love making had been great, and she felt closer than ever to Mark this morning.

"Sleep good?" he asked when they settled back into a contented cuddle. "After we..."

"Mmm..." Tracy answered.

"Me too." He picked up Evan's picture and studied it again. "You guys look a lot alike."

"My hair is longer," she said with a giggle.

"Not much," he laughed, making back and forth comparisons between her brother and her.

"Thanks for agreeing to go meet him."

"All by myself, without you." Mark put the picture aside and gave her a serious look. "Oh, Tracy, I just really wish I had a better feeling about this, my going there alone. I mean, I still don't see how it will—"

"Don't," she said, pressing her finger against his lips. "Please don't back down now. I need you to do this."

"I'm not backing down. I promised I'd go and I will."

"But you're going to hate it, aren't you? And then you're going to hate me."

"Probably," he teased. Then added seriously, "I'm playing for keeps here, Tracy. Whatever matters to you, matters to me. Learning about this agoraphobic brother of yours last night, I see how much he matters to you. I also see how much frustration and hurt you've been going through because of him. I want you to know that you're not alone in dealing with him anymore. You've got me now and I'll help in any way that I can."

Though Tracy adored Mark's thoughtfulness, she couldn't help wondering if he would still feel the same after becoming more directly involved with the situation.

"Okay?" Mark asked for her trust.

Suddenly she bolted from his arms, pulled on her robe, and headed for the bathroom. "Do you know how late it is!"

During her shower, Tracy tried to enforce her reasons for believing she could have a future with Mark. Last night's talk went well. He seemed okay about Evan. He respected her concern for her brother. He was willing to put some genuine effort into dealing with the situation.

Okay, sure, she'd had a lot of stuff to cope with in her life...losing both her parents, Evan's agoraphobia, several failed relationships, and big financial problems a while back. But Mark had come to her as something wondrously above all that, and if she didn't let herself truly trust in him and believe in the happy world they could have together then maybe she just plain didn't deserve any happiness whatsoever.

When she left the bathroom, Mark was sitting on the edge of the bed, still looking at the picture of Evan. But when she started getting dressed, he turned to watch her instead. He smiled with a manly pleasure that made Tracy glad she had a good body and lacy underwear.

When the show was over, Mark came to give her a long kiss before heading to the bathroom for his shower.

Tracy checked the time. There was no way she was going to make her eight-thirty meeting with the hotel manager. She phoned him apologetically, asked if they could change it to nine, and he said sure, no problem.

Mark's shower took nowhere near as long as hers did. He was soon out of the bathroom, dressing before her and teasingly rubbing in the fact that she delayed her appointment in preference to him.

Admitting as much, she helped him finish buttoning his shirt. But by the time he pulled his sweater down over his head, her insecurity returned. "Tell me again that we're going to be okay," she said.

"We're going to be okay," he told her. "And as a symbol of that, why don't we put the ring back on."

"No. Not yet. I can't."

"Tracy…"

"Please understand, Mark."

It took him some time to reluctantly say, "Okay."

She dropped her look from him. "I'm sorry."

"Hey…" he said, putting his hand beneath her chin and raising it until their eyes met again, "I've never seen you like this, the way you were last night and this morning. So scared and insecure. Come on, honey. You've got a brother who won't leave the house, and a real nice boyfriend, me, who's going to go visit him and prove that I can get along with him. Then we're going to get married and live happily ever after…*the three of us*."

She smiled halfheartedly. "You're ridiculing my expectations."

"No. I'm getting the picture you want me to get and agreeing to do what you want me to do."

"And you're not mad?"

"I'm not mad. You've been honest with me, Tracy. I mean, once you told me what you were keeping from me, you were honest about it. And…so…I'm thinking that maybe now you can get honest with Evan, let him know the effect he's been having on your life, and finally put the guy in his place."

"Place? He's my brother, *that's* his place."

"And you're his lifelong keeper?"

"We're close."

"How close? Closer than you and me?"

"That's sick. Evan and me, we're brother-sister close. *You've* got a brother," she reminded him.

Mark gave a so-what shrug. "Yeah?"

"And you love him?"

"Yeah. Of course. Sure. But that doesn't mean I mentally take him with me everywhere I go, like I'm finding out you do with your brother."

"Jim doesn't have agoraphobia."

"No, he doesn't. Jim's healthy and normal, thank God. But even if he wasn't, you can—" Mark nipped the rise of his voice but hardly the crudeness, "be damn sure I wouldn't carry him around like a monkey on my back twenty-four hours a day every single day of my life."

Tracy withdrew in silence.

"Don't get me wrong," he said. "I'd do everything reasonably possibly to help the guy, I'd just be very careful about what was considered reasonable."

"I don't want to fight," Tracy said, fearing that maybe they'd never get beyond this.

"Neither do I." Mark stood looking lost as to what to say next and notably sorry for what he already had.

All Tracy had left to say was, "I want to feel secure with you, Mark, but security's not an easy thing with me."

"I'm going to give that to you, you'll see." He nestled the side of his face against hers and just stood holding her quietly for a long time.

After Mark left for his apartment, vowing he would chain himself to his computer for the rest of the day and desperately work to get past his writer's block, Tracy took a few moments to herself before going to her meeting. Later she would let Evan know about Mark's visit to Drendal. Though first she would have to explain to him just exactly who Mark *was*.

Chapter 4

▼

Mark chose to drive to Minnesota rather than fly. And it was good for his Dodge Shadow to let loose over the endless, fast interstates as to the stop-and-go, bumper-to-bumper commuting it did around New York City.

Though the roads were clear and dry, deep marshmallow sidelines showed a much greater accumulation of snow in the Midwest than there had been out East. Bare-limbed, skeletal trees and powdered evergreens trimmed the way to Drendal, which was a hundred and twenty miles north of the Twin Cities.

It was still hard for Mark to believe that he'd actually left New York, and Tracy, and was going off by himself to meet her brother with the strange problem. That he'd been so easily manipulated into doing something that made no sense. That being in love should warrant such senselessness.

He smiled sadly, already missing her and wondering when their relationship would ever be based more on time spent together rather than time spent apart. When they'd said good-bye, she'd looked at him with those big brown eyes of hers and told him to be careful. He still wasn't sure whether she'd meant with his driving or with Evan. Well, he considered himself a careful sort of person in general and really didn't foresee any trouble with either.

It was late Wednesday afternoon when Mark reached the quaint little town of Drendal. The business district was a mere two blocks. Storefronts had paned windows and calligraphy-painted name signs. Streets were narrow, with old-fashioned light posts and barely any traffic. People bundled in warm clothing were passing along the sidewalks edged with high snow banks. Workers with ladders and cartons were taking down Christmas decorations from the holiday three weeks past.

Though Mark considered himself a devoted New Yorker, he was, at the same time, admittedly charmed by Drendal's innocent Norman Rockwell appearance. At least in the way that he could visualize the characters of one of his books dwelling there, but not himself.

At the other end of the short town, he rechecked the map Tracy had drawn for him and took a left onto Elwood. Three blocks that way, then right. He drove slowly on roads that weren't plowed nearly so well as the ones behind him. The spaces between houses widened and the landscape turned more rural. He watched for landmarks.

There, on a corner of the next intersection he spied the boarded-up vegetable stand. And across the road was the large fenced-in field that Tracy said belonged to a neighbor who had once kept horses. Beyond that was the gray, two-story house that was hers and Evan's.

Mark found the driveway beside the house too deep with snow to drive into. He passed it, found a place where he could turn around, then went back to park in the road.

As he was pulling into place he saw someone coming from the house out toward the mailbox. He left his car and hurried around the front of it. From the picture he'd seen of Evan, he recognized the young man with longish, dark hair to be him. Except, if this guy had agoraphobia, how could he be outside?

"Hi! Are you Evan Lawton?" Mark called from the road.

"Uh, yeah…that's me," the guy answered reluctantly, stopping right there. Drawing his unzipped jacket closed, he stood staring at Mark as if he were staring at an alien from outer space.

"Oh. I wasn't sure. I mean, I didn't expect to see you outside. But that's good, great." Mark waded through snow that was well over his shoes and went close enough to offer a handshake. "I'm Mark Rydell."

Evan's eyes were as round and as dark as his sister's, but far more wary and mysterious. He made frequent glances back at the house, as if making sure it was still there. Tracy had said he was friendly, but though he shook hands with Mark he hardly expressed any pleasantry.

Evan left Mark and walked the remaining short distance to the mailbox. Mark felt slighted, as though his coming all the way from New York was nothing special after all. Though he really didn't expect a medal or a hug or anything like that, a smile or a couple of welcome words would have been nice.

With a handful of envelopes and nothing at all to say, Evan started for the house, backtracking the path he'd made on his way out. Mark, feeling very uncomfortable, followed in his own silence.

When they reached the back door of the house, which was on the side toward the snow-laden driveway, Evan glanced over his shoulder, surprised at finding Mark there. "You're...coming in?"

"W-well...yeah...if that's okay." Mark cringed at the guy's odd sense of kidding, if it was, in fact, kidding.

"Do I know you?" Evan asked.

"Not really, not yet," Mark played along.

"Do I want to?"

"Probably not." Mark was really beginning to think there might be something a whole lot more wrong with this guy besides agoraphobia.

Hesitating with his hand on the doorknob, Evan threw another suspicious look back at Mark.

Okay, that was it. Mark was ready to say fine, the hell with it, good-bye. Friendly, my eye. There was no sign of friendliness in Evan thus far. If Tracy's brother was opposed to having him, no way was he staying. Yet, when Evan opened the door and stepped inside the house, Mark hurried in behind him.

The kitchen had a warm, homey, farmhouse feel that in itself lent much more welcome than Evan had. The bottom half of the walls were a tan tongue and groove, and the top half a small-print wallpaper. The cupboards were also painted tan. A table and four chairs stood upon a braided rug in the center of the room. Next to the sink was an open doorway revealing an uncarpeted stairway that led to upstairs.

Leaving his jacket on, Mark stayed put just inside the door, wondering if there might be a motel in the vicinity. He watched Evan, also in his jacket, sit down at the table. Though Evan's face had a healthy robust color from being out in the cold, his breath seemed notably laborious, hands and arms quivery.

"You okay?" Mark thought he should ask.

"Yeah," Evan said.

"You don't look okay."

"Take your coat off if you want," Evan offered, sounding questionable as to whether he actually meant it or not.

"Maybe I'll just keep it on," Mark said, "since I'll be going back out for my luggage anyway."

"Luggage?"

Evan seemed so befuddled about it that Mark even more seriously considered a motel.

A big gray tabby padded into the room, ears pricked, tail swishing, green eyes checking out the visitor. "Mir-oww."

Evan made introductions. "My cat Remington. Rem, Mark."

The cat chanced his nearness to Mark in order to get at the tracked-in snow on the entrance rug. He sniffed it from several directions. Tested it with the quick flick of his tongue. Looked up at Mark again. Eyed Evan. Back to Mark. Then was soon licking his snow treat as enjoyably as a child licked ice cream.

Mark didn't much care for cats but supposed there was always a certain amount of fascination in watching them. He watched Remington for something to do, but with no desire to pet him.

"This is from my sister," Evan said of one of the envelopes he'd brought in. "Do you mind?"

Mark thought it very weird, this guy's swing from rudeness to politeness. "No, go ahead. Tracy deserves priority."

"You *know* my sister?" Evan exclaimed.

Something was definitely missing here, Mark determined. Keeping by the door, with his jacket on, he was seriously thinking that he should just leave Drendal completely, even the motel idea, and drive straight back to New York. Evan was acting as if he had absolutely no idea who Mark was or what he was doing there. But Tracy had told him. Hadn't she? He was supposed to know. How could he not know?

Remington swiped against Mark's legs, approving him now and endowing him with his scent. Mark gazed down at him and stepped aside.

When Evan finished the letter, he looked at Mark in a whole new way. As if something was suddenly clearer to him. Something that turned him from confused to amused and caused a smile to spread across his handsome young face.

"What's so funny?" Mark asked curiously.

Evan flagged Tracy's letter at him. "This tells me who you are and that you're coming here for a stay. Good timing, huh?"

"You just got that letter? But Tracy sent it last Thursday. You should've gotten it sooner. So you didn't even know who I was before now?"

"I only go out to the mailbox once a week," Evan explained.

Annoyed as he was, Mark felt at least somewhat closer to this guy's problem. Yes, okay, evidently going out to get the mail was such an ordeal for him that his only means of dealing with it was by keeping it as limited as possible. Like once a week. Like today. So then why hadn't Tracy phoned him rather than written? She who was supposed to be so knowledgeable and accommodating of her brother's problem. And why hadn't she ever told Evan about her boyfriend before this? That was strange, almost unforgivable. Mark was miffed at how she'd handled this. Really miffed.

Anyway, Evan was looking a lot better now. More relaxed and comfortable about what was going on. He actually laughed about his prior skepticism. "I was wondering what you were about. Had no idea who you were as you came trudging through the snow toward me. Like I was suppose to know who Mark Rydell was. Like I was suppose to be okay with your coming up to the house with me like that. And coming inside. Talking about luggage."

Mark had to laugh too. "It was kind of funny."

"Yeah," Evan agreed, putting Tracy's letter back in its envelope.

There were still parts of the puzzle missing, as far as Mark was concerned. "So Tracy never mentioned me to you before this, the letter that said I was coming for a stay?"

There was a sorry look on Evan's face as he shook his head.

Mark apologized, "I'm sorry my turning up was such a shock to you, Evan."

"But there *is* something familiar about you," Evan said. He shook his finger at Mark until it came to him. "*Dances With Wolves*."

"Huh? Oh, yeah." A modest smile escaped Mark. "I guess some people think I resemble Costner's earlier days."

"I do. I definitely do," Evan said, notably excited by it. "Tracy picked up the video for me some time ago. You see it?"

Mark nodded.

"I've seen lots of Kevin Costner movies," Evan carried on, "but I think *Wolves* was definitely the best."

"Well, I put a lot into that one," Mark said jokingly.

Evan stood up from the table, extending his hand to him. "New start?"

The two of them shook, laughing at their situation.

Evan finally took off his jacket, hung it on a wall hook, and bent down to get his cat. As he swooped the animal up affectionately, he asked him, "Hey, Rem, what do you think about all of this, huh?"

Mark watched the two of them responding to one another. Snuggled face to face, Remington purring and Evan cooing. Mark found himself viewing yet another Norman Rockwell scene.

"So why would you even let me in your house if you didn't know who I was?" he still wondered about Evan's doing that.

Evan returned Remington to the floor, brushed a collection of cat hair off his navy blue shirt, swept his own dark shoulder-length hair back from his face, and gave Mark a grin. "Because all the while I was trying to think if I was somehow supposed to know you, since you really seemed to know me. But I wouldn't have allowed the luggage. That was where I would have drawn the line. If I couldn't figure out who you were or what you were doing here, no way was I going to let you bring in any luggage."

"Speaking of which," Mark said, reaching behind him for the doorknob, "I'd better go get mine now, if that's okay with you."

Evan was fine with that. "Right, sure, go ahead. I...I'd help you, but I—"

"Oh, thanks, no, that's okay. I can manage by myself in two trips. No problem. Don't have that much. Except, I did bring along my typewriter and a carton of writing supplies."

"Writing supplies?" Evan asked.

"I'm a writer," Mark said. "But I guess if you never heard of me until now, in that letter, what you did hear probably wasn't that inclusive. Yeah, I'm a writer. That's what I am, what I do."

Evan nodded with quiet amazement.

Mark's amazement wasn't as quiet. "I just don't get it! This secrecy of Tracy's."

"She can get a little weird sometimes," her brother allowed.

Weird, right. Mark was really starting to question where the true placement of that term lay in this family. "I guess I should explain that she and I met last summer."

"I know. She said that in the letter."

"Right, the letter." Mark resented how Evan's introduction to him came just short of their actual meeting. Tracy had had six months to tell Evan about him, but she'd let it go only to end up cramming it scantily into a last-minute letter. From their talk last week he supposed he understood her reasoning for not having mentioned Evan to him until lately. But there was no reason, as far as he could tell, for her not telling Evan about him. He would call her later and confront her about it.

Meanwhile, Mark went for his luggage. Back outside into the cold and down the trodden path to his car at the road. The grim grayness of late afternoon had deepened into night and it was starting to snow. More snow, as if there wasn't enough already.

Mark was a long way from New York. A long way from feeling comfortable about this visit to Drendal, to Evan, to things Tracy had said and not said. And somehow, unfortunately, he knew that phoning Tracy probably wasn't going to straighten out a whole lot either. He was disturbed at how she'd handled this, at how and why she'd kept him and Evan in the dark about one another all this time. He loved her, but was miffed at her. Plus also, right now, he was tired and hungry and unable to stop worrying about why a guy like Evan should be ladened with agoraphobia.

He stood at the back of his car, not yet opening the trunk but just taking some time to think in the incredible quiet. Large snowflakes billowed down upon him and around him, bestowing a kind of celestial peace onto the world, onto the moment, onto him.

Chapter 5

▼

"I'm glad your trip went well, Mark, and the map I made you was of help." In pajamas and socks, Tracy sat curled on her hotel bed with the phone. The switch felt odd, her being in New York and Mark being in Drendal.

"The letter you wrote Evan was an even bigger help," he said.

Tracy dismissed his sarcasm in that he'd only just arrived at Drendal and was no doubt travel fatigued. "Did Evan make you a nice supper? He's an excellent cook."

"He's preparing something now."

"Oh, right, it's an hour earlier there. So he's with you in the kitchen as we speak?"

"Actually he went upstairs to put my room in order and left me stirring the spaghetti sauce. I'm stirring as we speak."

Tracy laughed. "So how is Evan? How did you find him upon your arrival?"

There was a pause before Mark answered, as if he found the question difficult. "When I got here he hadn't the slightest notion of who I was, *that's* how I found him."

Tracy shifted her position on the bed and put the phone to her other ear. "But I wrote him a letter."

"A letter, right," Mark confirmed. "Which he got today, same time as I arrived. Of which he opened and read, learning who I was and that I was coming for a stay, all as I stood right here in this kitchen."

Tracy laid her head back against the pillows and sighed. "But I sent it last week. "Right after you agreed to go. Before the weekend. "He should've—"

"You didn't know that Evan only goes out to the mailbox once a week?"

She played with the phone cord. "W-well, I—"

"I was surprised that he went out at all, and you're surprised that he only goes out once a week?"

"I...I guess I didn't consider that."

"I thought you knew him so well."

"I do. It's just that you can't fit Evan's behavior into a precise pattern all the time. There are exceptions and degrees with agoraphobia."

"As with you and me obviously," Mark said coolly.

Tracy was not feeling as happy about this phone call now as she did upon first picking it up and hearing Mark's voice. "What does that mean?" she asked of his remark, not exactly sure she wanted to know.

"I don't know," Mark backed down.

"I should have told him about you long before this."

"Yeah," Mark agreed. "Why didn't you?"

"It's complicated," was all Tracy could say, realizing that it was beginning to look more and more like a mistake, her sending Mark to Drendal. At least, for sure, the way she'd gone about it. "Mark, I wish we didn't need to be apart."

"Your idea, remember?"

"I know. Please don't be mad."

"I'm not mad. It's just that at first, after the letter, Evan and I kind of laughed about things, you know? But now, I just don't know about all of this, Tracy."

"Everything came up so fast. Your proposal, my telling you about Evan, my asking you to go visit him. I guess I didn't handle any of it very well."

The line went quiet. For a long enough time that Tracy felt the need to ask, "Mark, are you still there?"

"Yeah," he answered.

"Say something," she urged, aching for a better conversation than this.

"Tracy," he came back hesitantly, "I don't know what else to say."

"Tell me you love me," she suggested.

Following what sounded like Mark tapping his spoon against the edge of the pot a few times, he told her sweetly, "I love you."

"Are you sorry for ever getting involved with me?"

"A little," he laughed. Then added, "No, not sorry. Just a little overwhelmed at how when I purposed to you *wham*, our relationship immediately went into a spin."

"I know," she said. "I didn't mean to spoil things. But Evan, he's there, he's just always there for me to have to deal with in one way or another. That's how it is. And I need you to understand that, Mark."

"Okay…yeah…I guess I sort of understand why you never told me about him until a week ago. Though you wouldn't have had to be, it seemed you were afraid of how I might react and how it might affect our relationship."

"Which it has."

"Tracy, we're okay. We're working on this together now and we're still okay."

"Okay," she said, putting her trust back into him.

"So you probably never mentioned me to Evan before now because he wouldn't have approved, or something like that, huh?" Mark assumed.

"It's—" she began, without knowing where she was going.

"—complicated, I know," Mark finished for her.

Tracy watched it snowing outside her window. Though it was night and dark out, the snow glittered against the backdrop of hotel lights across the way. "Evan lives in his own little world," she continued with the subject matter, "and I…I just don't tell him a whole lot about mine."

"Because he wouldn't be interested?"

"He'd be interested. Likely to the point of feeling how much he himself is missing in the real world."

"And might possibly want to get well? Could that be it, Tracy?"

"You don't think I want him well?" She felt hurt that Mark would think that.

"The thought's crossed my mind, yeah."

"I just don't want Evan feeling pressured, that's all. He doesn't need that. He can't handle that. I won't do that to him."

"Do?" Mark shot back at her. "He's twenty-six, right? Not six, Tracy. You make it sound like he's a child."

"You don't understand agoraphobia."

"More like I don't understand you."

"Let's not fight on the phone, Mark, please." She hated the friction Evan was already creating in their relationship. She knew it would be like this once she'd brought him into the picture. She *knew*.

"Tracy…no…honey, we're not fighting. I'm just…I'm sorry…I'm really trying to understand all this, but I'm not doing so well. I can't help feeling there's something, I don't know, something weird about how you look after your brother."

"Weird?" she said with a choke in her voice. "Evan's my brother. Don't use the term weird to describe my caring for him."

"Okay, change that to over protective."

Watching the falling snow outside her window was beginning to have a hypnotic effect on Tracy. How easy it could be to just totally lose herself in the effortless enthrallment. She closed her eyes for a moment to recapture her concentration. "Mark, maybe you'll feel protective about Evan too after you're there a while."

"He's a nice guy," Mark said. "Except for his not going outside, he seems okay."

Tracy took that as a good sign. "He *is* okay, yes!"

"I guess he does make one immediately adopt a sense of protectiveness toward him," Mark concluded, as if it came to him just now by surprise.

"Yes!" she cheered. "That's exactly what I wanted you to learn from your visit."

Mark laughed. "That to be around Evan is to want to protect him?"

"Yes!" Tracy was suddenly feeling so much better.

"So can I come home now?"

"Home?"

"Since I've learned what I was sent here to learn?"

Tracy reminded him, "I'm the one who's coming home soon."

"Not soon enough," he said hungrily.

"I know," she agreed about the wait. "But meanwhile, Mark, enjoy the country, do some writing, get to know Evan. Like you told me, we'll work together on this."

"The three of us," he affirmed.

Tracy smiled. "I like hearing you say that."

"It wasn't easy," he teased.

Watching it snow outside her window, and feeling wonderfully secure about their relationship again, Tracy needed nothing further at the moment except, "Mark, is it snowing there in Drendal?"

"Yeah. Why?"

"Because knowing that it's snowing where you are, at the very same time it's snowing where I am, makes me feel closer to you. Don't you feel that too, Mark? Don't you?"

He laughed. "I don't know. Yeah. Maybe. I guess."

"Can we not talk for a few minutes and just watch it snow together?"

"Sure."

Chapter 6

▼

"Maybe you'd better not come over today, Laurel. I have a house guest." Evan cast an anxious look at the stairway while speaking lowly into the kitchen phone. Though it was five o'clock on the morning after Mark's arrival, and Mark was presumably still asleep upstairs, Evan was especially quiet.

"House guest?" The girl spoke as secretively as he did, because at her house, across town, she had her father to be wary of. "Who, Evan? Who's there?"

"My sister's boyfriend from New York."

"Boyfriend? I didn't know Tracy had one."

Evan drew a deep breath. "Neither did I. Till yesterday. Till he dropped in, told me his name was Mark Rydell and that he and his luggage were here to stay for a while."

"I thought Tracy was scheduled to be out East for a time yet."

"She is. She sent Mark here alone. Wants him and me to spend some time together, get to know each other."

"She sent him alone?" Laurel said, as if she, too, found the event strange.

Evan checked the stairs again.

"It doesn't seem right," Laurel continued with concern.

"I know. It makes me very suspicious." Evan cupped his free hand around the end of the phone, ensuring that his whispered words got through to her. "Tracy doesn't know about us, you and me. At least I don't think she does. But it's like maybe she suspects something and sent her boyfriend back here alone to—"

"Spy on you?"

"I don't know. Maybe. We have to be careful, Laurel."

Remington, curled in a ball on the rug by the back door, suddenly opened his eyes, raised his head and pricked his ears.

"Wait a minute," Evan told Laurel. He looked up at the ceiling and listened. He wondered if Remington, with his super cat hearing, heard Mark moving around up there. He, himself, heard nothing. Anyway, Remington was already shutting his eyes and laying his chin back down over his forelegs.

"What's wrong?" Laurel asked.

"Nothing, I guess," Evan decided.

"Evan, I really don't think your sister's boyfriend is here to spy on you. And even if Tracy did find out about our relationship, I doubt that she'd be a problem."

"How can you say? You don't know her. You've never even met her."

"I know about her from you, and she seems very nice."

Nervously shifting his weight from foot to foot, Evan reminded her, "The biggest problem is your father. We both know how he'd react if he found out about us. He'd break us up, Laurel, you know he would. So on account of him we need to continue keeping this a secret. From everyone. Even from Tracy and her boyfriend."

Laurel Timmons lived on the opposite side of town, with a stern over-protective father who had his own ideas about who his daughter should or shouldn't see. He didn't know she was seeing Evan Lawton and would never permit it if he did. He'd heard enough town's talk about this strange guy who'd had agoraphobia for five years to make up his mind that he didn't like him and certainly didn't trust him. He warned Laurel not to go anywhere near the guy's house, because it was hard telling what to expect from someone like that and she'd best stay clear of him.

Unbeknownst to her father, her job at Dave's Pizza had her delivering pizza to Evan's house one day, which turned out to be the beginning of an ongoing friendship between the two. "Evan," she said reassuringly, "maybe it would be all right to let Tracy and her boyfriend know about us."

He massaged the tension in his forehead. Rechecked the stairs. The ceiling. The stairs again. Feeling that danger was about to spring out at him any second.

"Just Tracy and Mark, no one else," Laurel said.

"It's not a good idea," Evan disagreed.

"But their knowing, it wouldn't get back to my dad."

"It could!" He caught himself getting louder out of desperation and immediately cut back to a whisper. "We can't take the risk, Laurel. I don't know what I'd do if your father broke us up. And he would, you know, if he had any idea that—"

"Okay, okay, Evan," she gave in, "we'll continue being careful. If we have to, we have to. How long is Tracy's boyfriend staying?"

"I'm not sure." Evan's chest felt tight, legs weak. He drew an ultra deep breath, trying to force more oxygen into his lungs. Though leaving the house was a catastrophic ordeal for him, it didn't seem fair that he should be having a panic attack here and now while merely standing in the kitchen. He took support against the counter. It helped some. "I wish we didn't have to worry about this. I wish I could just face up to your father and—"

"It's okay, Evan," Laurel said, mindful of his limits and his needs. "We don't have to worry. We're not going to let anyone break us up. We'll do whatever we have to. If that means being careful forever, then we will."

"Forever," he said, as if it were a prison sentence rather than a comfort measure.

"Are you all right?" she asked.

He tugged at his sweatshirt, as if it were the pressure he felt to his chest. But the shirt was loose, the gripping coming from the inside, not outside, of him. "I'm a little nervous," he admitted.

He looked at the stairs. From there he slowly moved his gaze to the sink. Then to the back door. The cupboards. Refrigerator. Stove. This was it. His world. So small and limited, that he had to wonder how it ever managed to include Laurel. But it did, in a fragile sort of way. A way in which, not to lose her, he had to be careful, so careful.

"Evan," her voice beckoned through the phone to him with that amazing ability she had of rescuing him from himself, "we're going to be all right."

"I know," he said and swallowed hard.

"So don't worry, okay?"

"Okay." He gave Laurel a smile that she couldn't see and he didn't feel.

After hanging the phone back onto its wall base, Evan swooped Remington up off the floor, sorry about giving the cat a startle but needing him close right then. Remington easily conformed and was soon purring in the wrap of his master's arms.

Chapter 7

Just as Laurel was hanging up the phone in the kitchen of her house, her father walked in, saying, "Kind of early for a call. Who was it?"

"It was Dave from Dave's Pizza," she lied. "He…he wanted to verify a schedule change with me."

"At five A.M.?" Parker Timmons, fifty-four, overweight, thinning gray hair and a gruff disposition, stood in his blue-striped pajamas and bare feet.

"Sorry if it woke you, Dad." She tightened her robe belt and brushed her sandy brown hair back from her face. Since this was only a half hour ahead of his regular wake-up time, she suggested, "I'll make you some breakfast."

"What kind of schedule change?" His interest stayed on her phone call. That was the problem with him, he was always too overly interested in what was going on with her, her schedule, her life. "Do you have to go in later and stay later today?"

"No. Well, I was suppose to," she lied some more, "but then the schedule changed back to normal, so now I'm back to my regular time. Bacon and eggs? Or oatmeal?"

"Oatmeal."

"Good choice," she approved, as per the diet he was on. She fetched the round Quaker canister out of the cupboard. When she turned back, she found the familiar set look on her father's face that signified his stubbornness toward choosing anything else in life so lightly.

"Dave's Pizza doesn't open before eleven." Parker's brow furrowed as he continued trying to piece together the facts of a story he obviously didn't get. "Why would Dave call so ungodly early about any sort of schedule change?"

"I don't know," she said as if it were do big deal.

"You sure it was him?"

"Do I seem confused?"

"Doesn't make sense," Parker said amidst a yawn, "his phoning like that. What the heck's wrong with the guy?"

"Dave's just that way. He's as devoted to his pizza operation as you are to your financial services at the bank."

"I've never phoned anyone at five in the morning regarding work," Parker grumped. Then dropping the matter, he left the kitchen, saying, "Going to get my shower. I'll have cinnamon toast with my oatmeal."

Popping two slices of bread into the toaster, Laurel gave a big sigh of relief for having made it through that scene with her father. Now she could only hope that Evan would manage all right with his houseguest.

Chapter 8

Mark awakened to the sound of…something. Not sure what, he lay perfectly still in bed, listening, trying to decipher it. Hammering? Pounding? Knocking? No, actually it was more like hard fast footsteps against the uncarpeted stairs just outside his room. Footsteps clumping up the stairs—clump, clump, clump. Footsteps slamming down the steps—slam, slam, slam. Up again. Down again. Over and over. Though he figured out the source of the sound, the why of it was a separate mystery.

He blinked his eyes more clearly awake and toward the window. The edges around the window shade were still dark. What the heck time was it, anyway? He turned on the nightstand light and squinted at his watch. Five-thirty.

He rolled out of bed and hurriedly pulled on his clothes. He'd slept well for his first night in a new place. At least until this five-thirty aggravation cut him short about three hours. His given room had been Tracy's parents' room. The assorted pictures on the walls and dressers, of a boy and a girl growing up, were undoubtedly her and Evan. Interesting. Touching. He would take the time later to look them over more closely.

Going into the hall, he caught a glimpse of Evan turning on the top step and fleeing back down again. Why? Why was this guy making noisy, senseless, up and down repetitions on the stairs? If the purpose was to annoy his visitor, it worked.

Mark stood waiting for Evan's upward return. Which didn't happen. Thus the quiet became the strange new sound. Quiet…yes…for a few moments…until a rattling sound began in the kitchen. He slowly, curiously, ventured down the stairway.

Evan was washing dishes at the sink. Sleeves pushed up, dark hair brushing his shoulders, seemingly unfazed by how early it was.

"What were you just doing on the steps?" Mark asked him in the way an adult reprehended a misbehaved child.

Evan glanced around, surprised at first but quick to smile. "Good-morning, Mark. Sleep okay?"

"Fine. Until...what *were* you doing?"

"Steps. I was doing steps. Twenty runs up, twenty runs down. My morning workout. Good for the heart. How's your heart, Mark?"

Mark's answer was a moan.

"Want coffee?"

"Yes." Mark sat at the table. Remington was soon brushing against his legs, purring, eyeing him with that green-eyed whiskery look, no doubt wanting to be petted. But Mark rejected him with a look that, on its own, was effective enough to make the cat give up and go away.

Evan brought coffee and cereal to Mark, then returned to his dishwashing.

Sitting there half awake, eating an exceptionally early breakfast, Mark began to do a silent mental rating of how he observed Evan's state of being thus far. Some of it was normal, some of it abnormal, all of it confusing.

"What's wrong?" Evan asked, catching his studious look.

"Last night...I was pretty beat..." Mark said with a mouthful of Wheat Chex, "but I was thinking...maybe today...you and I could talk some?"

"Sure. Okay," Evan agreed easily. "About what?"

"Us. You and me."

"As to your purpose for being here?" Evan switched from washing to drying dishes now and setting them into the cupboard.

"Purpose?" Mark threw the question back at him.

"There is one, right?" Evan said. "I mean, you wouldn't come all the way from New York to visit someone in Minnesota you didn't even know unless there was a purpose."

"Tracy's the purpose," Mark established. "She wanted me to meet you, Evan. That's all." Wheat Chex were good. He hadn't had them in a long while. Toasty, crunchy, nutritious. He kept the spoonfuls coming.

"Are you a doctor?" Evan asked him.

Mark laughed amidst his chewing. "No...I told you...a writer. Why would you think doctor? Do I look like a doctor?"

"I don't know," Evan said with solemn consideration.

"Aren't you having breakfast?" Mark pushed the box of cereal across the table in Evan's direction.

"Had mine already." Evan closed the box and put it in the cupboard.

"A real early bird, aren't you?" Mark jested.

Remington, still hanging around, meowed at the word bird.

"He doesn't speak English," Evan explained to Mark's amazement, bending down to pet the cat, "but he understands it."

Mark laughed. "Ahh, where did you get such a smart cat?"

"A gift from Tracy. Three years ago her friend's cat had a litter and Tracy asked if she could have one of the kittens for me. Her friend said sure. So she went to choose one when they were six weeks old. Tracy was crazy about all three of them. Looked them over, studied them, asked them outright, 'Okay now, which one of you guys wants to go live with Evan?'"

"And the little gray one said me," Mark supposed.

"Actually he said meow."

"Oh, right, understands English but doesn't speak it," Mark corrected himself.

When the dishes were done Evan went directly to his next task. "Got laundry to do now. You got anything to put in?"

"No, not yet. I'm fine, thanks."

Evan went to the small alcove at one end of the kitchen, that appeared to have once been a pantry, and opened a door that led to the basement. Remington went with.

While finishing his cereal and savoring his coffee, Mark pondered Evan's lifestyle, wondering how it had ever come into the dire boundary of agoraphobia. He wondered what could be done to help him. And why, in five years, there hadn't been something.

Eventually Mark walked over to the basement door and peered down the narrow stairway. A single, bare light bulb hung over the bottom step. The sound of the automatic washer hummed and swished, and the scent of laundry detergent drifted through the air. He slowly started down, cautiously lowering one foot after the other against the creaky steps.

Evan looked boyishly young, sitting there on the cement floor playing with Remington. The cat was comical in his leaping, pawing, chasing, and attacking the shoestring Evan waved around.

"How's the laundry going?" Mark interrupted, sitting on a step.

Evan glanced over at him. "Ten more minutes to go."

"Looks like you two are having fun."

Evan laughed, swerving to one side as the cat totally missed his leap at the shoestring and plowed into his shoulder instead. "It's Rem's playtime whenever the washer is running."

Mark nodded. "He did seem eager to come down here with you."

"A creature of routine."

Yeah, Mark thought, *as is his master*. He felt a deep emotional tug to his heart, watching Evan and Remington. And with it, his concern over Evan's condition was growing. Like, if Evan could be this happy and free playing with his cat, then why couldn't he be as happy and free in the world outside? How could anyone have agoraphobia without actually acquiring claustrophobia? As this phobia matter drew him more and more in, Mark found himself wanting answers and solutions.

When the washer stopped Evan got up, removed the damp items from it and hung them one by one onto the clothesline stretched across the basement. "No dryer," he explained to Mark as he pinned up a pair of jockey shorts, a tee shirt, a pair of socks, a towel and a shirt.

"That's it?" Mark asked of the skimp collection.

"I keep up with whatever there is. A load a day."

"Right," Mark said of Evan's meticulous manner.

When the guys started up from the basement, Remington bound from step to step, passing both of them and reaching the top first. The cat went to his litter box at the back corner of the alcove, sniffed it, stepped into it and diligently scratched some additional coverage over the wet spot he'd left earlier.

"Got cleaning to do now," Evan stated to Mark, notably driven by time and schedule. "Then we can have that talk if you still want to."

"Sure." Mark watched him take some rags, spray cleaners and the vacuum cleaner off to the living room. Company or no company, the guy had his work to do. And Mark had to wonder if this obsessiveness was actually part of his illness or his wellness. "Evan," he called to him, "I'm going upstairs to shower."

"Okay," Evan answered. "Leave the shower curtain open when you're done."

Mark peered around the kitchen doorway at him in question.

Evan stopped dusting and gave him a look. "For Remington. He likes to sit on the edge of the bathtub and watch the water drops roll down the shower walls."

Before Mark got all the way upstairs rock music came blaring from the living room stereo. He smiled, taking the music thing as a sure sign of normalcy in a twenty-six year old. It told him that Evan was not yet too far gone to be helped.

Even with the bathroom door shut and the shower water spraying forcefully down on him, Mark could still hear the drums, the guitars and the screaming vocals. Which was fine. He wasn't so old that he didn't like a little rock 'n roll himself now and then, though usually not so early in the day.

After his shower he opened the bathroom door. Remington zoomed in and straight up onto the edge of the bathtub. The gray cat sat there cocking his head from side to side, fascinated with the water droplets trickling down the shower walls. It made Mark laugh, and for a few moments he, too, watched the droplets.

By the time he went downstairs again Evan had finished his cleaning and the music was off. Whereas Mark had just begun feeling the first real onset of his own energy kick in for the day, Evan had already exercised, made breakfast, washed dishes, done laundry and cleaned. As Mark brought his hands together into a clap, indicating the official start of his own morning, Evan, from the other end of the kitchen, looked wryly amused that it should only come about so late.

"Guess I'll call Tracy," Mark decided.

Evan nodded and left him alone to some privacy.

Mark stood to the wall phone, dialed the long-distance number, felt an excited rush when Tracy answered, and told her, "Hi, it's me."

"What's wrong?" She sounded scared.

Which scared him some in return. "Nothing that I know of, why?"

"We just talked last night."

Mark leaned against the cupboard, stared down at the floor, took a deep breath. "It's just that I was a little upset about things last night, but this morning I'm feeling a lot better. How are you, Tracy?"

She laughed, relaxing to the fact that this wasn't some critical emergency. "Fine. I was just about to go meet with the first-shift, east-wing housekeepers."

"Housekeeping has already been taken care of here," Mark stated with a grin.

"What?" she asked.

"Tracy, I'm feeling fine, except why is it that I feel farther apart from you when you're in New York and I'm in Drendal, than when I was in New York and you were in Drendal?"

It brought another laugh out of her. But she was serious in saying, "Sorry, Mark, I really don't have time to figure that out right now. I'm working, remember? And running late besides."

"Okay. I won't keep you. I'm just glad I caught you for a minute. Love you," he ended softly.

"Love you, too. See you soon, Mark."

"Soon," he said.

"Bye."

"Bye, Tracy." Mark put the phone back and strolled into the living room, which was directly off the kitchen. It was a cozy, oblong room. Browns and rusts, comfortable furniture, lots of plants, a beamed ceiling, and a large oak desk on the side wall.

"Have a good talk?" Evan was sitting on the couch, holding Remington.

"Yeah, sort of," Mark said.

"It was short."

Mark went to the front window to check on his car. Holding the curtain aside, he was appalled with what he saw. "Damn!"

"What's wrong?" Bringing the cat with him, Evan came to look for himself.

"The snow plow went by and plowed me in, that's what's wrong. Look at it!" A deep ridge of snow walled the entire length of the driver's side of his Shadow. "They don't much care how they plow here, do they?"

"It's the road. Your car's sitting in the road. It snows and they plow the roads. That's how it is, Mark."

"Got a shovel?" Mark headed for the kitchen.

Evan followed him. "Yeah, outside the back door."

"Great. Got *two* shovels?"

"W-well, yeah…but sorry, I'm afraid I can't—"

"That's right, you can't. Sorry. It's okay. Look, Evan," Mark said, pulling his jacket on, "I know about your being a…a home-bound person. It's just that yesterday you were all the way out to the mailbox at the road."

"I manage to go for mail once a week, that's it. I…don't shovel snow."

"Right." Mark wrapped his scarf around his neck, dismissing the possibility of obtaining his help.

He went outside alone, shutting the door behind him and grabbing the shovel out of a snow bank. *Damn*, it was cold out. Much colder than New York had ever seemed. He worked his way out to his car by shoveling the new-fallen snow out of the rutted walk path as he went.

The snow atop his car was light and fluffy and easy to whisk off with his car brush. But the snow that had been pushed up to his car off the road was heavy and packed. Mark scooped and heaved, shovelful after shovelful, up and over to the yard. His heart and lungs pumped vigorously, and his breath puffed white clouds into the air before him. He made frequent glances back at the house, expecting to catch Evan peering smugly out at him. But there was only ever Remington in the living room window.

When Mark finally got his car cleared off, he went inside the house to check with Evan about doing the driveway.

Evan wasn't in the kitchen. The house was silent. "Evan!" he called.

"In here," Evan's voice came from around the corner.

Mark kept his shoes on but stomped off the snow and wiped them dry before leaving the rug at the back door.

Evan was in the living room, sitting on the chair by the desk, ashtray balanced on his crossed leg, smoking a cigarette. "What's wrong?" he asked of Mark's sense of urgency.

Mark gave an embarrassed shrug. "Nothing. "I...I just wondered where you were."

"I don't go too far, you know," Evan ridiculed his own phobia.

"I didn't know you smoked."

Evan took a deep drag, then exhaled slowly and satisfyingly. "One cigarette a day. Nine A.M. That's it."

Mark checked the time. It was a couple minutes past the hour. "One a day?" he questioned the preciseness.

Evan drew another drag, looking rather lofty, as if he were smoking something stronger than a common cigarette. But an ordinary pack of Marlboros lay on the desk top.

Mark supposed the guy's simple-pleasured highs from simple things were due to his limited lifestyle. "Yeah...well...I won't interrupt you. I just thought...I mean, if it's okay I'd like to shovel out the driveway so that I can park my car up there while I'm staying here."

"Sure. Go ahead."

"Okay." Mark started back to the kitchen. Stopped. Took a chance on, "You wouldn't happen to have a snow blower, would you?"

"No," Evan answered.

With a sense of adventure, Mark returned to the outdoors and reclaimed his shovel. Feeling driven, determined, and surprisingly exhilarated, he took on the driveway like a challenge he willed himself to either meet or die. Like what else was there to do around there anyway?

It was hard work, moving an accumulation of snow that had built up and sat half a winter. Mark was using muscles he didn't even know he had. Good workout. In spite of the pleasure he was getting out of shoveling, time seemed to pass with a sense of ongoing sameness.

It was a pleasant surprise when Evan shouted from the back door, "Hey, Mark! It's ten o'clock! Coffee break time!"

Mark speared his shovel into a snow bank and went to the house. Inside, Evan had two mugs of hot coffee waiting on the kitchen table and a brick of cheese on a plate with a knife beside it. Mark stomped his shoes on the rug, wiped them, kept them on and went to sit down. Remington was right there to feast on the tracked-in snow.

Mark took off his gloves and opened his jacket. Cheese and coffee, how quaint. He'd never heard of cheese with a coffee break. He wondered what all these quirks meant about Evan. It was like from moment to moment you just didn't know what strange thing to expect next from the guy.

"It's cheddar," Evan said to Mark's staring at it. "Go ahead, slice yourself some."

"Right." Mark risked it. Ate some. Found it amazingly hit the spot. And supposed it probably offered a greater energy kick than a sweet roll or a doughnut. He smiled approvingly.

Evan cut a slice for himself. "How's the shoveling going?"

"Oh, all right," Mark said wearily. Then jested, "I doubt there's more than eight or ten hours of work left out there."

"Wish I could help you," Evan sounded like an apology.

"Yeah, me too." Mark took a second piece of cheese. "Actually, more than the shoveling, I'm still wondering about that one cigarette a day of yours. No more, no less?"

"You're not going to tell me to cut down, are you?" Evan asked.

"No," Mark laughed, "can't see the harm in one. Nor the value."

"One seems to suit me just fine."

Evan was so serious about that one cigarette a day routine of his that Mark chanced he might answer as equally seriously to, "Don't you miss getting out of here? Don't you ever feel like you—"

"I feel fine, Mark," Evan was quick to assure him and steer the subject away from himself. "It's you we should be worrying about. Like have you ever done this much shoveling before?"

"No. My apartment has underground parking."

"Better not push your New York body too far," Evan said with a smirk.

"We're not exactly wimps in New York, you know." Mark took another drink of coffee, relishing the warmth spreading throughout his body.

"Just take it easy, all right?"

Mark nodded but kept his resolve. "I feel compelled to finish the job."

"Your wanting to park in the driveway, that must mean you're planning to stick around for a while." As Evan lifted his own coffee mug and drank from it, his dark mysterious eyes stared over the rim at Mark.

"A while, yeah. If that's okay with you."

"No problem," Evan said. "Other than we're apt to get a whole lot more snow for you to deal with."

Mark moaned amidst his laugh.

Soon he was outside working again. The challenge of finishing the driveway spurred him almost as much as finishing a writing project. He felt alive to a whole new degree. Scoop and heave, scoop and heave. Arms and back proving they definitely belonged to him, were under his command and still had the ability to work this hard. Breathing in, breathing out, of surely the coldest, freshest air that had ever cleansed his lungs and soul before. And the most amazing part of all this was that he was having sort of good a time at it.

It was a long driveway, extending past the house and out to a shack-like garage that stood semi-buried behind an even deeper section of piled-up snow, indicating its non use so far this season. Though Mark had no intention of clearing away that much snow now, he couldn't help wondering what was in the garage, if there might possibly be room in there for his car, and why Tracy never used it to shelter her car when she was home. By the looks of it, she parked in the road between snow plowing. Her car right now, of course, was at the Duluth airport.

The next time he took a break, to lean idly against his shovel handle, Mark spent a few minutes just staring at the house. He didn't understand this phobia of Evan's. How anyone could acquire it. Or tolerate it. How Evan could lead such an imprisoned life and, despite a few strange quirks, still manage to be so amiable and content.

Mark shook his head, coming only to the conclusion that though he didn't know any reasons or solutions for Evan's condition, he did know that the driveway wasn't going to get done by his standing there day dreaming. He started shoveling again.

At noon a purple car pulled up in front of his car in the road and parked at the foot of the driveway. A DAVE'S PIZZA sign was attached to its roof. A girl got out, carrying a red insulated-wrapped package, and came bounding up the near-finished driveway toward Mark.

"Hi," she said cheerfully, passing him and going for the house. She was a cute bright-eyed girl, with sandy hair tufting out of the rim of her parka hood. Her bubbly personality seemed to express that she loved her job, her life, the world. "Pizza delivery," she needlessly explained of her visit, by then already standing on the back stoop and knocking on the door.

Mark watched in a nervous wait well after she'd disappeared into the house and the door had closed behind her. Minutes passed. Long minutes. Enough minutes that made him wonder if maybe he ought to go in and check on matters.

But was that really his responsibility, to check up on Evan and the pizza girl? No, stupid thought. Yet as he resumed his shoveling, at a much slower pace now than before, he kept a watchful eye on the back door.

Chapter 9

▼

Inside the kitchen Evan was holding and kissing the pizza girl. She was still in her zipped-up jacket and boots, but there was no time to get any cozier or more intimate. Time was limited. He was just glad for this brief moment together, brought about by his idea of ordering out a pizza. "Laurel, I had to see you, had to take this risk."

"I couldn't believe it when Dave told me I had a delivery here," she said with a shudder. "I thought you wanted to be careful."

"I do." Amidst their closeness and exchange of deep looks, Evan was almost afraid to blink per chance she might disappear. "If you delivered Avon instead of pizza this would never work."

"Oh, Evan," she gave way to a cute little laugh and tightened her arms around his neck as they kissed again.

"I hope Mark likes pizza," Evan said thoughtfully.

"Everybody does," Laurel stated.

"Yeah, I guess."

"He seems nice, your sister's boyfriend out there."

"He is. It's just that…who asked him here, you know? I mean, not me. Tracy did, but she's not even home. Mark Rydell just shows up out of the blue one day and now I…I'm suppose to rearrange my whole life for him."

Laurel held Evan's face between her hands. "You don't have to rearrange anything. It's your house, your life."

Evan's eyes shifted away from her and to the back door. "I don't trust him. I don't want him to know about us. We probably shouldn't be together like this right now."

She giggled and motioned to the box she'd put on the table. "Far as he knows, I only delivered a pizza, right?"

Evan stayed serious. "I don't want anyone wrecking things for us, Laurel. Mark's knowing could do that."

"I'm only the pizza delivery person," she reminded him, arms back around him and holding so tightly to him that it seemed like maybe, in spite of what she was saying, she, too, was actually afraid.

They kissed again. Tenderly, as if their togetherness and this moment were so very fragile.

The tremor starting through Evan's body made him face the ugly fact that he was the fragile one. It wasn't fair that he should get a panic attack here and now, with Laurel, in the house. It wasn't like he was attempting a trip to the mailbox or to anywhere. He was only in the kitchen. With his girlfriend. Unfortunately sometimes the boundaries of his phobic life squeezed in on him even tighter than usual, as to where he felt there was no safe place for him. He hated his problem. And himself for having it. He gulped a gasp-like breath and stepped back from her.

"Are you all right, Evan?" she asked, with the compassion she always showed whenever the strangeness came over him.

"This can't be easy for you," he told her, ashamed of himself, his handicap, and the secrecy their relationship depended on. "How did you ever become involved with someone like me?"

"Maybe," Laurel said sweetly, "it was because in the last few months you ordered out endless pizzas from Dave's. And because I ran all of those deliveries. And because you always paid good tips. And because we always wound up having stuff to talk about."

Holding her, Evan wished he could be so much more for her. "I'm not sure those are enough reasons."

"They're enough for me."

"You deserve better."

"You *are* my better," she said.

They kissed a last time.

He paid her for the pizza.

She had to leave.

Evan watched her go down the driveway to that sick-looking purple car of hers, wishing he was going with her and leaving everything else behind him. Wishing that to leave could only be that simple rather than an inevitable head-on collision into the very core of his problem. Thinking about it made his hands clammy, mouth dry, swallowing difficult.

Pushing the back door open farther, he shouted at Mark, "Hey! Come on in! We're having pizza for lunch!"

Chapter 10

▼

Even if it hadn't been lunchtime, Mark was done shoveling. Good and done. He moved his car from the road up into the driveway, which he'd managed to clear as far back as the rear line of the house, then just stood for a few minutes admiring his accomplishment before going inside.

When he entered the kitchen Evan was pouring a glass of milk for each of them. "You did a good job out there, Mark. You must be hungry. Hope you like pizza. You do, don't you? I mean, I think everybody does, don't they?"

"Yeah, sure, I like it." Mark took off his jacket and shoes, then peered once more out the door window at the driveway before going to the table.

Evan came to sit across from him, bringing a paper napkin for each of them but forgetting their glasses of milk on the counter.

Mark guessed what was boggling his mind and went to get the drinks himself. "Cute delivery girl. Sure seemed like she was in here a long time."

Evan slipped a self-conscious smile, shifted on his chair, said nothing.

"Well, it's such a small town," Mark allowed, sitting back down, watching him, wondering about him, "I suppose everybody knows everybody and has a lot to talk about each time they run into one another."

"Change," Evan said like an answer, even though Mark really hadn't been asking. "For the pizza. I paid her and she was making change for me."

Though Mark gave a nod, he had a pretty good idea something other than making change had been going on. "If there was any trouble making change," he teased, "you could have called me. I'm good at making change."

"There wasn't any trouble," Evan said, opening the pizza box lid to an appealing cheese and pepperoni rimmed with golden crust and an aroma to die for.

Each of them took a slice and started eating.

Deciding he'd best let up about the delivery girl, Mark focused on the food. "Hey, this is great!"

"You don't have good pizza in New York?" Evan asked, his fingers catching up the gooey string of mozzarella dangling from his slice.

"Not this good, no. Least none I've had."

"Welcome to my world," Evan boasted.

"No kidding," Mark said with a laugh. "Dave's Pizza, Drendal, Minnesota...who would've guessed they had the best."

"What's New York like?" Evan asked, as if it were impossibly beyond him.

Mark took a second bite and talked with his mouth full. Big...stirring...exciting."

"More exciting than Minneapolis, no doubt."

"No doubt," Mark said. He wiped his mouth with his napkin and studied Evan curiously. "So it sounds like you've at least been to Minneapolis, huh?"

"A long time ago," Evan said, as if it were something he'd just as soon forget.

"Well, you'll have to come see New York for yourself some time."

"I don't think so."

Of course he wouldn't go to New York, Mark knew. Not with agoraphobia. Maybe he could make it out to the mailbox once a week, but that was it. Like Evan couldn't imagine New York, Mark couldn't imagine the restriction of agoraphobia. "How'd you get there, to Minneapolis?"

"I told you," Evan said, staring at the slice of pizza he was still holding but no longer eating, "it was a long time ago."

"What happened? What changed everything for you?" Mark kept on.

Evan put his pizza down, wiped his hands on his napkin, said nothing.

Mark hadn't meant to badger him. That's not what his visit was for. But it was really hard not to become analytical about it. Because how could anyone withdraw, as Evan did, from the world beyond the kitchen door, or the mailbox, or from ever going anywhere further with the pizza girl than the kitchen?

Mark reminded himself that he was only a houseguest and had no right to be razzing Evan. Or pitying him. He took another bite of pizza, safely saying, "Hey, this is really, really great."

Evan nodded, though seemed to be done eating.

Remington, sitting on top of the refrigerator as if he were king of the hill, watched over the guys.

"I still can't believe all the snow I moved out there," Mark got back to commending himself for it as he helped himself to a second slice of pizza.

"Yeah, it was a lot." Evan seemed pleased to have the attention off of himself. "So how you feeling now?"

Mark grinned. "Good, in a broken down, exhausted sort of way."

"It was probably way too much for you to tackle at one time," Evan said.

Mark gave an immense nod, as in no kidding. And then before he knew it he was remarking, "Could've used some help out there, that's for sure." Damn, he'd done it again, stabbed Evan with his own phobia.

Evan lowered his eyes and seemed to disappear.

Mark had meant to be more careful, to start weighing his words ahead of saying them. And yet, he wondered, was that really what Evan wanted, expected, of him? Soft-siding? Pampering? Avoidance of his problem like it was something totally unapproachable or shameful? God, this was difficult.

Holding on to the hope that Evan would truly prefer directness, Mark pressed, "How did this happen? How did you become this way? I'd really like to know, understand."

Head down and silent, Evan was somewhere else.

"How did this agoraphobia thing start with you?" Mark nevertheless kept on, trusting that his persistence would show compassion rather than disrespect. "I wish you would tell me."

Neither words nor movement nor expression came from Evan. It was spooky. And sad.

Mark left him alone for a few minutes and ate some more pizza. But he didn't feel good about letting Evan alone. It felt every bit as wrong as did his bugging him. So eventually he spoke out again. "I'm sorry you have this problem, Evan."

Evan responded to that. "Everyone has problems."

"Yeah, I guess," Mark partially agreed, "except not with leaving their homes."

"No, I suppose not."

"It bothers me, Evan," Mark said, "that you're living such an imprisoned life here."

"It's not your problem. Don't be bothered."

"What bothers me the most is that it doesn't seem to bother you that much."

"How do you know it doesn't bother me?" Evan's dark eyes seemed to get darker.

This was good, how they were getting into it now. Hopefully it meant that Evan might be opening up enough to accept help. Proceeding a bit too eagerly however, Mark stumbled over his own words. "Because…because you…I mean, the way you…"

"You've been here one day," Evan's voice rose. "You don't know me."

"That's right, I don't. But Tracy told me stuff."

"Tracy sees what she wants to see."

Mark nodded all too knowingly. "She sees you as okay and wants me to see you as okay. But you're not, are you?"

Evan swallowed hard, rolled his eyes, and answered, "Yes and no."

"Let's talk about the no part." Mark leaned forth on his chair, as if being a few inches closer to Evan might better his chance of getting through to him. "How can you let yourself be a prisoner to this house."

"I'm not a prisoner," Evan said, defending his life as if he actually had one.

"I'd say yes you are a prisoner when you can't even walk out that door." Mark motioned toward the back door, daring Evan to prove his freedom.

"I can walk out that door any time I want." Evan straightened himself against the back of his chair and nervously gazed across the room.

"Maybe that you don't want to is the problem."

"Mine or yours?" Evan asked.

It was a double-edged question Mark chose not to answer.

"What's it matter to you anyway, what I do or don't do?" Evan fended.

Mark chose a drink of milk over answering.

But Evan already thought he had it figured. "Tracy sent you out here to work on me, didn't she?"

Mark downed his entire glass of milk, then sat playing with the empty glass for a few moments before emitting in half truth, "The only work I may get into out here is my writing."

"Writing," Evan said suspiciously. "Like an article on me?"

"No. I'm not that kind of writer. I write fiction."

"Maybe I *am* fiction," Evan said smartly.

"Meaning that your phobia is merely an act?" Mark asked in a lawyerly manner.

Evan sprung away from the table, ending their talk right then and there and going for the stairs. Remington, as though he'd been listening all along with complete loyalty to Evan's side of the case, leaped from the refrigerator, to the counter, to the floor, and followed his master up the steps.

So much for open communication, Mark concluded disappointedly. Left alone, he resumed eating. But either the pizza had lost its original good taste or he'd lost his original good appetite, because it sure wasn't the same now. He felt ashamed of talking to Evan the way he had, suggesting his phobia wasn't real, driving him off like that. He had no right. He barely knew the guy. The point of his stay was supposed to be to get to know him, not psychoanalyze him. He shouldn't have said half of what he did to him. And yet, then what should he say? He honestly didn't know.

When he'd eaten his half of the pizza, he covered the lid over Evan's half, left the table and went to the door window to look out at the cleared driveway and his Shadow parked there upon it. Pride once more swelled over him for the good job he'd done.

As his gaze eventually slipped back to the stairway, so did his concern slip back to Evan. He considered taking the remaining pizza up to him and making amends for all the wrong things he'd said, then secondly he decided it might be best to just leave well enough alone for now.

Mark shuffled his weary, aching body into the living room and carefully lowered himself to the couch. Since the sun had gone under and stayed under, the afternoon had turned to a faded gray beyond the window sheers. The blandness easily encouraged him to shut his eyes. Except when he did it was in exchange for lonesome, mental visions of Tracy. Which made him wish, all the more, that she were here in person with a hug and a kiss and some helpful guidance in this Evan situation, because he sure wasn't handling it as well as he ought to.

He remembered how he'd gotten into this. Tracy's idea. Abetted by the fact that he loved her enough to go along with it. Okay, it was that simple. And the reminder helped him be less hard on himself about it. She wanted him to get to know and accept her brother, his phobia. A sound request, Mark logically reconsidered. Shouldn't be that big of an ordeal. Except how quickly he'd already found that to know and to care about Evan involved a whole lot more than simple acknowledgment or blind acceptance. Something within his own heart and conscience was pressuring him to believe that Evan could get well, and that just maybe he, all the way from New York, was the intended one to help him do so. Mark realized this was becoming more than just a favor to Tracy. It was starting to feel like his own personal mission to save Evan.

His head ached as much as his back and arms. From the snow, the cold, his confrontation with Evan, the responsibility he'd undertaken. He needed some aspirin but didn't feel like getting up to look for it. He didn't want to move. Couldn't move. Which made him feel as much a prisoner to the couch as Evan was to the house. He wondered if there was a phobia name for that.

Chapter 11

▼

Upstairs, on his bedroom phone, Evan called the New York Howell Hotel. He needed to talk to Tracy. Now.

"Too many rings," he noted to Remington, who was sitting beside him on the edge of the bed, ears pricked with interest. "She's not answering in her room."

He cut that call and dialed the lobby desk. The clerk paged Tracy, tracked down her whereabouts in the hotel and brought her onto the line.

"Evan?" she answered, sounding alarmed.

"I don't need a baby-sitter, Tracy!" he immediately shot off to her.

"Evan, what's wrong?"

"Or a therapist!" he added.

"What's going on? Calm down and tell me what's going on."

"That's what I'd like to know." Evan was overwrought with a degree of anger he wasn't used to and didn't know how to handle. Plus he was already sorry he'd hastily phoned Tracy.

"This is about Mark, right?" It didn't take her long to determine.

"Of course it's about Mark," Evan said, so sharply that it startled Remington. He soothed the cat with some petting.

"I don't want you to be upset," Tracy said, though she sounded more than a little upset herself. "I realize it was kind of a shock, your not reading my letter about Mark until after he'd arrived. I'm sorry about that."

"I'm not upset," Evan lied. "I just don't get the point of Mark's being here. Your letter, late as I read it, never did give any actual reason for his coming here."

"But it did," Tracy insisted. "I explained that Mark and I are considering marriage and…and I want the two of you to get to know each other first."

Evan gave a curt laugh. "That's not a reason, it's a joke. Shouldn't it be more important for him and you to get to know each other than him and me?"

"We'll be a family, Evan," she said in that motherly manner she so commonly used on him. "We'll all need to get along well with one another if we're going to—"

"Live together?" he grimly speculated the rest of her sentence. "You're planning to officially move him in here?"

While the line hung silent for a few moments, Evan raked his fingers through his hair, rolled his eyes upward, and shook his head over and over.

When Tracy got around to answering, it didn't seem to come that easily for her. "I don't know…probably…we'll see how things go."

"You don't have to stay here, Tracy, after you and Mark get married. You can move wherever you want to. I'll be all right, you know. Don't always think you have to juggle your life around for me."

When she didn't respond, Evan knew that juggling was precisely what she was trying to do. "You don't need to be my keeper," he told her, "and neither does Mark."

"I'm sorry, Evan, if Mark's giving you a bad time."

"I don't like being studied—"

"I warned him not to do that," she said,

"—like an animal in the zoo."

"I'll talk to him, okay? Get him, put him on the line."

"I can't do that." Evan started petting Remington again, this time more as a comfort to himself than to the cat.

"Why?" she asked.

"He's downstairs."

"So go down and—"

"I can hardly go tell him that my big sister wants to talk to him about leaving me alone, can I?"

"Oh, Evan," Tracy sighed sympathetically. Then more assuredly, "Don't worry. It's going to be all right. Mark's a nice guy and he's not there to harass you, believe me. Give him a chance. That's all I'm asking. Listen, I'll tell you what, hang up now and then in a few minutes I'll call back and talk to Mark. Let it ring so that he'll have to pick it up."

"I don't know," Evan said, shutting his eyes tightly as a means of helping him concentrate. When he opened them, he found Remington staring at him quizzically. "Okay," Evan gave in to Tracy's idea, "but first, how come you never told me about Mark before this if you've known him for six months?"

"I should have," she confessed. "I just never got around to it."

"Now, all of a sudden, it's important."

"Yes, it is."

"Well, it's not that important to me," he let her know.

"Evan, please," Tracy coaxed.

"When are you coming home?" Evan asked, wanting a measure of how much longer he was going to have to put up with this stupid situation.

"I leave for New Jersey tomorrow. I'll be home in about a week. Hang in there, okay?" she said encouragingly. "Mark's a nice guy, you're a nice guy, the two of you should be able to get along just fine."

"Okay," Evan said, finally realizing he had no choice in the matter.

"I'll see you soon," she promised.

He hung up the phone and dropped back flat across the bed. Remington nosed against his hand then licked it. Evan paid no attention to the cat. He wasn't feeling well. Uncontrollable flash thoughts, far more disturbing than the problem of Mark, were jolting his mind. Ones of Sam...blood...a darkened back street. Horrid, reoccurring memory attacks he couldn't stop, change, or come to any certain terms with even now after all this time. And as always, they turned him sick, sorry, and intensely bothered.

Chapter 12

▼

Tracy had been in the hotel kitchen talking with Travini, the head chef, when she'd been summoned to the phone. After talking with Evan, and before returning to her work, she excused herself and went up to the privacy of her own room to call Mark.

She sat at the desk, worried as to what exactly was going on between him and Evan. Her plan didn't seem to be going as she'd hoped. Mark had only been in Drendal for one day and Evan seemed really stressed. She didn't like that her brother was upset. It was the last thing she wanted, the last thing he needed. She had so hoped this together time between the guys would be good. She had depended on Mark to make it be.

The phone rang and rang. Of course Evan wasn't answering and Mark was undoubtedly hesitant to do so.

Maybe she wasn't supposed to let anyone else into her life. Maybe that's what all these times meant of nothing ever working out, with Mark or any other guy before him. None of her ex-boyfriends ever accepted Evan's situation and the effect it in turn had on her life, why should Mark? Except, she'd really hoped he would be different, better.

"Hello," a groggy voice finally answered her call.

"Mark?" she asked.

"Tracy?" he asked.

She laughed. "You didn't sound like yourself. Don't I sound like myself either?"

"No...I mean, yes...I mean, I was just surprised. The phone was ringing and ringing and it didn't look like Evan was going to get it and I thought I probably should but it took me a while to get on my feet and out to the kitchen and..." He paused to breathe. "It's good to hear you, Tracy. I've just been dreaming about you."

"You were sleeping?"

"Napping."

"Are you okay?" she asked with new concern.

"Yeah. You?" he returned the question.

"Yes. Why wouldn't I be?"

"I just talked to you this morning and didn't expect this."

"Like twice a day is too often for us?"

"That's not what I meant," Mark said.

She leaned back on her chair, took a deep breath, composed herself. "Mark, I'm only calling to...to see how everything is going there."

He laughed. "Not much change since this morning." Then seriously he stated, "Tracy, I like your brother, he's okay, but I just don't think I understand him."

"You're an understanding person, Mark, please try."

"Evan's life shouldn't be the way it is," he summarized the problem.

"Unfortunately it is. You've got to understand that and accept that. It's the reason you're there. Why can't you just—"

"Okay," he interrupted, "maybe I understand it, but I can't accept it."

"Mark, please," Tracy pleaded over long distance, "don't disrupt Evan's life. Just be nice to him. Relax. If you relax, he'll relax. And so will I."

"That's why I'm here, to relax?" he said, mixing a laugh into his complaint. "I'm sorry, Tracy, but I'm finding that just a little bit hard to do. I'm having to watch everything I say to him, when I don't even know what to say to begin with."

"You're a writer, you should be good with words."

"I tend to get accusing with him."

"No, Mark, no," Now Tracy found herself whining over long distance and stopped it right there. "It's the last thing Evan needs, to be accused. Just accept his problem and him for what they are. Can't you please do that?"

"I like Evan. I do." Though Mark's certainty seemed to rise for a moment, it didn't last. "Except that...what he's doing to himself makes me feel really sorry for him on one hand and furious on the other. I...I just don't know here, Tracy. I just don't."

The wearisome sound of his voice was causing Tracy to worry as much about him as she did about Evan. "Mark, what's wrong? You sound so tired or sick or something."

He moaned. "A little tired and sick, yeah, otherwise okay. It's from all the shoveling."

"You did some shoveling?"

"Yeah. Some. The driveway, so I could—"

"The driveway? The whole driveway?" she shrieked.

"Except for the part right in front of the garage."

"Why did you do that?" Tracy scolded. "There was a half a winter's accumulation on the driveway. You could have parked in the road like I always do."

"I wanted to park in the driveway."

"You'd kill yourself to park in the driveway?"

"It's okay. I'm okay. I'll be okay." His voice lifted and almost seemed to bubble now. "I actually think it did me some good. I sort of enjoyed it."

Tracy broke into a helpless laugh. "Enjoyed it?"

"Yeah, sort of."

"I don't want you to have a heart attack."

"I'm thirty-eight, not fifty-eight."

"You're used to New York apartment living. Don't think you can turn into a country boy in one day. Take a long hot bath, a couple aspirins, and rest. Okay?"

"Okay, doc," he said.

"Another week," she reminded him, trying to make their separation sound like practically nothing. "Relax. Get to know Evan. Do some writing. I love you, Mark."

"Love you too, Tracy."

After hanging up the phone, Tracy sat there for a while with a smile on her face and a renewal of hope in her heart. She was lucky to have two such wonderful guys in her life as Evan and Mark. She loved them both so dearly. Now all she needed was for them to become friends before they became brothers-in-law. That was her goal, her absolute necessity. She trusted Mark with the matter. At this point she had no *choice* but to trust him.

"Please," she nevertheless prayed for further reassurance.

Soon she left her room and her daydreaming to go back down to the hotel kitchen. Travini had been about to show her the newly installed supply cupboards, explain the rotation system used at hectic dinner times, and go over the menus for next month.

Chapter 13

Mark returned to the couch and collapsed back into the same state of bodily surrender he'd been in before Tracy's call. His muscles were becoming more stiff and sore by the minute. It wasn't fair that he should have to pay this hard for his master achievement, his sort-of good time. He closed his eyes. Moaned. Knew he should go upstairs for aspirin and a long hot soak in the tub. But that would require an amount of effort he wasn't sure he had. A few minutes. He just needed a few minutes to think about it, work himself up to it. Maybe ten minutes. Maybe thirty.

Since he didn't fall asleep this time, he eventually forced himself back up onto his feet. He walked out to the kitchen with more physical discomfort now than when he'd gone for the phone. He dragged himself up the stairs, resenting how easily Evan had raced up and down them that morning. He also resented that a few hours of snow shoveling had wiped him out this much. How could he be so out of condition? Whatever was happening to him? Time, he supposed. Age. The fact that he wasn't twenty-six, but thirty-eight. Two notches away from forty.

Evan's bedroom door was shut. Mark passed it, feeling twinges of guilt. He had to do a lot better than he had so far with Tracy's brother. For Tracy's sake. Evan's sake. Maybe his own sake. This was a test, according to Tracy, and so far he wasn't rating very well. Think. Evaluate. It shouldn't be that difficult. Any test should depend on honesty, shouldn't it? What test didn't? Okay then, to not follow his own natural instincts on this would be like cheating on a test. Wouldn't it? Therefore he ought not do any less than be himself, only himself, if this were to be a worthy test.

After a twenty-minute soak in steaming hot water Mark felt more limber, wonderfully soothed and drowsy. He retreated to his given room and dropped onto the bed. A little more rest…and then…maybe later…he and Evan could talk about…well, something. Surely they could find something permissible to talk about.

The next time Mark opened his eyes it was to total darkness. *Can a person go blind from shoveling snow?* he panicked. He strained to see, but couldn't. *Whoa,* this was scary. And then…he considered that it could be night.

He felt for the bedside light and turned it on, glad to have regained his sight but squinting to the shock of brightness. He checked the time. Ten-thirty? He'd slept several hours only to wake up and find it was bedtime?

Every muscle in his body protested as he got out of bed and hobbled toward the door. The therapeutic effects of aspirin and a hot bath were long gone. Hours of non-motion caused the stiffness and soreness to really set in. He peered into the hallway, hearing voices, faintly, from somewhere. He stood listening. They were coming from the kitchen. Evan had company this late?

Curiosity got the best of him. He had to go check. He walked to the top of the stairs and quietly began to sneak down. Well, he guessed it wouldn't actually be sneaking if he was simply going to the kitchen for a snack. After all, he'd missed supper.

Just as he got to the last step, he caught sight of the back door going shut. Someone had just left.

Lit only by a nightlight, the dimness of the kitchen seemed to further enhance the mystery. Evan stood against a cabinet, looking as if he'd been caught, or almost caught, at something. He offered no explanation.

Though he was dying to know, Mark restrained himself from asking. "Hi."

"Hi," Evan said as simply. "You slept a long time. Guess you were wiped out."

"I never want to look at a shovel again, let alone use one."

Evan laughed. "Rest was good. You needed it. Feeling any better now?"

"Not as tired, but twice as sore." Mark walked across the room to the back door. Looking out the window, he saw a car backing out of the driveway onto the road with a DAVE'S PIZZA sign on its roof.

He turned to Evan. "You ordered another pizza?"

"Did you say you wanted more pizza?" Evan rearranged the question. "There's still some left in the refrigerator. Or stew, maybe you'd prefer stew. I made stew for supper, which you missed. You must be starved. I didn't wake you. Thought it was best to let you sleep."

"Uh...uh..." More interested in what might be going on between Evan and the pizza girl than in food, it took Mark a few moments to switch his thoughts. "I'll have some stew, thanks."

Evan took a ready-portioned bowl of it out of the refrigerator.

Mark slowly lowered himself onto a chair at the table. "You said you made it?"

"I did."

"You're very good at cooking, Evan."

"I am," Evan credited himself.

Mark grinned. "Except for pizza, huh? Don't suppose you could make pizza comparable to Dave's, right?"

Evan set the stew inside the microwave, shut the door and pressed the appropriate buttons. "Six minutes should do it. It's late for me. I'm going to bed. Good-night, Mark."

"Mir-oww." Remington appeared out of nowhere and tagged up the stairs after him.

Mark sat alone at the table. In the quiet, low-lighted kitchen. In Drendal, Minnesota. He'd just gotten up from a long sleep and wouldn't likely be ready for more for some time now. Whatever would he do the rest of the night? After his ten-thirty dinner?

The aloneness made him start doubting his being and meaning all over again. How he'd come there to meet Evan, finding that he liked him just fine, sure, but wasn't allowed to help him. *No, hadn't dare.* And he loved Tracy, sure, but she was running this weird test on him as if he were a used car she wasn't quite sure of buying. And his profession was writing, but his last published book had been over a year ago, with still nothing new and promising in the making. He felt so idle. Useless.

The microwave hummed to the heating of Mark's late night meal, sending out an appealing aroma to tantalize his empty stomach. He got off his chair, moaning at the effort, and went to have another look out at the clean shoveled driveway and his Shadow parked there upon it in the moonlight of one very cold winter's night. In spite of the problems weighing on him, he found there was an amazing amount of comfort and coziness to be had in this farmhouse kitchen. He gazed about, absorbing its worth.

The microwave beeped. His food was ready. And he was starving.

As he started toward the appliance, he found Remington had returned and was sitting on the bottom step, cute-faced and quizzically watching. Deciding right then and there that cats weren't really so bad after all, Mark acknowledged him with a friendly, "Hey, Rem,"

"Mir-oww," the cat responded.
"Oh, you smelled the stew, did you? Like to share some with me?"
"Mir-oww."
"I'll get another bowl."
"Mir-oww."
"You're welcome."

Chapter 14

Wincing at the soreness in his back and arms, Mark pulled the covers up over his head, hoping to shut out the clamoring noise of Evan's step routine early the next morning. The covers hardly did it. He could still hear the annoyance…up the stairs, down the stairs, up, down, again and again. He resented the time, location and form of Evan's exercise. Also the fact that someone else could be so vigorously active when he himself could barely move.

As he slowly and carefully repositioned himself in bed, every movement a painful account of yesterday, his right foot bumped against a solid lump in the covers. Something was on the bed, on top of the quilt. Groaning, he reached to turn on the nightstand light, discovering…

It was Remington on the lower right corner of the bed, curled in a ball as rightfully as if he owned the space. The door must not have been shut tight last night and he'd freely wandered in and claimed a spot. He raised his head and gave Mark a look.

"Yeah, yeah," Mark acknowledged him. "Share some of your stew with a cat and he automatically expects you to share your bed."

Mark dropped back onto his pillow, letting every muscle in his body relent. Then he sighed with the contentment of lying still again. The step stomping ceased. Finally. Good. Maybe a couple more hours of sleep would be possible now.

After a few minutes of not falling back to sleep, Mark checked the time. Five forty-five. He'd slept all of yesterday afternoon and part way into the night, had supper, and was awake from then until somewhere around four AM. Now, just when he'd been sleeping well again, Evan's exercise regimen woke him.

Figuring what the heck, he got out of bed, dressed, and with Remington scuttling ahead of him, went downstairs.

"Hi, Mark. How you feeling?" Evan, washing dishes at the sink, greeted him as cheerfully as if yesterday's tiff was long forgotten and today was a brand new beginning.

"Guess I'm fortunate to still be able to move," Mark said. "How come you always have so many dishes to do this early in the morning?"

"Not so many. Just the few from my breakfast. I eat my cereal, do my steps, wash my dishes. I like to keep up."

"Keep up, right." Mark watched Remington weave around Evan's ankles. "I woke up with your cat on my bed."

Evan nodded, stepping over the cat in order to reach a towel off the end of the counter. "Rem likes you."

Still standing in place just off the steps, Mark said, "I suppose it's nice, getting your workout out of the way so early."

"The steps, yeah. Sorry if I disturbed you."

"No, not at all," Mark said pungently. "Us New Yorkers are used to noise."

"They do steps there?" Evan asked, finishing his task at the sink and turning a serious look back at him.

Mark's silence was his answer.

"Maybe you'd like to give it a try, the step thing," Evan suggested.

Mark shook his head. "No thanks. I had enough exercise yesterday to last me a while." Though he'd sort of enjoyed the vigorous shoveling as a diversion, and despite his writer's block, he was missing his writing.

Evan took a notebook out of a cabinet drawer and sat down with it at the table. On his way to the door window, Mark looked over Evan's shoulder, seeing that it was a collection of hand-written recipes. Man, this guy sure liked to cook. But since he would no doubt be doing laundry soon, as per his routine, Mark thought he should mention, "Evan, I've got a few things now that need washing, if you want to add them to yours."

"Actually I'm going to be pretty busy this morning," Evan said. "I was thinking that maybe you could do the laundry today, if you wouldn't mind."

"Oh...uh, sure...that's fine. What are you going to be busy with?"

"Cooking."

"This morning?" Mark was surprised.

"Yeah, soon as the groceries arrive." Evan left the table and took his cookbook over to a counter. "Wilson's promised me an early delivery."

"That's how you get things? Deliveries?" As soon as Mark asked he felt foolish for doing so and answered it himself. "Right. So what are you going to cook?"

"Chicken Primavera."

"Sounds fancy." Mark peered out the door window. Both his Shadow and the driveway appeared to be intact. He stepped over Remington, now curled up on the entrance rug, and went to pour himself a mug of coffee. "You know, Evan, I've already found you to be a excellent cook, but please don't feel you have to continue out-doing yourself on my account."

"It's not for you," Evan said.

Mark gave him a questioning who-else sort of look.

"It's for Mrs. Quillo's luncheon," Evan explained. "She's coming by to pick up the prepared food at eleven. I'm just hoping the groceries get here soon." He nervously checked the wall clock. It was barely six.

Only halfway getting it, Mark asked in puzzlement, "Have you ever done this before, cooked food for people to pick up?"

"Yeah."

"Really?"

"Yeah."

"Often?"

Evan nodded while tying on a white chef's apron. "Sort of."

"Oh. Kind of like a little side business?" Mark was getting it now.

"Kind of," Evan said, fastening his long hair back with a rubber band.

"Wherever did you learn to cook so well anyway?" Mark asked, after which he finally took a drink of the coffee he'd been holding.

"Here in this kitchen," Evan answered.

Mark cracked a smile. "I mean how?"

"Recipes. Practice. Liking to work with food." Evan took two bowls down from the top shelf of a cupboard, set them on the counter, then impatiently went to stand at the door window to watch for Wilson's.

"Well, the spaghetti and stew I've tasted so far have been sensational," Mark complimented him, "but this Chicken something or other sounds gourmet. That's got to take a special knack. Plus where do you even get recipes like that?"

Flicking a look from one end of the room to the other, as though the place was under tight scrutiny, Evan quietly disclosed, "It's…a secret."

Chapter 15

▼

Tracy took a final stroll through the New York Howell Hotel. This time without a clipboard and list of questions for the staff. This time to say good-bye. At this point she'd made her rounds to everyone except Alex Roso, the hotel manager, and the kitchen help.

As she approached Alex in the main lobby, he pulled a long-stemmed yellow rose out of the desk arrangement and gave it to her.

She sniffed it, touched it to her cheek, and smiled. "Thank you, Alex. You're always so thoughtful."

He stood there in his navy suit, red tie, perfect posture and professional grandeur, giving her a fond, uncle-like smile. "It's been our usual pleasure, having you here and about, Tracy."

"And, as usual, my report to Mr. Howell on this hotel will be excellent in all respects. Keep up the good work."

"Our intentions," he assured her.

"Of all the Howell Hotels, New York's my favorite," she stated sincerely.

"And of all our guests, you're our favorite," he said in the same way to her.

They shared a laugh over their mutual admiration society.

"I'll be back in a few months, you know," Tracy reminded him.

"Your regular room will be available to you."

"It's a wonderful room," she said. "But of course all rooms in a Howell Hotel are wonderful."

"Of course," he readily agreed. Then giving her a wink, he added, "Though some rooms, like some guests, are particularly special."

Tracy's eyes teared. "*You're* special, Alex. Thank you. I'm going to say good-bye to the kitchen staff now, then I'm off to New Jersey. See you next time, okay?"

"Next time, yes." Alex Roso gave her a warm, parting hug.

She left the lobby, walked down the hall past the dining room and through a back door to the kitchen. It was mid morning, with the crew at its lightest. There were just two cooks, one waitress, one waiter and a dishwasher on duty. They stopped their tasks when Tracy entered, immediately lending her their full attention.

She stood beside the center island. "Guess it's that time. Time for me to be moving on. Once again my report on the New York Howell has met its usual excellence. And once again the kitchen rates four stars out of four."

Everyone clapped and cheered at their score. Tracy laughed and clapped along with them.

Travini, the chief cook, stepped forth to hand her some papers. He was sixty-ish, with a kind round face, twinkly eyes, and white hair edging the rim of his white hat. "Here, for your brother, more of Howell's exclusive recipes."

"Oh, Travini, thanks. Evan always loves getting these. He's almost the cook you are."

He shook his finger at her. "Remember, the recipes, they do not go any further than the Howell Hotels or your house."

"No, of course not. Privileged material." Tracy folded them and clutched them to her chest.

"And…" Travini added considerately, "if he has any questions he can call me here any time on the 800 number."

"Okay," she said, standing there with her rose in one hand, recipes in the other, eyes misty again. Who would have thought a hotel field manager's job would be so emotional? She broke a smile, saying, "I have to leave now. You guys keep up the good work. Because along with its elegant rooms and superior service, the Howell is especially known for its exquisite dining."

"It's the special recipes, known only to the hotel *and to your brother*," Travini stated with a grin.

She waved the papers appreciatively. "Thanks. Good-bye, everyone. See you next time."

She'd already had her suitcases brought down to the front door earlier, and as she went there now she found her cab waiting to take her to the airport.

After a week at the New Jersey Howell she would then be able to go home to Mark and Evan. She looked forward to that, expecting by then to find them good friends, and no obstacles in the way of her marrying Mark. Thinking of it made her wonderfully excited and anxious.

Chapter 16

Mark did the laundry. No problem. He'd been a bachelor looking out for himself for a long enough time to know perfectly well how to do the task. His stiff and sore muscles had improved considerably since he'd first gotten up, and he didn't feel half bad now. While the washer ran its cycle, he carried out Remington's play routine with him on the basement floor. The cat was in his crazy glory, chasing the shoestring around in circles, batting at it, biting at it. It made Mark laugh and feel child-like.

After hanging the washed clothes on the line he went back up to the kitchen to find Evan well into his cooking. The groceries had arrived while Mark was downstairs. He'd heard the truck in the driveway, the knock at the back door, extra footsteps across the floor.

Bowls, pots, pans and food were everywhere on the counters and table now. Washed broccoli and carrots were draining in the sink. A curly-looking pasta was in bubbling water on the stove. Evan was dipping chicken parts into a yellowish batter that contained little green flecks.

Mark shook his head, still so amazed over Evan's cooking ability. It hardly fit with the first image the guy projected. Yet here and now, with his dark hair in a ponytail, a white bibbed apron around his slim frame, concentration in his face, and precision in his hands, Evan displayed a masterful expertise in the art of food preparation.

Mark picked up a spice bottle off the counter and read the label. The fact that the name was impossible for him to pronounce indicated its rarity, at least to him. "A one-horse town like Drendal carries *this?*"

"Tracy got it for me in Duluth," Evan said, setting the baking dish of green-flecked chicken into the oven. "And actually, Drendal does have quite a few horses."

Mark grinned. "I suppose it does." He went to the door window for a look out at his car. It was still there in its place on the neatly shoveled driveway. And no, there was no new fallen snow as of yet. "So Evan..." he began.

"Yeah?" Evan glanced up from the ten things he seemed to be doing at one time.

"I'd like to get out of here for a while later on. You know, cruise through town and a ways out of town, check out the whole general area."

"Okay," Evan said easily.

"Could I talk you into going with me? I mean, you could just stay in the car, you wouldn't even have to get out."

"No," Evan's answer was quick and automatic, "you go ahead, Mark."

"But I could use your—"

"No. Sorry."

Mark was as disappointed for Evan as he was for himself. But he dropped it in exchange for asking, "So is there anything I can do to help you here?"

Evan gave an embarrassed smile and shook his head no. "Actually, I manage much better by myself in the kitchen."

"Oh. Sure. I'll get out of your way. Listen, maybe I'll set up my typewriter at that desk in the living room and try to do some writing this morning."

"Okay." Evan said.

Mark strolled into the living room. Remington was grooming himself in a spot of sun coming through the front window. He took his typewriter out of the carton, set it upon the desk and plugged it in. Rem continued his bath, not the least bit distracted.

Mark rolled a sheet of paper into the machine. Then sat staring blankly at it, with no words coming. The writing of *Street Winder* had gone so well, and had become a much bigger success than his first book, *Ryan*. It made enough money for him to quit his classy investments job and devote himself full-time to the expectation of book number three and all the endless thereafters. Except that book number three still hadn't taken off. And his savings were dwindling. And he'd bought Tracy an expensive ring and asked her to marry him. And...what the hell did he think he was doing? Getting ahead of himself like this, living in a dream world, riding on the coattail of one really good book? Thinking that his love of writing and his love for a woman were enough? Like believing automatically made it so. What he still needed to do was pass Tracy's so-called test with Evan. Plus buckle down to creating at least the first draft of book three.

Gazing at the falling-asleep cat on the floor, who was tired from his playtime, Mark mindlessly sought his advice, "Hey, Rem, give me a good story idea."

Remington was still awake enough to give Mark a slit-eyed look and a faint meow.

Mark interpreted it as, "Oh, you're saying I should write about this cat in a fish market who has enough money in his little cat pocket to buy anything he wants. Yeah, that could work."

Okay, seriously, back to his typewriter, Mark placed his fingers upon the keys. He typed T R A C Y. Which had nothing at all to do with any idea for a new book but was the only thing, the only letters, that came to his mind.

He missed her so much. And still could not comfortably comprehend why she was out East and he was here. So far the time he was spending with her brother wasn't making a whole lot of sense. He was getting to know Evan, sure, okay, that. But how much was there to really know about the guy? Other than the fact that he stayed in the house, ran his life on pretty much of a set routine, was a great cook, and didn't really seem to give a damn about expanding his life to the outer world. Nor was Mark permitted to pressure him any in that direction. And that was it. What more was there?

Mark found himself to be in the middle of a two-sided situation consisting of Tracy's side and Evan's side. He was actually beginning to wonder which of the two had the worse problem and needed the most help. And what sort of help at that. Test…this was all part of Tracy's so-called test. As of yet he hadn't found any answers. He still wasn't totally sure of the questions.

He stared at his idle fingers positioned on the keyboard. Then at the letters he'd typed so far that spelled Tracy's name. Then he typed some more letters, S H I T.

Evan, the master cook, worked steadily in the kitchen until nine o'clock. Then he came into the living room, sat on the arm of an easy chair, and lit a cigarette. "You ever smoke?" he asked of Mark's watching him.

"I quit a couple years ago," Mark said proudly.

Evan exhaled a gray haze. "Does my smoking bother you?"

"One cigarette? No, I think I can handle it."

"Good."

"So Evan, are we having a ten o'clock coffee break today?" Mark felt an uplift just thinking about it.

Until Evan replied, "Sorry, don't have time this morning. Got a lot to do yet. But you can help yourself."

"No, no, I wouldn't want to impose. That's okay. I can skip it. I've got a lot of writing to do here anyway."

After Evan finished his smoke and returned to the kitchen, Mark got on with his typing, NO COFFEE BREAK TODAY. SHIT.

This was stupid. He was getting nowhere, would never get his third novel written this way. He felt distant to creativity. Had no direction or base. If he were at least at his own base, he might be able to think like the writer he was suppose to be. He could definitely think a whole lot better on a computer rather than a typewriter, and in New York rather than Drendal.

He left the desk, feeling restless, and took a walk around the room. He stopped to gaze out the front window. No additional snow coming down. Yet. A part of him was glad, another part surprisingly disappointed. He gazed back at his typewriter, then down at Remington, who was contentedly basking in the sun with no further want. Then he went to stand in the kitchen doorway to watch Evan. He felt envious that both Rem and Evan were doing something and he wasn't.

Although time was assuredly going fast for Evan and slow for Mark, eleven o'clock arrived at precisely the same time for both of them. And an attractive looking woman of probably forty-something arrived to pick up her luncheon order. Mark watched as inconspicuously as he could from the living room. This whole event had him totally fascinated.

"Well, you've done it again, Evan," the woman raved happily, setting an empty carton and two empty baskets onto the kitchen counter.

"Hope everything's all right," the chef said, dishing his cooked specialties into plastic containers, then setting them into the carton and baskets.

The woman, in tight purple slacks and a white furry jacket, sashayed around to Evan's side of the table, cooing, "It will be fine, dear, as usual. I can always count on you."

Maybe Evan was afraid of the outside world, but he hardly seemed afraid of women…at least not of the young one who delivered pizza yesterday and this older one for whom he'd cooked today.

Mrs. Quillo cozied up to him, as if doing so was a familiar practice of hers. She slid one hand up his chest and her other hand down his arm. Then kissed him. Not in a friendly thank-you-for-your-help way, but more like ooh, baby baby.

Interesting, Mark thought from his stakeout. *Very interesting.*

Evan took Mrs. Quillo's attention placidly, as though it was a typical means of payment, nothing more. Then the woman also paid him with a substantial looking amount of cash, and he thanked her as if that, too, were nothing more than typical.

Mark could no longer keep from going all the way into the kitchen. "Can I help carry this stuff out to your car?" he offered, stealing the woman's attention away from Evan.

Evan made introductions. "This is Mark, my house quest. Mark, Mrs. Quillo, one of my clients.

She and Mark observed one another from across the room.

"A house guest," the woman said, giving him a smile of approval.

"A client," he approved her as well.

Mrs. Quillo winked at Evan as she left the kitchen with her two baskets of food. Mark, following after her with the carton, grinned and raised his eyebrows up and down at Evan a couple times.

As Mrs. Quillo's car left the driveway, Mark returned to the house, exclaiming to the master cook, "Just how often do you do this anyway?"

"Do what?" Evan was already underway with the clean up.

"Cook for people."

"Oh, only once or twice a week."

"Only?" Mark exclaimed. "For different people each time?"

Evan gave a casual shrug. "I have a clientele of eight. They have a lot of bridge games and committee meetings and stuff combined with luncheons."

Evan acted as if it were nothing. As if an entire morning of cooking, received by a sexy kiss and a handful of money and a clientele of eight were nothing. Fact was, maybe this phobic person wasn't so proficient in the regular world, but within the limitations his own world he seemed to be doing quite all right for himself.

Mark eagerly asked, "How do they hear about you?"

"Who?"

"Your customers."

Evan, with his hands in dishwater, responded simply, "Oh, I don't know…they just hear…and call."

"And they all, in addition to giving you money, give you a kiss?"

Evan laughed. "No. Only Mrs. Quillo."

"Because?" Mark probed.

"Because she's the type of person who pays really well. Know what I mean?" Evan tried to insure the meaning of what he was saying in the look he gave Mark.

But Mark wasn't getting it.

Evan further explained, "Money isn't enough, in her estimation. She…needs to give something of herself, in addition to the money, in order to feel satisfied."

"Satisfied. Yes." Okay, Mark was sort of getting it now. "And how nice, for her, that you're so obliging." He carried some dirty pans and bowls across the room to Evan at the sink. "I think I'll go for that drive into town now."

"Okay," Evan said, working a scour pad over one of the greasier pans.

"Why don't you come with me," Mark coaxed.

"No," Evan said.

"Why not?"

"You know why."

"You sure?" Mark tried one last time.

"Sure," Evan verified with a nod.

"But you won't mind if I go?"

"No."

Mark put on his jacket and left.

Chapter 17

▼

Evan stood alone in the kitchen amidst the after mess of his morning's cooking. A panic attack was starting within him, set off from simply being asked to go somewhere. He wasn't used to anyone asking him. The few people he still had any association with had pretty much given up asking. Only now there was Mark, who had dropped into his life, his meager little world, and asked lots of things. Mark, who repeatedly, insistently, preferred treating him as normal.

Evan took his hands out of the sudsy water, wiped them on a towel and stared at how they were shaking. Agoraphobia. That's what he'd unofficially been diagnosed with. A fear of open places, of leaving the house. So why was he having a panic attack now, when he hadn't even gone anywhere, had only been asked to go? Maybe, for a moment, he'd wished he'd gone, tried to imagine himself going. But he hadn't and was still only right here where he always was, where he was supposed to feel safe and okay. Except that he didn't. Because more and more lately his okay place seemed threatened.

Evan gazed around at the sad disarray of the kitchen and the amount of clean up still facing him. He didn't mind the work. He liked work. It was just this down reaction he was having from contending with Mark. It had never been easy for him, contending with people. Especially not now, these days, with his agoraphobia. He hoped Mark understood why he'd been unable to go with him, but doubted that he did.

Suddenly Evan was thinking about Sam. His deceased friend Sam. And the cold harsh fact that Sam never had the slightest chance to even begin to understand anything in that last moment of his life.

Everything was closing in on Evan. His mind felt crowded, overwhelmed with all he needed to deal with. It was a lot. Too much. He couldn't do it. But had to. In a quick flare of frustration he grabbed the wooden mixing spoon off the counter and fired it across the room. It hit the wall with a sharp crack, followed by a second crack to the floor. He bolted back, startled, as if he hadn't been the one who'd thrown it and didn't know who did.

Where was this coming from? What was happening to him lately? This was something new, throwing a spoon across the room. He had to be careful, couldn't afford to get any sicker than he already was. Agoraphobia was one thing, anger another.

He looked around for Remington. He'd last noticed him at his food bowl, but he wasn't there now. "Rem…" he called. "Rem…"

He found the cat crouched behind the corner wastebasket, ears flat, eyes distrustful, tail swishing. Evan picked him up, cuddled him, touched faces with him, felt his little cat heart beating hard. "Sorry, Rem. I didn't mean to scare you. Guess I scared myself too. But it's okay now…it's okay…it's okay…"

Chapter 18

▼

Mark drove into town alone, still not fully understanding why Evan wouldn't come with him. What was the big deal about leaving the house and going into town anyway? It wasn't like going out into the streets of New York City, for cryin' out loud. What could possibly be so frightening about Drendal?

He drove slowly, looking from one side of the street to the other, not wanting to miss anything. There was a feed store, drug store, barbershop, post office. Dave's Pizza. He smiled with familiarity to that one. Passing it, he saw that it wasn't just a take out and delivery, but an eat-in as well. Okay, great, he'd go there for lunch after his tour.

He saw Wilson's Super Market, from which Evan had ordered his groceries, a hardware store, gas station, clothing store, video store, another restaurant, bar, bank. Amazing how much was crammed into two blocks. Drendal was clearly self-sufficient, in it's simple little way.

Mark was about to make a turn and head back to Dave's when a red brick building, just around the corner and down from where he was, caught his attention like a happening meant to be. DRENDAL LIBRARY. He hung a right and went to park in its lot, hoping he might find something professionally concrete to read about agoraphobia.

He climbed the outer steps, opened the door and entered the library. It was small and orderly, with the smell of paper and print and the sound of quiet reverence. An elderly woman behind the checkout counter looked up pleasantly and gave a nod.

"Hi," Mark whispered, crossing before her, pretending to know precisely where he was headed.

There was only one reading table and two chairs, but a surprising number of bookshelves. He started down the first aisle.

"Something I can help you find?" the librarian called over to him.

"Psychology section," he answered.

"Last row on your left and part way down the top section."

"Thanks." They had one. A small-town library like this actually had a psychology section. Mark was impressed.

Suddenly the librarian was beside him. "Any certain type of psychology?"

"Something on phobias."

"Phobias…oh, yes…let's see." She traced her finger along the book edges, tilting her head to see through her bifocals.

Mark turned the search completely over to her. It was almost like she was grateful for having something to do anyway. Meanwhile, he started wondering if the Drendal Library possibly carried a copy of his own book. No, not very likely, he felt sure. Yet couldn't resist asking, "You…you don't happen to have a copy of *Street Winder*, do you?"

"Excuse me?" The woman looked away from the books and briefly at him.

"*Street Winder*," Mark repeated.

"Doesn't sound like psychology."

"No. It's fiction. Adventure."

"Oh." She started to pull a particular book off the shelf, reconsidered, shook her head no and stuck it back. Regarding *Street Winder* again, she asked, "Who's the author of *Street Winder*? I'll check for it in another section when we're done here."

"Mark Rydell," he said, wishing it sounded as impressive as Dean Koontz.

"Rydell…Rydell…mmm, I'm not sure. I'll look in a minute."

"No…uh…that's okay," Mark backed down modestly, not wanting to make this into something bigger than it was. "I, uh…don't want to read it anyway. Actually, I was only wondering because…well, I wrote it."

The librarian straightened her glasses and gave him a whole new look. The age lines on her face crinkled into a smile. "You're…? Oh, my my, how honored to have you here, Mr. Rydell. I surely do hope we have your book."

He felt embarrassed, unworthy, wished he hadn't mentioned it. "Well, I'd understand if…I mean…I know this is a small-town library and—"

"But we keep up, Mr. Rydell. We do keep up with the literary world. It's our civic duty."

"Right. Sorry." He hadn't meant to sound like a New York snob.

"Let me just help you here first and...here." She withdrew a book from the shelf and handed it to him.

Mark took it, looked at it, shook his head no. "This is on panic. I wanted—"

"Phobias, yes. They're a form of panic, you know."

"Yeah, sure, what am I thinking?" He managed to make it sound more like something he'd forgotten rather than just learned.

By the time the nice lady had gone over the entire psychology section, she'd selected a total of three books for him.

"Thanks," he said, then followed her across the aisle to the fiction section.

"*Street Winder*...Rydell..." She began her next search.

It won't be there, Mark was sure in his mind. Even though it had made the best-seller list, he still wasn't that well known of an author. He couldn't expect...

"Yes!" the woman suddenly exclaimed, pulling the book from the adventure section, second-to-the-bottom shelf. "Here it is."

"Really?" Mark couldn't contain his surprise.

The librarian kept the book in her own grasp, merely holding it out to show him. He stared at it, as if this were the first time he'd seen it. But it was only the first time he'd seen it in a library. He was newly proud of the cover, a night picture of a troubled-looking man strolling down a busy city street.

The woman carried the book with her to the front counter.

Mark followed, telling her, "No...no, I don't want to take it out."

"Oh, but I do," she said. "I'm going to read it myself."

"Oh." The thought of her doing that discomforted him. Because there was no way a woman of her age and stature was going to understand such a book, or him for writing it. "Are you sure? I mean...well...let me put it this way, if it were a movie it would have an R-rating."

"Mr. Rydell," she said, with an eye-twinkling look back at him, "I'm over sixteen and can well use a little R-rating in my life."

Mark smiled and surrendered to the idea. He laid his three panic books onto the counter.

"Wouldn't happen to be agoraphobia you're going to study up on, would it?" the librarian asked him.

Mark's mouth dropped. How could she know that? Of all the phobias there must be, why would she assume that one? He stood there feeling uncomfortably revealed. First by this person's enthusiastic intention of reading *Street Winder*, and secondly by her ability to read his mind.

She laughed, with an edge of small-town knowing. "Evan Lawton. You're wondering about *him*, right? Quite a case, yes. One we're all wondering about."

"You know him?" This wasn't New York, Mark reminded himself. Everybody knew everybody here, no big deal.

"Of him. I know of him, not actually him himself," she explained. "And of what acquaintance are you to him, if I may ask?"

"Friend," Mark answered simply. "Just a friend."

She nodded her head of white hair. "About time some friend got technically interested in helping that boy. His sister certainly hasn't done anything for him in all these years that she—"

"I really need to get checked out and be on my way," Mark interrupted, resenting that she seemed to think she knew a thing or two about Evan and Tracy, when it was probably no more than the brunt of small town gossip.

The librarian opened the first of his three books, removed the slide-out card and stamped a return date on it.

Standing by, Mark jokingly offered, "I suppose you're going to tell me now that I need a library card."

She peered at him over the top of her glasses. "Yes, of course, but I take it you don't have one."

He grinned sheepishly. "Just a Visa card."

She poked her glasses back in place and broke a slight grin herself. "But you're not buying these books, Mr. Rydell, you're only borrowing them. You'll need to apply for a library card."

"Then how long before I get it?" he asked.

"About five minutes."

"Great."

"Soon as you answer a few questions," she added dutifully.

"Are they difficult?"

"I'm sure you'll pass." She handed him an application form and a pen. Also, she opened *Street Winder* to the title page and motioned for him to sign it as well.

When Mark left the library, it was with eager enthusiasm to plunge into the panic books and learn all he could about Evan's problem. As soon as he sat into his Shadow he flipped through a few pages of each book for a quick preview. Though the light was bad and his look was hasty, the word agoraphobia seemed to frequently jump out at him. It was going to be interesting, learning what this was really about. And beneficial, he hoped, toward helping Evan.

Despite the intrigue, he finally forced himself to set the books aside. Later he would get into them nonstop, but right now he was hungry and was going to go have some of that good pizza.

He wasn't expecting to know anyone at Dave's. But as he walked into the restaurant he found the girl who'd delivered pizza to the house yesterday working as a waitress. Actually he didn't know her, they'd only said hi to one another in the driveway as she'd jaunted past him. Evan, on the other hand, seemed to know her quite well.

"Hi," he said to her as he slipped into a booth.

"Hi," she said, with that perky little smile of hers, bringing him a menu, wearing a non-uniform outfit of jeans and a blouse. "I know I've seen you somewhere before, but…oh, I know…at one of my deliveries yesterday. You were shoveling snow at the Lawton's. You're Tracy's boyfriend from New York, aren't you?"

"Evan explained me to you?" Mark pretended to be more surprised than he actually was. "You deliver pizza to a house and the customer gives you an automatic run-down on the person shoveling his driveway?"

She giggled. "Well, this is a small town. There are no secrets."

"I can think of one," he couldn't help saying, though immediately regretted the way it clouded her pretty face.

A husky middle-aged man in a business suit, carrying his top coat over his arm, got out of a back booth and came their way. "That was a good lunch, honey," he said, pausing beside the waitress. "Got to get back to work now. See ya later."

"Okay," she said. "See ya."

He put his check and money into her hand, cast a searing look at Mark, that felt almost like some sort of warning, then left.

"Whew!" Mark said as an after effect. "I'd watch out for that one."

"He's my dad," the waitress said.

Mark cringed at having made yet another mistake with her. "Sorry."

"It's okay," she responded casually, "I do need to watch out for him."

"Because of you and Evan, right?" Mark was pleased with himself for having figured as much.

Not so pleased with his discovery, Laurel's expression dropped.

"Come on," he said, "you small-town people can't fool a New Yorker like me. Something's going on with you and Evan, and your dad doesn't know about it nor would he approve. Right?"

She stood beside Mark's booth, still clutching the menu she hadn't yet given him, fear in her eyes, distrust in her voice. "H-how do you know so much?"

"You and Evan, the two of you seem very secretive, which only tends to draw more attention to you, you know? From me anyway."

Laurel looked sadly threatened.

Mark smiled softly, hoping to assure her he meant no harm. "It's okay, don't worry, I won't say anything to anyone. Especially not to your father. You can trust me with your secret."

She brightened a little.

Without ever looking at the menu, Mark told her, "I'll have a medium size cheese and pepperoni and a large Coke."

She nodded, turned and started toward the kitchen.

No more customers came into the restaurant. Mark was totally alone. Country music wailed through the ceiling speakers and a spicy, tomatoey aroma drifted through the air. He had plenty of time to think. And now with a new person to think about. Along with his concern for Tracy and Evan, it seemed he'd taken on the pizza girl.

Fifteen minutes later she brought his pizza.

"Can we talk?" he quickly asked before she could get away. "Please sit down with me for just a minute?"

She seemed both curious and scared. "No...uh...I..."

"I'm from New York," he quipped, "but hey, really, I'm a nice guy. I care about you and Evan, and I'd like to talk to you about that."

She took the seat opposite him.

"My name's Mark," he began.

"Laurel."

She was studying him now in that quizzical way so many people did upon meeting him. He decided to cut ahead of her asking and offer, "Costner...people say I'm his twin."

"Who? What?" It seemed that she hadn't been thinking that after all.

"Nothing." Mark gladly dropped the matter, actually feeling good about having maintained his own identity with her now as well as with the librarian. "I thought your job was running deliveries, not waitressing."

"I do whatever is needed of me here. Deliveries, waitressing, dish-washing, floor scrubbing, whatever."

"You make any of the pizzas?" he asked.

She broke a smile. "No, not that. Only Dave does that."

Mark took a slice of pizza, inviting her to, "Help yourself."

"No thanks," she declined, but seemed interest in watching him eat.

"Evan can sure cook," Mark said. "Have you ever tasted any of his cooking?"

Laurel's reluctance to answer seemed an obvious give away to the fact that sure, she'd spent enough time with Evan to have sampled his cooking but didn't want to admit it. She shifted uncomfortably on her side of the booth, as if her spending time with Evan was something she should feel guilty about.

"Evan's a good guy," Mark stated.

The girl nodded carefully, as if trying to protect what little she might still have left of her secret.

"So how do you handle his problem?" Mark ventured asking, not meaning to pressure her but feeling the need to move forth.

"Problem?" Laurel asked innocently.

"Yeah, his not going out, his phobia."

The girl shrugged and shifted her position again.

"He has agoraphobia, you know," Mark said.

Laurel nodded. She knew. In fact the obvious immensity of her knowing was beginning to show that this was as much her problem as it was Evan's.

"How long have you known him?" Mark asked.

"A few months."

"Must be hard, keeping it a secret. I mean, this being a small town where everyone seems to know everything that's going on. And your dad, he looks pretty fierce."

"He's not so fierce as he looks." Laurel's quickness to defend her father denoted her love for him.

"But he could react fiercely if he found out about your seeing Evan, right?"

She lowered her gaze, not answering.

Mark needed her as a link. And maybe, just maybe, she, too, needed a supportive link to handling this whole Evan situation. "You can talk to me," he coaxed gently. "I bet you really want to talk to someone, don't you?"

As if with that he'd turned the magic key, she began to open up. "Dad and I just moved here a year ago. He works at the bank, and I've got this job at Dave's. I make a lot of deliveries out to Evan." A look of adoration came over Laurel's face as she emitted, "He *loves* pizza. My deliveries to his house gradually turned into little stays, visits with him. He gets lonely. Nobody else goes to visit him. We talk, you know, him and me, and...and enjoy each other's company whenever we can."

"But your dad doesn't know, does he? Nor would ever approve, right?"

Laurel's fessing up seemed both difficult and satisfying to her. "Dad's heard all about Evan through talk from the townspeople, about this guy who never leaves his house. He's decided that Evan's strangeness is something to be wary of. He would never allow me to—"

"Have a relationship with such a person?"

Her look indicated no.

"I didn't think this type of father existed anymore," Mark said, shaking his head and taking another slice of pizza. "He sounds pretty extreme. But then I'm not a father. Maybe a father does feel such protectiveness toward his daughter."

"Neither of my two older sisters have good marriages," Laurel explained. "Dad worries about them. He doesn't want me making a bad choice that could mess up my life as much."

"Evan's such a risk?"

"In Dad's estimation, yes."

"Has he ever met Evan?"

"No."

Mark tipped his head sideways. "Don't you think that would help?"

"No," she said.

"Because Evan's not a bad person," Mark reasoned, "he just doesn't like leaving his house."

"Evan's a wonderful person," Laurel verified, with much more punch than she'd shown thus far, "and I'm not going to give him up. Therefore I can't let my dad find out about us."

"So you'll go on hiding this forever?"

"Maybe."

"How?" Mark kept at her. "I mean, where can you expect this relationship between you and Evan to go?"

"Go?" she asked resentfully. "It's just there, and that's it."

"Which is making you just as much of a prisoner as he."

Laurel closed up again.

"I don't mean to scare you," Mark said, though he could see how much he already had. As a matter of fact, he realized fear seemed to be the whole pitiful price this girl was paying for caring about Evan.

"I don't understand what your intentions are," she said nervously.

Mark had to be careful. Had to earn her trust. He could see how much he needed to help her now as well as Evan. "First of all," he said, slipping a smile into his words, "I'm not a threat to your secret. Believe me. You can relax about that. And secondly, I'm thinking that maybe you and I together can help Evan overcome his phobia."

"Evan's inability to leave his house is very real," she said against it. "I don't think we can force him to do it."

"No, not force, Laurel. I'm saying that maybe there are ways, steps."

"Such as?" she asked, becoming more drawn in.

"I'm not exactly sure of the steps yet, Laurel," he had to say, "but I'm going to find out and I'd like to have your support. What do you say?"

Though she gave it some thought, doubt still lingered on her face.

"I'm on your side here," Mark assured her. "Yours and Evan's. I think you guys just really need someone on your side, okay?"

"Like you?" she asked in the manner of a challenge.

"Yeah," he said in the manner of a happening. "Me."

Chapter 19

▼

Following her talk with that Mark guy, who she'd come to realize reminded her of someone but she couldn't think who, Laurel pondered his words throughout the remainder of her work shift at Dave's. He had all these high expectations for Evan. And while that tended to inspire her some too, and give hope to Evan's normality, it saddened her to think that her simple, uncomplicated acceptance of Evan's problem might no longer be enough.

With so much new stuff going around in her head, Laurel waited on her customers in somewhat of a daze. And later into the evening, when she was in the kitchen fetching a Dave's everything-on-it for a group of teenagers, the tray tipped from her hold and sent the pizza splattering face down onto the floor.

"Laurel!" Dave blasted her. "What the hell you doing?"

It was as if he thought she'd purposely dumped the pizza on the floor.

"I'm sorry," she said, no less shocked than he was. She'd never dropped a pizza before.

"It's okay, it's okay," his tone immediately softened. Not a yeller by nature, Laurel's thirty-something boss looked from her to the mess and back to her again, starting to laugh. "Jeez! I don't know which looks worse, the floor or you."

"I'm so sorry," she apologized again, close to tears. Laurel's distress came from more than a ruined pizza. For hours her mind had been more on Evan than on her job.

"It's okay." Dave looked as if he sensed there was something deeper going on with her, but he didn't ask. He grabbed some paper towels and a trash bag and began cleaning the floor.

Laurel stood there completely absorbed in her thoughts of Evan. Wondering whether he would still be himself if he overcame his agoraphobia or if he would thus become this different person who she wouldn't know as well, like as well, or who maybe wouldn't like her as well. Was he ready to deal with all the possible side affects of being cured? Was she? The possibility of her losing him through his losing his phobia was frightening. And yet, she bravely reminded herself, Evan's conquering his phobia was what mattered.

"Go talk to the customers," Dave instructed her.

"W-what?" Her mind snapped back to the here and now.

"Apologize for the delay," he said. "Give them some complimentary bread sticks. I'll start a new pizza for them."

She nodded and went through the swinging door.

"It's not ready yet?" a boy from the awaiting table complained to her empty-handed approach.

"Sorry. There's been a delay."

"Delay? We've never been given a delay at Dave's before."

"A delay," she verified, firmly but nicely.

"I don't believe this," another boy scowled. "This ain't normal. Not for Dave's. What happened? What does it mean when you say…"

The rest of his words trailed off to a faint nothing, following the word normal. Laurel was once again consumed with thoughts of Evan.

Seven-thirty finally came. Jana, her replacement, arrived right on the dot. And on the very same dot Laurel slipped into her jacket and out the door. She would drive home, wait until her father went to bed, then sneak away and go to Evan's house.

Chapter 20

▼

Evan had been glad when Laurel phoned to say she would come over later that night. He waited at the kitchen table for her, holding Remington on his lap, petting him, listening to him purr. It was after eleven. Mark had gone to bed an hour ago. Evan had pretended to go, then sneaked downstairs later. The house was still and dark but for the low night light.

When Laurel's car pulled into the driveway, Evan dumped the cat and was to the door in a flash.

The girl he was crazy about got out of her car and came running to him. He pulled her inside the kitchen, held her close and kissed her. Eventually he helped her out of her parka. And then they just stood there for a long time without talking, exchanging deep eye messages.

Remington meowed around Laurel's ankles for attention until she stooped to stroke him and tell him hello.

"Are you okay?" Evan asked, seeing a saddened look on her face when she stood back up.

"Yeah,' she obviously lied. "You?"

"Yeah," he lied as well. "So you got away all right without your dad knowing?"

"Evan," Laurel began, paused a moment, then continued, "I don't like having to keep our relationship secret."

"I know," he agreed, "me neither. I'm really sorry about that. But I don't know how else we can manage it." He put his arm around her and walked her into the living room. It was darker in there, with only a dim glow in the doorway from the kitchen night light. They sat close together on the couch.

"I feel safe…right here…right now," he murmured between their kisses.

"I know…me too…" she said. "But Evan?"

"Mmm?" he responded, with his hands moving over her sensually.

"Evan…no," she said, stopping him.

It wasn't a good sign, Evan thought, how she was pushing him away now.

"Evan," she said, "Mark knows about us."

Evan didn't want to talk about Mark or about anything. He wanted the rest of the world beyond him and Laurel to disappear. But this was definitely not going his way.

"Did you hear me?" she asked of his silence.

Evan moaned.

"We need to talk about Mark," she said.

"No, we don't."

"Mark knows about us."

Evan finally gave up trying to make more out of Laurel's visit than a discussion about Mark. He settled away from her and into the arm of the couch. "Mark knows?"

"He figured it out," she said, "he just figured it out."

Evan was surprised, yet not surprised. "I know he's been watching everything pretty closely."

"It's okay," Laurel said, "he's on our side."

"Side?" Evan questioned.

"Yes. Ours."

Sometimes Laurel could be too sweet and innocent and trusting for her own good. Like now, about this, about Mark. Evan didn't trust him. Not at all.

"Mark came into Dave's this afternoon and talked to me," she continued.

"He never told me he was at Dave's."

"He thinks he can help you," Laurel said.

"Like who asked him?" Evan sprang to his feet, distancing himself from the couch, from Laurel, from the subject of Mark.

"He really cares about you, Evan."

"He doesn't know anything about me," Evan scowled, walking around the dimly-lit room.

"He knows enough to know that he wants to try and help you."

Evan stopped at the window, took a look outside, then turned back to Laurel, who was still sitting half hidden on the dark couch. "I knew it. I knew there was a purpose behind his coming here."

"Mark thinks you and I deserve a normal life together," she reasoned.

"Right," Evan said, "like it will be real normal if your Dad finds out about us."

Laurel got to her feet and stepped into the path of faint light coming from the kitchen. Her expression was very serious. "Normal as to your leaving the house," she clarified.

Evan felt robbed of what little security he thought he'd still had in his life, including the trust he'd put in Laurel. "Mark's a meddler," he concluded. "I knew that right off about him."

"Don't you want us to be normal, Evan?" Laurel pleaded out of this need she now seemed to have.

Evan looked at her, studied her, no longer understood her. Something, by the way of Mark, had come between them. It was strange, how her claiming to want something so good could make him feel so bad.

She came to embrace him and tell him, "I love you, Evan. I love you just the way you are, you know that. "But I want you to—"

"Be normal," he said, nodding, knowing, sickened.

"I was going to say have more freedom in your life."

Evan felt forsaken. "My freedom is in staying here, right here, where I'm safe and…and free to be myself. That's my freedom. I thought you knew that, Laurel."

"I do. But—"

"Don't have doubts, please don't have doubts." He backed away from her, letting her know in a manner of warning, "Because if you do, that makes you my enemy."

"I will never be your enemy," she said.

Evan ran a hand through his hair, letting his gaze drift past Laurel and into the darker area of the room behind her. "Everything's changing."

"Maybe some things," she said softly, "but not us."

When she laid her hand on his arm he flinched away. Because he had to wonder now if she was pitying him for the way he was or resenting him for the way he wasn't. Either possibility appalled him.

The night was ruined, as far as Evan was concerned. Mark's fault. He didn't try stopping Laurel when she cut her visit super short and went for her jacket to leave. But he did stand at the kitchen door window a long while after her car backed out of the driveway and drove off.

When Evan finally went upstairs, his head felt painfully overloaded and pressing at him to make decisions. He paused in the hallway outside of Mark's shut door. He hated the invasion this guy's presence had made on his quiet simple life, and he held him totally responsible for the problem now wedging between himself and Laurel.

On a sudden whim Evan pounded several times on Mark's door, then opened it and walked in.

Startled out of his sleep, Mark fumbled for the bedside light. "What? Evan, what's wrong?"

Evan stood just inside the room. "You know!"

"No...I don't...I'm asking."

"Oh, you know all right!" Evan shouted.

Mark sat part way up, squinting and shaking his head no.

"Stay the hell out of my business!" Evan ordered him, clenching and unclenching his fists at his sides.

"Your cooking business? But I only helped Mrs. Quillo carry her stuff out to her—"

"Your talking to Laurel about helping me. I don't want or need your help, Mark. You have no right interfering like this."

"Evan, I don't mean to interfere, believe me."

"It's what you've been doing though, right from the start. Ever since you came here." Evan pointed a gun-like finger at him. "It's why you came here, isn't it, to try and turn everything around."

"No, of course not."

"My life was fine before you," Evan said. "I don't need a whole lot, want a whole lot. Just to be left alone. That's all. Just leave me and Laurel alone!"

Mark, in his underwear, was now getting out of bed to argue the case. "Evan, how can you be fair to Laurel when you can't ever leave this house? Don't you want to overcome this phobia of yours? Because you can, I truly believe that you can."

Not wanting to hear it, Evan wheeled around and left Mark's room. He stormed across the hall to his own room and turned on his stereo full blast. Rock music jarred the tranquillity of night, and he flopped down onto his bed in a glory of drums and guitars.

Remington started coming into the room, stopped at the deafening noise, and left on a run.

Chapter 21

When Tracy phoned Mark from the New Jersey Howell Hotel Saturday she didn't get the enlightening response she'd hoped for. To his short, cold tone she asked, "What's wrong?"

"Wrong? Nothing." There it was again, short and cold.

Sitting on the edge of the bed in her slip, she was better warmed by the morning sun coming through the window, "I can tell by the sound of your voice that something is."

He tried dissuading it with a laugh. "Oh, really?"

"You sound grouchy."

"Grouchy? I just laughed."

"It was a grouchy laugh." She lifted her coffee cup off the room service tray and took a sip. She'd already finished her croissant and juice, and had, with this last cupful, polished off a whole carafe of coffee.

"It's early, Tracy," Mark justified. "Maybe it's just a little early for me. It's an hour earlier here than in Jersey, remember."

"Not so early that you should be grouchy."

"I—"

"You what?" she prompted.

"—missed a half night's sleep."

"Because you were thinking of me?" she asked playfully.

"No, because I was listening to rock music."

"You like rock that much?"

"I didn't say I was liking it."

"Then why did you—?"

"How are things going with you, Tracy?"

"Things are going fine here," she said. "I'm just about ready to go meet with the hotel registrar. Except for my suit, I'm ready." She gazed at her mauve outfit draped over the back of a chair.

"Great."

"You sound annoyed, Mark."

"The music did last a long time last night."

"This music thing…do you want to explain it or do I have to try and guess?"

Mark sighed. "So far I think your brother and I are annoying the heck out of each other."

Tracy sighed with her own annoyance. "I sent you there to get to know him, accept him, smoothen the way for whatever life you and I might want to have together."

"My proposal to you shouldn't have to depend on your brother."

"I need to know that the two of you can get along."

"There's just this…this little friction now and then."

"Friction," she said uneasily.

"Friction, yes," he verified.

It was getting late. Tracy had to let things go for now. "I have to say good-bye and start work."

"Work…ahh, yeah…" he said dreamily, "how I envy you."

"Have you done any writing since you've been there?" she took the time to ask.

"Yeah. Some. A few words."

"Good. I'd like to read them when I get home."

"No, I doubt that you would."

She gazed out the window at the beauty of the new day, trying hard to own up to it. "Don't be silly. I love your writing, you know that…finished book, rough draft, whatever. I loved *Street Winder*, didn't I?"

"Yeah, you did. So did I. I'm afraid I'm not living up to that one yet."

She got off the bed and reached for her suit. "I have to finish getting ready and leave for my meeting. I love you, Mark. Take care."

"Love you too, Tracy. Bye."

Tracy finished dressing, aching with the need for things to be right between Evan and Mark. She'd thought Mark finally was someone mature and loving and caring enough to cope with the family situation he'd be getting into. Now she wasn't sure. She had these clouded thoughts that maybe she should never have gotten serious with him in the first place, and that maybe she would never be able to have a life of her own aside from Evan.

A few minutes later she was hurrying down the hall toward the elevator.

"Hey! Hi, Tracy!" A bellhop coming her way recognized her and greeted her enthusiastically. "It's good seeing your beautiful face around here again. How are you?"

She realized just how upset up she actually was, finding that she couldn't even utter a single word back to him. She was only able to manage a slight nod and a stiff smile.

No longer able to keep back the tears that had been threatening since her talk with Mark, she tucked her head down, turned and fled back to her room. She had to compose herself, get a grip. She had a job to carry out at the hotel and she couldn't let her personal life get in the way like this. She had to do something about it right now.

She sat down to the desk and made a second long distance call to Drendal.

"Howell residence," the butler answered.

"Hi, Webber. It's Tracy. May I speak to Howard, please?"

"One moment, Miss Tracy," he said with his usual formality.

She used the wait to take deep breaths, reach for a Kleenex, blot her eyes, blow her nose.

"Tracy, hello," her boss soon came on the line, sounding concerned. "What's wrong?"

"Howard, I wanted to ask if…if it would be all right for me to wind things up sooner than planned here and come home?"

"You're in Jersey now?"

"Yes."

"Tracy, are you sick?"

"No."

"But something's wrong," he knew her well enough to detect and to care.

"Yes," she admitted reluctantly. "Sort of. But not here. It's about some family problems back home."

"You always told me you didn't have family around these parts."

She'd just gotten caught in her own lie, because Howard knew nothing of Evan. Nothing. Not even that he existed, let alone lived in Drendal with her. Though she'd spoken of her brother to some of the hotel employees amidst her managerial inspections, she'd never mentioned Evan to her boss. "Well, not exactly my family," she protected one lie through another. "I meant family problems of a…a dear friend of mine."

"Here in Drendal?"

"Yes. There's this terrible fight going on between her and her husband and I...well, she sort of needs me there right now."

"Sounds serious."

"It is."

"Anything I can do?" he offered kindly.

"Let me shorten my work here and come home sooner. That would really help me, Howard. The Jersey Howell always has wonderful ratings anyway. I can't imagine finding any snags this time."

"Of course, Tracy," her boss readily granted her. "Tell you what, do a light run through, maybe get in an hour's conference with Rogan, and that will be sufficient. Then come home, you just come home."

"Thanks, Howard." She felt immediately better. She was glad she'd called, and was grateful for his understanding, though felt guilty that it should be to her lie.

She hung up and dialed yet another number, the airlines, to change her return flight to an earlier date. She was confident that going home ahead of schedule to check on Evan and Mark was the right thing to do. Her priority.

Chapter 22

▼

Mark was sitting on the couch, deeply engrossed in one of his panic books from the library, when Evan came in, sat by the desk, and lit his nine o'clock cigarette.

"Your sister called this morning," Mark told him. "I was right by the kitchen phone, so I answered. I think you were in the shower at that time."

Smoking, staring, contemplating...Evan was silent.

"She thinks it's great, you and I spending this time together," Mark added.

Evan blew out an especially hard puff of smoke.

"She wants us to get along," Mark said.

When Evan did speak, he was flippant, "She's probably hoping you've got me almost cured by now."

Mark closed his book with a hard slap. "You know, Evan, I honestly think she doesn't *want* you cured."

Evan put out his unfinished cigarette in the ashtray.

"Sorry," Mark said with immediate regret, "it's just an assumption."

"You're a visitor here," Evan stated, "you don't have the right to make assumptions."

Mark drummed his fingers against the book cover. "Oh, I'm more than a visitor, Evan. Eventually, hopefully, I'll be your brother-in-law."

"Which still doesn't give you the right to go around analyzing me and reading those books."

"I think it gives me the right to care about you."

"I don't need your care."

"Plus the right to try to help you," Mark continued.

"I don't need your help." Though Evan tried to sound confident, his shoulders drooped and his gaze stayed at the floor.

"You're wasting your life away with this agoraphobia thing," Mark insisted. "You can do better for yourself, Evan. I know you can."

Evan glanced up for a second, then back down. "This isn't your business. Don't concern yourself."

"Too late, I'm already involved." Mark tried a calmer tone of voice, "I just want to help you, Evan."

"I can't believe Tracy did this to me."

"She didn't do anything to you," Mark said. "Nor did she want me doing anything to you. Wanting to help you is strictly my idea. Mine."

Evan salvaged his half a cigarette out of the ashtray and relit it.

"Come on…" Mark coaxed, setting his book onto the end table next to him, "you do want to get over this problem of yours, don't you?"

"Problem?" There was a surprising glint of humor in Evan's voice and the way he raised eyes.

Mark grinned, pleased for that much.

"And I suppose you know the solution," Evan smirked.

"I'm studying about it."

Evan took a drag off his cigarette then exhaled heavily. "Problem or no problem, I'm fine. Don't waste your time on all that reading."

"I don't understand why you're so against overcoming this."

"And I don't understand why you think you have to understand."

"You could expect a whole lot more of yourself, Evan," Mark said, leaning forward. "Look, just admit you've got a problem and that's half the cure right there, believe me."

Evan took him on. "Okay, I've got a problem." He rolled his dark eyes, as if waiting for something miraculous to happen. When nothing did, he gave Mark an I-know-better look.

At least Mark could see that Evan had spirit, which was a good sign. "I really believe there's hope for you," he said encouragingly.

Evan crushed his cigarette stub in the ashtray and left the room.

Remington leaped up onto the couch beside Mark. It was unusual that the cat hadn't taken after Evan but rather chose to stay there with him this time. Mark scratched the cat's back with one hand and took up his book with the other.

Chapter 23

Evan felt stressed all day. Like who wouldn't be, subjected to the psychiatric surveillance he was under? At least that's what it seemed like, the way Mark looked at him and spoke to him since checking out those books from the library. Since the books, the New York pretend-doctor had become obsessed with curing him. Evan avoided him as much as possible, except for lunch and supper.

Laurel came over unexpectedly that evening. She'd gotten off work at seven-thirty and drove straight from Dave's. Evan wasn't sure what to make of her visit, following their disagreement last night, but he welcomed her in and assisted her out of her jacket.

"I've been thinking about you all day," she said with the sweetness of wanting to make up.

Somehow Evan couldn't bring himself to admit that he'd been thinking of her, too. In fact, he had trouble bringing himself to say anything after having practiced silence the whole day. He just stood there gazing helplessly mute at her, fearing that he may have permanently lost his voice, like maybe another phobia besieged him.

"It's cold outside," Laurel said, shivering and hugging herself.

Evan gave a nod.

"It was a busy day at Dave's," she said.

Though he stood there feeling like a jerk for not embracing her or talking to her, he couldn't seem to rise above his insipid mood.

"Were you busy here?" she asked, glancing around the kitchen as if she might see a specific sign of his accomplishments.

It was a dumb question, but before Evan could even begin to answer, Laurel noticed Mark in the living room and called hello to him.

"Hi, Laurel," he called back.

The two of them knowing each other tormented Evan. Feeling sure that they were plotting something against him, he finally found enough voice to smartly ask Laurel, "Did you come to see me or him?"

"You're acting crazy here, Evan," she said.

"Crazy, yeah," he scoffed in a whisper, "Mark's driving me there."

"Don't say that," she whispered back.

"I was all right until he came here."

"You're all right now," she insisted.

Evan shook his head. "I can't leave."

"Leave? What do you mean?" Laurel's voice rose above a whisper.

"The house. No matter how much you and Mark think I can leave, I can't."

"Oh, Evan, no, that's not what we—"

"It's what you're up to, you and him, isn't it?" The more he studied her the more he was sure. "Change Evan, fix Evan, make Evan normal, right?"

"We're not up to anything," she said, touching his arm.

As if her hand were fire, Evan flinched away from it. "You and he had a talk."

"So?" she said, more as a statement than a question.

"It was about me," Evan charged her further.

"Isn't anyone allowed to talk about you, be concerned about you?"

Evan glanced over at the stairway, feeling a dire need to escape. He even started toward it, but then stopped himself, took a deep breath and turned back to Laurel, saying, "You and I were okay till he came here."

"We're still okay," she said.

"Everything's changing."

"Why don't you like Mark?" she asked, whispering again.

"I do. I just don't trust him. And now it looks like I can't trust you either."

A knock at the back door interrupted them. Evan went to answer it. He hadn't heard a car. Hadn't ordered groceries. And no one ever came to visit other than Laurel. He couldn't imagine who...

He swung the door open to a huskily built man in notably bad temperament.

"Yes?" Evan asked.

"Where is she?" The guy's face and shoulders swelled even larger as he tried maneuvering a look beyond Evan. "I know she's here! Her car's in the driveway!" Suddenly he was shoving his way through the doorway, past Evan, and into the kitchen.

"Hey!" Evan protested. "What do you think you're doing? Who are you?"

The intruder stopped and glared back at him. "Parker Timmons, Laurel's father."

"Oh," Evan said in a small voice.

"And I know who you are," Parker said, "you're the one who hasn't been out of this house in five years. Yeah, I know all about you. I also know that Laurel's car has been spending a lot of time in your driveway. A lot more than—"

"You're spying on your daughter?" Evan fired at him.

"Don't need to. A couple employees at the bank, they—"

"Dad!" Laurel cut in. "What's this all about?"

"That's what I aim to find out!" he told her. Then continued to Evan, "They live out this way. Not many people around here have purple cars. I always get the word when someone notices Laurel's purple car parked in this driveway. Even in the dark the color jumps out in the flash of headlights. Someone informed me of this particular occasion tonight when I ran into him in the drugstore. I just thought I'd come check it out for myself."

"Hello." Mark came strolling out from the living room, making like he had some sort of rightful place in this.

It seemed Parker recognized him but couldn't quite make the connection.

"Dad," Laurel said with a nervous laugh, "I'm not here to see Evan. You thought that? No, I'm here to see Mark. You remember seeing him at Dave's yesterday, don't you?"

Parker rubbed his chin. "Oh...yeah...that's where."

As Laurel left Evan's side to go stand by Mark, she told her dad, "I apologize for not introducing the two of you at that time, but I knew you were in a rush to get back to the bank. Anyway, this is Mark. Mark, my dad."

Parker's look switched back and forth between Mark and Evan. Although it seemed like he kind of bought Laurel's story, he didn't seem relieved. And he still had a question for her, "So exactly just how often and how late have you been keeping time out here?"

"Pretty low, keeping check on your daughter this way," Evan criticized him, even though this was supposedly Mark's fight now.

"Looks like I haven't done enough of it," Parker said.

"Y'know," Evan further contributed, "Mark's been my house guest for quite some time now and I don't like it that he and his friend Laurel should have to feel threatened by nosey people. He's a good person. You'd better call off your hounds."

"Okay...I'm sorry if I...I got the wrong impression about this," Parker said.

"Same impression, wrong guy, don't you mean?" Evan asked.

Laurel, under her father's watch, linked her arm through Mark's to further promote the idea of them being a couple.

Parker gave a dubious nod. "So it's you and the house guest, huh?"

"Yes," Laurel lied and turned up a cute smile at Mark.

"I love pizza," Mark instilled himself deeper into the charade. "And I guess I have ordered it pretty often since I've been here. It's how Laurel and I met, her bringing all those pizzas out here. I haven't had the chance to meet many people in town so far."

"Where you from?" Parker asked him.

"New York."

"Big Apple." Parker was notably impressed with that.

"Yeah," Mark boasted.

As if Parker was determined to find fault in at least something here, he asked Mark, "Aren't you a bit old for Laurel?"

Mark smiled awkwardly. "Yeah, maybe a little."

"But you do leave the house, right?" the father verified.

"I do," Mark replied, after which he flashed a sympathetic look across the room at Evan.

"So why haven't you ever been to our house?" Parker asked Mark. "To pick up Laurel? Or meet me? And why didn't you speak to me at Dave's yesterday, even though I was in a hurry?"

Laurel told him, "Maybe he's been reluctant. You can't blame him, because I told him how disapproving you are of every guy who's ever been interested in me."

Parker shook his head. "No, honey, no. Only guys who—" He shot another crude look at Evan.

Evan wanted to boot the guy's ass out the door. With Mark right behind him. He wanted his quiet, simple life back. He wanted Laurel to himself.

"So what's the purpose of your stay here?" Parker started in on Mark again.

Good question, Evan thought, as anxious as Parker was to hear the answer.

Mark unlinked his arm from Laurel's, only to place it more affectionately around her shoulder. His display of naturalness with her was making Evan nauseous.

"Writing," Mark came up with his answer. "I'm a writer and I came out here to this peaceful location of Drendal to do some writing. I've known Evan for a long time," he added.

"Long, long time," Evan exaggerated.

Parker's eyebrows arched. "A writer...oh...anything published?"

"*Street Winder*. Before that *Ryan*. I'm working on my third."

Evan hated how Mark stood there making points with Laurel's father, pretending to be her boyfriend and doing such a good job of it. Yet the hastily thrown-together plan was undeniably working and he had to be glad for that.

Parker took to rubbing his chin again with his further study of Mark. "You look like a writer. I'm sure I've seen your picture somewhere, haven't I? In a magazine? Newspaper maybe?"

"*Dances With Wolves*," Evan offered.

"Huh...?" Parker didn't get it.

"Costner, yes!" It was Laurel, not her dad, who finally matched Mark's resemblance to the actor. She smiled and studied him in a whole new way.

Parker didn't seem impressed by the celebrity connection. "Well," he said, "Sorry for barging in like this. You know how some things just get a person riled."

"Tell me about it..." Evan mumbled to himself.

The way in which Parker's attention returned to Evan was as if he considered agoraphobia a contagious disease. Something he needed to protect his daughter from.

"It's me and Mark," Laurel reminded him. "Evan doesn't even stay in the room when Mark and I are together."

"I go down in the basement and sit by the furnace," Evan padded the picture grumpily.

"I'm sorry this situation caused you such distress," Mark told Parker, then flicked a nasty look of warning at Evan.

Laurel's dad backed himself to the door. "I'll just be going now. Sorry I intruded. Nice meeting you, Mark. See you at home, Laurel." He gave Evan a last look, with no words, then left.

Evan turned a narrowed look on Mark.

"Hey, don't do that mood on me!" Mark said. "It wasn't my idea to make me the boyfriend."

"It was mine," Laurel took responsibility, "and a good one at that. A very necessary one." She came over to Evan, making like everything was all right now.

But as far as he was concerned, it wasn't. He rejected her closeness.

"Come on, Evan..." she urged him to lighten up, "what else were we supposed to have done? We needed a cover right then and there and Mark was it."

"He didn't have to like it so much," Evan complained.

"Like it?" Mark objected. "I saved your neck. You're the one who should have liked it."

"Anyway," Evan continued, "I'm not so sure Timmons believed it."

"He was just surprised that things weren't the way he thought they were, that's all," Laurel reasoned.

"I know the feeling," Evan scoffed.

Laurel went for her jacket. "I've got to go."

"You barely just got here," Evan said. "Your dad didn't demand that you leave, so why leave?"

"This isn't about my dad." She zipped up her jacket and left.

Evan closed the door behind her, then turned back into the kitchen with a grating look at Mark. "Look what you've done."

Laurel's new boyfriend threw up his hands. "Done? What have I done?"

"You changed everything between Laurel and me."

"I don't think so, Evan."

"Think again"

"That lie we just handed her father was to save what the two of you have."

"I'm talking about before Timmons ever came over. About your having had a talk with Laurel yesterday. About your filling her head with notions about how, maybe, I can get over this problem of mine."

Mark shrugged. "That's not a good thing? I thought it was, Evan. I honestly thought it was. And I'd really like to fill your thick head with as much."

Evan's breathing became shallow. His body tightened, ached, trembled. He needed an escape from the cause. He started toward the stairs.

"You can do it, Evan," Mark's voice followed him. "I'm sure that you can overcome this phobia if you want to."

"*Want to?*" Evan stopped and turned back. "You think that's all there is to it?"

"No, on the contrary, I think there's so much to it that you can't begin to handle it alone. Shouldn't have to. Don't need to. But it seems Tracy's pretty much always left you alone with it, hasn't she? I think it's time you had some help."

Evan lit a cigarette.

"I don't believe this." Mark grinned, watching him.

"What?" Evan snapped.

"That's your second cigarette of the day, plus it's evening, not morning, and you're smoking it in the kitchen, not the living room."

"So?" Evan resented the amusement Mark seemed to be finding in him.

"So, it proves that you can break routines."

Evan leaned against a counter edge. He wasn't sure what was happening here. Except it felt like he was being taken in. And he had no defense. Nor anyone to trust. Maybe not even himself.

"Evan, let's get out of here," Mark suggested enthusiastically. "You and me. Let's go into town for a couple beers. What do you say?"

Evan didn't answer. He only took another drag off his Marlboro.

"I'm sure it would be a difficult ordeal for you, but not impossible," Mark coaxed. "And I'd help you."

Evan said nothing.

"I guess your answer is no," Mark eventually made of the silence and went for his jacket off the wall hook. "But if you change your mind," he gave Evan a last look, a last chance, "just walk on in and join me. I'll be there for you and I'll take you back home whenever you want."

The amateur psychiatrist left.

Evan went to the kitchen door window and gazed through it at the vast outer world. He watched Mark's car disappear down the road toward town. And then, for a while, he just stood there staring out into the dark empty driveway.

When he left his post at the door, Evan paced around the kitchen table several times. As if it were a game, Remington took to following him, making little meows up at him.

Evan thought about the stuff Mark had said, weakening and wondering now if maybe he should start trying harder to believe in it.

Suddenly, on a fast whim seeming to come from a source beyond him, Evan grabbed his jacket and tore out the back door.

Outside.

Down the stoop.

Into the driveway.

Moving in a sense of unrealness.

By the time he actually realized what he was doing, he was past the mailbox and well into the road. He stopped, checked his whereabouts as if he were in dire danger. He looked back at the house, which seemed to be a mile away.

He stood there. Not moving. Only breathing. That was enough to handle right now. More than enough. His cold, bare hands hung at his sides. The wind tunneled into the front opening of his jacket. He waited, like something really bad was about to happen...or already had.

Sam. A flash thought of Sam. God, he was so sorry about him. But it was too late about Sam. That was then and this was now. He had to think about now. Right now this minute.

Evan tried to picture himself walking the whole distance into town, into the bar, joining Mark there, laughing and swigging a few beers with him. Jukebox music would be playing. People would be coming and going and talking. Evan would be among them. Or stuck there was more like it. A gripping sensation would no doubt come to his chest. Anguish would show on his face. People would look at him strangely and ask what was wrong. Some of them would know.

He took two more steps. Breathing in, breathing out, not getting ample satisfaction from either. It wasn't that long of a walk to town. He remembered that it wasn't. Another step. Another standstill. The road seemed to be more of a force against him than a path of direction. He felt sick.

He turned around. It no longer mattered that he'd failed, only that he get back to the house as fast as he could. He returned to the house on a run.

Remington met him at the door, meowing happily at seeing him again. He entered the kitchen, slammed the door shut behind him, picked up his cat and held him closely.

Chapter 24

Tracy's flight arrived Monday morning, eleven forty-five, at Duluth's airport. She took her car out of the long-term parking lot and drove to Drendal, glad she'd decided to come home early, eager to see the guys. She was surprised at how much more snow accumulation there was in the area now than when she'd left.

When she got to the house she found how nice it was being able to park in the driveway. Mark had done a good job shoveling. She was impressed at his having undertaken the huge task. She was hoping to be equally impressed at how well he and her brother were getting along.

"Hello! Surprise! It's me!" she called, going in the back door.

It was quiet. No one had been expecting her. No one came rushing to greet her. There was only Remington, napping on a kitchen chair. He awoke to her entrance, jumped down, stretched, yawned, and meandered across the floor to her.

Tracy swooped him up and snuggled face to face with him. "Hi, Rem…it's so good to be home."

By then Mark was coming from the living room, looking more alarmed than happy at seeing her. "Tracy! What are you doing here?"

"I live here." She was still in her coat, still holding the cat, wishing her surprise had been a bigger hit than this.

Evan came down the stairs, stopping on the bottom step, looking even more stunned than Mark. "Tracy…"

She laughed from her place by the door. "Come on, you guys, I knew I'd surprise you, coming home early, but I thought it would be a happy one." She put Remington down, pulled off her cap, and shook her hair free.

Smiling at last, Mark came to give her a hug and a kiss. "It *is* a happy surprise, I'm just not sure it's real."

She looked beyond him, at her brother still standing glued to the bottom step. "Evan, how are you?"

"What's wrong that you're back this early?" he answered with his own question.

"Finished my work sooner than expected. Hey, it's good to see you, too," Tracy mimicked his tone.

Evan left the stairway, broke into a sheepish smile, and came to give her a hug. "Welcome home."

"Thanks," she said. "Hey, the driveway looks great. It's a real treat, being able to park in it." As Tracy took off her coat and boots, Mark watched as though her every move fascinated him. She was enjoying looking at him as well.

"I could have cooked something special, had I'd known you were coming," Evan told Tracy, noticeably bothered by it.

But when Tracy caught the tumultuous look he shot Mark, it became more apparent to her that what was really bothering him had more to do with the houseguest than with food. "Well," she said lightly, "I had lunch on the plane but you can still make me supper tonight. Oh and here..." She reached into her briefcase.

Evan took Travini's recipes she handed him and brightened considerably. "Wow. Thanks. These will probably call for a new grocery delivery, but meanwhile I've got the makings for tuna casserole tonight."

Everyone noticed and laughed at how Remington's ears perked at the word tuna.

Tracy stepped into the living room, pleased at seeing Mark's typewriter on the desk and some paper in it. She went to have a look, only to find the paper was blank.

"It's been a slow day," Mark, beside her, explained.

"I thought you'd be writing up a storm."

"I am," he quipped. "The solid white paper shows it's about a snow storm."

Tracy didn't find it funny, his joking about his writing. She hoped it mattered more to him than that. "You don't find Drendal a good place to write?" she asked.

"I've been a little distracted so far."

"With shoveling snow."

"Among other things," he said mysteriously.

Before Tracy could even begin to make anything out of it he pulled her into his arms, told her he was *very* glad she was home, and kissed her much more passionately than he had in the kitchen. It gave her the sense of security she was looking for.

Until she opened her eyes again and found Evan watching from the kitchen doorway. The forlorn look on his face immediately imposed a sense of guilt onto her. She broke away from Mark, feeling sorry that Evan should be so alone without anyone special of his own. "The house looks great," she praised him. "And so do you, Evan."

Her brother shrugged and said with a scowl, "Mark thinks I need a haircut."

"I never said that!" Mark denied it.

"I didn't say you said it," Evan clarified, "I said you thought it."

Mark flipped a hand in the air. "Oh, like now you know what I'm thinking?"

Evan turned up an irksome grin. "Yeah…I think so."

"Well, you don't," Mark said, totally blind to the fact that Evan was only teasing. "I don't give a shit about your hair, the fact that it swipes against your shoulders when you cook or that you toss it back from your face like some girl. Maybe the only thing that disturbs me about it is the fact that you can't leave this house to go get yourself a decent haircut if you wanted to. Which I doubt that you do anyway."

Tracy had only been home ten minutes and the guys were into it right before her eyes. It put her in the middle, pressured her to take a side. Choosing Evan's, she raved at Mark, "You don't know anything about hair!"

"I didn't say I did," he pleaded. "I just—"

"Evan has the right to whatever style or length he wants," she said.

"I never criticized his hair."

"I kind of think you just did."

"Okay, until now…" Mark admitted meagerly, "only because he provoked it."

"Oh, right, I'm the bad guy," Evan protested.

"No, of course not," Mark said, "you already made it perfectly clear that I am."

Tracy left the living room, picked up one of her suitcases from the kitchen and started up the stairs. "I'm taking a shower."

Remington tagged after her.

It bothered Tracy that Mark not only criticized Evan's hair but blamed it onto his agoraphobia besides. Lots of guys have long hair. Her brother looked good with his. Anyway, if he wanted it cut she could do it for him. Or he could have a barber come out to the house. His keeping it long was by preference. Not by neglect, not by agoraphobia.

She let the hot shower water spray down over her for a long time. Soaking her hair, massaging her shoulders and back, and easing her travel fatigue. When she was done, she would retackle the task of trying to fix things between Evan and Mark. Somehow she would have to, because the guys had to get along a whole lot better than this before she would ever agree to marry Mark.

Strange…how in order to make a separate life for herself aside from Evan, she felt it necessary to make sure he was included in it. Balance…that's what was needed between her and Evan and Mark. Because…that's the way it had to be. Because…she was Evan's big sister and all that he had. He had no job, no friends, no life. And she would never desert him. She would desert her own life's dreams first. Pretty much had, up until now, until Mark. She wasn't getting any younger. If she was ever to have a family, maybe Mark was her last chance. Sad…she thought, how this had to be such a desperate proclamation rather than a joyous one.

When she finished showering, Remington jumped up onto the edge of the tub to watch the water droplets trickle down the shower walls. Silly cat. He was such a wonderfully silly cat. He brought a laugh out of her, which lifted her mood even more than the shower had.

Wrapped in her terry robe, feeling all dewy and relaxed and ready to deal with the world again, she started down the hallway toward her room. As she passed her parents' room she saw Mark stretched out on the bed. She stopped, met eyes with him, and felt surprisingly aroused. He patted the bed for her to come join him. A sense of girlish demureness mingled into her adult desire. Not that she wouldn't like to go to bed with him right now, but…

"C'mere…" he coaxed, softly and seductively.

She decided to at least go sit by him. But when she got there he pulled her all the way down against him, expecting much more.

"No…Mark…no…" She pushed her way back up.

"What?" he asked, disappointed.

"It's…my parents' room."

"But they've been gone for—"

"I know…but Evan…he's downstairs…right below us."

"So let's go to your room," Mark suggested.

This wasn't as easy for her as it obviously was for him. "No. No, Mark. We can't. Please understand."

"Is it because Evan and I shot a few harsh words at each other?" he asked.

Though that was part of it, she answered, "No."

"Because you and I shot a few?"

Another part, yes, but she said, "No, not really."

"What then?"

Poor Mark. He looked so sad and dejected, more victim than bad guy. It made Tracy wonder how much good her coming home was actually going to do. She'd hoped to bring so much more with her than this. "Give me some time, Mark, okay?"

His tenderness turned to anger. "Like we have so much, you and I! Like we always have so much!" His eyes were off her now and staring at the ceiling.

Tracy was just about to leave, to go to her room and get dressed, when she noticed the books on the nightstand. She picked them up, one by one, reading off their titles, "*PANIC DISORDERS, DON'T PANIC OVER PANIC, ESCAPE YOUR PANIC*. What the hell is this?"

"Books," Mark answered. "They're only books, Tracy. Don't get so riled."

She was very riled. These books were like hard evidence to what she'd so far only suspected. "You're playing psychiatrist to my brother?"

"Uh...well, I..."

"You don't have the right to do this."

Mark rose onto an elbow, insisting, "He can be helped, Tracy."

"These books assure you of that?" she scoffed.

"No, I figured that much out all on my own before I ever got the books."

She slammed the books back down onto the nightstand.

"Tracy...honey..." Mark was trying his trust-me look on her, "Evan can get over his problem with some help."

"Nobody asked you to go this far."

"Like I could avoid it?" He got off the bed, confronting both her and the issue straight on. "Come on, I really don't think you'd want me to do that, would you?"

"I wanted you and Evan to like each other. That's all I wanted."

"If I didn't like him," Mark reasoned, "I probably wouldn't care so much about helping him."

"I hate the friction going on between the two of you."

"I know," he agreed, "me too. But Tracy, there's always a certain amount of friction in any sort of healing process."

"Why can't you just accept Evan's problem the way I want you to?"

Mark shook his head to the impossibility he obviously considered that to be. "Because I can't. And I don't know how you can. Or he can. Or why anyone should."

"He's not your brother," Tracy reminded him, "he's mine."

"He's my soon-to-be brother-in-law," Mark reminded her as well.

She raised her chin. "And heaven forbid that you should get into a family where there's an abnormality that you can't fix."

Mark's look grew deep and analyzing. "I don't think you want Evan better."

"What a terrible thing to say."

"It's a terrible thing to suspect."

"You still don't know me, do you?" Without giving Mark a chance to answer, Tracy continued, "Of course I want Evan better. I just don't like seeing him upset, or pressured, or hurt. That's what I'm fighting you on. He's had a rough time with his life. But he's content and secure now."

"There should be a whole lot more than contentment and security in the life a twenty-six year old, don't you think? Don't you, Tracy?" Mark picked up one of his library books and held it in the air with eminence.

Think. Think. No one had ever pressured Tracy to think as hard as Mark did. As if she hadn't already done plenty enough hard thinking all her life. Although the conclusions had always been the same. "Evan is the way Evan is. Mark, I told you when we were in New York that if you couldn't accept my brother and get along with him then—"

"Yeah, I know," he verified, "then you and I wouldn't likely work out either."

"I think you're failing the test," she said.

He lowered his eyes, shook his head and moaned.

"I don't want you to fail it," she said. "I wish there didn't even have to be a test."

"You know," he said with a coolness that burned, "maybe all of this is really your test. Yours, Tracy. And maybe you're the one who might be failing."

Mark's manner really shook her. He was never like this in New York, before knowing about Evan. She missed the way their relationship had been back then. "Make this work out, Mark, please? It's not that difficult."

Chapter 25

▼

Later, in jeans and a sweater and feeling considerably better after some alone time in her own room, Tracy headed downstairs. Passing Mark's room this time, she saw he was lying on his bed reading one of his panic books. Whether or not he was aware of her, he didn't look up.

With music coming lowly from the living room stereo, Evan was working busily in the kitchen. Pots and pans and bowls and food were everywhere, the way he liked it. He was definitely happier now than earlier, and broke into a big smile as she joined him.

She pulled a chair up to where she could sit and watch him. She loved watching Evan cook. Marveled at his skill. Envied it. Though had to ask, "Isn't it kind of early for making supper?"

"The main course, yeah. But this is dessert."

"Oh," she said.

"Angelino's Apple Cake."

"Mmm…the recipe I brought you from the Chicago Howell last summer."

Evan added diced apples to a bowl of batter, gave it a few more stirs, then poured it into an oblong pan. "This is only the second time I've made it." He set the pan into the oven, telling her, "I'm glad you're home, Tracy."

"I wanted to surprise you and Mark."

"That you did."

"So what do you really think of him?"

Starting on the kitchen clean up, Evan answered lightly, "Mark? He's okay."

"I mean," she said, putting the cover on the flour container, "except for that little ta-do about your hair, are the two of you getting along all right?"

Evan turned to her with one of his irksome grins, which could usually mean just about anything.

"Because," she said, putting the flour container in the cupboard, "I want this to work out."

"I just don't get why you would send him out here ahead of you like that."

"I didn't send him out here to work on you, Evan, believe me. Only to get to know you before he and I get married. That's it. Maybe it was a mistake."

"What? Sending him out here or planning to marry him?"

"Don't joke about this, Evan."

Evan gave her a slanted look.

When Mark came downstairs, Tracy scooped Remington up off the floor and carried him with her into the living room. Mark followed them.

When Tracy put Rem down, she was surprised at how he immediately went trotting over to Mark. She was even more surprised when Mark bent down to pet him. "I thought you disliked cats," she exclaimed.

"Maybe the one benefit of my visit here so far has been my overcoming that."

"How wonderful," she said, "that you should be getting along better with the cat than with Evan. Or, at the moment, with me."

"Well, at least Remington isn't moody, like some people."

"I'm not moody!" Tracy snarled, sending the cat fleeing behind an easy chair.

"Calm down," Mark said, "you're making Rem nervous."

"He's depressed."

"Rem?" Mark questioned with a frown.

"Evan. He wasn't like this before my trip out East."

"So you're saying it's your fault for leaving?"

Oh, how Mark could twist things around. "No, yours for coming here."

"Which, you seem to keep forgetting, was your idea."

"You're affecting my brother's stability."

"Don't you think maybe your brother's life is just a little too stable?"

It sounded to Tracy like something Mark had drawn from one of his library books. "You're putting a lot of pressure on him. I cautioned you that Evan can't take pressure. It only makes him worse."

"Hey, hey…slow down." Mark gave her a moment to do so before saying, "You're talking in circles here, Tracy. You feel sorry for him, just like me, I know you do. Plus you want to help him, just like me, I know you must. But you're letting sorry get in the way of helping, can't you see that?"

"I love Evan," was all she had left to say.

"I thought you loved *me*," Mark said.

"You know what I mean. He's my brother."

"Brother…right," Mark verified coldly.

"And you're—"

"I'm what?"

"—the guy I'm hoping to marry if—"

"If?"

"—if everything works out."

Mark grasped his head between his hands and moaned. "We've become a triangle, haven't we? You, me, Evan."

"I was afraid this would happen," Tracy said, nodding at the painful account. "That what you and I have for each other wouldn't stand up to Evan's agoraphobia."

Mark's eyes and voice hardened. "I think it's you who won't stand up to it, Tracy. Not us. Not me. Not Evan. You."

She suddenly noticed Evan standing in the kitchen doorway. Surely he'd caught a good part of their talk.

"Evan," Tracy went to him in her mothering manner, "it's all right. Mark and I were just clearing the air about some things."

"Nothing sounded very clear to me," he made of it, flicking his gaze back and forth between the two of them.

Tracy walked past him, into the kitchen, and fetched her coat off the wall hook. "I'm going to drive out to Howard's and check in with him."

"Now?" Mark asked, following her. "You just got home."

"He's always anxious to see my reports as soon as I get back. It's hours till supper, I'll be back by then."

Evan, resuming his kitchen work, seemed fine with her leaving.

Mark, however, was bothered, and caught a hold of her coat as she started putting it on. "Don't go."

"I have to," Tracy said.

"Don't be mad," he whispered closely to her. "Come on, we can work this out."

"I'm not mad." She pulled free of him, finished getting into her coat, and took her briefcase off the chair.

"All the more reason to stay," Mark coaxed.

It almost worked. She was almost going to stay and trust him all over again. But a stronger inner force made her open the door. "Howard let me come home early. The least I can do is get his reports to him earlier now. I'll be back by six."

Chapter 26

Howard Howell lived seven miles outside of Drendal's downtown in a mansion in the hills. Each time Tracy drove there she newly found it hard to believe that she actually worked for such a rich eccentric who owned nine hotels and was currently in the process of finding a location for number ten. And it would make her smile, that despite his status he was so incredibly likable and down to earth.

Webber, the butler, a tall thin elderly man who'd been with Howard forever, let her in. "Mr. Howell is in his office, Miss Tracy." He assisted her out of her coat and hung it in the foyer closet.

She stepped out of her boots and into the shoes she'd brought with. "Thanks, Mr. Webber." She always liked seeing how close to smiling she could bring him. Close, ahh yes, but never quite to the brink of cracking his professional formality.

"Tracy…Tracy…" Howard looked up from behind his mahogany desk and the game of solitaire he had going. He was a charming, handsome seventy-year old, with a full head of white hair, thick mustache, and a trim physique. He smiled warmly. "It's so good to have you home. Now maybe we can have a real game of cards."

"Hi, Howard." Purse tucked under her arm and briefcase in hand, she walked toward him, across the wood-paneled room lined with bookcases and file cabinets, centered with his desk and two extra chairs, and accented with numerous plants. "How are you?"

"Not so good," his pleasantry faded.

Tracy stood before him with concern. "What's wrong?"

"Just not feeling so well," he said, followed by a heavy sigh.

She put her purse and briefcase on a corner of his desk and took a chair across from him. "I'm sorry. What is it? What can I do for you?"

"Two weeks…two weeks," he said, shaking his head gravely, as if the end of him were closing in.

Tracy was scared to ask, but had to. "Till what?"

"Sterling and Bryce from Minneapolis are coming up to discuss the building site choices for our newest Howell Hotel."

In her estimation that was something good, not bad. She helped herself to a lemon drop out of his candy jar, then held the jar across to him. "So, that's great, isn't it? This is the meeting you've been waiting for, right?"

Though Howard popped one of his favorite pacifiers into his mouth, his frown remained.

It puzzled Tracy, since ordinarily an event like this energized him rather than stressed him. She hoped he wasn't getting sick, doing too much since his semi retirement several years ago. Though he'd given up his actual physical position at Howell Hotels' executive head-quarters in St. Paul, he'd kept very involved with the business from his home in Drendal.

"A luncheon here with a meeting to follow," he said, as if it were a major problem.

She smiled reassuringly. "This is nothing you haven't handled before."

"I know," he said dimly, "except these guys are…shall I say…of a much different caliber than any of those I've dealt with before."

"Caliber?"

Howard picked up his cards and set the deck aside. "Sterling and Bryce…you know their reputation. I'm not sure we'll be able to come to terms with them. Or them with us."

"Of course we will, Howard. It'll be good. You'll see."

"I can only hope so," he said, managing to give her a slight smile.

"You've got more than hope to bank on," she said.

"You will be here to join me for the battle, won't you?"

It was hard to tell if Howard was making a request or a demand. Either way, his old eyes glistened with need. "Howard, you've got Richard for that."

Leaning part way across his desk, he pleaded, "I need you both, Tracy. You more than Richard. So say yes."

"That's silly. Richard's your right-hand man, I'm only your field reporter."

"You're a woman. A very attractive woman. You can help woo these guys into our terms a lot better than Richard can."

Tracy gave her boss a slanted look. "Howard, that's sexist and unfair. Come on, you're a better businessman than that."

"Please?" he asked, sounding much more like a grandfather now than a boss. Which he well knew, and often used, as his best means of getting through to her.

Tracy fell into a helpless grin and found herself telling him, "I'll be here."

He leaned all the way back in his chair again, nodding with satisfaction. "Thanks, my dear. Now tell me, how's your friend doing?"

"Friend?" Her mind went blank at the subject change.

"The one with the marital problems who you came home to lend your support to," Howard reminded her.

Tracy nodded in reference to her lie and padded it further. "Oh, I'm going to stop by and see her later today."

"Later?" Howard sounded both surprised and disappointed. "You should be there now. You needn't have come here until later."

She played with the closure on her briefcase, snapping it open and shut, open and shut. "No...uh, that's okay...we have something worked out."

"And that New York boyfriend of yours," Howard jumped a whole 'nother track, "are you and he working anything out yet?"

Tracy swallowed hard. Funny, how she'd told him about Mark but never about Evan. Not so funny, how it was really getting more and more tricky keeping her truths, lies and secrets straight. "Mark...he's, uh actually right here in Drendal."

"Here? He came back with you?"

"Uh...well...he's going to be staying here with me for awhile." She couldn't quite determine if Howard's reaction was happy, disapproving, or puzzled.

Then there it was, that grandfatherly nature of his coming through to her again. First in shock, "Staying with you?" Followed by acceptance, "Well then, bring him around so I can meet him."

"We'll see," was the best she could tell him.

Howard laughed, as though he took her to be teasing. "We'll see? That's all you can give me is a we'll see? As if I might or might not deserve the honor of meeting your beau?" Then he bluntly let her know that he expected better. "I thought our relationship, yours and mine, went a lot deeper than business, Tracy. More like family, seeing as neither of us have any family around here."

She was already worrying ahead to the further complication of introducing Mark to Howard while still keeping Evan in the background. But she smiled stiffly and said what she had to for the moment, "Okay, yes, I'll bring Mark around."

"That's better," Howard said. "You know, I always hated thinking of you being so alone. And now you're not."

Tracy's guilt intensified. Howard loathed lies. Honesty was an absolute must with him, his world, everyone he dealt with. Yet she'd always let him believe she lived alone. She'd never mentioned that she had a brother. It just seemed so much simpler that way from the beginning. And since Howard rarely mingled with any of the townspeople, it seemed very unlikely that he'd ever hear anything about Evan through them. Which had always insured Tracy peace of mind toward keeping her family secret from him. Except for the guilt. But then there was always the guilt for Tracy anyway, no matter what she did or didn't do.

At the time she started working for Howard, two years ago, she had been so tired of always having to try and explain Evan's problem to people, because whenever she did it only drew sympathy or strange looks or unwanted advice. That, to her, seemed more of a burden than keeping things to herself. Thus she considered how nice it would be to work for someone who didn't even know Evan existed, to go off for at least part of her day feeling free of questions and concerns related to him. Dear sweet Evan...along with loving him so, she needed her breaks from him. And that's exactly what she'd been managing to get, as far as this job went, by keeping him a secret from Howard. It worked well, except for the guilt.

In an effort of getting off the subject of her personal life, Tracy opened up her briefcase for the reports she'd compiled and brought home from out East.

Howard told her once more, "It's so good having you back, Tracy. I always miss you very much when you're away."

The office door opened and Richard, who also worked for Howard, entered in his usual sprightly manner, wearing a burgundy sport coat over a black shirt and pants set. "Tracy, hey! Saw your car in the driveway. I've been out running errands for Howard. He never said...I mean, I didn't think you were due back for a while yet."

Richard was several years younger than she. Somewhere in his twenties. Boyish and disarmingly cute. With a stubborn, senseless, going-nowhere crush on Tracy ever since they'd both begun working for Howard around the same time.

"Hi, Richard," she greeted him. "I finished my inspection sooner than planned."

His eyes played flirtatiously at her. "Hey, no complaints. Good to see you. So, any special problems with New York or New Jersey?"

"Nothing big."

"Good." He dropped into the chair next to hers.

"Tracy accomplishes her tasks quickly and efficiently with no monkey business," Howard told Richard.

"You're insinuating that I'm a monkey?" Richard responded smartly.

"Insinuating?" Howard dished it back, straight-faced and in that way he had of making one wonder if he was joking or serious. Then he rose from his desk, saying, "Excuse me, you two, I need to get some papers I left up in my bedroom. I'll be right back. And I'll have Webber bring us in some coffee."

"With cookies?" Richard asked, childlike.

"Cookies," Howard agreed, leaving the room.

Tracy disbursed a warning to Richard, "You think you're kidding around with him, but actually you're rubbing him the wrong way, you know?"

"Rubbing…ah, now there's an interesting word." He looked at her in that way again, like a sweet allowance to distasteful words.

Despite his appeal, she told him, "You rub me the wrong way too, Richard."

"Aww…" he drawled playfully, leaving his chair and going to perch himself onto the windowsill behind Howard's desk. From there, legs dangling just short of the floor, he shook his head, smiled confidently, and continued, "It's okay, Tracy, I'm not pressuring you. It's not my style. I'm patient. We'll take things slow."

"Richard, I told you a while back that I'm involved with a guy named Mark from New York and that we—"

"New York's a long way off."

"He's here. At my house. He's asked me to marry him."

"Whoa! The big M word. So what happens to me now?"

"You, Richard?" her voice screeched. "There's never been anything between you and me, which you very well know. I'm getting tired of this game of yours. Aren't you?"

His grin said no. "Come on, what about these vibes I'm getting?"

"Vibes?"

"Yeah."

"There are no vibes, Richard."

"Then, tell me…" He hopped off the windowsill and came closer to her. "Why do I always get this flip-flop sensation in my stomach whenever we're together?"

"Mmm…" she only pretended to ponder it. "Could be a nervous reaction as to your knowing that I've done my work and you haven't done yours."

"It's not about work."

"Then, I can't imagine."

"I think it's your signals."

"Signals?" she dared ask.

"I keep getting these signals from you, Tracy."

"I don't do signals," she said with straight clarity. "If I were interested in you, Richard, you'd be getting something much more than signals."

Hands in his jacket pockets, eyes holding steadily on her, mouth in a crooked smile, he was still obviously set on believing what he wanted to believe.

Howard returned with a handful of papers. Webber followed him in, carrying a tray of coffee and cookies.

Richard helped himself to a cookie.

The meeting was about to begin.

Chapter 27

As soon as Tracy awoke Tuesday morning, she jumped out of bed and hurried to the window. Though it was still dark out she could see that it was snowing. It felt like a homecoming gift for her, because she so loved the snow and never found it to be as beautiful anywhere else as it was in Drendal.

She stood at the window a long time, until she grew chilled in her nightgown and went for her robe on the foot of the bed. She thought about Mark. The fact that she hadn't slept with him last night, his hurt look as they'd said goodnight to one another in the hall before going to separate rooms. Evan was the problem, not just that his being in the house affected their privacy, but that she and Mark so differed about what was best for him.

Since Mark was basically an understanding, kind-hearted person, Tracy had hoped he would handle the situation better than any of the self-centered, jerks she'd dated before. However it seemed to be those very qualities of Mark's that made him decide he should help Evan, could help Evan, would help Evan. Which, as far as she was concerned, was turning out to be more hindrance than help to the matter.

Though it was way earlier than her usual time to go to work, Tracy felt anxious to get going. After her bathroom time, she returned to her bedroom and dressed in her brown wool slacks and a tan sweater. Continuing to be especially quiet, so as not to wake Mark or Evan, she started downstairs. Remington, curled on the top step, arose, stretched, meowed, and followed her to the kitchen.

"Poor baby..." she cooed to him, "we all had our doors shut tight last night and you had no one to sleep with, did you? Poor baby had to sleep on a cold hard step."

"Mir-oww," he responded.

There was still plenty of dry Cat Chow in his food bowl, but Tracy put fresh water in his water bowl. She herself wasn't hungry, but she would be ready for a mug of hot coffee when she got to Howard's.

As she was putting on her boots and coat, Mark suddenly, soundlessly, appeared at the bottom of the stairs with a stunned look on his face.

She flicked him a smile tinged with guilt. "I'm not running out on you, I'm only going to work."

"In the middle of the night?" He left the stairs and came toward her.

"It's not night, it's morning," she said, buttoning her coat.

"You even beat your brother's morning regimen."

"Well, Howard, too, happens to be an early bird."

Remington meowed. Tracy laughed, scooped him up and hugged him.

"Should I get in line?" Mark asked.

"Line?" She gave him a puzzled look.

"The way I see it," he grumbled, "Evan's first, then your job, then the cat, and then, maybe, me."

She put Rem back on the floor and was just about to step forth to give Mark's pouty mouth a kiss when the thundering clamor of Evan doing steps began.

The brother made a flash appearance on the bottom step, said a chipper good-morning, pivoted and charged back up. Clump, clump, clump—up. Slam, slam, slam—down. Up again, down again. Back and forth. Shattering the quiet, as well as the significant moment Mark and Tracy almost had.

"Maybe you should think about getting carpeting for those stairs," Mark said.

She gave him a quick kiss and left.

Outside Tracy found the snow to be deeper than it had appeared from inside. It glittered like diamonds in the throw of light from the kitchen window, while the rest of it lay in the dark like a smooth, grayish-white blanket. She trudged through it to her car.

She sat in behind the steering wheel, stuck her key into the ignition, and turned it. An easy start, no problem. As the engine ran in a warm-up idle, she stepped back outside and used her long-handled brush to clean off the roof, hood and windows.

A few minutes later, back inside the car, she geared into reverse.

Whirr, whirr, zizz. She wasn't moving. Though the engine roared, the tires merely spun in place and went nowhere.

Whirr, whirr, zizz. The car was stuck.

She sat there. Waited. Tried again. Nothing.

Mark came out, grabbing a shovel from the snow bank by the house and motioning for her to hold on a minute.

Tracy watched him in her rear view mirror, in the glow of red taillights, as he cleared an area behind her car. What a really nice guy he was, she knew and appreciated. It was Mark's nature, being nice and helpful and giving of himself. It shouldn't surprise her, and certainly shouldn't disturb her, that he wanted to help Evan. So why did it? Maybe, she thought, because Evan had always been her problem to deal with, and if she couldn't fix it she didn't want someone else coming along thinking that they could. She guessed if that were true it made her a selfish, insecure person, at least where Evan was concerned. Except, no one knew Evan, and what was best for him, better than she did. Not even Mark. And she just didn't want to risk the chance of her brother getting worse from pressures he couldn't handle.

When Mark had shoveled a good portion of snow away from her back wheels he came up alongside the car to give her the go signal.

Tracy lowered her window. "Thanks, Mark."

He nodded, smiled and motioned for her to try backing up now.

Before she did she grabbed the front of his jacket and pulled him down to where she could meet him through the open window for a kiss. It was a much better kiss than the little good-bye peck they'd had in the kitchen.

Stepping away then, so that she could leave, he said, "No charge for the shoveling, lady."

"Thank you, sir." She shifted into reverse. The car moved backwards down the driveway. Though it caught some snow, turning onto the road, it wasn't enough to get stuck. She waved at Mark, then ventured on her way.

It was still dark. Still snowing. Still a beautiful sight to her, although driving in it was hardly her favorite means of enjoying it. She hoped she hadn't made a mistake, thinking she had to go to Howard's this early. Ahead of daylight. Ahead of snowplows. Ahead of spending more time with Mark.

Chapter 28

▼

On his way back to the house, Mark caught a glimpse of Evan looking out from the over-the-sink window. A sad scene. He entered the kitchen, met by the aroma of freshly brewing coffee and the comforting warmth of the house. Remington came to lick the tracked in snow.

"Coffee's going and I'm cooking breakfast," Evan said. "Hungry?"

Mark checked the ungodly time. "Sure."

So far today there didn't seem to be any friction between the two of them. It almost seemed that Evan began every day with a fresh attitude, no matter what. Maybe it was the step routine that jump-started him so well.

Soon there were scrambled eggs, sausage, toast, juice and coffee on the table. Mark and Evan sat across from each other. Evan was quiet. Mark felt like chatting, but all that came to his mind were questions pertaining to Evan's phobia and he didn't think he should go there right now.

After breakfast Evan insisted on doing the dishes and laundry and cleaning by himself, even though Mark offered to help. Unneeded, Mark went up to his room and laid on his bed to do some more reading in the panic books from the library.

He found the study on agoraphobia to be fascinating. It seemed there were far more people than he would have imagined with the disorder. He read about therapy and medication and recovery. It was reassuring to know there was help and hope for these people. For Evan.

At nine o'clock Mark put his books aside and got off the bed. All that reading made him drowsy. He had to move around some. He pulled open a dresser drawer and took out the box with Tracy's engagement ring. After a few moments he opened it, took out the ring and stared at it. There had to be a right time for this, there just had to, he told himself.

When he went downstairs, he found Evan in the living room having his daily cigarette.

Evan met looks with Mark through a thin puff of smoke, and Remington, curled in the middle of the floor, perked at his entrance.

"Did you notice that it stopped snowing out?" Evan asked.

"Yeah. I'll go shovel after a while."

"You don't have to, you know. I can call a service to come do it."

"When you've got me?" Mark exclaimed with a grin.

Evan grinned back. "That's right, you enjoy it, don't you."

"At least my muscles have stopped screaming." Mark went to the desk and sat down at his typewriter. It felt so ancient, looking at a typewriter instead of a computer.

"How's the new book going?" Evan asked.

"It's not. I'm afraid I've got writer's block."

"What's that?"

"Something that happens to all writers at one time or another, where you can't think, create, work. You're just blank, and it's tough to get going again."

"Oh," Evan said. "Well, maybe it's because you're in a different setting than your usual writing place."

"Actually, my block started while I was still in New York. It's…been an awfully long block." He placed his fingers on the keyboard and clicked off a fast line of letters.

"That sounds good," Evan observed from across the room. "What is it?"

"The alphabet."

"Oh. You know, I'd like to read something you've written."

"Come look."

"No, I mean a book. Have you actually completed any books?"

"Two. *Ryan* and *Street Winder*."

"Really?" Evan was in awe.

Mark laughed, supposing it did sound impressive. "*Ryan* didn't do so well, but *Street Winder* made the best seller list."

"What's *Street Winder* about?"

"Adventure. This homeless person is living on the streets in one of the highest crime areas of New York City. It's about all he must go through to survive, and in the process how he manages, at the same time, to help others."

"Where can I get a copy?"

"Well, I didn't see it on the drug store book racks the other day, but I did surprisingly find it in Drendal's library."

Evan's moan indicated the impossibility that was for him.

Mark gave him an understanding look. "I'd go check it out for you, but I'm afraid the librarian herself has it right now. Tracy has a copy. But I'll tell you what, Evan, I'll call my publisher and special order a copy out to you for your very own. I mean, if you want."

"Yeah, I do. Really. Thanks." Evan seemed genuinely enthused about it.

"I'll even autograph it," Mark added laughingly.

"You'd better."

Mark turned his typewriter off again. Heck with the writing. Things between him and Evan seemed to be going better than the writing right now, and maybe it was more important for him to concentrate on that. It was, after all, the purpose of his being there.

He stood up from the desk, stretching hard enough to feel some soreness still deep in his arms and back, though to a much duller degree than yesterday. And now another major workout awaited him. "Guess I'll go do the driveway. Then…well, maybe you and I can have a real talk. Call me for coffee break, okay?"

Evan gave a nod.

Mark felt like an old trooper at this shoveling chore now, compared to that first day he'd done it. He'd learned the benefit of having a system. Like first he would shovel behind his car, move the car back, shovel before it, move it ahead. Then he would start at the house end of the driveway and work his way down to the road, hoping the snowplow would have gone past by then so that he wouldn't have to shovel the edge twice. Daylight had fully opened and the snow had stopped falling for now.

Mark was feeling especially good. About the kiss Tracy had given him earlier. About he and Evan communicating better. About the new day. The new snow. Even about shoveling the new snow.

With his frequent glances at the house, he so wished Evan would come outside and help him. It wasn't that he needed help, but he thought it would be good for Evan.

A little later, as though Mark's thoughts had been telepathic, Evan surprisingly came out the back door. He was a sight to behold, wearing his jacket, pulling on his gloves, smiling tensely.

"Hi," Mark threw him a casual welcome.

Evan pulled the other shovel out of the snow bank by the house and used it as a cane to assist his walk into the driveway. When he stopped, he then stood in place using his shovel cane to lean on. The sick look coming into his face implied that he would not be using his shovel to shovel.

"Are you okay?" Mark asked him.

"Sure," Evan lied. He stood there until it seemed he could no longer take it, and then he went back in the house.

At their coffee and cheese break later, Mark and Evan kept a conversation going about a variety of things. The snow, Tracy's being home from out East, the differences in laundry soap, Remington's silliness as he played with his toy mouse on the kitchen floor, and eventually Evan's going outside.

"Sorry I wasn't able to help you out there," Evan apologized.

"No, that's okay," Mark assured him. "Your coming outside was a good step in the right direction for you.

Evan sighed. "I didn't get very far."

"Hey, you tried. Give yourself some credit."

Clutching his coffee mug between both hands, Evan stared down into it. "You don't know what it's like, Mark."

"No, probably not, I guess I can't even imagine."

Evan's eyes lifted again as he explained, "I get weak. Short of breath. I sweat. Shake. Feel endangered. Weird, huh?"

"Yeah," Mark agreed.

"Out there," Evan continued, "it was like suddenly I knew I had to get back inside the house or I'd die."

After finishing off his second piece of cheese and quietly thinking to himself for a few minutes, Mark expressed to Evan, "You noticed that I was out there shoveling and that I was perfectly safe, didn't you?"

"But that's you, not me," Evan had his own reasoning.

"What about if I, me, a safe person, were to stay right beside you, lending you continual assurance of your safety?"

Evan held back reluctantly.

"Okay, listen," Mark proceeded, "you were out there for ten minutes. What if you were to go out again for…say twelve minutes? And walk just a little farther in the driveway this time?"

"I don't know," Evan said.

"You survived that outing a few minutes ago. You did. It was difficult, sure, but you survived. Do it again. Prove it wasn't a one-time thing."

"I don't know," Evan said.

"I think you do know a lot more than you credit yourself with."

Evan's eyes shimmered. "Twelve minutes?"

Mark held up a promise hand. "No longer. I'll time it with my watch."

Evan gave it some serious thought. "Okay."

When the coffee break was over, the guys put on their jackets and left the house together. The fact that it had started snowing again made them burst into a mixture of moans and laughter.

Evan took up the shovel he'd had before, using it once again to assist his walking.

"How you doing?" Mark, right next to him, asked.

Evan didn't answer. Mark could see that he was concentrating on his every step along the driveway. It was almost as if he were thinking about this way too hard. If he could just relax more and think less this could be a lot easier for him. But then Mark supposed it to be the way of the phobia.

He motioned out the distance Evan had so far covered and praised him for it. "Very good. You're doing just great."

Evan bent forth, rammed his shovel deep into some snow, and held it up for Mark to see. Then he heaved the load off to the side. Another scoop, another heave. By the third one his eyes looked a little strange and his balance wavered. Mark dropped his own shovel and went rushing over to his side.

Evan was again using his shovel to lean on. "How many minutes?"

Mark checked his watch. "Eight."

Evan started back to the house, four minutes short of twelve.

Mark watched him, wishing he could convince him how good he'd done. His prior ten minutes, plus this eight, made a total of eighteen. Which was a lot better than zero. It was definite progress. Whether Evan realized it or not himself, he'd made a worthy start toward getting back his freedom.

Chapter 29

Evan was relieved to be inside the house again. It felt as if he'd just saved his own life by retreating to the security he knew and needed. He closed the door, then turned back to look through the door window at the driveway he'd just left. He didn't belong out there. The phobia demon saw to that and was surely laughing hideously right now at the control it had over him.

With his jacket still on, he sat down at the table. Remington wove around his ankles, checking him out, sensing his anguish, seemingly affected by it. Evan brought him up onto his lap, assuring him, "It's okay, Remy, it's okay."

Chapter 30

On her drive home from work that night, Tracy stopped at Drendal's drug store. She'd had a headache all day at work, and since Mark had used up what aspirin there'd been at home, she needed to pick up some more.

"Bottle of aspirin, that's it, Tracy?" Leo Kalen, the pharmacist, verified of the single purchase she put before him on the counter.

"Yes, that's it." She resented his asking. It was dumb of him to ask. As if she wouldn't have bought more items if she'd wanted more items. "Just aspirin."

"Good for what ails "ya," he said, like an old country doctor.

She nodded, opened her purse, and took out her wallet.

"So how's the winter been treatin' ya, Tracy?" Leo chatted on.

"Great." She forced a polite smile. She knew and dreaded what this small talk of his was leading up to. She wasn't going to get out of there as freely as she'd hoped.

As he rang the sale on the cash register, Leo Kalen commended her with, "Smart idea, keeping a good ol' bottle of aspirin on hand."

Tracy paid him, took her purchase without a bag, and turned to leave.

Then it came. The inevitable, friendly, well-meaning, not-to-be-forgotten question from the man behind the counter, "How's your brother?"

"Fine," Tracy answered without stopping or looking back. "Evan's fine."

"Shouldn't have to live his life restricted to the house that way," Leo's voice followed after her.

Tracy hurried down the aisle of cold medicines. Then the first aid supplies. Then the magazines. She resented that people's concern over Evan's welfare always rose to the point of rudely insinuating that she should be doing a whole lot more about his welfare than what she was. She wasn't superwoman. Nor supersister. Yet people expected her to be supersomething. Always had, always would. Well, she could only do what she could do, no more.

"Shame about that boy, just a shame," the pharmacist managed to get in one more dig before she escaped through the door.

Tracy felt better outside in the crisp fresh air. The new fallen snow sparkled like fairy dust beneath the street light. God, it was so beautiful. She wanted to just stand there, blending in and becoming an actual part of the magic. Magic, yes, if only she could really find some magic in her own life. She'd so hoped Mark was it. Except maybe he was too much of a realist to be anything magical.

It was late, she had to get home.

Inside her car she opened the aspirin bottle, shook out two tablets, popped them into her mouth and swallowed them without water.

Then she drove off, realizing how ironic it was that she had the opposite phobia of Evan's...a fear of going home rather than leaving home. Home was where her responsibility to Evan's welfare always hit her the hardest, facing him directly rather than through other people. She had no answers or probable predictions that his life might ever again be any fuller for him than it was now. It hurt her and scared her to no end, but she had to keep pretending it didn't. She had to be much stronger when she was with Evan than when she was away from Evan, because she was the big sister, a long-standing title that meant she supposedly had the ability to hold everything and everyone together.

She turned off Main Street onto Elwood. Driving slowly. Breathing deeply. Thinking, magically, how easy everything would be if only she were superwoman.

Chapter 31

▼

Mark was glad when the weekend came and Tracy didn't have to go to work. Even though she'd cut her New Jersey trip short and flew home Monday, she'd still gone off to her job every day.

While she kept to herself in the kitchen most of Saturday morning, and he to his typewriter in the living room, it was good being at least that near to one another. However, were it not for the problem of Evan between them, things might have been better.

Tracy didn't seem to be doing anything particular out in the kitchen, other than avoiding Mark. And as for what little writing he did at the desk, it only turned into paper scrunches he tossed across the floor for Remington to pounce on.

The phone rang at ten forty-five. Tracy answered it in the kitchen and called to Mark, "It's for you."

He couldn't imagine who would be calling him. But when he got there, Tracy couldn't wait to inform him, "It's a girl. Guess you made friends here pretty fast."

He took the phone, sickened with a wave of undeserved guilt. "Hello."

"Hi, Mark. It's Laurel."

"Hi," he said to the pizza girl, not feeling any better that it should be her.

"It's about my dad," she began.

"What about him?" Mark asked, though wasn't sure he wanted to know.

"He thinks you're a nice guy."

Mark laughed and stood a bit taller. "Yeah, I guess I am."

"He wants you to come have dinner with us."

Mark checked Tracy's whereabouts. She was practically right behind him, arms crossed, watching, waiting, listening tentatively to his every word. Back into the phone, he told Laurel, "No, I don't think I—"

"I know Tracy's home, but maybe you can explain to her what happened and how important this is for Evan."

Mark considered the mood Tracy was already in. "No, I don't think so."

"Please, Mark," Laurel was desperate. "It would really help protect Evan's and my secret from my dad."

"Don't you think this has gone far enough?" he warned her, flicking another look back at Tracy.

"Don't you see," Laurel kept at him, "if Dad thinks you and I are a couple then it lifts the pressure off Evan and me getting found out."

"He needs to know the truth."

"No. Please no," she begged.

"I'm sorry," Mark said, nicely but firmly.

"I thought you cared about Evan, wanted to help him."

"I do," Mark said, nodding to himself.

"You don't understand what my father can do."

"He can't do anything. Don't be afraid of him or of the truth."

The phone line went silent, as though Laurel had finally given up or had at least run out of anything more to say. Mark felt sorry for her fearfulness. But he had his own fears to consider, such as Tracy standing right there anxious for an explanation to this. "I'm sorry," he told Laurel one more time, in closing, and hung up.

"So…" Tracy began in the very next moment, "you've been cheating on me."

Mark faced her squarely. "I suppose it looks that way, but—"

"Yes."

"A girl calling me doesn't automatically make it cheating, Tracy."

She crossed her arms. "What, then, does it make it?"

He motioned at wall phone. "That was Laurel Timmons."

"How nice of you to share her name with me."

"You don't know who she is?" Mark was surprised.

"No."

"She works at Dave's Pizza."

"You've been hanging out at Dave's Pizza?" Tracy exclaimed, making it into another sign of infidelity.

"I haven't hung out there," he answered carefully, "I was only there once."

"Once and the pizza girl's calling you?"

"She's Evan's girl."

"What?"

"Laurel, the pizza girl, is Evan's girl."

Tracy blinked her eyes. "What are you saying?"

Mark enunciated each word precisely, "I'm saying she's Evan's girl."

Tracy laughed and shook her head with disbelief.

"It's true," Mark assured her.

"But he…how could he…"

"Meet someone? Well, it seems he's been ordering out a whole lot of pizza over the last few months. And he and the delivery girl, they've gotten rather acquainted."

"I live here and never saw this?"

"You're away a lot, you know," Mark reminded her.

"Yeah, but—"

"You don't think it's possible for Evan to have a relationship because of his agoraphobia?"

"I didn't say that."

"But you were thinking it."

"You don't know what I'm thinking."

"I'm starting to get pretty good at it."

"Why was she calling you?"

Mark didn't know, until now, that Tracy had a jealous side. Certainly he'd never given her any cause to be jealous. Certainly it wasn't flattering to him. Nor funny. That look in her eyes, tone in her voice. He would never cheat on her for real.

He kept trying to set things straight. "Laurel's dad heard some rumors about her and Evan and he doesn't much like them. He knows about Evan's problem. Considers him a bad choice for Laurel. Actually, a forbidden choice. He came charging out here the other day, catching her here at the house. You should have seen him. To protect her and Evan's secret relationship, Laurel, on a whim, told her dad that it was me, Evan's houseguest, who she was seeing, not Evan."

"You?" Tracy hardly looked any happier for the story.

"A whim of an idea, just a whim," Mark told her.

"And you played along?"

"At the time, yeah."

"To a lie?"

Mark needed to sit down. He took a chair at the table. "Believe me, Tracy, the expression on Parker's face was enough to make anyone lie to save his self."

"And he actually accepted you as being the boyfriend?" Tracy kept at him.

"Yeah. I guess. He did think I was a little old for his daughter. But...well...yeah...he thought I was okay. He seemed relieved that I, not Evan, was Laurel's suitor."

"How nice," Tracy said coolly, "that he was relieved."

Remington brushed against Mark's legs, trying to get his attention, but Mark stayed focused on Tracy. "The reason Laurel called was that her dad wants me to come have dinner with the two of them so he can get to know me better."

"Yes, by all means, I think he should get to know you better." Tracy gave a little huff and tightened her crossed arms.

"I'm not going, of course," Mark stated.

"You're backing down just when this is getting good?"

"It's not getting good, Tracy. Because it's over. The lying is over. I told Laurel that on the phone."

"So when the father finds out that it's really Evan his daughter cares about after all, Evan's life will be in danger, right?"

Mark took a deep breath. "I don't think it's quite that threatening."

"But who knows for sure, right?"

At first Tracy had been upset thinking that Mark had been cheating on her. Now she was more worried about what might happen to Evan. Mark hated seeing her stressed. He left his chair and went to give her a hug. "I don't think there's anything Parker can do to separate Laurel and Evan. They're not exactly kids, you know."

Tracy slipped away from Mark's attempt to comfort her. "Well, maybe you know what to think, but I'm not sure I do."

Evan came down the stairs into the kitchen, immediately aware of having walked in on something. "What's going on?" he asked, shifting his look between them.

"Laurel called," Mark told him outright. "Her father wants me to come have dinner with them tonight."

"You going?" Evan asked.

"No, of course not," Mark snapped.

Tracy went over to her brother, acting as if she'd been betrayed. "You have a girlfriend and never told me?"

After the shock of finding that she'd found out, he merely shrugged and dished it back, "I guess just like you never told me about Mark, right? 'Least not until he was on his way here for a stay."

"I'm sorry about that."

"I'm sorry about Laurel."

"No, Evan," she reconsidered, "you needn't be sorry about having a girlfriend."

"Then why are you mad about it?"

"I'm not. It's just that—"

"I kept Laurel a secret from you because I thought if you knew about us it would be stressful for you, having to be careful to not to let it slip to anyone else."

"Don't you think I want to know everything that's going on with you?"

"Everything?" Evan tilted his head to the side.

Though Tracy looked embarrassed, she nevertheless waited to hear.

"Okay, everything," Evan complied. "So you probably should know that within my phobia I'm really a real person."

Tracy began wringing her hands nervously. "A real person. Of course you're real. I never thought that you—"

"Except for leaving this house, I'm normal."

"I…well…yes…but…"

"I do think about girls."

"Girls…sure…" Though Tracy nodded that she knew, it was evident she hadn't until now.

Mark felt like cracking a smile and cheering Evan on, but he contained himself and kept in the background.

"At least one girl," Evan went on telling her. "Laurel."

"Laurel." Tracy nodded again.

"I also think about leaving here, going places."

"Leaving?" That seemed to get Tracy more than the girl thing did.

"You never tried helping me leave the house, did you?" Evan said, walking past her and over to the door window to look out.

Tracy had trouble answering. "No…uh…because you…"

"But Mark has," Evan said, turning a sharp look back at her. "He's really tried."

Mark rolled his eyes and made a silent moan inside his head. Though he was glad to have won this much regard from Evan, it was undoubtedly going to cost him points with Tracy.

"Just don't blame me for being a little shocked here, okay?" Tracy pleaded to her brother.

"You mean to my having these feelings?" Evan smugly asked. "Or to Mark's wanting to help me?"

Ah-ha, Mark thought to himself, *score another point for the brother.*

Tracy's gaze went from Evan to Mark then back to Evan. "I...I'm just so amazed to see this much of a change in you."

"Amazed?" he asked. "That's it? You're amazed?"

As Tracy drew a deep breath and smiled in a sad sort of way, it became pitifully clear how much her place with her brother meant to her and how lost she felt without it. "When no one else understood you, Evan, or accepted the way your life had become, I did. You know I did. I've always had all the patience in the world for you."

It seemed as if he could only agree to part of it. "You've always accepted my problem like it's nothing. And you've kept *me* believing, all along, that it's nothing. Only it is something, Tracy."

"What's gotten into you?" her voice rose with frustration.

Evan expressed his pride quietly. "A touch of the outside world. Through Laurel. And Mark."

Tracy wasn't handling any of this very well, finding that others were apparently helping her brother more than she was. It made Mark cringe with guilt for his influence on Evan when he ought to be feeling good about it.

"That's your touch with the outside world?" Tracy asked Evan. "Liking some girl whose father may go psycho on you?"

Mark re-entered the conversation at that point. "I don't think Evan and Laurel should worry about him. I don't think there's anything Parker can do to break them up." He turned specifically to Evan. "But I do think maybe it's time you lay the truth on him, Evan."

"Truth?" Tracy shrieked at the idea.

"About him and Laurel," Mark said. "Maybe in time Parker will simmer down, accept Evan, get to like him in spite of his problem."

"And what if he doesn't?" Tracy said. "What does Evan have then? A broken heart? Maybe a few broken bones?"

"A chance to stand up for himself, for starters," Mark stated more logically.

"Stand up?" Tracy scoffed. "He hasn't done anything wrong."

"Exactly!" Mark said. "So why do you always make it seem like he has?"

"Me? I don't."

"I guess why should you expect other people to accept Evan's problem when you yourself can't even manage to?"

Tracy's eyes widened. "You don't think that I—"

"No," Mark cut her off. "It's plain to see that you don't accept it, never have."

"That's ridiculous!" she argued.

"Ridiculous indeed," he used it back at her, "because I don't think you've ever really given Evan half a chance to try to get better."

"And you step into this house thinking you know it all, don't you?"

"I've read some books, yeah. And I've probably learned a thing or two about agoraphobia from them, yeah."

"Books. You read a couple books and—"

"Three. Three books."

"Three books are suppose to top all the time I've spent dealing with this problem for real."

"That doesn't especially mean you know everything you should."

"I deal with Evan from my heart, not from books."

"Stop fighting about me like I'm not even here!" Evan shouted over the both of them. And then with the silent attention he'd acclaimed, he went for the steps with Remington following him.

Lowering her voice, but not her temperament, Tracy said to Mark, "You don't know everything about Evan. I'm just trying to say that you shouldn't go assuming what's good for him and what isn't like you're some sort of authority figure. Because you're not." She snatched her jacket off the wall hook and slammed out the back door.

Mark's being in the middle of this seemed to make him wrong no matter what he said or did. He seriously wondered if there was any possible way for him to pass this test? He grabbed his own jacket and went after her, still determined to try.

He caught her in the driveway and had to struggle with her to get his arms around her and keep them there. "Don't act like this, Tracy."

"Angry and hurt?" She tried writhing away from him but couldn't. "Like I'm not allowed to have my own personal feelings?"

"There's no…reason…for these sort…of feelings."

As Mark and Tracy continued struggling against one another, their white puffs of breath mixed together in the cold air.

"You're saying I'm a woman of no reason?" Tracy balked.

"I don't…like…fighting with you," he said, finally having to let her go.

"We didn't used to fight," she stated, standing there almost too still now on her own. Her dark eyes searched Mark's, as if trying to find the magic they'd known in New York.

"What's happened to us?" he asked, immediately realizing it was a stupid question.

"Evan," was her answer, *the answer.* She went stomping off from him, raving, "I knew this would happen. Which proves, doesn't it, that we don't stand a very good chance of having a life together, you and me, if our ideals are going to be so different."

He followed after her. "I think you're missing the real issue here, Tracy, which is, in fact, Evan himself, not us."

She chopped the air with her hands. "No, you're the one who's missing the issue! Because Evan's always been the issue to me. Always."

"Okay, good. We agree on that much, that Evan's the issue. Which means we both want to get him over this phobia of his, right?"

Tracy shook her head over and over, still refusing to believe it was that simple. Then she started marching about the crusty, crunchy driveway snow, arms flailing in the air with her frustration.

Mark followed her less dramatically. "Tracy, let's go inside and have some coffee."

"I don't want to go inside! And I don't want any coffee!"

"It's cold out here."

"It was pretty chilly inside."

"We'll talk this over."

"I don't want to talk anymore."

"We have to," he said, starting to shout. Then catching himself, calming himself, he repeated more softly, "We have to, Tracy."

"I want to build a snowman." She scooped up some snow from the embankment on one side of the driveway.

"What?" he exclaimed, puzzled at her sudden mood swing.

"A man...out of snow...you've never heard of it?"

"The snow's not sticky enough."

"Then I want to make a snow angel." She found a section of smooth snow in the yard beyond the driveway and plopped down backward into it. Lying there, she slid her arms and legs back and forth, impressing the shape of wings into it.

Mark watched, helplessly amused at her.

When Tracy finished she got to her feet and turned in child-like delight to look down at her creation. "Isn't it beautiful, Mark! Isn't it! You make one now!"

"I don't think so." He was amused at her playing in the snow, yes, but he didn't care to participate.

"Yes, Mark, you've got to," she urged him.

"No, Tracy, I don't want to."

"Haven't you ever done it before, made one?"

"No."

"Ever?"

"No."

She took pity on him. "I don't believe it. What kind of childhood did you have? Okay…come on…you've got to do it now."

She wouldn't let up until she'd directed him to the smooth snow next to her angel and steered him backward and down into it. It was to her satisfaction then, not to his, that he laid there foolishly staring up at the open sky.

"Now move your arms and legs back and forth," Tracy instructed him. "That's all there is to it. Yes. There. That's it. You're doing it. Good. Now get up. Be careful not to muss it. Here…take my hand."

She assisted him to his feet, then had him turn to see what he'd done. Together they stood looking down at their side-by-side angels.

"Aren't they beautiful," she said, as if their angels were the winsome representation of love and peace.

"Yeah," he agreed, though was actually looking at her now rather than the snow.

Chapter 32

Laurel, at her house, was also enchanted with the wonder of snow, though not that of outside. She sat in her bedroom, shaking up the snow globe her father had given her at Christmas. Within the glass ball was a snowman with black button eyes, a black hat, and a tiny red scarf around his neck. White artificial snow swirled abundantly around him and upon him. Then over and over, each time it settled, Laurel shook the globe again and watched the little snowman good-naturedly withstand another blizzard.

Poor guy, she thought, as though he were a real person imprisoned to the diminutive glass-walled world. She couldn't help comparing Evan to him. Because it was like Evan's house was his snow globe and everyone kept shaking up *his* life. And all he could do about it was stand there, in place, and take it. Amazing, how he and the snowman had so much in common.

Maybe, she thought, if she broke the glass globe she could rescue the snowman. But then wouldn't a snowman, in the real world, just melt away? Ultimately, there was no way to rescue a snowman. And maybe, she feared, no way to rescue Evan.

She held the globe preciously against herself. She loved the snowman. Loved Evan.

Chapter 33

Evan had been watching Tracy and Mark in the driveway for some time, glad to see their fighting had ended. They seemed really happy, frolicking in the snow like a couple of kids. He felt envious and wished he were out there with them.

"Hey!" he shouted to them from the back door. "Hey!"

His sense of urgency immediately brought them scurrying toward the house to see what was wrong. As they neared the steps, Evan, still grasping the door with one hand, swooped down with his other hand to grab some snow off the side mound and throw it at them.

Conveniently backed by a gust of wind, the one single blast of snow sprayed widely enough to catch Tracy and Mark both at the same time. Tracy screamed at the burst of icy fluff in her face. Mark, however, was quick to grab his own handful of snow and fire it at Evan in the doorway. Before Evan could duck, it hit him in the chest and exploded upward into his face.

Everyone laughed uproariously.

Still gasping for his breath and blinking his wet eyes, Evan stepped back into the kitchen and Tracy and Mark followed.

"I can't believe you did that!" Tracy exclaimed, giving him a playful jab in the arm.

"Maybe you'd like a replay," he offered.

"No!" she said, laughing all the more.

"And to think," Mark said, still brushing snow from his hair and neck, "how a short time ago all of us were standing in this kitchen bickering."

"It's the snow," Tracy claimed. "It has this effect on people. Turns them into children. Evan, come out and make an angel. Next to Mark's and mine. There's enough good snow left. Come on."

"No," he had to say, his moment of bliss already dissolved. Fun time was over. He'd gone his limit. He hated that more should be expected of him. A handful of snow outside an open door was one thing, but going all the way out across the driveway and lying down in it was another. How could Tracy ask it of him? He wanted her to treat him normally, sure, but only within reasonable bounds. His bounds. Which, he realized, were never enough. He headed for the stairs, needing to be alone.

"Evan!" his sister shouted at him.

He stopped, hung his head, waited without looking back.

"Evan," she said more softly.

On that he made a half turn and met eyes with her.

"I'm sorry," she told him. "I got carried away. It's okay, your not going out. I understand. You *know* I understand."

It wasn't right that she should feel the need to apologize for merely asking him to go out and make a snow angel. Thus her apology made him feel all the worse, all the lower. He proceeded up the steps, two at a time, fleeing to his safe place.

Remington joined him in his room, jumping up onto the bed beside him, nuzzling into him, purring.

So much of the time lately Evan's world seemed to be getting smaller and smaller, anxieties larger and more frequent. It was probably due to the new and unsettling thoughts he was starting to have of wanting to break free of his agoraphobia. He gazed around at the limit of his room, trying to regulate his breathing, wishing he were normal. He thought how nice his snow angel might have looked next to Tracy's and Mark's. But he realized, in sad actuality, that his life was way too complicated to contain anything so simple.

Chapter 34

▼

Tracy stood in the kitchen at the foot of stairs. She had never felt as upset over Evan's condition as she did right now. It was because of the snow incident. Because in that very short time, when Evan had scooped up some snow and thrown it at her and Mark, he'd seemed so wonderfully free and unbound. But then the moment was over all too quickly and it was harder than ever to accept the restrictions still gripping his life.

As though sensing what she was thinking and needing, Mark came to wrap his arms around her. She welcomed his comfort and stayed in his hold for a long while.

When they eventually parted she was calmer and ready to talk again. "Sometimes it's just so hard to know the right thing to say to Evan, you know? I'm always so afraid of hurting him."

"Yeah, I know," Mark agreed. "But I don't think weighing everything, being extraordinarily careful about everything, is helping him either."

"He needs gentleness."

"I think firmness."

Just like that Tracy and Mark were on separate sides again. "I suppose," she said smartly, "you're inferring to a kick in the butt."

"Not that firm."

"You don't get therapeutic results by force," she argued.

"I didn't say force, I said firmness."

"I believe in gentleness."

Mark sighed. "Sometimes too much gentleness can do more harm than good. Depending, of course, on the result you're after."

Tracy strolled over to the door, looked out the window, shook her head in frustration, then turned back to Mark. "You don't know Evan."

"I'm learning about him."

"You don't know agoraphobia."

"I'm learning about that too."

"Our always disagreeing on how to handle him makes me feel that we'd make a terrible set of parents."

"This isn't about a child," Mark said, "it's about a grown man."

Tracy hadn't meant to imply that Evan was a child. Yet Mark's statement made her realize that since her brother was eight years younger than she, and had, for as long as she could remember always been in one sort of emotional dilemma or another, maybe it did tend to keep him a child in her perspective. But the fact was, Evan needed her and she was always there for him. And that was the way it was. Mark didn't realize that if she lost that, her place, her purpose, her manner of handling everything as she always had, she would surely fall apart...and so would Evan.

"Mark," she said gently, despite her strong inner drive, "I know you must have a lot of ideas going around in your head for helping Evan, but you just haven't known him or his problem as long as I have."

"Which, I'd say, lends me a fresher perspective."

"All you care about is trying to change him."

"Change can be beneficial."

"Or harmful."

"I hardly think Evan would be facing any harm in the process of recovery."

"One great accomplishment on his part and right away more is expected of him. Faster than he can expect it of himself. And he retreats even farther back than where he'd been before."

"Sometimes for every two steps forward one has to take a step back."

"And that's worthwhile?"

"You have very little faith in potentiality, don't you, Tracy? Very little faith in Evan. Maybe, also, in me."

Her eyes started filling with tears. "You make me sound heartless."

"No, honey, not heartless. "Just maybe a little blind to the—"

"You stand there trying to make it sound so amazingly simple."

"If you care about Evan, Tracy, you try and help him to get better and live in the real world. That's it." He finalized the simplicity of it with a shrug.

"The real world?" she fended. "You know nothing about the real world, Mark, you're a fiction writer."

"That's a dumb remark."

"You write about make-believe people and think you can just as easily manipulate real people around in the world like you do in your stories. But, it doesn't work like that. Not with Evan. Not with me."

"Manipulate? More like you're the manipulative one here, Tracy. Like you have this control over Evan and you're trying to get it over me as well."

"No, you're mixing up the concept of control with the concept of caring."

"What do you want here, Tracy? Just tell me exactly what it is you want."

She threw her hands in the air. "I'm not much of a manipulator, am I, if I haven't yet made that clear to you."

"All right, listen…" He came over to her, catching her hands and stilling them in his. "Why don't you give me some background on Evan. Give me a reason why he is the way he is. There must be one. I want to know, understand. Let's discuss this completely, logically, then maybe you can make me see things your way. Could you…maybe…do that?"

"You're saying this rather smugly, Mark."

"No, Tracy, look at me, I'm sincere. Why can't you just get down to some real sincerity of your own here?"

She walked off, leaving Mark in the kitchen, and went up to her room, feeling upset and drained. Disturbed over the words sincerity, manipulative, control. Was she wanting and expecting way too much? Of herself as well as others? Or way too little?

Meanwhile, on top of everything else, she was trying to deal with how fast her biological clock was ticking. She knew if she was ever to have a family of her own she'd better stop thinking of Evan as the significant one in her life and start making more room for Mark. Amidst so many conflicts, there had to be a balance. Before it was too late.

Standing at her bedroom window, she looked out at the snow, thinking about the angels she and Mark made. If only Evan had gone out and made an angel too. If only the simple things were that simple.

Neither Tracy nor Mark nor Evan spoke more than a couple words to one another at supper and were equally quiet afterward in the living room. This whole togetherness plan of Tracy's had gone awry, enough so that it actually came as a relief when the evening broke at an early eight o'clock and everyone retreated to their rooms.

Chapter 35

Somewhere deep in the middle of the night, as Tracy lay in but a half sleep, she heard her bedroom door open and someone sneaking toward her through the dark.

Before she could turn around, the bed jiggled. It was Mark crawling in behind her, slipping an arm around her, fitting his body tight against the curve of hers. "Tracy..." he whispered, "I love you."

"I love you, too," she said faintly, as if she were responding to a dream rather than the realness of him.

"I miss you," he said in her ear.

This moment together could be so easy for them, Tracy thought, if only the problem of Evan wasn't in the way. But she couldn't deny that it existed and that it *was* in the way. Therefore she did nothing more than lie there, eyes closed, offering nothing.

Mark's arm tightened still more around her. "Tracy, your being right across the hall suddenly seemed a whole lot farther away from me than across the states ever had."

His breath, as he spoke, was warm on her neck. His chest, as he breathed, expanded and fell against her back. His male hardness pressed against her buttocks. It was obvious how much he wanted her right now. She wanted him too, but only when the timing was right. And this moment, for so many reasons, just wasn't it.

"Mark, I can't..." she said against the chance of this going any further.

"I know," he said, sadly acceptant.

Tracy felt enough satisfaction in just lying there close with him, doing nothing more. And she knew that Mark was trying to make it seem like it was enough for him right now too.

At least until out of a lengthy silence he gave a sigh and suggested, "Maybe I should go back to New York."

She clasped his hand. "No."

"Maybe it was a mistake, my coming to Drendal."

"Don't say that."

"I know you're worried about Evan. But maybe not enough. Maybe you need to get *real* worried in order to get drastic enough to help him."

"Is that what you are, drastic?"

"Yeah. Oh, yeah. I pretty much am. He needs help and I won't turn my back on that. I'm thinking, Tracy, that…well, maybe you need some help, too."

It took her a moment to respond. "I'm fine."

"No, you're not," Mark insisted, putting them back on the verge of yet another argument. "You're overly burdened by your brother's problem and resistant to fix it."

She knew he was right. No one had ever really looked inside of her or made her look inside of herself the way Mark did. She wasn't sure she liked what she saw.

"I think," he continued, carefully, "you're just not used to anyone helping you, are you? To someone actually standing with you, rather than against you, on your problems. You've been so alone for so long, except for those other boyfriends who—"

"They were nothing, Mark. Nothing."

"Okay. Good. I'm glad they were nothing. And that they're gone and I'm here. We're going to work this out…you, me and Evan. The three of us will be fine."

With no more words between, them they laid together motionless except for an occasional ever so subtle movement from Mark, letting her know he still wanted to make love with her if she should change her mind and show him just the slightest interest.

But Tracy was so tired and emotionally overwrought that she wanted nothing more than to snuggle right now. She appreciated Mark's not pressuring her, and eventually his quiet closeness soothed her to sleep.

When Tracy next awoke it was with a quick startle and confusion as to how long she'd slept. She remembered that Mark had been there with her, but she knew, without looking, that the bed space behind her was now empty.

Lying there alone, on her side, she stared into the snow glow coming through the unshaded window. Its chalky paleness seemed to match the dismal feeling in her heart. Mark had been there, and held her, and now he was gone. She didn't mean to treat him badly. Didn't mean to drive him away. He had to know how much she only wanted things to be right. She just wasn't sure how much her sense of right should actually include or exclude. Except...nothing could be so right as to the cost of losing him.

The bed quivered. It wasn't Mark this time. Remington had leaped up from the floor to claim a corner of the comforter. He kneaded and purred. And just as he settled into a contented ball, Tracy got up, telling him, "There's something I need to do."

A moment later she entered Mark's dark room and went to stand beside his bed. She didn't say anything. She just waited until he sensed her presence, saw her shadow, and sat up with dismay.

"Tracy."

"Can we talk?" she asked.

"Sure." He turned on the bedside light and patted the blanket for her to come sit.

"It's not that kind of talk," she said, keeping her distance.

Mark got out of bed and pulled on his pants. "What kind of talk is it?"

"Can we go downstairs?"

"Sure." He pulled a sweatshirt on over his head, then grabbed his shirt off the bedpost to give Tracy.

She welcomed the wrap of soft flannel over her nightgown.

Mark followed her down to the kitchen. She turned on the nightlight and sat down at the table. Mark sat across from her, looking worried.

"It's about Evan," she began. "You said you wanted some background on him, reasons why he became agoraphobic."

"And you chose now to tell me?"

"I don't know why I didn't tell you everything before. I'm sorry. I should have. You have the right to know."

Mark's hands closed over hers on the table. "I'm listening."

"Evan's problem started five years ago," she said.

"I know the when," Mark said, "I just need to know the why."

"We all lived here in this house. Me, Evan, my mom and dad. We were a happy, close-knit family. Except that at nineteen Evan got pretty independent, as nineteen-year-olds get, and he began thinking he could do better for himself than to stick around Drendal."

"So he thought he'd try Minneapolis," Mark said.

"How did you know that?"

"He told me he'd been there once some time ago. But that's all he told me."

Tracy left the table, filled the teakettle with water and put it on the stove to heat. "Tea or hot chocolate?" she asked Mark.

"How about a shot of something stronger, straight up," he suggested jokingly.

She set two mugs on the table and added a tea bag to each. "Evan got a job in Minneapolis. Made friends there. Became best friends with a guy named Sam. They were the same age. Worked at the same place. Lived in the same apartment building. Neither had a steady girl. They went skiing, hiking, to ball games, movies, concerts. The two of them, they were having one great time with life. Evan brought Sam back home here with him for a visit once. We all liked him. We were glad Evan had such a good friend."

"The story doesn't sound bad so far," Mark commented.

The teakettle started to whistle and Tracy brought it over to the table and poured the hot water into the mugs. "No, it was a great story…until one night, a year later, in Minneapolis, when Evan and Sam were leaving a bar and—"

"And?" Mark coaxed.

"Walking to their car…"

"Yeah?"

Tracy sat down and sipped some of her tea, hoping it would work fast to settle the queasiness in her stomach. She looked across the table at Mark. He looked a little sick himself. "They were mugged," she told him. "By two guys. One with a gun. Evan handed over his wallet willingly. But Sam resisted and was shot."

"Jeez!" Mark said.

"Sam fell, bleeding, to the ground. The muggers took his wallet off him and fled. Everything happened in a matter of seconds. Evan dropped beside Sam, cradled him in his arms and held him. He watched him die. He was helpless to do anything more. Sam's life ended so abruptly. And, to another degree, so did Evan's."

"Wow…" Mark moaned and shook his head. "Rough one. Very rough. Did the cops ever get the muggers?"

Tracy drank more tea then nodded. "Yes. Evan had to go to court. He got sicker and sicker from everything. He was stressed out to the point of missing more and more work, or doing so badly when he was at his job that he eventually got fired. And then he was on the verge of losing his apartment. And then…"

"Then?" Mark prompted, totally mesmerized.

"We told him to come home, to just come on home. But he was in such bad shape that he could no longer make a decision, let alone a move. So one day Mom and Dad started down there to get him. To just go and get him and bring him on home. On their drive to the city they…" Tracy paused and swallowed hard. "They were in a big car accident. Both were killed on the scene."

Mark sighed. "Oh no…"

Tracy continued, "I had to go tell Evan. He took everything as his fault. About Sam and then about Mom and Dad. I couldn't convince him otherwise. But I did manage to bring him home."

"And he developed agoraphobia."

"Not immediately. But as time went on, he began keeping to the house more and more. Kind of as if his going out in the world only insured harm. I mean, he knew better, and we, he and I, had talks about it, but he just sort of seemed to shut down."

"And stayed home."

Tracy left the table, her tea, and Mark, and strolled over to the door window to look out at the night.

Mark came beside her.

"I guess you're wondering why I never got help for him," she said.

"Yeah, I guess I am," he admitted. "Why?"

"Because at first I thought Evan had had enough to deal with. Sam. Court appearances. Losing his job, his apartment, a good deal of his health, Mom and Dad. I thought it was best to just leave him alone. Let him be, let him rest. Let him keep to himself as much as he wanted, needed. What was the harm? Home was good, an okay place for him. But then a lot of time passed and Evan still kept to the house. Eventually he regained his health. He became stronger, happier, and seemingly content. It was good, seeing Evan better in those ways."

"So you let him be."

"I still wanted him to see a doctor, but he wouldn't, and finally I gave up, yes, and decided to just let him be."

Mark's arms came around her. He nuzzled a kiss into her neck. "That was a lot for Evan to have gone through. I guess I can better understand now just where he's coming from."

"But not where he's going," Tracy said. "That's the hard part."

"Evan's going to get to wherever he wants to get, I have no doubt about that. It's where *you're* going that most concerns me."

"Me?" she questioned.

"You told me about all that Evan went through and how much both he and you have had to deal with ever since. Thing is…it seems as if you care more about what happens to his life than you care about what happens to your own life."

Tracy stood peacefully in his arms for only a couple of minutes. Then she left him and went back to the table to finish her tea.

Mark retook the chair across from her, rejected for the second time that night.

She looked at him over the rim of her mug. "Sorry. I don't mean to keep doing this to you. You're right…I need to get a better sense of myself before I can fully give myself to you." She reached for his hand. "I love you. Whatever problems Evan has or I might have, I do love you, Mark."

He lifted her hand and kissed it.

The timing seemed good, and Tracy felt like telling him more about her past. "I had a meager little job at Drendal's post office when all this started with Evan. But it barely paid enough to support the both of us. I…I had this new responsibility all of a sudden that was throwing everything off balance. It was hard, just really hard. When the job with Howard Howell sort of popped up out of nowhere, I got it and it was like two prayers were answered for me at once."

"Two?" Mark questioned.

"In addition to making the higher income I needed, I was working up in the hills, out and away from the regular townspeople and working with someone who knew nothing about Evan and therefore wouldn't be continually asking about him. It was good. For me. I've managed to keep Evan a secret from Howard all this time." She shamefully dropped eye contact with Mark in adding, "The truth of it is, I'm not really sure if all this shows how much I've cared about Evan or only how much I've wanted to escape from him."

Mark saw it in a nicer way. "I think the truth of it shows the stress you've been under and how badly you needed a break from it."

"What's going on?" Evan asked, startling Tracy and Mark by his sudden appearance at the bottom of the steps.

"Evan," Tracy said with a gasp. "Sorry if we woke you."

"You didn't." He rubbed his eyes, yawned, then bent down to tie his tennis shoes. "It's time for my step workout. I'm just surprised, finding you two sitting here."

Tracy and Mark checked the wall clock, amazed that it was already five A.M. Then they looked at each other, shook their heads and laughed.

Evan began pounding the steps.

Remington came meandering out of nowhere, meowing for attention.

Chapter 36

"Then that's it, you're leaving?" Howard was speaking to his cook Anthony in his office as Tracy arrived for work Monday morning.

"I'm sorry, Sir," the slight-framed, middle-aged chef told his boss. He said hello to Tracy then left the room in a quick, crisp manner.

"Sounds like trouble," she interpreted of the partial discussion she'd caught.

"He's leaving, quitting his job just like that."

"No, I don't believe it."

"His mother is very sick and he needs to go to her."

"Oh. Well, that's understandable."

"Guess where his mother lives. Hawaii."

"Oh," Tracy said, detecting Howard's suspicion.

"He says he won't be back, regardless of his mother's outcome. Says he's turning this into his retirement. Just like that. Just when I had it planned for him to cook Beef Bourguignon for my business luncheon next week."

"Good timing, huh?" Tracy concluded sympathetically.

"I'll have to find a replacement, but I'll tell you, no one could possibly cook that French dish like Anthony does."

"The business meeting," Tracy said, "it's not going to be based on the luncheon food. You shouldn't get upset if you have to change the menu."

"No," Howard said stubbornly, "it must be Beef Bourguignon."

"We'll find you a new cook comparable to Anthony," Tracy said like a promise she wasn't so sure of. Then pulling the New York and New Jersey managerial reports out of her briefcase, she asked, "Where's Richard? Don't tell me he's late again."

Howard checked his watch, sighed heavily, and sat down at his desk. He filled two mugs of coffee from the carafe and handed Tracy hers. "I don't know about Richard, I just don't know about him. But tell me, what about that boyfriend of yours from New York?"

Tracy's heart skipped a beat.

Howard was studying her intently. "How's it working out, him staying here at your place?"

After a sip of coffee, she said evasively, "Oh, I don't know."

"How can you not know?"

"Mark and I, we've been doing some arguing."

Howard frowned. "Arguing? What an awful waste of time. What could you possibly have to argue about?"

"Ev—" Tracy caught herself in the nick of time from saying Evan. She had never told Howard about her brother and wasn't about to now. Evan was something she still intended to keep out of her work place. "Everything," she said, crinkling her nose and shaking her head, hoping to make it seem more silly than serious. "We're just sort of arguing about everything."

"Well, I guess all young couples go through their share of disagreements," Howard allowed her. Then with a twinkle in his seventy-year-old eyes, he added, "If you love each other, you'll get through yours. You do love each other, don't you?"

Her smile was her answer.

"Don't let anything come between that."

"No," she said.

"I had a love once," Howard revealed of his past with some notable pain. "A long time ago. Lost her. Never had another. Don't let that happen to you, Tracy."

She was amazed. Howard had never ever before mentioned anything about his having loved and lost. It was a side of him she would never have imagined, and certainly wouldn't have expected him to share. But it seemed he brought it up now, despite his discomfort, to warn her that love was fragile.

"How old were you?" she asked, curiously.

"Thirty five."

"And you never loved again?"

"Never."

"I'm sorry."

He smiled sadly. "Me too. I'm guess I'm just trying to say watch out, Tracy. Don't make a mistake that could haunt you for a lifetime."

"Mark and I will be okay," she said, as if to assure herself as much as Howard.

"I know you will." Though he picked some papers up off his desk, his eyes remained on her. "I am going to get to meet him, right?"

"Right." Tracy motioned to the reports. "Should we get started or wait for Richard?"

"You know, Tracy, for a field manager you're actually in the office a good deal of the time. And Richard, for being my right hand man around here, is usually out of the office a good deal of the time."

Tracy laughed at the truth of it but reasoned, "I don't think he's cut out for restriction."

"One should hardly consider a job restrictive."

"Maybe the term restrictive differs with each individual."

Howard rubbed his chin pensively. "You're right. We all have our own personal boundaries."

Boundaries, yes. Tracy was now thinking of Evan's boundaries more than Richard's. And also of her own boundaries with Mark, because of Evan. Suddenly she was more eager than ever to plunge into her work and direct her full concentration onto that. Howard, studying her reports, was also ready now.

Richard finally arrived at ten to eleven. The day was half over, as far as Tracy and Howard were concerned, and the looks they gave him sharply conveyed it.

"Sorry I'm late," the well-dressed young man apologized. Today he was wearing tan cords, a white shirt and a beige sweater vest. Nice clothes were but the first impression of Richard. The second one was his unrefined manner. He dropped himself haphazardly into the chair next to Tracy, slid down to his tailbone, propped one foot on the rim of the wastebasket, and yawned.

"You have an explanation?" Howard asked him, as if already knowing there could be nothing satisfactory.

"Car problems," Richard said. "It snowed again last night, you know."

"A half an inch at most," Tracy established against the trauma he was trying to make of it.

Richard grinned sheepishly. "Snow is snow. My car just doesn't handle it well."

"I think," Howard said, "the problem is more you, than your car.

Richard took his foot off the wastebasket and straightened himself taller in his chair. "Well, I'm here now so let's get the ball rolling, what do you say?"

"The ball has been rolling for several hours," Howard informed him. "We're about ready to break for lunch." He left his desk and walked across the office toward the door. "If Anthony's not off packing yet, I'm going to go see if he can whip something up for us. Tracy, if you want to go over that Jersey snag with Richard, I'll be back shortly and then the three of us can kick it around."

"Yes, Sir," she said to him, while glaring at Richard.

The unfazed Richard left his chair and casually perched himself upon the corner edge of Howard's desk. Paging scantily through Tracy's reports he claimed in a manner of relief, "I was *hoping* I'd make it in time for lunch."

In her mind Tracy made her usual allowance for him. Despite Richard's annoyances he was the kind of person you couldn't help worrying about, caring about and endlessly putting up with no matter what. Knowing him was kind of like having another brother. "You're skating on thin ice here, Richard," she warned him.

He laid the papers aside and picked up one of Howard's pens to teeter between his fingers, intrigued with the rubbery illusion it gave.

"How could you be so late?" she scolded. "Why do you always have to be so nonchalant about this job?"

He put the pen down and next picked up the glass paperweight to play with. "I'm just a nonchalant guy, what can I say?"

"Anthony's quitting," Tracy informed him.

Richard accepted it easily. "I've always hated Anthony's salmon croquettes."

"Howard's not in a good mood today. I'd be a little careful, if I were you."

Richard put the paperweight down and removed himself from the desk, seeming more amused than serious. "Careful…yes."

"If you care about your job, yes," she said. "He's not real happy about your work attitude. You've got a good job here, Richard. Why do you keep pushing it? You're always pushing things with Howard."

"As with you?"

"Excuse me?" The instant she asked, she knew she shouldn't have. She hardly wanted to open up the matter of Richard's silly little crush on her.

"Well?" He was pushing now for her answer.

She wrung her hands together. Her gaze left Richard and drifted over to the bookcases, then the file cabinet with the philodendron plant, the window, the ceiling, anywhere but him. Until finally she said, "Yes, okay, me too. Pushing, pushing…why can't you ever just take things the way they really are?"

"How are they, Tracy?" he asked, as flirtatiously as ever. "I thought you and I…well, that we liked each other."

"We do," she answered cautiously, meeting eyes with him again.

"I mean *liked*."

"I have a boyfriend. You know that, Richard."

"Yeah, yeah, as if I haven't heard enough about this writer guy from New York." Richard was pouting, like a child who couldn't have his way.

Tracy wished she had kept Mark as much of a secret from Richard as she'd kept Evan a secret from him. "This writer guy and I are going to get married," she said.

"As in Mr. and Mrs.?" Richard's face held a pathetic look of rejection.

"Yes."

"When?"

"Eventually."

"Which means you're not married yet," he said. "Which means there's still a chance for you and me."

Tracy shot out of her chair. "There is no chance, Richard! None! You should know by now this talk of yours bounces right off me. I'm not interested in a romantic relationship with you. I never have been, never will be. Look elsewhere."

His self-assurance withered into an insecure slouch. "Right," he said out the side of his mouth, "like there's a whole lot of elsewhere in this teeny tiny town of Drendal."

"You're not a prisoner here. You have free evenings and days off and Duluth's not that far away."

"Duluth probably gets more snow than Drendal does," he scowled.

"If you dislike snow so much, why aren't you living in California?" Tracy was beginning to suspect that there was something more to this argument than Richard's job, or the snow, or his flirtations, but she couldn't determine what. "I don't understand. You're young, you're smart, you're free…and there are other places and other jobs to be had, Richard. If you're not happy here, what's holding you?"

He gave her that deep, troubled, poor-me look.

She hated when he did that to her. "No…please…don't tell me that I'm your hold."

"Tracy, I—"

"Because I don't want to hear it."

He motioned at their whereabouts. "This is hardly the place to talk."

"There is no right place to talk about us, Richard. Not here, not anywhere. If that's what this is about, I don't want to hear it."

He shook his head. "No, it's not what this is about. At least not all of it."

She moaned, doubtful but curious. "So okay, tell me what then."

"It's…not important," he changed his mind.

Damn him for the guilt trip he was successfully laying onto her. "It is important," she insisted, caught in the trap. "We're friends, you and me, aren't we? Richard, come on, if you've got something bothering you, of course I want you to—"

"Go out with me and we'll talk about it," he coaxed.

Okay, he'd hooked her and was now trying to reel her in. *Damn him.* "Richard, I've told you, you're too young for me."

He seemed enlightened. "So that's it? I mean, about us? The age factor rather than the Mark factor?"

"I can't go out with you, Richard."

"Then I can't talk to you about—"

Howard's return to the office ended Tracy and Richard's conversation right there.

"Lunch in twenty minutes," he announced. Then muttered on and on, more to himself than anyone else, "Don't know what I'm going to do…Anthony's leaving…puts me in a bad predicament…bad…"

Tracy was thinking about that moment right before Howard came in, wondering what Richard was so desperate to talk to her about. She was almost wondering if she should go out with him, play the game his way just to find out. Unless it was only a scheme whereas he would wind up calling it a date. Curious as she was, she wasn't sure to what extent. Or risk.

"Now then," Howard began to Richard as he situated himself at his desk, "Tracy has reported to me that there's just a slight problem in the Jersey Howell's lobby restrooms."

"Really?" Richard said, far too seriously to actually be serious. "All right! Let's tackle it. Wrong color toilet paper? Towels too scratchy?"

Chapter 37

Mark sat at the living room desk before his typewriter, bound and determined to get his next book underway. If only he had his computer, this could be so much easier. He glanced down at Remington, sitting on the ream of paper he'd put on the floor moments ago, and chuckled at the cat's simple pleasure.

This desk was a simple pleasure, Mark thought, running his hand along the edge of it. He'd loved this desk the very first moment he'd laid eyes on it. It was big, old, worn, and rich with character. An inspirational place to write. *Come on*, he urged himself.

When finally Mark's creative juices began to flow, his fingers came alive against the typewriter keys and fluent words filled the paper. *Yes*!

He had several pages written when Evan wandered in about noon, shuffled over to the couch, dropped down heavily onto the cushion, and lit up an off-schedule cigarette.

Mark tried to continue his typing, now that he'd made an accomplished start, but he felt Evan staring so hard at his back that it interfered with his concentration. Finally he whipped around to ask, "What?"

"I didn't say anything," Evan said defensively.

"I can hear you thinking."

"Sorry."

Mark typed a few more words. Stopped. Apologized, "No, I'm sorry."

"I was just wondering," Evan explained, "what it's like being a writer. Or for that matter, having some sort of life."

"It's hard work, being a writer," Mark said, turning to Evan again. "Or for that matter," he laughed, "having some sort of life. Writing is very rewarding when you create something. I suppose sort of like what your cooking does for you."

"There's not much to following a recipe."

"Ahh, yes, there is. I think you have to have a certain knack for it. Because I know that merely following a recipe isn't enough to make someone a masterful cook."

Evan nodded somewhat agreeably, then took a long drag off his cigarette.

"And as for having a life," Mark said, "you do have one, Evan."

"Do I?" Evan doubted.

"Yeah."

"Limited."

"Doesn't have to be." Mark turned off his typewriter.

"So you really think you could help me?" Evan asked with a passion for wellness that Mark had never before heard from him.

"Help you with what?" Mark couldn't resist teasing.

Evan was serious. "You know…going outside."

Mark resumed his own seriousness. "Sure, I'd be glad to help you. Evan, I hope it's okay with you that last night…actually I guess it was this morning…Tracy told me about what happened to you five years ago. She told me about Sam and your parents. I'm sorry, really sorry."

Evan lowered his head.

"Hey…" Mark said, "if you ever want to talk about it with me I'd—"

"I don't talk about it," Evan said.

"Oh."

"So when should we go out?" Evan's voice lifted with the subject change.

Mark shrugged. "Now?"

Evan popped up from the couch.

"When you're finished with your cigarette," Mark said. "I need to go upstairs for something anyway. I'll be right back."

Mark was much more interested in helping Evan now than he was in his writing. In his room, he hurriedly paged through one of the books from the library, refreshing his mind with some of the particulars he'd read earlier. It was a good sign, Evan's asking for help. But Mark had to be careful of how he lent it.

When he felt prepared, he went downstairs. Evan was putting on his jacket.

Mark put on his own and the two of them started out the door together. "Any certain place in mind?" he asked.

"No." Evan's voice sounded weaker and less determined than before. But he was trying and that was the main thing.

"How about the mailbox?" Mark suggested. "Pretend it's the day you go out for the mail. Come on, I'll stay beside you."

Evan gazed off toward the road, as if it lay far beyond his means. As if he didn't think he could make it, even though he was already managing to once a week. He looked sideways at Mark. Mark gave him a go-ahead nod. Evan started down the driveway and Mark stayed with him.

It was a long, painstaking journey for Evan. Mark could almost feel the ordeal it was for him.

When they reached the mailbox, Evan proudly, but nervously, opened and shut the box door several times. "Mailbox…no problem."

"Great, Evan. You're doing great." Mark looked about in search of another goal. "The car. How about a short ride in my car?"

Evan eyed the Shadow. "I don't know."

"Very short, Evan, I promise."

Evan said nothing, did nothing.

"Evan…" Mark coaxed.

Evan was staring past him at the car.

When Mark touched his arm, Evan flinched. Mark left him there and went by himself to his car at the other end of the driveway, hoping Evan would follow.

Mark got into the car and waited, trying not to seem overly anxious about this. He watched for Evan in the rearview mirror.

It took a long time for Evan to decide, approach the car, open the passenger door and get in. He looked very uncomfortable.

Not wanting to put any more expectation on him than necessary, Mark overlooked Evan's not buckling his seat belt. He started the engine.

Evan took a stiff look over his shoulder to see where the car was backing.

"You don't need to be scared," Mark said. "I'm a good driver."

Evan nodded.

"How long has it been since you've been in a car?" Mark asked.

Though Evan opened his mouth, no words came out. Breathing seemed to be all he could manage.

"You're all right, Evan," Mark assured him, "because you're with me. And I'm your friend. You can trust me. I won't let anything happen to you." *God, this is like talking to a three-year old*, he thought.

The car backed out of the driveway, turned, and started down the road.

Evan gripped the door handle. "I can't do this."

"A short ride," Mark said. "Your house won't leave our sight, I promise."

He took Evan's silence to mean okay.

They slowly passed along the fence surrounding the neighbor's property. When they reached the next driveway, Mark pulled in, backed out and headed home again. Evan was hyperventilating.

The instant the car stopped in the driveway, Evan got out and made for the house.

Mark stayed in the car for a while. Thinking. Feeling overwhelmingly responsible for Evan's welfare. The mail truck pulled up along the road. The carrier dropped a delivery into the mailbox then drove on. Mark left the car and went to check it out. There was an electric bill, an advertisement, and Evan's copy of *Street Winder*. It would have been nice if the mail had already been in the box when Evan opened it ten minutes ago.

Mark walked back to the house. Evan wasn't in the kitchen or the living room.

Mark stood at the foot of the stairs and called, "Hey, Evan! Your book came. I'll put it on the kitchen table."

There was no response.

"Okay?" Mark verified.

No answer.

Chapter 38

Tracy entered the house that evening to a dark and empty kitchen. She flicked on the light, took off her boots and hung her coat on a hook. "Hey! Where is everybody?"

"In here," Mark called from the living room.

Okay, yes, she heard his typewriter clicking and headed toward the sound. "Hi. What's for supper? she asked, finding it strange that there was no sight or smell of anything in the making.

Mark, at the desk, stopped typing and gave her look. "Evan didn't feel like cooking tonight."

"Didn't feel like cooking? Evan *always* feels like cooking. What's wrong? Something's wrong."

"Nothing. Nothing is wrong."

"Mark, come on, that's not my brother." This was turning into an argument Tracy didn't mean but couldn't help. Mark was doing that *I know Evan better than you do* thing to her. "If Evan doesn't feel like cooking, it means something is definitely wrong."

"Calm down, okay?" Mark suggested all too easily.

"Where is Evan?"

"Upstairs."

"Why?" she asked.

"Why?" Mark questioned her question. "Like he has to have a good reason for being upstairs?"

Tracy gave a huff and crossed her arms. "Something's wrong. It's not like him to not feel like cooking."

"Just allow him a night off from cooking for once, okay? I think…tonight…Evan wants to send out for pizza." Mark pulled the paper he'd been working on out of the typewriter and added it to the pile of others on the desk.

"Pizza," Tracy verified.

Mark grinned. "I think maybe he wants to see the pizza girl."

"Laurel," Tracy said through a sigh. She took a stroll around the room, picked up a couch pillow to plump, straightened a picture on the wall, rearranged a plant on an end table. "I had a very rough day at the office."

"Come on," Mark made jest of it, "how rough can one old eccentric guy be?"

Accentuating the mood she was in, Tracy spun back to him with, "Oh, it wasn't Howard that made my day so rough, it was Richard."

Mark seemed more amused than disturbed. "The kid who's suppose to be Howard's right hand man?"

"The *kid* has this big crush on me and—"

"Whoa! You never mentioned crush before." *Now* he was disturbed.

Tracy guessed she wanted Mark to feel as disturbed over Richard as he was making her feel over Evan.

Mark shook his head, not so much that he wasn't getting it but that he wasn't liking it. "Are you telling me this because I posed as Laurel's boyfriend?"

"No. You wondered how my day at the office could possibly be so rough and I'm just telling you that Richard is the reason."

Mark squinted at her. "So I'm suppose to feel sorry for you? Or jealous? What? Obviously you want me to feel something here."

"Forget my day." Tracy knew that putting it off now would rile him all the more. So she did. "How was yours? I see you got a lot of writing done." She went to the desk and flipped through some of his pages.

"Compared to yesterday, yeah, but far from enough."

From there Tracy went to look out the window. She was surprised to see it was snowing a lot harder now than when she'd driven home. "Wow…" she said, more to herself than to Mark, feeling a rush of childlike delight over the scene. Watching it snow never failed to strike her as awesomely as if she were seeing it for the very first time.

"I took Evan for a ride in my car today," Mark, from behind her, said.

She spun back to him with alarm. "You what?"

"Ride. In the car. A very short one."

The strange undercurrent she'd felt ever since she'd gotten home was finally coming into account. "That's what this is about. Why he's upstairs in his room and not cooking supper. He had a nervous reaction, didn't he?"

Mark rocked his head in a so-so way.

"Didn't he?" she demanded.

Mark gave a slight shrug. "Sort of."

"How could you do that to him?"

"It was his idea. Sort of."

"Pressured by who?"

Mark ran his hand through his hair. Took a deep breath. Sweetened his voice to cover his guilt. "Tracy...honey...the guy's got to get out of here one way or another."

Tracy was unbending. "I told you over and over not to interfere with his problem. Only to accept it, him, the way things are. But no, you can't see that, can't do that, can you?"

"No, I guess not," he admitted.

"I'm sorry I ever suggested that you come here."

"I can leave for New York in the morning," he offered.

"What's wrong with tonight?" she threw back at him, only to regret. There was shame behind the tears coming to her eyes. "I'm sorry. I don't want you to go back to New York, Mark. I want us to work this out. I really do. It's just that...Evan doesn't need pressure. Pressure is bad for him. You must have upset him really bad."

"He's not a child, Tracy."

"I know. He's my troubled adult brother. But I'll tell you what I also know...that I'm able to deal with Evan a whole lot better than you or anybody else might think they can."

"And you have some actual proof of this?" Mark was giving her that know-it-all library look of his.

The differences between her and Mark were getting worse. "How can we ever get married this way?" she said, with it sounding more like a statement than a question.

Mark was equally unbending. "If you can accept Evan for the way he is, why can't you accept me for the way I am?"

"You weren't this way in New York," she claimed.

"Neither were you."

"Because that was before Evan."

"He's really not the problem here, is he, Tracy?"

"Of course he is! What do you think we've been arguing about?"

"I should have never left New York," he said.

"Right," she scoffed, "like we could've easily gone on forever having a long-distance affair."

"Maybe I liked you better that way."

"Do you want to fail this test, Mark? Are you purposely trying to fail it?"

"Screw the test!" he shouted.

Evan appeared in the kitchen doorway. Though it was obvious he'd heard a good portion of their argument, he casually announced, "I ordered out pizza. Hope that's okay with everyone."

Tracy forced a happy face. "Pizza. What a great idea!"

Chapter 39

Tracy hadn't been home long before Richard came by unexpectedly. She couldn't believe it when she answered the knock at the back door and found him there. He'd never been to her house before, nor had a reason to be there now.

"Richard!" She felt a major headache coming on.

From the look on his face, catching her off guard almost seemed to be his purpose. "Hi. Hope you don't mind my stopping by like this, but I thought the conversation we'd started earlier deserved finishing." He was covered with snow and hunching his shoulders against the wind.

Though she felt like screaming, Tracy had no choice but to motion him inside. Evan and Mark were curiously standing by. "Guys, this is Richard, my coworker. Richard, Evan and Mark."

Pulling off his gloves, Richard acknowledged Mark with, "Ahh...the boyfriend from New York."

"Ahh..." Mark mimicked him, "the boy who's a friend."

Richard shifted his look to Evan.

Tracy had never told him about her brother. Never planned to. She had intended to keep Evan as much of an on-going secret from Richard as she had from Howard. And it had worked until now.

When Richard looked to her in question of Evan, she only said, "I can't believe you drove here through all that snow. You hate driving in the snow." Rather than suggest he take his jacket off, she just brushed the snow off his shoulders.

"I know," he agreed, equally amazed with himself. "And not only is the snow coming down hard out there, but it's blowing like crazy too. It didn't seem bad when I started out, or I wouldn't have started, believe me."

"That's Drendal country for you," Mark stated.

Richard nodded at him, then looked at Evan again. "So you're a friend from New York too?"

Tracy cringed, rolled her eyes and said a silent prayer.

"No," Evan answered.

"Oh," Richard said, hardly satisfied. "Well, I just thought—"

"I'm Tracy's brother," Evan told him. "I live here."

"Brother?" Richard shot a puzzled look at Tracy.

Okay. There. The truth was out, her lie split open. Unless she could still cover it with another. She smiled at Richard and gave it a try. "Come on, I've mentioned Evan to you before."

Richard was quick to disagree. "No, you haven't. Not ever."

Tracy nervously tried to sluff it off with a laugh.

Studying Evan again, Richard asked him, "So how come I've never seen you around?"

Evan flashed Tracy an uneasy look. And Mark was giving her one of the same.

The best thing to do was to get Richard out of there. As a direct hint for him to leave, Tracy told him, "We can talk at the office tomorrow."

"Or now," he suggested firmly.

Though this was evidently urgent enough for Richard to brave a snowstorm and impose upon her privacy, Tracy allowed him no extra credit. "I think we pretty well wound things up this morning. I really don't think there's anything more."

"There's a lot more," he said, eyes glistening with a degree of desperation she'd never seen in him before.

Okay, *now* he was starting to get to Tracy. Maybe he did deserve the opportunity to say whatever he'd come there to say, but not with Mark and Evan present. She would take him into the living room where they could have some privacy and get this over with.

Before she could suggest it, another car drove up into the driveway. Tracy looked out the window, seeing a DAVE'S PIZZA sign on the roof of the car parking behind Richard's. Evan opened the back door.

The delivery girl, who Tracy easily assumed was Laurel, came into the kitchen carrying two large insulated packages. Just walking from her car to the house, she was covered with snow.

"Are you okay?" Evan anxiously asked her.

"Yeah...I think so...it's terrible out there."

He took the pizzas from her and set them onto the table. "I had no idea it was that bad when I phoned in the order or I wouldn't have," he apologized.

"I had no idea it was so bad out either until after I'd gotten underway." As if the snow ordeal hadn't been enough for the girl to contend with, she seemed additionally nervous finding three other people in the room besides Evan.

"You're safe now," he assured her tenderly.

Laurel turned her attention back to just him. "I could hardly see where I was going at times. I almost went off the road by Randall's place."

Evan put his arms around her. Even though he looked just as upset as she was, he managed to comfort her. "It's okay. You're here now and you're okay."

The pizza girl began to calm down. As she relaxed, Evan did also.

Tracy was totally amazed that this relationship had happened behind her back. For sure she wasn't the only one who had been keeping secrets.

"The storm came on really fast," Laurel said. "I don't think anyone knew about it until it was directly on us."

"Well, you're not going back out in it, that's for sure," Evan told her. "You're staying right here."

"Here?" Her eyes shifted from him to Tracy, as if the decision might be more up to his sister.

"Yes, of course you're staying," Tracy validated it, then officially introduced herself. "Hi, Laurel, I'm Tracy, Evan's sister."

"Hi," Laurel responded pleasantly. "Yes, I figured that's who you were."

Though Tracy found the pizza girl easy to like, she still found it hard to believe she was Evan's girlfriend. "You're very brave to have made it this far in the storm. But we certainly won't let you go back out in it."

"What about me?" Richard, in a whiny voice, asked of his own welfare.

This was no time to boot anyone out the door, not even Richard. Tracy was forced to tell him, "Better stay. Looks like a real blizzard developing out there."

"Thanks." Settling in, he took off his jacket, bent down to pet the cat that was brushing against his ankles, and removed his wet shoes. "Pizza, great, I love it."

Tracy made the newest introductions, "Laurel, this is Richard, with whom I work. Richard, Laurel."

As the two guests said hello to one another and compared notes on the rough driving ventures they'd both just encountered, Tracy set the table with plates and napkins and glasses of water for everyone. Evan went to get the desk chair from the living room. It felt so strange, preparing the table for five. Stranger yet that one guest should be Richard and one Evan's girlfriend. The pizzas, though still under wrap, smelled wonderful. And in spite of all she'd dealt with since getting home from work, Tracy was hungry.

Before sitting down to the table with the others, she stepped over to the door window for one more check on the weather. Right at that moment another car was turning off the road and pulling up behind all the other cars in the driveway. A man got out, and with his head tucked down against the blustering storm came forging his way toward the house.

"Oh, oh…" she moaned, somehow feeling it might be Laurel's father. She opened the door to him.

"Is Laurel all right?" the big man clamored, as if he feared for his daughter's life. Standing on the stoop, jacket unzipped, muffler blowing out from his neck, more snow than hair on his head, he tried to finagle a look past Tracy into the kitchen.

"Yes, of course she's all right," Tracy said. Then, despite her resentment of who he was and why he was there, she politely motioned for him to come in.

He entered the kitchen, met by startled looks from the group at the table.

"Dad!" Laurel exclaimed from her place beside Evan.

"I'm Parker Timmons," the man established to Tracy.

"Of course you are," she said. "And I'm Tracy Lawton."

Standing just inside the door, Parker spoke to his daughter across the room. "When the weather started getting bad I called Dave's to tell you I'd come pick you up. I didn't want you driving home in it. But Dave said you were making a delivery out here. Laurel, how could you take a chance like this? Mark," he spoke to him next, "how could you let her do this?"

Before Mark could answer, Laurel reasoned to her father, "It wasn't that bad when I started from Dave's."

"Well, it's plenty bad now," he said, "and we're on the opposite side of town. I don't want you driving in it." More closely evaluating the scene he'd walked in on, it now registered with him that Laurel's coat was off and she was sitting closer to Evan than to Mark. His disturbance grew.

"She's okay here," Evan said.

"Yes," Tracy added, "we told her to stay until the weather clears."

Parker gave Mark, the supposed boyfriend, sitting way around the table from Laurel, a whole new look.

"You don't have to worry about her, Mr. Timmons," Mark offered.

"A father worries," the man said like a set rule.

"Right." Mark didn't argue it.

Parker's look settled back on his daughter, the fact that she was sitting next to Evan rather than next to Mark. "Come on, Laurel, get your coat. I'm taking you home."

She left the table as if she had no choice and went for her coat.

"Really, you don't have to go," Tracy sincerely insisted to both the father and daughter. "Please stay."

Ignoring her, Parker Timmons opened the door and Laurel followed him out.

Evan was upset and looking like he wanted to do something but didn't know what. Tracy shared the feeling.

She, Mark, Richard and Evan crowded together in the open doorway to watch Parker and Laurel trudge down the driveway and become virtually lost in the thickening snowstorm.

Though the headlights of Parker's car soon cut through the stirring whiteness, the vehicle remained in place.

Soon the car lights went off and Parker and Laurel came back to the house.

"Blasted snow!" Parker snarled, entering the kitchen behind Laurel. "Visibility has worsened. It's become so bad out there, I decided we shouldn't try to go anywhere in it."

Evan was giving Laurel a look of relief. Mark was giving Tracy a look of amusement. And Richard was taking another look out the window.

"Man!" Richard said excitedly, bursting into laughter. "Looks like a north pole movie scene out there. This night has sure turned into an adventure."

Tracy latched onto his exuberant spirit and tried to pass it on to the others. "An adventure, yes! That's what this night is. We have plenty enough pizza, plenty enough blankets and places to sleep. Nobody's going anywhere in this storm."

"Not even me?" Richard tested the extent of her hospitality.

"Stay," she ordered him.

Richard turned to Evan. "Going to be a lot of shoveling in the morning, huh, Evan?"

When Evan didn't say anything, Tracy told Richard, "He won't be going out. He has a cold."

Richard took something out of his shirt pocket and went across the room to give it to Evan.

"What's this?" Evan hesitantly accepted the small wrapped something.

"Cough drop," Richard said. "Just happened to have one on me. Sometimes I eat 'em like candy."

Evan gave it back to him. "I don't have a cold."

"But Tracy said you—"

"No," Evan said, breaking her lie and letting her know, with a look, that this was something he had to do.

Richard was also giving Tracy a look, letting her know how confused he was. "But I thought—"

"What I have is agoraphobia," Evan said straight out.

Richard took a step backwards. "*God*, what's that?"

Tracy flagged her hands at her brother, trying to stop him from saying anything more. As if there *were* anything more. "We need another chair at the table."

When Evan went to get one, Richard closed up to Tracy, gasping, "What's ago…agoff…?"

She felt sorry and guilty for the way the truth of this had come out. In a whisper, she told him, "Fear of open places. A phobia that has Evan bound to the house."

Richard's mouth dropped. Neither asking nor saying anything more, he stood in a silent stupor.

Having already known about Evan, Parker was only too eager to sound off about him. "It's insane, if you ask me, how anybody can possibly—"

"Evan's not insane!" Tracy said in an angry hush.

Parker argued, "Anyone who doesn't go out of the house for five years sounds pretty insane to me. Insane enough that I'm damn glad to have found out it's Mark Laurel is seeing and not your brother. Good Lord, I don't know what that would have done to me, let alone her."

Tracy watched Richard's reaction to hearing that Mark, rather than Evan, was Laurel's interest. The guy looked so perplexed. When he finally seemed about to speak again, she passed him a quick, silent signal not to.

She checked the doorway, glad Evan wasn't back from the living room yet but suspecting he'd probably heard most everything from around the corner anyway. She gave Laurel's father a grating look.

Parker gave up on Evan and focused on Mark, seeming okay with him, or at least with what he thought him to be. "You seem like a decent sort of guy for Laurel, Mark."

"Thanks," Mark said.

"You and I will have to get to know one another now."

"Uh…yeah…sure," Mark agreed uncomfortably, extending his look beyond Parker to meet with Tracy.

Tracy, in turn, looked to Richard. He was not only having trouble comprehending that Evan was her brother and had this weird thing called agoraphobia, but was now also trying to comprehend why Parker was talking like it was Mark who was Laurel's boyfriend and not Evan.

Richard shook his head. "Man, I feel like I'm in the twilight zone."

"We all are," Tracy said, unable to explain it any other way right now.

Evan brought a sixth chair into the kitchen, eyes down and antisocial.

"Okay, let's eat," Tracy said. "All of us are warm and dry and safe from the storm and we have to be thankful for that. We really do."

"Amen," Richard added and was first to the table.

Chapter 40

▼

Evan hated Parker's attitude. He hated Laurel's pretending to be Mark's girl. He hated that Tracy hadn't previously told her coworker Richard that she had a brother. Most of all, he hated how crowded this house had become. He preferred being alone. Life was so much simpler to deal with when you were alone. He gazed around the table. Tracy and Parker to his right, Mark and Laurel across from him, and Richard to his left. It was a strange night, a strange gathering, and he had a disheartening feeling that it was going to get a lot stranger before it was over.

When all the pizza had been eaten and everyone else had gone into the living room, Evan stayed by himself in the kitchen. He lit a cigarette, his second one of the day, and stood against a cupboard, staring over at the stairway, thinking of making a getaway.

Remington suddenly came padding into the kitchen as if he'd been driven out of the living room by too many people and voices coming down on him.

"I know just how you feel," Evan consoled him.

The cat went scampering up the steps, and Evan was just about to follow him when Richard came into the kitchen.

"Hey, there you are."

"Yeah, here I am," Evan mocked Richard's delight in finding him.

"There's something I don't understand…" Richard began, with that same muddled look he'd had all through dinner. "My first impression earlier tonight had been that you and Laurel were…uh…something. Then her old man gets here and it's like all of a sudden it's Mark and her who are something. That's following my prior understanding that Mark and Tracy were something. Plus my other prior understanding that Tracy lived here alone and had no family. I don't get it. Everything's so mixed up."

Evan didn't like Richard's trying to sort things out and wished he'd go back into the living room. But he just stood there, expecting an explanation.

"All of this is due to my agoraphobia," Evan felt pressured to say. "It tends to create problems, lies, messes."

"So it really is you and Laurel."

"Shh…" Evan signaled for Richard to keep his voice down. "Her dad doesn't know. We've got to keep this a secret from him."

Richard leaned against the cupboard opposite Evan. "He's down on you because of your—"

"Agoraphobia," Evan filled in the word for him. "Most people who hear about me automatically consider me weird. Evan, the weird one."

Richard grinned. "Hey, I can relate to that. Some people take me as weird too."

Evan's eyes widened. "Really? What've *you* got?"

"Attitude, I guess. Something about my attitude. Something that tends to rub some people the wrong way. Howard Howell, for starters. Like right now you could say my butt's on the verge of getting fired."

"Sorry," Evan said.

"And Tracy," Richard added.

"Your attitude rubs *Tracy* wrong?" Evan was now the muddled one.

"I can never seem to say anything right to her, you know?"

"You…you've got a thing for my sister?" Evan exclaimed.

"Shh…" Now it was Richard, reminding Evan to keep his voice down. "Tracy's always made it perfectly clear that she wasn't interested in anything more than a work-friend relationship with me. It's just…I feel like I just never get the chance to say to her how I—"

"Your intention for coming here tonight, right?" Evan gathered.

"I came here tonight," Richard said, "because Tracy and I started a conversation at Howard's earlier that never got finished and I was hoping to get back to it."

"But I thought you said you already knew about her and Mark."

Richard drew a deep breath, smiled briefly, then turned serious again. "Yeah, I did know about her and Mark. I mean, I thought I knew, till I got here and found him linked as Laurel's boyfriend. That threw me."

"Yeah, I can imagine. But don't blow our cover, okay?" Evan asked.

Richard nodded, and Evan nervously checked the living room door.

"Parker doesn't like me," Evan said. "In order to see each other, Laurel and I have to lie."

"You just don't seem the type to lie," Richard said, as though he were still adding things up in his head that weren't coming out right.

"Everybody's the type if they have a reason." Evan finished his cigarette and put it out in the sink. Then he stuck his hands in his pants pockets and stood staring at the floor. "Laurel's my reason."

"Well, I say too bad if her dad doesn't approve of you," Richard voiced his opinion. "You have to tell him the truth about you and Laurel. You have to."

Evan's gaze lifted, but not his spirit. "It's not that easy."

"You and Laurel have your rights. Tell him."

"Thing is," Evan worried openly to this person he barely knew, "maybe he'd take Laurel away from here, from Drendal, and then I'd—"

"No, he couldn't do that. Not if she didn't want to go. And I doubt that she would. I've noticed the looks she gives you, even while pretending to be involved with Mark. Parker himself is bound to notice too. So take a stand. For her. Because we're talking love here, aren't we?"

Evan swallowed hard and gave a careful nod. "Yeah. Love. I think so."

"All right then, that's not something you should have to hide. It's something to feel happy and proud about. I envy you, Evan. I'd never hide anything so wonderful, if I ever had anything so wonderful."

Evan felt overwhelmed. "Nobody's ever envied me before."

"You've got a lot. Don't lose it."

Listening to Richard was raising Evan's courage to the point of wanting to take Parker on. Yet when the guy came walking into the kitchen a moment later, Evan lost his nerve.

"I need a glass of water," the big man said, lumbering past the two guys, going to the sink, unaware that they'd been discussing him. "That pizza sure has made me thirsty."

Evan fetched a clean glass out of the cupboard for him. Then behind Parker's back he froze in silence.

Richard, standing by, just shook his head.

Chapter 41

Sitting in the corner easy chair, Tracy watched Parker Timmons return to the living room. His having gone for a drink of water made her realize how thirsty she was too. She got up, excused herself, walked past Mark and Laurel's togetherness on the couch and went to the kitchen.

"Where's Evan?" she asked Richard, who was alone, gazing out the door window.

He turned at her voice and smiled for seeing her. "Evan? He uh, went upstairs. Took off all of a sudden, looking like some kid about to cry."

Tracy well knew the look, the mood, of her brother. She'd seen it building throughout the evening but hadn't been able to save him from it. She got her drink of water at the sink, trying to think what, if anything, she might be able to do for Evan.

"This seems like a good time for our talk," Richard said, coming over to her.

Her thirst quenched, she put the glass down and turned to give him a warning. "No, it's not a good time, Richard. It's not good at all. Besides, I told you that talk was finished."

"Okay, okay, maybe *that* talk is over," he partly agreed, "but maybe there's something else I want to talk to you about."

Though Tracy curiously wondered what it could be, she didn't want to get involved in any discussion, any subject, with Richard at this time. There was already enough to deal with right now in this house. She shook her head no.

"It's about my job," he nevertheless told her, with a needy look on his face.

"Job?" Tracy was helplessly lured by the subject.

Richard sat down at the table.

She took the chair next to him, realizing out loud, "You're worried about getting fired, aren't you."

"No," he said. "I'm considering quitting."

Tracy looked at him in a whole new way.

"Guess you don't know me as well as you thought, huh?" he said.

"I knew you were somewhat dissatisfied with your job, sure, but I never thought it was this serious."

"Well, it is." Richard shifted on his chair and gave a shrug. "No challenge. No diversity. Same thing day in, day out. Howard holds me back like I was twelve years old. He doesn't trust me with the big stuff. You know that, Tracy. He never lets me make a single decision. Has me running errands, sharpening pencils, nodding yes and no to decisions he's already made. It's a flunky job, that's all it is. I'm a well-paid flunky, who really doesn't feel too good about it at the end of the day, let me tell you."

Tracy could see it, now that he'd pointed it out to her, yes, and it saddened her.

"I think I really do have more to me than he gives me credit for," Richard concluded.

"Explain it to Howard," she eagerly advised him. "Just tell him that you—"

"He knows."

"Maybe not. No, really, I don't think he does. I think he's totally misinterpreting this…this dissatisfaction of yours. I think he sees you as a lazy goof-off, Richard. You've got to be more assertive. You've got to prove him wrong."

"He sees me the way he sees me and that's it," Richard said.

Tracy leaned closer to him, looking deeper into his eyes. "Listen to me, Howard thinks you're uninterested in your work, when in fact you're only bored and are craving more work, more responsibility. You're going to have to talk to him."

"I'm no good at getting through to people."

"Richard, yes, you are."

"I sure haven't been very good at getting through to you, have I?"

Suddenly their discussion jumped tracks, from his job back to her. "That's different," she said, "entirely different."

"I've been as much of a joke to you as I've been to Howard."

"I have Mark," she reminded him for the umpteenth time, wondering why he couldn't, wouldn't, accept that.

"I knew you before Mark and I never stood a chance then either."

He was serious. He'd been serious about her all along. "Come on, Richard. We're friends. That's all we've ever been, all we can ever be. You know that. Besides, I'm too old for you."

Richard looked pathetically wounded.

"You need to get out and find a nice girl closer to your own age," Tracy continued with concern. "The trouble is, you never go anywhere or do anything in your free time."

"Like there's a whole lot of places to swing in this teeny tiny clown town."

"Duluth isn't that far away. Go to Duluth for a weekend now and then."

"Yeah," he said with a curt laugh, "sure."

Trying to get through to him, she put her hand on his arm and shook it gently. "Where's your sense of adventure? A little while ago you were calling this snowstorm an adventure, even though you hate snow. I liked that side of you, Richard. Use that spirit to search farther than me for a girlfriend. And to stand up for your job."

A smile escaped him. Tracy smiled too and leaned in to give him a hug.

Right at that moment Mark came walking into the kitchen. "Am I interrupting something?"

Tracy quickly rose from her chair and away from Richard. "We were just talking. About an office problem."

Mark nodded trustingly, in spite of how it looked. "Where's Evan?"

"Upstairs," Tracy said. "He, uh, isn't much for crowds. And it has gotten rather crowded around here."

Mark was studying Richard more intently now. As if, on second thought, he was re-evaluating the scene he'd just walked in on and was starting to accumulate some questions.

Richard got up to leave. "Guess I'll go join Laurel and her dad in the living room."

"Evan's pretty upset," Tracy told Mark. "It's not easy for him, you know, watching you pretend to be Laurel's boyfriend. For that matter, it's not easy for me either."

"Oh, really?" Mark said. "Like it's easy for me, coming into the kitchen and finding you huddled with Richard."

"We weren't huddled."

"Huddled and smiling," he called it like he saw it.

"You were huddled pretty close to Laurel on the couch," she dished it back to him.

"A show for her dad, you know that."

"Right. And how very convincing you've been."

Mark was staring at her now with as much desperation as Richard had a few moments ago. It was like everyone in this whole evening was desperate about something.

"This game has to end," Mark said. "I don't like lying to Parker Timmons. Nor do I like what's happening between you and me."

"Nothing's happening between us that you're not making happen."

"This is not a good time for a fight, Tracy."

"Then why are you starting one?"

"I'm not. I'm just frustrated, very frustrated."

She nodded. "How do you think I feel about Evan most of the time?"

"This isn't about Evan right now," Mark said. "You and Richard, there seems to be something between the two of you."

Tracy sighed with the guilt of Mark's having gone where she'd led him. "Okay tonight, when I first got home from work, I was angry at you and I admit I tried making you feel jealous about Richard. But now I'm telling you there's absolutely nothing to it."

"Which is why he happened by tonight?"

"We had something important to discuss, that's all."

"*Very important*, from how the two of you were huddled together at the table when I came into the room?"

"We weren't huddled!"

"Sitting very close," Mark emphasized.

"He's a kid!" Tracy said.

"Exactly!" Mark agreed.

Tracy threw up her hands.

Before they could exchange any more hurtful words between them, Parker came walking into the kitchen catching the intensity therein and looking curiously disturbed as to just what might be going on between his daughter's boyfriend and Tracy. "I…I came out to…to get another drink of water," he said, suspiciously observing the twosome.

"I'm not Laurel's boyfriend," Mark blurted out the truth to him.

"What?" Parker came to an abrupt stop in the middle of the room.

"I am." Evan appeared at the bottom of the stairs, enforcing the truth and bracing himself for its outcome.

Laurel came from the living room, looking scared. Richard was with her.

Everyone stood around the kitchen staring at one another. No one spoke. It was like someone had died. Or was about to.

Eventually Laurel walked past Tracy and Mark, past her father, and over to stand beside Evan. A simple, quiet gesture that said much more than any words could have.

Chapter 42

▼

Finding out that things weren't at all as he'd been led to believe, Parker Timmons demanded. "What's going on here?"

Evan, holding hands with Laurel at the foot of the stairs, took the question, the responsibility, as his. "Laurel and I have been seeing each other. We knew you'd disapprove, so we kept it a secret. The other day when you came here, Laurel panicked and told you it was Mark she was seeing, not me. Tonight we pretended the same. Until now. I'm sorry for the lie, Mr. Timmons. I'm also sorry there was a need for it."

Following Evan's speech, the kitchen fell silent. Everyone waited for what might happen next.

The truth was out and Evan knew he had to deal with whatever that brought. He felt like turning and fleeing up the steps, except surely that would be one more thing Parker could use against him. He also craved a cigarette, but he figured Parker was probably as against smoking as he was against agoraphobia and Evan decided that he best not rile the guy any more than he already had. There was nothing more he could do now but stand there and wait, like a criminal facing his judgment.

When Parker finally spoke to Evan, it was with an eerie calmness. "This was my first notion, you know, as to what was going on out here, that Laurel was seeing you. I had a hard time trying to believe it was Mark and her."

"We didn't like lying to you," Evan said, "but we had to."

"The lie began as my idea," Laurel, still holding hands with Evan, confessed to her father.

Parker's eyes held hurt and disappointment. "How could you do such a thing to me?"

"Because I love Evan. And because I knew you wouldn't understand. So I tried to protect him, us, from you."

"Protect?" Parker broke his repose. "Haven't you got this backwards, about who needs protection from whom?" He looked at Evan as if he were looking at a rat in the sewer.

"I have agoraphobia," Evan said, "that's all."

"And you want to subject my daughter to that?"

Before Evan could answer, Tracy lashed out at Parker, "Stop trying to make this into some sort of filth!"

Parker gave her a look as piercing as the one he'd been giving Evan. "I'll say and do whatever I have to protect my daughter."

"I believe your daughter's old enough to make her own decisions," Tracy said.

Parker shook his head. "No, I'm sorry, I can't accept any of this."

"We don't need your acceptance," Evan spoke more bravely than he felt.

"See how far you get without it," Parker warned him.

Evan raised his eyebrows and lowered his voice, "We've gotten pretty far already."

"You slimy creep!" Parker started toward him.

Tracy stepped into his way. "Don't talk to my brother, in our house, that way!"

She stopped him physically but not verbally. Thus he kept at Evan with, "How many other young girls have you lured into your sick, secluded world?"

"Dad!" Laurel shrieked.

"Look at him," Parker said, pointing his finger at Evan, "the guy hasn't been out of here in what, five years?"

"That doesn't make me a slimy creep," Evan argued. "I take showers and wash my clothes just like everybody else."

"I wasn't referring to your hygiene. It's your mental state that bothers me."

"Dad!" Laurel said again. "You've got no right talking to Evan like this!"

It bothered Evan that Parker was paying no mind to his daughter's desperation, nor to the fact that he was causing her far more misery than anyone else was. In another spurt of bravery, Evan told him as much. "You don't care about Laurel's feelings, only your own distorted ones."

"I care enough about Laurel to want to save her from you," Parker argued.

"Save?"

"She doesn't need to be mixed up with someone who has mental problems."

Evan grinned at the irony. "I think it's more your mental state, than mine, that's scaring her."

"Mine's sound," Parker boasted. "Solid as a rock."

"Hard to tell that from listening to you," Evan disagreed.

"Evan," Tracy interrupted in her big-sisterly way, "this isn't going anywhere. Anyone can see there's no getting through to this man."

"On the contrary," Parker spat back at her, "things have gotten through to me quite clearly. A bit late, perhaps, but that all the more proves how wrong it—"

"I have to live my own life," Laurel sounded off to her dad.

Parker glowered at Evan. "Not with him, you don't."

"Evan's a nice guy," she said. "Give him a chance. You don't have to approve of him but at least be polite, can't you?"

"All right," Parker agreed all too sweetly, giving Evan a phony smile. "So you like my daughter, do you?"

"Yes," Evan answered guardedly.

"How nice. So what sort of dates have you taken her on?"

Evan said nothing to the obvious put down.

"And how many times have you picked her up at her house?"

Evan said nothing.

"And by the way, what barber do you go to?"

Evan said nothing.

"Exactly how do you make a living? Or do you?"

"He cooks," Mark came out of his long silence to speak up for Evan on that. "And he's wonderful at it. People pay him to cook for them."

Parker was surprised, but hardly satisfied, and continued badgering Evan, "Do you have taxes withheld? Do you have medical insurance?"

"Stop it!" Tracy ordered him.

Parker justified his questions as, "I'm checking him out as any father would check out his daughter's so-called boyfriend."

"He doesn't need to be checked out," Laurel said.

"Can't you see what you'd be getting into with this guy," her father warned. "What's he got to offer you except maybe a little cheap hanky-panky when you deliver pizza out here and—"

"That's not how it is," Evan told him.

"You want me to believe that the two of you haven't—"

"The two of them are crazy about each other," Richard entered the conversation at that point. "Anyone can see that."

"Crazy…ahh, yes," Parker sneered, "that's precisely the word I've been looking for."

"Evan doesn't deserve this," Richard said.

"Nor does my daughter deserve him."

"What she doesn't deserve," Richard shouted, "is you for a father!"

"Richard!" Now Tracy had to restrain him also.

Evan stood impressed that Richard, someone he barely knew, would stick up for him like that. He sort of wished Tracy hadn't shut him up just yet.

"Why don't we all go into the living room, sit down and talk this over sensibly," Mark suggested.

"There's nothing to talk over," Parker grumbled. "And there's certainly nothing sensible about it."

"Just because you don't approve of me," Evan said, "don't think you're going to keep Laurel and me apart."

"That's exactly what I intend to do," Parker stated, looking ready to tear into him with a whole lot more than just words.

Evan swallowed hard, imagining the squeeze of Parker's hands around his throat.

"Speaking of exactly," Mark lit into Parker, "what is it exactly that you have against Evan?"

The man laughed, as if it were only so obvious. "Look at him. Come on, what kind of guy can he possibly be, locked up in this house for years? Unhealthy, very unhealthy."

"I'm not locked up," Evan said.

"Mentally, yes, you are," Parker insisted. "Which is pretty scary. Unusual. Weird. How could you possibly offer Laurel a life when you've none yourself?"

"Stop it, Dad!" Laurel dropped hands with Evan and used them to cover her ears. "I love Evan. Whether you like it or not. And whether or not he ever leaves this house. That's the way it is. You can either accept that or lose me."

Parker looked long and hard at his daughter, as if maybe he was finally listening to her. But then at a loss for his own words, he just walked away and into the living room.

Evan breathed easier, now that he and Laurel had taken their stand.

Until she left his side, saying, "I've got to go talk to my dad."

"Talk?" Evan didn't understand. He surely thought everything had been said.

"I need to explain to him," she said, leaving the kitchen.

Evan was disappointed. Like maybe he'd lost Laurel after all. Like maybe her father was too strong an influence for her to break free. Tracy, Mark and Richard all stood staring at him, waiting to see how he was going to handle this. Evan didn't want to have to handle anything, or think, or decide. He wanted simplicity. But simplicity was not an easy thing to acquire. He wasn't even sure if he knew what real simplicity was anymore. Not since...

A flash thought of Sam zapped him. He closed his eyes at the attack. But its vision only intensified. Blood. Darkness. The weight of his friend sinking to death in his arms. Gone. Over. Done with. Why?

Evan opened his eyes again, sickened by a bad memory he couldn't let go of. He tried to realize that this was here and now, whereas he still had the chance to be careful, to avoid another mistake, to not lose Laurel. He tried to slow his breathing, clear his mind, be strong.

It was soon obvious that Mark was battling his own complexities, in how he suddenly scowled at Tracy, "So are you happy now that I'm no longer posing as Laurel's boyfriend?"

She lashed back at him, "I don't know, because now I'm not so sure I want you as mine." She left the kitchen and went up the stairs.

It left Mark in the same state of affliction as Evan. He stuck his hands in his pockets. Sucked in a deep breath. Gazed up at the ceiling. Shook his head. Exchanged a look with Richard. Then with Evan. "Any laundry to do?" he asked.

"No," Evan had to say, having already done it that morning. But thinking quickly, he snatched the hand towel off the stove handle and gave it to him.

"Thanks," Mark said and headed for the basement.

"I'm sorry about everything, Evan," Richard said when it was just the two of them left in the kitchen.

"It's not your fault, not your problem," Evan told him.

"Part of it is. The part of how I reacted when you told me you were Tracy's brother and that you had that...that agro thing."

"You were just startled, that's all."

"Yeah, at first, I guess," Richard said sheepishly. "Now I...I just really have all this concern for you."

"Concern?"

"Yeah."

"You don't need to be concerned. I don't like people getting concerned about me."

"Life can be cruel," Richard stated, as if he knew first-hand.

"Yeah," Evan said.

"So how did you get this phobia?"

No, please, not another amateur psychologist starting a work-up on me, Evan thought to himself. He'd hoped Richard was beyond that.

"I'm sorry," Richard said, as if reading Evan's thoughts. "I'm sure you've had enough of this tonight."

Evan brushed his hair back from his face and gave an appreciative nod.

"Wanna get drunk?" was Richard's next question.

"What?" Evan wasn't sure he'd heard right.

"Drunk," Richard repeated.

"We don't have any booze in the house."

"Try my car," Richard said.

"Your car?"

"Got an unopened fifth of vodka out there."

"In the snowstorm?"

Richard laughed. "I think we can make it that far, Evan. Come on."

If ever Evan needed an escape, over all his escapes, it was now. Though it'd been a long time since he'd gone the alcohol route, tonight seemed surely worthy of that direction.

The two of them put on their jackets and went out the back door.

Consenting to Richard's idea didn't automatically mean it was easy for Evan. Panic seized him, as usual, leaving the house. Yet for all the stress that had been going on inside, he tried to think of going outside as merely a trade off from one discomfort to another. Like he was going to feel miserable no matter what he did, or where he was, so what the heck.

He followed closely behind Richard. The snow was coming down so heavily, and blowing so ferociously, he could barely see. He didn't suppose Richard could see much either. It was kind of like the blind leading the blind. He grabbed a hold of the back of Richard's jacket.

When they got to Richard's car, Richard opened the passenger side for Evan. Then as he ran around to the driver's side, he made loud whooping sounds as if couldn't get there fast enough.

Too tense to let out any whoops of his own, Evan just got inside and closed the door after him. It was dark in there, as the front windshield was completely blanketed with snow. And at most probably only a couple degrees warmer in there than outside.

As soon as Richard got into the car, he turned to pull a bag off the back seat. "We'll stay out here and drink. Okay, Evan? I think we both need a break away from all that's going on inside the house. Right, Evan?"

"Right." Evan heard his own voice answer vaguely, as if he were in a dream.

Though the inside of the car was cold enough to see your breath, it was at least free of the falling snow and biting wind.

Richard opened the vodka, saying, "Sometimes you just gotta say piss on it all and call time out." He took a hardy drink then handed the bottle to Evan.

Evan took his first swallow of hard liquor in five years.

Chapter 43

Tracy sat on the edge of her bed crying. Over everything, everyone. Mostly Mark. He wasn't the person she thought he was, hoped him to be. She had so wanted and needed him to see things as she did. For a time she thought he had, but it was plain now that he didn't. She felt let down, deserted, and scared.

She worried about what was going to happen to Evan. His life was such a pitiful struggle. He was so badly misjudged. There were the cruel put-downs from Parker Timmons, unreasonable expectations from Mark, and the shock with which Richard reacted on meeting him. No one knew or understood Evan the way she did. Except, maybe, Laurel.

Even from the second floor Tracy could hear the humming-knocking agitation of the washer in the basement. She smiled fondly that Evan should be doing his therapeutic laundry at this time. His meticulous compulsion for doing housework helped him cope with the limits of his agoraphobia. But now, maybe, Laurel would start to put a little more balance into his life so that he wouldn't feel such a need to scrub the kitchen floor twice a week, wash clothes every single day and dust the furniture almost continually.

Tracy left her bed and went to have a look out the window. The blizzard wasn't letting up any. In fact it seemed worse. This had turned into quite a night, inside as well as outside. She guessed, despite the stress of it, she felt good having offered food and lodging to three storm victims. Ironically, it couldn't have been a more unlikely threesome than Laurel, her father and Richard.

There was a knock at her bedroom door and Tracy went to open it, expecting it was Laurel needing a girl-to-girl talk right about now. But to her surprise it was Mark.

"Hi," he said, standing there with a smile as sweet as spring.

Tracy's anger toward him melted into a warm, helpless smile of her own. "Hi."

"I was hoping we could talk."

She nodded, stepping aside, letting him in. "Listen," she laughed, "you can hear the washer all the way up here. Evan's doing one of his escape bits."

"It's not Evan," Mark told her. "It's me. I'm the one doing laundry."

Her eyes widened at him. "You?"

"Learned it from Evan. Good stress reliever. Only...it didn't exactly do the trick for me. So I came up here instead. Let's not fight, Tracy." He pulled her close and kissed her.

Mark's love and affection was exactly what Tracy needed. She didn't want to fight anymore either. She only wanted things to be simple and secure. They seemed to be that way right now.

Except...the sound of the washer was soon triggering a new concern she couldn't ignore. "If Evan's not doing laundry, then where is he and what is he doing?"

"Let's not start in on him again," Mark said.

"Was he in the kitchen when you came up?"

"No."

"And he's not up here either?"

Mark shook his head, suggesting, "He's probably in the living room with Laurel and her father and Richard."

Tracy found that difficult to imagine, but nodded hopefully. And then she returned to the pleasure of hugging and kissing Mark, until the matter of Evan again came between them.

Tracy pulled away from Mark, saying, "I have to find him and know he's all right. This is a very painful time for him and..."

She ran off amidst her sentence. Down the hall, down the stairs, through the kitchen, Mark following.

"Where's Evan?" she asked, bursting into the living room and finding just Laurel and Parker.

"I thought he was upstairs," Laurel said, with her own concern rising.

"No. He's not upstairs and he's not in the basement. And where's Richard?"

"Whose turn is it to watch those two anyway?" Parker tried making jest of it.

Tracy turned to Mark with a sinking feeling. "Oh my gosh, no!" She brushed past him, going for the kitchen door.

Mark hurried after her. "They left? You think Evan left with Richard?"

She squinted out the window into the obscure visibility. "Richard's car is still there. I think maybe they—"

"I'll go check." Mark was already getting into his jacket.

"I'm going with." She whirled around in a fit of nervous energy, reaching for her own coat.

"No." Mark stopped her. "You stay here."

"But, I have to see if—"

"I'll handle it." He went out the door by himself.

Chapter 44

▼

Evan and Richard had both downed a lot of vodka in the forty-five minutes they'd so far spent in the car. Evan was feeling wonderfully oblivious to all the things that originally bothered him, thanks to Richard's idea of coming out there to drink.

Suddenly there was another thumping sound besides the drums in the tumulus radio music. Someone was pounding at Evan's door. He opened it, surprised to find Mark. "What are you doing out here?"

"More like what are *you* doing out here?" Mark shouted over Bon Jovi.

Evan offered the vodka to him. "Chill out, okay?"

"I'm chilled enough, no thanks." He dipped his snowy head and shoulders part way inside the car, shunning the bottle Evan kept shoving at him. "We've been worried about you."

"How about me?" Richard quipped. "Anyone worried about me?"

His childlike question brought a laugh out of Evan. And then Evan's laugh, in turn, started Richard laughing.

Mark remained the straight man. "You guys are getting smashed."

"We're on our way, yeah," Richard admitted. "Wanna come along?"

Evan stuck the bottle back in Mark's face.

Again he pushed it away. "This is crazy, you guys sitting out here. If you want to drink, come on inside the house and do it."

"We're okay here," Evan insisted.

"In case you don't know it…" Mark began.

"What?" Evan cupped his hand to his ear.

"There's a blizzard going on out here!" Mark shouted over the music.

"Not in the car there isn't," Evan said, causing Richard to burst out laughing again. And that was all it took to set Evan off again as well.

Mark shook his head at the two of them. "If you guys fall asleep..." He stopped and started over more loudly, "If you guys fall asleep out here you'll freeze!"

"Not with all this antifreeze in us, we won't." Evan's logic started another round of laughter between himself and Richard.

"We're not going to fall asleep," Richard promised Mark, then closed his eyes and dropped his head to his shoulder, pretending that he just had.

"Come in the house!" Mark ordered. "You can bring the bottle! Come on!"

"Leave us alone!" Evan said. "We're fine right here!"

"Would you mind closing the door?" Richard asked Mark. "It's getting drafty in here. Either get all the way in or all the way out, but just shut the door one way or the other, okay?"

Mark got out and headed back to the house.

Evan pulled the door shut and downed another good swallow of booze.

"Mark doesn't know what he's missing." Richard accepted the bottle from Evan and took a drink. Then he reached forth to lower the radio volume, "How does it feel being away from your house? Seriously, you okay, Evan?"

"This *is* my house. I've moved." Evan hadn't meant it to be funny, but when Richard laughed it started him laughing all over again. He couldn't remember the last time he'd laughed so much.

"You know," Richard said, finally laughed out and simmered down, partly due to the soft ballad playing next on the radio, "I don't have many friends in Drendal, and it means a lot having met you, Evan."

Evan nodded, not letting on that he felt more scared than honored with the responsibility of having a friend. Sam had been his friend, and look what happened to him. "Have you ever been shot, Richard?"

Richard was stunned.

"Or known anyone who was?" Evan added.

Richard shook his head no.

"Anyway," Evan said, without explaining, "other than Laurel and you, I haven't had a friend in five years."

Richard took another drink of vodka. "I can't imagine what it's like, having agoraphobia? Hey, I pronounced it right, didn't I?"

"It's an ugly word, isn't it."

Richard laughed. "Yeah. So is the word loser. That's me, a loser."

"No, you're not. You have a job, you live in the real world, you're free."

"You have a girlfriend, a sister and a nice home."
"But…I'm a prisoner here."
"We're all prisoners of something, Evan."

The next song on the radio switched back to rock 'n roll and Richard turned up the volume. The pulsing beat filled the inside of the car. While outside the deepening, drifting snow seemed to have brought the world to a halt.

Chapter 45

"But they'll freeze out there," Tracy fretted when Mark returned to the house without the guys.

"I don't think so," he said, hanging his jacket on the wall hook and stomping the snow off his shoes.

Remington came from out of nowhere to enjoy his treat.

"If they don't come in by another hour or so," Mark vowed, "I'll go back out there and somehow make them come in."

"How long does it take for someone to freeze?" Laurel asked fearfully.

"Don't worry about them," her father said. "They're not children, they know what they're doing."

She gave him a bitter look. "You'd probably *like* for them to freeze to death. Especially Evan."

"No, honey, no..." Parker's voice softened, "what kind of person do you think I am?"

Laurel raised her chin. "I'm not sure I know."

"Hey, come on," Tracy interrupted the start of a fight, "we're all pretty tense here tonight. The storm, our personal conflicts, our—"

"Conflicts?" Parker flared up again. "That's an understatement."

Tracy smiled and nodded in agreement. "Okay, despite our understated conflicts, why don't I make us some hot chocolate and we'll all go in the living room and try to relax."

"I can't relax until Evan and Richard come inside," Laurel stated.

"Well, we have to!" Tracy said. "Now...please get out the cups, second shelf in the cupboard behind you."

Chapter 46

Evan was cold and shivering. Though the car heater was going, its performance was up against some harsh weather.

"So Evan, what's going to happen with you and Laurel?" Richard asked, sitting behind the steering wheel with a notable shiver of his own.

"Nothing," Evan answered. "Probably nothing."

"She loves you. You love her. Don't say nothing."

"Her father disapproves."

"Stand up to him, Evan."

"Maybe...if I were normal...it would be easier."

"Then be normal, Evan."

Evan gave Richard a look.

"I mean it," Richard said.

Leaning his head back against the seat, Evan moaned, wishing it was only that simple.

"Hey, sorry," Richard apologized, "I'm suppose to be cheering you up, not cutting you down. Here." He handed the bottle of vodka to Evan.

Evan refused his turn. "I think I've had enough."

"No you haven't, not yet. I'd really like to see you get over that wall around you."

Evan was amused. "You can actually see my wall?"

Richard laughed. "Yeah."

"Prove it."

"High. Ugly. Topped with barbed wire."

"That's it. Wow, you really do see it. But...I wish you didn't."

"It's okay, friends share things like this."

"Friends." Evan nodded.

"Hey, let's show that asshole Timmons just how normal you really are," Richard suggested.

"Okay," Evan agreed bravely.

"You have to take back your freedom, Evan. It's right there waiting for you. All you have to do is take it."

Evan straightened up in his seat and rolled down his window. He welcomed the cold air on his face, laughing and taking it like a power feat. "Freedom! Yeah! I feel it! How about you, Richard?"

"Just a minute." Richard rolled the window down on his side of the car, and with the wind coming from that direction caught a blast of snow in his face. "Yeah! That's it, Evan! We've found it! So what do you suggest we do with it?"

Evan opened his door and got out.

Chapter 47

▼

Tracy had had all the waiting she could take. She'd finished her hot chocolate and was going crazy. Though she, Mark, Parker and Laurel were sharing the wait together in the living room, each was in totally separate emotional places. Talk was difficult. Everyone avoided looking at one another. The tension was heavy.

Finally she got to her feet and started out of the room, exclaiming, "I'm going to go bring them in!"

Mark followed her to the kitchen and stopped her from putting on her coat. "I won't allow you to go out there in that storm."

"Allow?" she said, glowering at him. "Get out of my way!"

"You're not doing this, Tracy."

"Watch me!" She struggled away from him.

Though she managed to get one arm into a coat sleeve, Mark kept her from getting into the other one. Their scuffling stopped upon their noticing some strange sounds coming from outside. Together they went to the door window.

What they managed to see, through the stirring blur of white, was Evan and Richard, out of the car, yelling and playing in the snow like carefree kids with no concern of the storm.

"What are they doing?" Tracy shrieked.

Laurel and her father came from the living room. Mark opened the door part way, and all four of them crowded into the drafty opening to watch.

Though Tracy knew they were drunk, and was not particularly happy with that, she couldn't deny the pleasure she felt seeing her brother functioning so freely in the outside world. It tugged at her heart, making her smile and cry both at the same time.

Caked with snow and waving his arms, Evan looked like a come-to-life snowman. Stepping high, bounding in circles, hooting and hollering unclear things, it almost seemed as if the long pent-up demons of his phobia were hereby being spewed from his soul.

Noticing his audience, Evan called to the group in the doorway, "Hey, come on out! The weather's fine!"

"It's even better in here!" Tracy shouted back. "Come in, both of you, and have some hot chocolate."

Evan gave Richard a playful shove, landing him into a snow bank.

"You're drunk!" she shouted. "And there's a blizzard going on out there!"

Half buried in a pile of fluff, Richard managed to free his right foot enough to ram it into the side of Evan's left foot. Evan's legs caved from under him and he fell fast into as much snow as Richard lay in.

The guys were laughing so hard they couldn't get themselves back up. The more they tried, the more they kept falling down.

"You have to admit, they do make it look fun," Mark commented to Tracy.

She nodded and laughingly agreed.

"I've never seen Evan like this." Laurel, peering over Tracy's shoulder, was enjoying the show as well.

"Idiots!" Parker grumped.

After all the effort it took for Evan to finally get back onto his feet, he then went to purposely drop down backwards into a deeper section of snow before Mark's car. He laid so still at first, it seemed he'd passed out. But then he was moving again, arms and legs spreading back and forth, open and closed, against the snow.

"What the hell you doing?" Richard yelled at him.

"Making an angel!" Evan yelled back, as if it should only be obvious. "Haven't you ever made a snow angel?"

"Yeah! Sure! Haven't *you*?" Richard got up and stood over him in obvious doubt.

When Evan was ready to get up, he again had so much trouble doing it that Richard had to lend him a hand. And then he turned to look back down at his supposed angel, but there was nothing more than an indistinguishable mess rapidly filling with more snow.

Tracy exchanged a knowing look with Mark. *They* had made angels the other day, and Evan had watched them. Not until now, under the influence of alcohol, was he himself able to attempt it. It was both astonishing and heartwarming, seeing him like this. Mark, beside her, seemed equally affected. Evan's spontaneity was like a miracle happening right before their eyes.

Tracy felt the guilt of not realizing until now how very much her brother had been longing for his freedom all along. It seemed, in time's passing, that she'd lost track of what normality even looked like on Evan anymore. He'd become agoraphobic and that was that. She'd always thought acceptance showed strength. She hadn't meant to become so absorbed in the forbearance of his problem as to overlook the curing. But sadly enough, it seemed she had.

"I'm going to bring them in," Mark decided, grabbing his jacket.

Out there in the blizzard, his endeavor to round up Evan and Richard became more of a circus act than a rescue mission. After just so much of their darting out of his reach, throwing snow in his face, and knocking him into snow banks, Mark laughingly broke down and played the game their way. Thus when he did manage to apprehend the two snowmen and bring them into the kitchen, he, by then, was a snowman himself.

While Parker stayed back grumbling to himself, Tracy, Mark and Laurel worked together as a team getting Evan and Richard out of their jackets and shoes, brushing snow out of their hair, toweling their faces. Then as the two guys sang an off-key rendition of *Winter Wonderland*, the team assisted them upstairs to Evan's room.

Once Evan and Richard became still on their shared bed, their eyes fell closed and they were out in seconds.

As for everyone else's sleeping arrangements, Tracy invited Laurel to share her room with her, and she assigned Parker to the living room couch. She loaned Laurel a flannel nightgown and gave her a fresh towel and washcloth. Then before getting herself ready for bed, Tracy took two blankets and a pillow downstairs to Parker.

When she got back upstairs, Mark was waiting for her in the hall. Neither had anything more to say to one another. But that was all right. The night had been exhausting, and getting some sleep seemed to be the most immediate need of them as well as everybody. They merely said goodnight, kissed, and went to their separate rooms.

The house fell silent but for the wind hissing beyond the windows. Despite the unrelenting storm going on outside, inside the house was warm and cozy and peaceful at last.

There would be new ways to perceive Evan's problem now, Tracy thought to herself, lying there next to Laurel, trying to sort out at least some of tonight's discoveries before giving in to sleep. There was a new awareness of his desire to be helped. And new possibilities for accomplishing it. Though surely not by his drinking. She smiled as Evan's display of freedom replayed over and over in her mind.

Chapter 48

▼

Somewhere deep in the middle of the night Evan awoke with a horrendous headache, profound thirst, and a strange sense of confusion. Turning from his right side over to this left side, he found he was not alone in bed. The shadowy outline of someone, he didn't know who, lay next to him beneath the covers. He strained his eyes to see. But the blankets were too high, the room too dark.

He got out of bed and stood in place for a minute, getting his bearings and holding his head. Then he walked around to the other side of the bed to get a better look at who he'd been sleeping with. It was Richard.

The happenings of earlier evening, one by one, started replaying in his mind. How he'd told Parker the truth about Laurel and himself. How Parker got so worked up over it. Then Laurel went into the living room to comfort him. And Tracy blew up at Mark and went running off to her room. Mark, in frustration went down to the basement to do laundry. And Richard suggested they get drunk.

Evan found his jeans over the back of the chair. The legs were still a bit damp from the snow, but he pulled them on, tolerating the discomfort as a better alternative than looking for a dry pair.

On his way to the door, he bumped hard into a corner of the high dresser. His gasp of pain accompanied the thud. Rubbing his arm, he glanced back over at the bed to see if Richard had awakened. He hadn't. Good. Then he waited a moment, listening, hoping he hadn't disturbed anyone else in the house.

He thought some more about earlier. How he and Richard had trudged through the blizzard to get to Richard's car. How they'd sat out there in it a long time, drinking vodka, listening to music, talking. Evan learned that Richard was not the secure person he first appeared to be. Behind his visual confidence, were many insecurities.

Evan smiled to himself, genuinely thankful for this new friend, and for the way the two of them were able to relate to one another. Except he had to wonder now whether it was Richard's secure side or insecure side that suggested they get drunk.

He remembered Mark's coming out after them and making them go inside the house. Evan supposed it was good that someone had cared enough to look out for their welfare, since they weren't doing very well at it themselves. But he still couldn't remember who had gotten them up to bed. Nor could he remember climbing the stairs. Or lying down next to Richard.

After using the bathroom, Evan stole quietly down the hall, down the steps, and into the kitchen. The snow outside cast a pale glow in through the windows.

He went to the refrigerator for a glass of milk. Remington was soon there, winding around his ankles, meowing. Evan poured some milk into a bowl for the cat and into a glass for himself. One glass wasn't enough, so he poured a second. When he'd quenched his thirst he put the carton back into the refrigerator, the empty glass into the sink, and went over to the door window to check on the storm. Though it was less intense now than it had been earlier, it was nevertheless still snowing, still blowing.

He heard the steps creak. At least he thought that was what he'd heard. He flashed a startled look in that direction. Watched. Waited. Wondered who else besides himself and Rem was awake and coming down in the middle of the night.

It was Laurel, soon appearing at the foot of the stairs, wearing a long white gown, looking like an angel. The awesome sight of her made Evan feel like he'd died and gone to heaven.

"Evan..." she whispered his name in her angel-like voice, "I heard something. I thought maybe it was you."

"I bumped into my dresser. Sorry."

She came toward him. Evan wasn't sure if she was walking or floating.

"You didn't wake me," she said, putting her hand on him as if she were testing the realness of him as well. "I haven't been asleep yet."

"You haven't? What time is it?"

"I don't know. Late. Really late."

"You look beautiful," he said, as if he were seeing her for the very first time.

She giggled quietly. "In a flannel granny gown?"

"Yeah," he said with a sigh. "So where are you sleeping? I mean, not sleeping?"

"With Tracy."

"I'm with Richard."

"Strange night, huh?"

"Very strange."

She held her finger to her lips. "My dad, he's sleeping in on the couch."

Evan flicked a nervous glance in the direction of the living room.

"So why are you standing down here in the kitchen?" she asked.

Returning his look to Laurel, Evan was smitten with how her eyes glistened. He wondered if it was from the snow glow shining through the door window or the emotional effect of this rendezvous. Angel eyes.

"Evan?" she said.

"Oh, uh, I woke up thirsty and came down for some milk," he explained. "Luckily I did because it seemed Rem was thirsty for milk too."

"A hangover, huh?"

"I don't think cats get hangovers. Actually, they don't drink anything that would cause a hangover in the first place."

"You," she said, giggling again. "I meant you."

"So are you mad at me?" he felt the need to ask, though she didn't act like it.

"No."

"Maybe you *should* be mad. I must have acted like a real idiot out there earlier."

"You were having fun, you and Richard, that's all."

"I was drunk."

"I don't think anyone's ever seen you have such a good time before."

"It was Richard's idea, the drinking."

"I'm sure," she said.

"We did have fun," Evan admitted, nodding and breaking a smile. "I really felt like I was somewhere, Laurel, you know? Away from here, away from myself. Just really somewhere. It was nice. Only now I'm right back where I was before. Nowhere."

She snuggled against him and Evan held her. She was soft and warm and desirable. She was his fix of the moment, making everything seem right. Like it didn't matter that a storm was going on outside. Or that the linoleum floor was cold beneath his bare feet. Or that Parker Timmons was as close as the next room. Or that morning would come in a few hours and shed a harsh light on reality. Right now was right now and all that mattered.

"You *are* somewhere, Evan," Laurel said. "You're right here, with me, and that's enough."

"For now," he compromised.

"Don't feel threatened by my dad," she pleaded. "It's good that he knows the truth about us. We don't have to keep our relationship a secret anymore. We're free."

"Yeah, I guess. It's just that there's all this stuff lately."

"What stuff?"

Evan didn't like that Laurel seemed scared. And that it was he, rather than her father or any other person causing it. He kissed her forehead tenderly. "Stuff that Mark's putting into my head."

"But it's good stuff, right? I mean, he's trying to help you, right?"

"Yeah. It's just…these changes…they…"

"You and I will never change how we feel about each other. Will we?"

Evan gave Laurel a serious look. And then he began kissing her deeply and passionately. They held each other so tightly their bodies seemed to become one. When the moment lightened, Evan gave a sigh ahead of saying, "I often wondered what it would be like spending the night with you, but I never thought it would be like this, in the kitchen, with your father right around the corner."

Laurel giggled quietly against his chest. "It's romantic, being here with you like this. I've never felt closer to you. I *love* this moment."

They kissed again. And again. Evan loved the moment too, except, "Laurel, haven't you ever wondered what it would be like if I could go out in the world and do all the ordinary things that ordinary people do?"

"Maybe. A little. Sometimes."

"Why does that have to be so difficult for me?" Though he loved her so much for loving him just the way he was, lately Evan was feeling less and less acceptant of himself.

"If we never go anywhere farther than this house, that's fine with me," she said.

They just started to kiss again when…

"What the hell's going on out here?" Parker's voice suddenly shattered their intimate moment. The big man filled the living room doorway.

Evan and Laurel dropped arms from one another. They were caught. Caught good at doing nothing wrong.

"As I'm sleeping right in there," Parker raved, motioning behind himself, "you two are in the very next room from me going at it."

"We were just standing here watching it snow," Laurel told him, as if he actually deserved an explanation.

Parker was nodding in a way that well indicated he'd already made this into something a whole lot more. "It's not enough that the guy you get mixed up with has agoraphobia but that's he's a drunk besides?"

"I'm not a drunk," Evan stated. "Until tonight, I haven't drunk in five years."

Parker continued to Laurel, "And what kind of respect does he have for you when he gets you down here in the—"

"We weren't doing anything," Evan said.

"Well, then luckily I came out here and put a stop to it just in time."

Evan put a finger to his lips. "You're going to wake everyone."

"Good. I'd like to see what the rest of the household thinks about this."

"We weren't doing anything," Laurel insisted.

Parker proceeded all the way into the room now. Though the snow glow bathed just as softly over his face as it did over Laurel and Evan's, it hardly had the same enticing effect. "You weren't raised this way, Laurel, sneaking around with—"

"We weren't sneaking," Evan said. "You're the one who came sneaking up on us."

"I'm a father trying to protect his daughter, that's all."

"C'mon," Evan said, giving Laurel a nudge, "let's go back to bed."

Together they started across the kitchen toward the stairs.

"Wait just a damn minute here!" Parker rang out at them.

"Separately," Laurel clarified. "I'm sharing Tracy's room with her, and Evan's sharing his room with Richard."

"Oh, uh, well…" For a moment Parker actually seemed to feel a bit sheepish. But in the next instance he was his thundering, commanding self again. "You're sleeping down here! On the couch!"

"So then where does that leave you?" Evan questioned him. "I mean, I guess if you exchange sleeping places with Laurel, that leaves you sharing the bed with my sister."

"I'll sleep in a living room chair," Parker blustered. "And you can be damn sure I'll keep an eye on my daughter for the rest of the night, that's what I'll do. Till morning, when we can go home."

Despite the Parker Timmons take-over, Evan momentarily felt he had a lot to be grateful for. He told Laurel goodnight, gave her a smile and the wink of his eye, then went up the steps alone.

Chapter 49

Tracy made breakfast the next morning. Pancakes were the one thing she could master almost as well as Evan and therefore undertook it without waiting for him to come downstairs. He would hardly be in condition for cooking anyway, she figured. Poor Evan, he was likely going to be suffering one heck of a hangover.

It was nice, looking outside and seeing it so calm after the blizzard. Though the sky was a grim gray, the snow was bright and clean and new. And the windswept drifts were as smooth and miraculously formed as if the storm had been a masterful artist working through the night.

While Mark, Richard and Parker sat in the living room barely talking to one another, Laurel lent Tracy a helping hand in the kitchen. Kind of curious, Tracy thought, how the girl kept smiling to herself and making frequent little glances over at the steps. Also curious was how Tracy had come downstairs earlier and found Laurel dressed and just standing at the back door staring dreamily out the window. It was the kind of curious behavior of someone in love.

Tracy still couldn't get over the fact that Evan had a girlfriend. That in spite of his agoraphobia he was actually carrying on a romantic relationship. While she, because of his agoraphobia, was having trouble managing a romantic relationship of her own.

She peered into the living room. Mark was sitting in the easy chair by the front window, holding Remington on his lap. She loved Mark so much. He meant so much more to her than any other guy she'd ever been involved with. He was different. Special. And he loved her enough not to be scared off. At least not yet. But Tracy knew she'd better start concentrating more on him and what they had together if she didn't want to lose him. She was finally, seriously, beginning to realize that she had a life of her own, aside from Evan's, to work on.

When the food was ready, everyone but Evan came to sit at the kitchen table. Though there was very little conversation, everyone had a hardy appetite.

Parker pretty much kept his eyes down as he ate. Laurel continually watched the stairs for Evan. Richard seemed to feel surprisingly well, for all the drinking he'd done last night. And Mark, sitting directly across from Tracy, kept sending her his seductive Costner smiles.

The roar of the snowplow passed down the road, no doubt leaving a good-sized ridge of snow at the foot of the driveway behind Parker's car. It would be a lot of work getting all five cars cleared out. Tracy hoped the breakfast she served would be substantial enough fuel for whoever tackled the job.

When Evan finally came downstairs, everyone stopped eating to look at him. Saying nothing, he went straight to the refrigerator and poured himself a tall glass of orange juice. After several thirsty swallows, he took the remainder of his drink with him into the living room.

Laurel left the table and went to join him.

Though Parker was notably agitated, he kept quiet and finished off his second helping of pancakes. Richard, as thirsty as Evan, downed his umpteenth drink of water. Mark forked one more pancake for himself off the serving plate in the center of table. Though Tracy desperately wanted to go into the other room and check on Evan, she decided she'd best leave that to Laurel.

It was Mark who first broke the long stretch of table silence. "Well, Richard, guess it's up to you and me to dig out the cars. What do you say?"

"Right." Richard seemed as ready and eager to get out there as Mark was.

"I'll help," Parker surprisingly offered.

"We've only got two shovels," Mark said, sounding sorry to have to turn him down.

Parker left the table and went for his jacket, saying, "I've got one in the trunk of my car."

"Hey, great!" Mark cheered. "We can sure use your help."

As the three guys ventured out into the cold white aftermath of the blizzard, all prior indifferences fell secondary to the immense task requiring teamwork. Tracy watched from the door window for a while.

She was washing dishes at the sink when Laurel returned to the kitchen. The girl took a dishtowel and began drying. As the two worked side by side, they kept an interested watch through the over-the-sink window at the crew in the driveway.

"Is he okay?" Tracy asked her about Evan.

There was both love and pain in Laurel's smile. "Yeah."

"His condition must be very hard on you," Tracy sympathized.

"On him, not me."

"Of course it's hard on Evan," Tracy said, "but certainly it's got to be difficult for—"

"We had a moment last night, me and Evan," Laurel told her in the way that women shared secrets.

"Moment?" Tracy was unsure of what that meant, or if she really wanted to know.

"Here in the kitchen."

"Kitchen?" Tracy's gaze swept imaginatively over the room. The table.

"He came downstairs for a glass of milk," Laurel said, taking a plate out of the draining rack and wiping it with her towel. "I heard him and came down also. We stood together in the dark, by the door window, watching it snow, listening to the quiet of the house. It was wonderful. Romantic. Until my dad came out here and caught us."

Tracy was only glad the moment they'd been caught at had been so innocent. "What did he say? Do?"

"He ended our moment right then and there. Said a lot of cruel things to us." Laurel put the dried plate into the cupboard and took another from the draining rack.

"Your dad, has he always been so strict?" Tracy asked.

"With me, yeah, his youngest daughter."

"Must be very difficult for you."

"Very."

Tracy rung out her dishcloth and went to wipe off the table. "You know, just because my brother has agoraphobia doesn't mean he's not a good guy."

"Dad won't see beyond Evan's phobia."

"But you do? See beyond it?" Tracy returned to the sink, observing Laurel's expression.

"I think being able to see beyond one's problems is a sign of real love, don't you?" Laurel spoke with pure adoration.

Though Tracy nodded, she honestly knew that she wasn't, herself, so easily seeing beyond the problems of herself and Mark. She envied the simplicity with which Laurel loved Evan.

Chapter 50

By noon the guys had all five cars shoveled out plus the entire driveway cleared. Mark's back was sore, but not to the degree that followed that first day he'd moved so much snow. It pleased him, knowing he was acquiring some stamina. Parker's stamina, for being hefty and older, held up very well. The man certainly shoveled his fair share. And Richard, following his night of heavy drinking, worked amazingly hard.

One by one the over-night house guests left. Parker, Laurel, Richard. And then Tracy, too, left for work without there having ever been time for her and Mark to have a worthy talk. Anyway they'd managed to share a nice good-bye kiss, which definitely insured that their relationship was heading back in the right direction.

As Mark later sat relaxing in the living room, feeling particularly good about everything, Evan came in, sat down, and lit up an off-schedule cigarette.

No doubt still recovering from last night, Evan shifted uneasily, as if the cigarette wasn't especially helping that much. For the way he kept staring across the room at Mark, it seemed as if he were trying to work himself up to saying something. Eventually he got there. "Mark, can we talk?"

"Sure," Mark responded eagerly.

"I want you to help me."

"Help you?"

"Yeah, you know, get over this problem of mine."

"Problem?" Mark couldn't resist teasing.

"My phobia," Evan said seriously.

"You surpassed it pretty well last night," Mark reminded him.

"Last night doesn't count."

"No, I suppose not. Okay, so what have you got in mind?"

Evan shrugged, took a deep drag off his cigarette, exhaled, shook his head. "I don't know. I guess maybe just something more than what I've done so far. I don't know what. But I won't quit this time, Mark, I promise."

"You sound determined."

"I am."

"I'll try to help you, sure," Mark said. "But Evan, I think besides my help you really might want to consider getting some professional counseling and—"

"No."

"—maybe some medication."

"No."

"Why?"

"This isn't New York," Evan stated.

"What does that mean?" Mark didn't like how this was starting to sound like an argument.

"For one thing," Evan reasoned, "Drendal is small, limited."

"I'm sure we could find you a doctor in Duluth. I'd drive you."

"No doctor."

"But, Evan."

"Just you. You said you'd help me. I just need you."

"Just me," Mark verified reluctantly. Though he'd certainly hoped to set Evan up with some professional help, he supposed he could try to be a good second best. On a lighter note, he laughingly brought up last night's event again, "Man, you sure were having a blast out in that blizzard."

Evan laughed as well. "Guess I put on quite a show, huh? But you know…it felt good, what Richard and I did. What I was able to do. The talk Richard and I had."

"Is last night what made you decide to beat your agoraphobia?"

"Sort of. Yeah. But not just because of my drinking and being out in the snow and talking with Richard. Not even because of any stuff that happened before that, such as Parker cutting me down. It was more like later on…like my being together with Laurel in the middle of the night."

Mark's mouth dropped. "You and Laurel were together in the night?"

"In the kitchen. In the dark kitchen. Standing by the door. Watching it snow. It was nice. It made me realize I want a lot more than that for her and me. I realized that if our relationship is to grow, to even survive, I'll have to conquer my phobia."

It was great, finally hearing Evan say he wanted more out of his life. "You'll do it," Mark assured him. "Look at the progress you've already made."

Evan took a drag from his cigarette and exhaled it instantly. "It's just—"

"Just what?" Mark probed, the way any good psychologist worked his patient.

"You know," Evan started, stopped, smiled awkwardly, then continued, "I'm not even sure if I really have agoraphobia or whether it's more like I've just worked myself into this deep rut of a lifestyle."

"Whichever," Mark said, "the cure's the same. You work yourself out of it."

Evan crushed the remainder of his cigarette in the ashtray and stood up. "Do you know how nervous I'm feeling right now?"

"Yeah, I think so," Mark said, also standing. Then changing his mind, he added, "Actually…no…probably not…but I'm almost sure it's a good kind of nervous you're feeling right now, Evan. And I'm very proud of you."

Chapter 51

It felt so different to Tracy, being around Richard at work that afternoon. After the strangeness of last night. As if his coming to her house wasn't unexpected enough, there was the surprising talk they ended up having, his finding out about Evan, his getting himself and Evan drunk, his spending the night. She knew that Richard felt different about her now too. They'd shared some really deep stuff between them that put their relationship on a whole new level of maturity and respect.

Howard didn't seem to notice any change between her and Richard. He was too preoccupied with the problem of having just lost his cook. It upset him to no ends. He couldn't see how he would ever survive without Anthony. Especially without Anthony's Beef Bourguignon at his luncheon meeting next week.

When Tracy volunteered to make a soup and sandwich lunch for Howard, Richard and herself, Howard seriously offered her the cook position in addition to her field manager job. Double pay, of course. She turned him down, knowing how fast he'd tire of soup and sandwiches.

After lunch in the kitchen, leaving Webber to do the dishes, Howard, Tracy and Richard went back to the office.

"We've got our needs and expectations tightened up on paper," Richard said to Howard in reference to the new hotel plans. "You've just got to relax about the food part. Everything will be fine."

"I wish I were that confident," the boss said in his gloom.

"Trust me, Howard. I'm your right-hand man, aren't I?"

Howard rubbed his chin and mumbled something to himself.

Richard ignored the obvious put down. "You're far more important to this deal than Anthony's cooking, believe me. These guys aren't coming here to eat, they're coming to discuss a new hotel location and lock a deal. And we're ready for that."

Tracy watched and listened to the newer, more assured, side of Richard. Something had definitely come over him. Funny, it was as if his getting drunk and playing in the blizzard last night had worked wonders on him. Though she smiled approvingly at Richard's new manner, Howard was unfortunately playing no more mind to him than he ever had.

"Anthony…" Howard said with a heavy-hearted sigh, "now there was my right-hand man. Why did I have to lose him? Why now?"

"You'll get another cook," Richard assured him.

Howard rose from his desk, as slowly as if the weight of the world were on his shoulders. "Another cook? Ha! As if there were another Anthony out there."

Tracy joined Richard's force. "Howard, we'll find you one. Okay? Don't worry."

Howard was none the more soothed. "I should have stayed out of the business end of all this once I'd officially retired."

The fax machine across the room beeped and began printing. Howard went to it.

"Howell Hotels is your business and you have the right to stay active in it for as long as you so desire," Tracy told him.

"I have executives all over the country who have become far better at this than me." Howard gave the fax report a scant look then dropped it into the wastebasket.

Tracy and Richard signaled to one another behind his back that they would retrieve it later.

"Maybe I'm getting too old for all this," Howard said, plopping back down into his chair and landing with a moan.

"You have us, Tracy and me," Richard reminded him. "Just let yourself rely on us a little bit more, okay?"

Howard re-evaluated him with a look. As if finally, maybe, he was listening. Then handing Richard a pencil, he said, "Here, put a point on this for me, will you?"

"Yes, sir." Exaggerating the importance of it, Richard took the pencil over to the electric pencil sharpener as if he were on a mission from God.

It was past five o'clock when Tracy and he wound things up with Howard and left the big house together. As they walked out to their cars in the front driveway, Richard invited her to have a drink with him at Wiley's Bar in town.

"I don't think that's a good idea," she answered automatically.

"Fine," he gave up easily.

Ironically, it was just that, his not pressuring her, that made Tracy change her mind. As he was getting into his car, she told him, "Okay, one drink."

He smiled slyly, as if pleased to have found a way to reach her at last. "Okay."

"Meet you there," she said, getting into her own car, hoping he wasn't just tricking her into this being a date.

"You know where Wiley's is, don't you?" he asked before she shut her door.

"I know where it is," she said.

The first thing Tracy did when she got to the bar was phone Mark to tell him where she was and that she'd be home a little later. He sounded puzzled but okay with it.

She hadn't been in Wiley's for quite a while, though some time back it had been the most frequent date place her second-to-the last boyfriend used to take her. It was a typical small-town bar. Plain, quiet, nothing at all like some of the fancy places she'd been to with Mark in New York.

When she joined Richard in a booth, he had a beer waiting for her and a way-too-serious look in his eyes. "Thanks for letting me stay at your place last night," he said.

After sipping some of her beer, Tracy down played the event. "My not throwing you out in that blizzard was a necessity not a nicety."

He laughed. "Okay, so you were forced to let me stay. But thanks anyway."

She smiled and eased up some. "You're welcome. And strange as it may seem, thanks for doing what you did for my brother."

"Getting him drunk?"

"Yeah. Though I hated you for it at the time, I know now that it released something in Evan. And maybe something in me as well."

"You?"

"I'm just saying thank you, Richard."

"I'm not sure I understand what I did for *you*," he said, studying her, "but okay, yeah, it's nice hearing you say it was something. As for Evan, he was pretty down after his confrontation with Timmons. Having some mental anguish of my own at the time, I suggested he and I do some serious drinking."

"And now, here, it's you and me drinking," Tracy concluded.

"Yeah," he said, with a little too much pleasure.

"As for today at the office," Tracy got on with the real matter at hand, "I'm sorry that Howard belittles you so. I don't think he realizes it."

"It's nothing new," Richard said. "Whether or not he realizes it, or you notice it, it's an every day occurrence that I realize and I notice all the time."

Tracy played with her neck chain. "I don't know why he does that to you. You don't deserve that."

Richard smiled appreciatively.

She sipped her beer. "It was really difficult for me when you suddenly showed up at my house like you did last night. Having you find out about my brother the way you did."

Richard nodded. "How many other people have you kept him a secret from?"

"Howard."

"You're kidding!" Richard exclaimed. "Old honest Howard? I can't believe your lying to him of all people."

"I know. But I had to." Tracy took another drink of beer.

"I thought you and he were so close."

"We are. It's been hard keeping this from him. But I—"

"Knowing he's such a stickler for honesty?"

"I've felt guilty," she admitted, "if that's worth anything. I just felt, when I first started working for him, that I needed to be free from…from the burden of having a brother like Evan."

Richard frowned. "Burden?"

Tracy looked away from him in shame. "I know. I'm terrible. But Evan's having this phobia for so long…that most people can't begin to understand or accept…it's put me up for some cruel encounters. Evan and I, the two of us, were dealing with his problem just fine. What was hard was other people, outsiders, their pity or stupid solutions or misconfigured wonderings and criticisms…and questions, questions, questions. I thought if I just had a place to go each day where I wouldn't be under pressure and—" She stopped talking to catch her breath.

"What about Mark?" Richard asked anxiously.

Tracy's eyes were tearing as she confessed, "I never told him about Evan either. Not until he asked me to marry him. Then I had to. And once I did, I thought it would be a good idea for him to get to know Evan and prove that he could accept Evan's situation before he and I moved on with our relationship. So I asked him to come to Drendal by himself, ahead of me, and spend some alone time with Evan. He agreed, but I'm afraid he went a little overboard with it."

"What do you mean?"

"Mark sort of got into this mode of thinking that he could help Evan, change Evan, cure Evan."

"And that's bad?"

Tracy fingered the rim of her glass and stared into her beer. "It can be, yeah. Sometimes you just have to accept things for the way they are and make the best of them. That's all I wanted Mark to do, regarding Evan. We've had some crude arguments over this. I think maybe, now, finally, we're okay again. But I'm not sure."

Richard reached across the table for her hand. "I'm sorry, Tracy, that all this has been so painful and complicated for you."

"I don't need you to be sorry, Richard. That's exactly why I never wanted you to know about Evan in the first place."

"Maybe that's what I'm the most sorry about, your feeling that you had to keep his problem so secret. Like it was something to be ashamed of."

"I'm not ashamed of Evan. That's never been it."

"You know, Tracy," Richard began, leaning back in his seat again, "I think you're just as scared of life as Evan is. Right?"

It was more true than Tracy cared to admit. "I have a life. A job. A boyfriend. I travel. I—"

"You pretend you're little miss perfect in your perfect little world, don't you? Ignore your problems and therefore they don't exist."

Mark had said as much to her, yes. And now Richard.

"Which is why you're turning into a lonely, frustrated spinster," Richard concluded.

"*Spinster*?" Tracy shrieked.

"Cruel word. Sorry. But you should have a home and family of your own by now instead of hovering over your brother. I think that sadly shows how afraid of life you are, Tracy. While Evan's been hiding his life away, you've been hiding your life away behind his."

Tracy nervously glanced around, hoping that no one else in Wiley's could hear them. "Where on earth is all of this coming from?"

He shook his head, dropped eye contact with her, and took a drink of beer. "I'm sorry. I'm not sure. I guess I got a little carried away, said a little too much."

"It was pretty evident you meant it."

Looking at her again, he tried to explain. "Maybe what I'm saying, Tracy, is that you should be glad you have someone like Mark. He cares about you and he cares about your brother and he wants to make life good for all three of you. As your friend, I don't want to see you lose that."

She smiled half heartedly. "You're right. I thought that if I pretended my world was okay, then it would be. Not only with Evan, but with Mark too. Now I'm starting to see myself more clearly, and I've got to tell you, Richard…I don't much like what I see."

"Mark's an understanding guy. You and he will be all right."

Richard, sitting there across from her in the booth, was beginning to seem more and more like this really great friend she'd had all along but never fully realized until now. "Maybe I should break up with Mark and take you up on that crush you've had on me for so long," she said.

He knew better than to take her seriously. "Tempting, very tempting. But I think we're beyond that now. I know that you and Mark are a match, a good one, so I give up."

She pretend to pout. "You give up? That's it? You're not going to fight for me?"

Richard laughed but kept his new resolution. "I only want what's best for you, Tracy. And I no longer believe that it's me. I'm settling for your friendship. I guess, honestly, that's all I ever really wanted."

She clinked her glass to his. "You've got it."

At eight o'clock Richard suddenly was shocked at something he saw behind Tracy. She turned in the booth to see for herself what it was. Evan was entering the bar with Mark.

She and Richard slid out of their booth and stood beside it with disbelief. Though Tracy spoke her brother's name, it was without sound.

Mark and Evan approached them slowly. For as stressed as Evan undoubtedly had to be, he was trying to act cool. Mark was beaming like a happy, but nervous, father watching his son walk for the very first time.

"Evan!" Tracy finally found her voice. She grasped her brother's arm for proof of his realness.

"Hi," he said through a stiff smile.

"What are you doing here?" she asked, shifting her look back and forth between him and Mark.

"Beer?" Richard asked Evan.

"Coke," Evan said, slipping into the booth.

"You're kidding," Richard said, though believed it more in the look Evan gave him. "Okay. Three beers and a Coke," he called over to the bartender.

Tracy sat back into her side of the booth and Mark sat beside her. Richard joined Evan across from them.

"However did this happen?" Tracy, still in a state of shock, asked Mark.

He hitched his chin at Evan. "His idea."

"Come on…" she doubted that.

"Relax," he told her through a grin that confused her all the more. "If Evan can handle this, so can you."

"Are you really okay?" she asked her brother.

He was busy checking out the entire inside of Wiley's from where he sat. The fact that only his eyes moved and not his head, proved to Tracy how tense he was.

"You're *not* okay, are you," she decided.

He still didn't answer. Didn't have to. She could see that he was feeling worse by the minute. The way he was starting to swallow too frequently, breathe too rapidly, tremble. Plus that headlock thing.

"Maybe you shouldn't have come here," she said. "I mean, it's great, Evan, but maybe—"

"I've got to get over this, Tracy," he said, more as if he were trying to convince himself than her.

"I know, but maybe you—"

"Don't discourage me."

"No, Evan, I'm not," she said with the guilt of doing just that.

"Glad you're here, man," Richard commended Evan. "Wiley's can sure use all the business it can get on a night this slow."

Though Tracy and Mark shared a laugh with Richard, Evan remained stone-faced. He was fighting a panic attack while trying desperately to hang on to the sense of normality he'd willed to himself tonight.

Tracy hated seeing him like this, suffering in the world outside of the security he knew at home. It almost made her feel like she was having something of a panic attack herself, just watching him. When she couldn't take it anymore, she blurted, "Evan, you look like you're going to pass out any minute. Maybe we should go."

"Maybe we should just leave this up to him." Mark coaxed her back against her seat.

The drinks came and Evan grabbed his Coke like a cure all.

"We took a drive this afternoon," Mark told Tracy. "Evan and me, a twenty-minute drive. Then tonight, learning that you and Richard were coming here, Evan suggested we come surprise you."

"Surprise?" Tracy exclaimed to her brother, smiling enough to let him think she was more happy than upset over this. She reached over to touch his arm. She felt him quivering but pretended she didn't. "I'm very proud of you. I am."

Evan soon came to a rude awakening, as if he'd suddenly had all he could take. He gave Mark a desperate look. "I think it's time for me to leave now."

Mark got out of the booth, readily meeting his need. "Okay. Let's go. You wanna drive?"

Evan followed Richard out of their side of the booth, answering Mark with a nervous laugh. "No…I don't think so."

Tracy felt a great sense of relief over the going-home decision, and an even greater one that her brother did not want to drive. She said goodnight to Richard and left Wiley's with Mark and Evan.

Chapter 52

▼

Tracy, in her car, followed Mark and Evan in Mark's car. She was exhausted and looking forward to getting home. Two nights in a row of pandemonium was enough. Last night it had been the blizzard and three over-night houseguests, each bearing problems. Tonight it had been going to a bar with Richard, for a talk like they'd never had before, and the shock of Evan walking in with Mark, trying to act like he was fine when he wasn't.

Tracy needed some peace and quiet. No more surprises. She was tired and drained. So turned around from how she thought and felt about everything a couple weeks ago.

When both cars pulled up into the dark, cleared driveway, Evan was quick to open his door and get out. Except rather than making a dash for the house, he slumped against the side of Mark's car and just stood there.

Tracy left her car and rushed over to him, trying to keep her own anxiety under control. "You did good, Evan. I can't believe you came into town like that. I bet you can't believe it either. But you did it. You did."

"I don't know," he said in a weak voice.

Mark came around the car, also praising him. "You did real good, Evan."

"Yeah…I guess…" Evan's breathing was rapid.

"Can you make it to the house?" Mark asked him, half kidding, half serious. "Or do you plan to spend the night out here?"

Evan managed a slight smile and began walking.

The three entered the kitchen. Evan first, then Tracy, then Mark. As they got out of their jackets and shoes, Remington came meowing and looking for tracked-in snow.

"I'm going to my room," Evan said wearily, starting up the steps. "There are leftovers in the fridge, if you haven't eaten yet, Tracy."

"Thanks. Okay. Have a good sleep, Evan," she called after him.

When she just stood there in silence for some time, Mark eventually read it as, "You're pissed off about my bringing him to Wiley's, aren't you."

"No," she said to his surprise. "I was just thinking how wrong I've been about over sheltering him." She surprised Mark even more by going to give him a kiss. A long, passionate kiss.

"I'm sorry," she eventually told him.

"Mmm..." he hummed, nuzzling her neck, "you've nothing to be sorry about."

She gently broke away from him, explaining, "About mistrusting your method of helping Evan."

"You have been rather set in your way," he said.

"I guess all Evan needed was a little nudging in the right direction. But I sure wasn't giving him that. I was, in fact, discouraging him, holding him back. Because whenever he tried something and failed and became miserable over it, I encouraged him to just accept his phobia to the point of staying comfortable and safe and..."

Tracy was struck, mid sentence, with guilt. She shook her head and sighed. "I just wanted to keep things simple. I guess maybe more for me than for Evan."

"You love him very much," Mark said. "I never doubted that."

Tracy walked across the kitchen and back again, sorting her words. "It's like, all of a sudden I had this sick brother to contend with. He had this weird sort of sickness that you couldn't possibly understand, could barely talk to anyone else about, couldn't begin to know what to do about. He and I, we went along hoping it would get better in time. Time...Evan just needed time, nothing else. Meanwhile his phobia became his way of life. He seemed content with it. He really did. Enough so that I managed to get on with my own life. Sort of. Until I'd bring someone else, some guy I liked, into the situation, and he'd meet Evan and...and..."

"Get scared off," Mark said.

She nodded. "Mostly because of my attitude though, not Evan. I know that now. But how slow I've been in realizing."

"I didn't get scared off," he reminded her. "Not by Evan, not by you."

"No, not you." She stepped back into his arms. "I didn't want Evan to come between us. Not you and me, Mark."

"He hasn't, won't," Mark assured her. "Evan's going to be okay, Tracy. And you're going to be okay. We're all going to be okay."

"I miss my parents, too," she said with a sad sigh.

"I know. I'm sure you do. Mine live in Arizona. I'll take you there and share them with you. I've told them about you and they're anxious to meet you."

"I like the sound of that," Tracy said, pleasantly imagining the event.

"Let's heat up your supper," Mark suggested. "You must be hungry, and I could probably eat a little more myself. Jeez, Evan's a good cook."

Tracy sat down to the table and watched him put together her meal. He did it as comfortably as if he were now a permanent resident, and she liked that. "I still can't believe how you got Evan to come to Wiley's with you tonight. Or how Richard managed to loosen him up so much last night. Or how he's acquired a relationship with a Laurel. These signs in Evan, they make me see how much I've missed his being a normal person."

Mark gazed back at her from the microwave. "He's finally seeing how much he's missed it too. But he also knows that he's got quite a ways to go yet."

"Yes," Tracy agreed.

"I told him I think he should see a doctor. That he probably needs some medication and counseling, because he shouldn't have to do this all alone."

"And?" Tracy asked, hopefully.

"He said no to all of the above. But we'll see. I mean, one step at a time, right? Today was a big one."

Tracy laughed. "Actually I'd say that last night, his drinking and playing in that snowstorm, was the bigger one."

Marked also laughed. "Guess we've got Richard to thank for that."

"I did thank him."

"That's why you went out with him tonight?" Mark asked.

"I didn't go out with him," she clarified. "We just had some stuff to talk about. Your coming there with Evan, that was to check up on me?"

"No," Mark said quickly. Only to add, "Well, yeah, maybe, sort of. But only after Evan suggested going there."

"There's this new level of honesty between Richard and me now," Tracy explained.

"Should I be jealous?" Mark asked.

"No. Richard's my friend. It's just that I never quite realized how much of a friend until lately. He...he's kind of like having another brother."

"Just what you need, another brother."

"Better another brother than another boyfriend, right?" she teased.

Mark left the microwave, came over to Tracy, pulled her up off her chair and into his arms. "Honey, I'm the only boyfriend you're ever going to have from here on."

Their kissing went way beyond the beep of the microwave.

Later, before turning in for the night, Tracy visited Evan's room. He was lying on his bed, eyes staring at the ceiling, Remington curled on top of him.

"Can I talk to you a minute?" she asked, sitting down beside him on the edge of the bed.

"Okay," he said, easily enough.

"Evan, I've been wrong about so much where you're concerned."

He gave her an unquestioning look. But he held direct eye contact with her as she made her confession.

"I haven't handled your situation very well. Not half as well as you have. My way of dealing with your agoraphobia on the outside was to keep it from Howard, my boss, and Richard, my co-worker, and Mark, my boyfriend, until I absolutely had to tell him. Denial seemed to be my best means of handling it. I'm not proud of that. Oh, Evan, I haven't tried to help you very much. Not like Mark or Richard have. I thought my responsibility was mainly to accept your situation the way it was."

Evan made no comment.

"I'm sorry," Tracy's voice quivered, "that I haven't been a better sister to you."

Evan gave her a soft smile. "You've been okay, Tracy. I have no complaints."

"No, of course you don't," she said, "because you're so easy-going and wonderful and sweet. But I haven't been all that I should have been for you."

"This has been my problem, Tracy, not yours. I'm just sorry that it overlapped onto you as much as it has."

"You deserve your life back, Evan."

He raised himself onto his elbows, causing Remington to meow and slide off of him. "So do you."

The brother and sister hugged.

"I'm going to be okay, sis, I promise," Evan assured her.

"I know," she said.

"You don't need to worry about me anymore."

"Whatever will I do with all my time?" she joked.

"How about giving more of it to Mark," he suggested.

"I can do that," she said.

Chapter 53

▼

Richard drove into Howard's driveway right behind Tracy the next morning. They parked their cars, greeted one another, and walked to the house together.

"Was Evan okay when you guys got home last night?" Richard asked, quick-stepping beside her.

"Yes and no," was the best Tracy could answer.

It was just barely getting light out. The winter air was calm but crisp. She shivered amidst a big yawn.

"I couldn't believe it when he came walking into Wiley's like that," Richard exclaimed.

Tracy laughed. "I still don't."

"He's going to be all right, you know, because he wants to be."

Tracy nodded.

"I wish you had told me about him long before this."

"I know. Me too. And I wish you had shared your job feelings with me before this too."

They reached the door and Richard pressed the bell. "I'm glad we had that chance to talk last night, Tracy."

"Me too," she said.

Webber opened the door. "Good-morning, Mr. Richard, Miss Tracy," he spoke in his ever-formal manner.

The two of them entered the foyer.

"Hey, Web, how ya doin'?" Richard greeted him with extreme casualness.

And Tracy, handing her coat to Webber, cheerfully sang. "Good morning, good mor-or-ni-ing…"

Richard laughingly continued with the next line of the song, "We danced the whole night through."

The two of them were determined that some day they'd make Webber crack at least a hint of a smile. So far nothing, but it was a challenge to keep trying.

"Mr. Howard is in his office," Webber said, taking Richard's jacket.

"And that would be?" Richard jokingly asked.

Webber blinked his eyes and motioned the way. "Down the hall and to your left, Sir."

Tracy and Richard were still snickering to themselves as they entered Howard's office.

Their boss was even more somber than the butler this morning. Sitting at his desk, he grumpily received them with, "Since Anthony's gone now, I had to make toast and instant coffee for my breakfast this morning."

"How awful," Richard dramatized it, exchanging a grin with Tracy, as if their problems should be so menial.

"Richard," Howard addressed him, "I want you to get right to it. Find me a cook"

Richard was notably thrown. "Weren't we going to go over our expectation list for hotel number ten? I have some good ideas."

"Tracy and I can handle that," Howard said. "I need a new cook, Richard. I need you to find me one. Use the kitchen phone."

Richard made a face. "The kitchen phone?"

"You have a problem with that?" Howard's tone inferred that he'd best not.

Richard looked at Tracy, then back at Howard. "It's just that we don't have much time to—"

"If I don't get a new cook by that luncheon meeting, and an excellent one at that, there won't be a meeting." Howard motioned for Richard to fetch him the report lying on top of the file cabinet.

Richard handed him the folder. "I thought later, like this afternoon, I could do the phoning, and this morning I could help you and Tracy tighten up our agenda."

"You're refusing my order?"

"No."

Howard pointed to the door. Richard made a sharp pivot and left.

Tracy felt bad for Richard, since last night she'd come to really understand what was going on in his head. She knew now that he took his job far more seriously than he was given credit for and had a lot more substance to him than the self-centered smart-aleck he usually came off as. She knew how he longed to prove his true abilities, given half the chance. She also knew, and had just witnessed the fact, that Howard was unlikely to ever allow him that opportunity.

"Well, Tracy," the boss began to her, "shall we get to work?"

"Howard?" She felt it in her heart and conscience to make a special plea for Richard.

"Yes?" The elderly hotel owner looked up from his desk.

"Maybe we should have Richard present when we—"

"Not you, too," he moaned. "Has everyone forgotten who's in charge here?"

"No, Sir," she cowered, and let it go at that.

"All right then, lets stop quibbling and get started." Howard motioned for her to sit down in one of the chairs across the desk from him. "You have your assignment, Richard has his."

Chapter 54

▼

Mark sat on the couch reading one of his panic books from the library, while Evan sat across from him smoking his nine o'clock cigarette.

"So what do I next?" Evan eventually asked, as a follow up to last night.

"I want to make you an appointment with a psychologist," Mark said.

"No doctor, no meds, no shrink," Evan firmly reminded him "Just me and you."

"You probably need a lot more than that," Mark advised, as much from his common sense as from his research.

Evan shook his head against it as he flicked his cigarette ashes into the ashtray. "I've made progress. You know I have. Due to you, Mark. Look at what I accomplished last night. All the way into town. Spent some time in Wiley's with you guys. I'd say that was good."

"Very good," Mark agreed.

"Okay, I'm saying I'm ready to move on from there now."

"Don't forget how sick you got from it."

"I don't need a doctor, Mark, I just need you." Evan was looking at him, depending on him like the cure to save his soul.

Mark laid his book aside. For as much as he wanted to help Evan, he felt suddenly overwhelmed by it. "That's a lot of responsibility you're laying on me. I mean, I haven't even finished reading all these books yet."

"It's more than the books, Mark." Evan shifted restlessly on the desk chair. "It's the confidence and strength you pass on to me. I gotta say you really bugged me at first, but now I don't feel so bugged anymore. I can see what you've been trying to do for me. I can see that it's working. Can't you?"

Evan's faith in him made it very difficult for Mark to turn him down. "Okay, no doctor for now, but we'll see later."

Evan crushed the remainder of his cigarette in the ashtray. "Not now, not later."

"Look, either you trust my judgment here or you don't. If I'm going to counsel you, you can't just pick and chose only the parts you want or don't want. Either you're with me all the way or you're not."

Evan gave a long hard sigh, rubbed his free hand against a pant leg, and after some thought said, "Okay…I'll go with the *we'll see later*. So what's my next step, doc?"

"Just call me Mark."

"Okay. Mark. So what do you want me to do? Take a walk? Like somewhere farther than the mailbox? And strictly on my own maybe?"

Mark got up from the couch, suggesting, "How about some shoveling?"

Evan also stood, motioning to the window with a laugh. "Shoveling? In case you haven't noticed, it hasn't snowed lately."

"Old snow," Mark explained. "The shoveling I'm referring to is the snow that's piled up deep in front of the garage."

"Garage?" Evan's eyebrows arched and his mouth dropped.

"Yeah, so we can get its front doors open."

"Doors…open…why?"

"Because I'd like to see what's in there." The curiosity Mark had had over it became even greater now because of Evan's uneasy reaction.

"What makes you think anything is?" Evan asked defensively.

"It's the car you used to drive five years ago before you got this phobia, isn't it?"

"How'd you—"

"I trudged through the snow and peeked through the garage window."

"Oh," Evan said.

"It's been sitting there idle all this time, right?"

"Tracy's taken it out and run it occasionally, before we got so much snow. It's in pretty good condition."

"Good," Mark said.

"Why is that good?" Evan asked.

"Don't you miss your car? Don't you ever think of driving it again?"

Evan shook his head despondently. "Oh, uh…I don't know. I don't think I'm up to it."

"No, not yet," Mark said. "I was just thinking that maybe it would be good for you to reacquaint yourself with your car. Get some fresh air and exercise shoveling your way back to the garage so we can open it and at least take a look at your car. Just a look. That's my assignment for you for today. What do you say?"

Evan broke a helpless smile. "I guess I have to say yes, don't I?"

"Yes," Mark said.

"Okay, yes. You will be out there with me, won't you?"

"Let's go." Mark started for the kitchen and Evan followed.

It wasn't bad outside, with the temperature in the mid teens today as opposed to yesterday's single digits. Mark and Evan each took a shovel from the snow bank beside the house and headed across the driveway to the deep, crusted section of snow extending about nine feet out from the front of the garage. So far that area had been used as a place to throw some of the snow cleared off the used part of the driveway, and it was really mounded up.

"You okay?" Mark asked Evan, after the first few shovelfuls had been hefted off to the far side.

"Yeah," Evan replied, though he didn't look it or sound it.

"So what are you going to do with your freedom when you eventually get it back?"

"I...I don't know," Evan said between labored breaths. "I guess that's...a whole 'nother problem, huh?"

"You've got a real nice girlfriend to consider for starters," Mark pointed out.

Evan stopped working for a moment to lean on his shovel handle. "So have you," he reminded Mark.

Mark smiled. "Tracy, yeah."

"I don't like how the two of you fight because of me."

"I think we're okay now," Mark said.

"Really?"

Mark rolled his eyes. "I think so."

Evan resumed his shoveling, speaking in spurts. "Look, don't hold it against her...that she wasn't always up front about me, okay? It's been...hard for her. My problem...it's been very hard for...for her to take. She...needed escape from my stupid situation...whatever way she could manage it, you know?"

"I guess," Mark agreed, bending, scooping, throwing snow to the side. "Except I don't much believe in turning one's back on one's problems. I've pretty much believed in tackling them head on."

Evan laughed at the understatement. "No kidding."

"You're going to be all right, you know," Mark told him, amazed at Evan's doing as much as he was right now.

"Tracy...she never expressed as much hope for me as you have. I mean...she'd always just tell me...my phobia...it was okay...things were the way things were. Like...as if I never had to worry about getting better. Like...as if I never was actually sick to begin with."

"Tracy's seeing things a lot differently now," Mark was able to say.

Evan stopped working, withdrew his pack of Marlboros from his pocket, lit a cigarette, and looked back at the house.

"Are you sure you're okay?" Mark asked, also taking a break.

Evan nodded between inhaling and exhaling. "I want you and Tracy to be okay, too."

"We are," Mark said.

"Because I'd hate to think of being the stumbling block between you two." Evan looked so worried, so responsible, so burdened beyond his agoraphobia.

"No, no," Mark assured him, "you're not, you couldn't be. Don't lay that onto yourself."

"I'm younger than Tracy. But still, I'm the brother. The one who should be looking out for her, you know? I never have. I've always been the weak one, the needy one. I've never done anything for her."

"Is that what this getting well determination of yours is about?" Mark suddenly began to wonder. "For Tracy?"

"No."

"Because if it is, that won't work, Evan. It has to be for you."

Evan took another drag from his cigarette. "It is."

"Good," Mark said, "because the best chance of your getting better comes when you do it for yourself and not for somebody else."

"I know. Yes. This is for me." Evan poked himself in the chest.

"Because?" Mark tested him.

"Because...I want Tracy and Laurel and you to be proud of me."

"No, Evan, no!" Mark scolded. "That's not wanting for yourself."

"It's not?"

"No."

"Like it's not enough that I'm at least out here like this, whatever the reason?"

Mark laughed, accepting as much. "Yeah. Of course. I guess. Okay, do it for the *squirrels* if you want to, as long as you do it." He motioned at two squirrels, which right at that time had stopped scampering about to observe the snow shovelers. They sat upright, still, and cautious, their little forepaws fixed together before them.

"They do seem to care, don't they?" Evan said, observing them as well. He tossed away his unfinished cigarette and resumed his shoveling, telling them, "Watch this, guys! Watch Evan work!"

Chapter 55

When Tracy went into Howard's kitchen to prepare sandwiches for lunch, Richard was at the wall phone in the corner, looking bored. He was obviously on an exceptionally long hold.

"How's it going?" she needlessly asked.

"Great!" he scoffed. "Most agencies I've contacted so far have never even heard of Drendal, let alone had anyone on file who would consider going this distance for a job."

Tracy opened a cupboard to get the bread, then the refrigerator for the ham, lettuce and mayo. "Damn Anthony for quitting at this time."

"His mother's fault for getting sick."

"Yes," Tracy sharply agreed. Only to add sympathetically, "Bless her soul, she needs him more than Howard does. And anyway, Howard's still got you and me."

"Work from you, schmuck from me," was how Richard saw it.

"Don't say that."

"That's the way it is, Tracy. You do the real work, I do the schmuck."

"All right, so do *you* want to make the sandwiches?" She offered the loaf of bread to him.

"No." He switched the phone to his other ear and exhausted a heavy sigh. "I'm not sure why he keeps me around. Except I guess there's always some schmuck to be done."

"Locating a cook for him is not schmuck." Tracy accidentally dropped her mayo-loaded knife on the floor, picked it up, put it in the sink, wiped up the smeary mess with a paper towel, and took a clean knife out of the drawer. "It's vitally necessary."

"When he has you?" Richard quipped of the scene he was watching.

This time the mayo made it from the jar to the bread, and Tracy next opened the package of ham. "I know you prefer having your hands on the actual hotel business, but—"

"Me? Help with the actual business?" he exaggerated his surprise.

"I think most of the time you tend to things so frivolously that it rubs Howard the wrong way. You don't take yourself seriously enough to expect him to."

"I'd say his being on the verge of firing me is pretty damn serious."

"Because you're always pushing him to that point, can't you see that?"

"Maybe I should quit, not wait to get fired."

Tracy shot him a disapproving look. "How many other jobs as good as this one are there to be found in Drendal?"

Richard returned the receiver to his other ear. "Who says I have to stay in Drendal? You're the one who's always telling me I should spread my wings. Maybe I will. I'm sick of this place, really sick of it."

Seeing him so down on himself scared Tracy. She was much more familiar and comfortable with the frivolous, egotistical side of him. "Be careful. Please be careful," she could only advise him. "Don't go doing anything you haven't fully thought through and might be sorry for."

When someone finally came onto the phone line, Richard responded, "Yes, I'm still here. Right. Drendal. It's...no, we're much farther north than that. Right. Yeah, lots of snow. Okay. Sure. I understand. Bye."

He hung up, giving Tracy an I-told-you-so look. "That was number nine. Think I should bother with ten?"

He answered his own question by dialing the next number on his list.

"Vegetable or chicken noodle?" she asked for his soup preference.

Richard flapped his elbows like a chicken for Tracy as he answered into the phone with, "Yeah, I'll hold."

Chapter 56

Mark and Evan shoveled almost non-stop until they had all the snow cleared away from the garage's double doors. Then they stood looking at one another in question of who should have the honor of opening them.

Evan took it as his and swung out both sides. A red Mustang was in the waiting.

"Wow, Evan!" Mark hurried forth to touch it, appreciating its realness after only ever having had a peek at it through the filmy garage window.

Evan slowly, dreamily, ran his gloved hand up across the hood and onto the windshield.

Mark strolled all the way around the vehicle, checking it out inch per inch. "How long do you think it's been since Tracy's driven it?"

"Last fall, before the garage got buried behind so much snow."

"And five years for you?"

It took some time for Evan to answer. "Yeah."

"So how do you feel looking at it and touching it now, having shoveled a ton of snow to get to it?"

"The snow was easy compared to…" Evan backed away from the car, shaking his head. "This ain't easy, Mark."

"I know. I'm sure it isn't. It's a big step for you, Evan. But you're doing good."

Insecurity had its claws into him again. "I've still got a lot more steps to take. I want my life back, but I'm just not sure if I—"

"I'm sure, Evan," Mark said, with enough confidence for both of them.

Evan gave him a dejected look. "But you're not me."

"No."

Though Evan stepped forth to touch his car again, he seemed to be a zillion miles away from reclaiming it. He gulped a deep breath. Then another. Another. Too much air, yet seemingly not enough. "I'm starting to feel like throwing up."

"Okay," Mark said, "let's consider this enough for now." He went around the car, took Evan by the arm and guided him away from the Mustang. "let's get out of here. Go to the house. Relax. You don't have to over-do it. Come on." Mark walked him out of the garage.

Evan complied on a note of sarcasm. "And maybe tomorrow Evan can open the car. And the day after that he can try the key in the ignition. And—"

"Knock it off!" Mark said. "Don't go blowing what progress you've made. You're tired. You've had enough for now. And that's okay. It's understandable. Be patient with yourself."

"Right," Evan scoffed, as he and Mark each pushed a garage door shut. "What's the hurry? It's only been five years."

"But only a few days that you've started tackling this," Mark pointed out. "It's good for you to be determined, but not pressured, Evan, that's what I'm saying."

Evan stood there in the newly shoveled area before the shed. His moment of quiet contemplation seemed to be a good sign. At least he wasn't running away. Or throwing up. Mark allowed him all the time he wanted.

"Are you sure you're not a doctor?" Evan eventually asked.

Mark grinned. "No."

"You're not sure whether you are?" Evan teased, in better spirits again.

"I mean no, I'm not a doctor," Mark clarified.

"It's just that sometimes your words—"

"Writer's words, not doctor's words."

"You have good words, Mark. You make them believable."

"Thanks."

"I started reading *Street Winder*.

"You did?" Hearing about his book actually being read by someone always tended to amaze and delight Mark. "So can I ask what you think so far?"

Evan gave a positive nod. "I'm impressed. It's great. I'm getting a lot out of it. It's really neat how this guy, out there alone on the streets amidst some very hard times, gets up enough fortitude to do good rather than bad, when he certainly could have gone the other way. Thanks for getting me the copy."

"You're welcome."

"And for signing it."

"Hey, always glad to acquire another fan."

"I've never met a real author," Evan told him in a state of awe. "Actually...I haven't met many people at all in the last few years."

"Come on, let's go eat," Mark suggested. "I'll make lunch for a change. I know it's not your style, but what do you say to a peanut butter sandwich?"

"With bananas," Evan requested.

Chapter 57

Evan was exhausted that night. It had been a long time since he'd breathed that much fresh air, worked that hard. He still couldn't believe he helped Mark shovel all the way back to the garage. The Mustang looked great.

After supper Tracy and Mark decided to take a drive to Duluth. They asked Evan to go with, but he said no. All he wanted to do, felt capable of doing, was listening to music in his room. The moody guitar song playing on his stereo fit like the soundtrack to his mind.

As the evening passed, he laid on his bed thinking about the day, and also, now, about what his tomorrows might hold in store for him. He wanted his life back, that much he knew, but he also knew that obtaining it wasn't going to be easy. Not with the demon still living inside him.

Sometime later the phone rang and startled Evan out of the semi sleep he'd drifted into. He reached across Remington, beside him, to grab the phone from the nightstand. "Hello."

"Evan…hi." The voice was male, slurred, unidentifiable.

"Who is this?" Evan asked.

"Yer friend."

"Friend?" The only name that came to Evan's groggy mind was Sam, and the possibility of it being a ghost sent an icy chill down his spine.

"It's Richard."

Evan raised himself to sitting, relieved that it wasn't Sam from the grave but newly concerned it should be Richard. "Oh…hi…what's wrong?"

Richard laughed and spoke in a drawn-out garble, "Why wood'ja think somethin's wrong? Thiz could be jus a…a friendly hi-how-are-ya call, couldn't it?

Doesn't have'ta mean somethin's wrong. Lighten up, Evan...jus lighten up...'kay?"

Evan ran his free hand through his hair. This felt like a dream he couldn't quite bring himself out of. "Not many people call me, that's all. If you're calling to talk to Tracy, she's—"

"I'm callin' ta talk ta you, Evan. C'mon...are we friends or what?"

"Yeah. Right. Friends," Evan responded. "So as a friend, are you going to tell me what's wrong?"

"Yer so determined...tha somethin' is...aren't you?"

"Are you drinking, Richard?" Evan asked, already certain he was.

Richard laughed again. "No...no, I'm not. Quit. Five miz ago."

"You've had too much, haven't you?"

"Y'mean...am I drunk?"

"Drunk, yeah."

"I...I don't do thiz all the time...I wan you ta understand, Evan. Do you?"

"Sure, okay," Evan gave him the benefit.

"Jus...don't go thinkin' I do...'kay?"

"Okay," Evan said.

"I mean...th'other night...an now...it's jus tha..."

"Where are you?"

"Home...second floor...McCully's duplex...upper Pine Road. Nothin' fancy...I mean, for the big bucks I make with Howell. Didge'ya know I make big bucks, Evan?"

"W-well...I figured you might, yeah."

Richard laughed. "Yet...here I am...in McCully's duplex...stuck in thiz plain an simple life. Know wha I mean, Evan?"

"Plain and simple...yeah, I know about that," Evan related.

"'Cause, Evan...I make good money...but wha good does it do me, huh?"

"I...um..." Evan shifted uneasily on his bed, not knowing what to say.

Richard readily filled in the space, "'Least I did make good money...when I still had my job...but I..."

"Had?"

"Yeah."

"You got fired?"

"No."

"You said *had*. Does that mean you quit?" With the phone still tight against his ear, Evan slid to the edge of the bed and put his feet on the floor. "Richard?"

"Not s'actly."

"What exactly *is* going on, Richard?"

There was a crash on the line, followed by some shuffling sounds. "Sorry…" Richard returned, "I dropped the phone…but izz okay now. You still there?"

Evan switched the receiver to his other ear. "Yeah, I'm here. Tell me about your job. Did something happen?"

"Y'could say I had a…a rough day at…at the office. Very rough."

"Such as?"

"Usual schmuck tha…His Majesty Howie gives me."

"I thought he was a nice guy. My sister gets along good with him."

"Well, yer sister is…la-de-da with him. But me…I'm nothin' more'n a joke 'round there. Y'know tha, Evan? An I'm really sick a puttin' in eight hours a day of joke time. I've had it, Evan. No more. So I—"

"You…did something, didn't you? What'd you do?"

"You bet. The ol' coot had it comin'."

"Had what coming?" Evan stood up, his free hand rubbing his head frantically. "Richard…what did you do to him?"

"Before I went home today…I wrote out thiz long letter ta Howard."

"Letter." Evan nodded.

"Man…I really sounded off ta him…on every single thing tha bugs me."

"Everything." Evan nodded.

"Yeah…the kind'a letter, y'know, Evan…tha one's sposta write in their worst anger…get it outta their system…then tear it up an throw it away th'out ever givin' it ta the person. Only I—"

"Gave it to him." Evan nodded.

"He was tired…said he was goin' up ta his room for an early retirement. Said g'night…he'd see me tomorrow…then went, leavin' me alone in the office. Guess he thought it was some notes tha I…I was workin' on. Or maybe…" Richard scoffed, "a comic book I was reading. I don't know. Anyway…fer sure…he didn't know it was a letter ta him. When I went home, I left it lying on his desk. Right there…so's when he comes downstairs in the mornin' he's bound ta see it…an…an finally know the truth of how the hell I feel."

"Now you're regretting it?"

"Yeah. Sure. I guess so. It was a whim. I get a lot a crazy whims. I guess… truthfully…izz not tha bad a job…y'know, Evan? Old Howie's really not tha bad a boss. 'Least…not like I have anything better. Truthfully…I need th' job, Evan. Y'know? What the hell was I thinkin'?"

"So go back over there and get it," Evan advised him.

"Yer kidding."

"I'm not kidding."
Richard moaned.
"Oh, right," Evan reconsidered, "you're drunk."
"I really chugged it down when I got home, Evan," Richard admitted. "Three times over wha I drank with you th'other night. I…I feel like I'm gonna…pass out…don't think I…"
"No," Evan newly advised him, "don't drive. Stay put. You just stay put." He turned himself in one direction and then the other, looking about his room for some sort of clue as to what to do. Feeling pressured. Obligated. To help Richard. But how? "Uh…let's see…what can we do?"
The line was silent.
"You there?" Evan checked.
Silence.
"Richard!"
"Yeah…I…didn't go anywhere."
"What's going to happen?" Evan asked.
"Wanna take a guess?"
Evan hated what Richard was doing, calling him like this, dumping the responsibility of this event onto him. Man, it wasn't his problem. Rubbing his head again, all he could suggest was, "Maybe it'll turn out okay."
"Know wha my guess izz, Evan?"
"No," Evan said.
"My guess izz…when Howie sees my letter in tha mornin' he's gonna fire my ass jus like tha. Not like he hasn't been thinkin' a doin' it anyway…but thiz will jus bring it forth sooner. Not like I haven't thought 'bout leavin' before either…but now…well…for sure…I'm out."
"What are you going to do?"
"I've already done it…wouldn't ja say?"
"I mean now, tonight, to retract the letter."
"Izz too late. Thaz what I'm sayin' here, Evan."
"But you didn't mean it, the things you said to Howel. It just sounds like you really didn't mean it. Like you only acted on an angry impulse."
Richard laughed hauntingly. "Yeah…I wish ta hell I hadn't done tha letter thing."
"Then you've got to get that letter off his desk. Now. Tonight."
"I…can't…I…don't think I…"
"Do you want me to help you, Richard? Is that why you called me?"

"Help me? No…Evan…don't worry…izz okay. I…just called ta sound off. Y'know? Haven't you ever jus felt like soundin' off 'bout somethin'…even though ya know izz not gonna get ya anywhere, change anything?"

"Yeah." With his shoulder holding the phone in place against his ear, Evan used both hands to put on his shoes.

"We're…a couple a…lost souls…you 'n me," Richard said, with his voice and spirit winding down, becoming faint. "We understand each other. We're both…tha kind that tha world shits on…and we jus take it…right, Evan?"

The length of the phone cord allowed Evan to get to the dresser for his car keys. "I've got to go now, Richard. So hang up. There's something important I need to do."

"Aw right…me too…gotta…yeah…tha room izz spinnin'…I…"

"Close your eyes. Sleep it off, Richard. Things will be better in the morning."

"Yeah…right…you still there, Evan?"

"Yeah, but I have to hang up now. Hang up, Richard. I'll talk to you tomorrow."

"Y'know, Evan…you're…like the brother I never had."

Brother, yeah. Sam had been like a brother. The loss of him struck Evan as sharply now as if it were brand new. The sound of the gun. The blood. The lifeless weight of Sam's body sinking in his arms, Evan felt sick. But there wasn't time for him to be sick. Maybe he hadn't been able to save Sam, but now there was Richard he could try to save.

Evan charged down the stairs and into the kitchen for his jacket. He wasn't sure where his strength was coming from that had him fleeing outside into the cold night, to the garage, to his car. He seemed to be moving ahead of thinking. And he wasn't actually sure if that was an indication of strength or stupidity.

Suddenly he was in the Mustang. He hadn't driven in years. Would he even remember how anymore? Would he get a panic attack along the way and have an accident? Before he could even begin to calm his doubts he turned the key.

The motor growled, as resistant to the cold as to it's lack of use. Nevertheless it started. Evan drove the car through the open double doorway and into the driveway. After a few minutes of idling, its roughness smoothened out and it was ready to go. He stared ahead into the path of headlights, beyond Tracy's car on the right. There was just enough space to squeeze by it. *He hoped.*

When he left the driveway and started on his way, Evan felt as if he were having an out-of-body experience. Because surely the real him was still back in his room, lying on his bed, wasn't he? He blinked his eyes, trying to bring his body and mind together as one, trying to believe these were his hands on the steering wheel, his foot on the gas peddle. He had to concentrate. Had to. Concentrate. Drive. Concentrate. Difficult. Concentrate.

Sam. More thoughts of Sam came gushing into his head along with everything else. He didn't want to think of Sam. Not now. Especially not now. It was such a nettling intrusion to what little concentration he did have. Richard. This was about Richard. He had to keep his focus on him.

And on his driving, of course. Except focusing on his driving made him start thinking about his parents, their driving to Minneapolis to get him five years ago. They never made it because of the accident. It was said they'd died instantly, but Evan couldn't help wondering if they'd had any one last thought before they went.

Focus. Evan fought to keep it on the here and now of his own driving and his intent of helping Richard. He tried to turn off the bad memories. Tried to dismiss himself from agoraphobia. Tried to make his breathing smoother, hands steadier. Tried to imagine himself as normal. Everything was going well. Evan was normal.

He took another look in the rear-view mirror, realizing he'd been taking *incessant* looks behind him. Which indicated he was much more concerned over where he'd come from than where he was going. He swallowed hard. Checked the mirror again. Kept going.

Chapter 58

It worried Laurel that she hadn't been able to reach Evan. She'd tried three times from the kitchen phone. No answer. He had to be there. He was always there. His not answering could only mean something was wrong. Something bad.

She returned to the living room. A commercial was playing on TV, but her father remained as glued to that as he'd been to the mystery program it had interrupted. Not one look or word from him all evening. No acknowledgment now, either, of her coming back into the room and sitting down in the chair across from him. No idea as to how alone and scared she was feeling.

Though Laurel's involvement with Evan was no longer a secret from her father, she still didn't have the freedom to talk about him as she would have liked or needed, particularly at this time. Ever since the big blow up at the Lawton's house the other night her father had gone the complete opposite way of saying almost nothing, which was actually worse.

Laurel checked the clock. She would wait ten minutes, then go try Evan's number again. She prayed that he would answer, that he was okay. Meanwhile, in her waiting, she sat hiding her feelings, pretending that she, too, was watching TV. But what she was really looking at, when she wasn't looking at the clock, was the little snowman snow globe she held in her hands. She wondered what would happen to Evan if the glass globe of his life should break. If he, like the snowman, would indeed melt.

Chapter 59

Though he'd never been to the Timmons' house before, Evan knew where to find it by its address. It was on the other side of town, about a mile beyond the business district. Though the roads through town were clearer than the outer ones, he drove them with even more caution. Slowly, clutching the steering wheel tightly, eyes in an earnest squint. Here there was the glare of more car headlights to contend with, stop signs to regard, and pedestrians to watch for. Though he was managing all right so far, he was functioning under a lot of tension. He wished he wasn't doing this. He wished he were back in his room. He wished he could stop thinking, shaking, breathing so fast.

Laurel had to be home. He knew it wasn't her night to work at Dave's, so she had to be home. He didn't know what he'd do if he didn't find her there. He needed her very badly right now.

Driving, driving...Evan still found it hard to believe that he was doing this. It was more like a dream. Not even his own, someone else's. But if it was a dream, and not his own, then why did his chest feel tight, his breathing shallow and his arms quivery? If his phobic reactions were this real, then he guessed what he was doing had to be equally real enough to cause them. *Stop thinking*, he commanded himself. *Be normal.*

Finally he was parking before the Timmons' house. There were still lights on inside. Good. He left his car and hurried up the walk. He slipped on a patch of ice, but luckily caught himself from falling. He went up the steps and across the porch. He stood at the door. His hand didn't want to leave his side, and he had to literally force it up to the doorbell. *Lift. Press the button.* He felt like a mechanical robot operating on a weak battery.

Laurel opened the door. "Evan! What are you doing here? How'd you get here?"

"Come with me, Laurel," he said desperately. "I need you to come with me."

She seemed to be experiencing somewhat of a panic attack of her own, for the way she looked, acted, sounded. "Where? What's going on? Evan, I can't believe you're standing here."

"I've got my car. I took it out of—"

"Car?" she exclaimed.

"Yeah. I took it out of the garage. I...I've been out of the house a lot today. Mark...he's been helping me. I'm okay, Laurel. Come on."

"I don't believe this, I don't believe this," she could only stand there saying.

"There's something I need to take care of right now," he said, rocking from side to side impatiently. "I need you to come with me."

Her eyes followed his every move. "Evan, I tried phoning you and you weren't there."

"That's because I was on my way here. I need you, Laurel, please."

"You're really scaring me, Evan," she said, putting her hands on him, trying to still his constant motion.

"Don't be scared." He tried to stand still for her but couldn't.

"*You* look scared, so don't tell me to not be."

Evan nodded. Yes, scared, he was. And try as he did, he couldn't keep it from showing. "Laurel, Richard's in trouble and I—"

"Who's there?" Parker joined Laurel in the doorway, disturbed at seeing Evan. "What the hell are you doing here?"

"I'm out of the house," Evan began defensively, "which makes me a normal person, doesn't it? Enough to earn the right to see your daughter now, right?"

"I...I..." Parker was totally thrown off guard. "Do you know how late it is?"

"Is that what's going to bother you next about me?" Evan said. "The time? It's always going to be something, isn't it? Well, I have no time right now. Laurel, get your coat and come on."

"No way! She's not going anywhere with you," Parker ordered.

Laurel put on her jacket and came outside to Evan. They left the porch together, with her father's anger burning at their backs. Evan kept hold of Laurel's arm, cautioning her about the icy spots on the sidewalk.

They reached the Mustang. He opened the passenger door for her then darted around to the driver's side.

"This is really your car?" Laurel asked when he got in behind the steering wheel.

"Yeah, really." He turned the key and pulled out into the road.

"And you know how to drive?"

He gave her a quick sideways look. "It comes back. I…just have to take it a little easy."

"I don't believe this," she said, buckling her seatbelt.

"I suppose you wonder where we're going."

"I do."

"Howard Howell's house, up in the hills."

"That hotel guy your sister and Richard work for?"

"Right."

"Something's wrong," Laurel determined.

"Yeah. Sort of."

"I knew something was wrong. I knew it the minute I saw you at my door."

Evan hoped she wasn't already sorry she'd come with him. "I'd rather not think of it as wrong. Just…important."

"It must be, for you to break your phobia like this."

With another brief look at her, he let her know, "It's…not exactly broken, my phobia. It's…still here…I still have it." Then with his eyes back on the road, he took a deep breath ahead of admitting, "I'm not feeling too good right now, Laurel."

"Want me to drive?" she offered.

"No. I have to. It's okay. I just…I needed you to go with me."

"You mentioned at my door that Richard is in trouble. So he's got something to do with this?"

"He's got everything to do with this."

"Well?" she urged for more when he didn't explain.

Evan's hands tightened on the steering wheel, as much to steady himself as the car. So far the car seemed to be doing much better than he. "Richard's my friend. And he needs my help. And…I hope you don't mind my coming to get you like this. I probably shouldn't have involved you, but it's just that—"

"Evan, it's okay. I'm here for you, whatever it is." She patted his arm. "Just explain more to me, please."

He could barely explain it to himself, let alone her. "I didn't mean to scare you, Laurel."

"You're scared, too."

"Yeah," he admitted through a half smile. "I guess I was hoping you'd be the calm one."

Laurel unbuckled her seat belt and snuggled closer to him. It seemed she wanted a kiss. Now, of all times. A kiss. While he was driving and trying to keep a good grip on the wheel and watching where he was going and…already feeling way too low on oxygen. But Evan understood about reassurance, about how when you needed it you needed it. Therefore he turned his head toward her, ever so slightly, just for a second, to meet lips with her. And *man*, just that quick the car got away from him.

The Mustang swerved to the right, skimming the snow banks along the edge of the road for some distance before he was able to straighten it back out. Laurel screamed and bounced back over to her own side.

"Sorry," Evan apologized, gaining control of the car again. "Guess I'm not up to kissing and driving both at the same time yet."

She rebuckled her belt, apologizing as well, "My fault. I'm sorry. That was so stupid of me. I shouldn't have distracted you."

"We're okay now," he said, keeping his eyes glued to the road.

"I know," Laurel said, sounding more like she *didn't* know. "So tell me why we're going to Howard Howell's house."

Evan owed her the truth. Even though he knew she wasn't going to like it. "I…I'm going to break in and steal something. A letter off Howell's desk that Richard left for him but since changed his mind about."

"Oh," she responded all too easily. She asked no further questions, as though she might've gone into shock. Anyway, it turned her quiet enough for Evan to fully concentrate on his driving.

Chapter 60

"Where can he be?" Tracy cried. "Oh, Mark, I knew we shouldn't have left him alone tonight. Something's happened to him. I just know something's happened."

When she and Mark had returned from Duluth and found Evan not home, Tracy immediately started going out of her mind.

Standing together in the kitchen, Mark tried to soothe her with an embrace. "Come on, don't get so worried right off. I'm sure he's okay."

"This isn't right, his not being home."

"He's getting better, you know that."

"Not *this* much better."

"I'm sure there's an explanation."

"Not a good one, I'll bet."

"Don't jump to conclusions."

Tracy broke out of Mark's arms. "Evan was really quiet at supper. That was a sign. I should have read more into it right then."

"Wait, I think I know," Mark said.

"Know what?" Tracy asked excitedly.

"I'll be right back," was all he said, leaving the house on a run.

She stood in the open doorway, watching him head for the garage. She couldn't believe that she hadn't noticed, until now, that the snow was shoveled all the way back to it and the double doors were standing open. Now she was *really* getting scared.

Mark came back to the house, verifying, "Evan took his car."

"No," Tracy moaned, "he's not up to that. How could you have let this happen?"

"Me? This is my fault?" Mark entered the kitchen, frowning at her. "I wasn't even here."

"I'm talking about before. Your influence on him before shoveling up to the garage doors. You got him interested in his car, didn't you?"

"I didn't tell you about this earlier," Mark confessed, "because I wanted to wait until he made a little more progress. But he...he's progressing much faster than I expected and—"

"With driving?"

"No. Well, we actually hadn't gotten that far yet. I mean, we shoveled the driveway all the way back to the garage, me and Evan together, so that he could just look at his car."

"How could you do that?" Tracy took another look out the door, hoping to find Evan returning.

"Because he had to do something, Tracy," Mark reasoned.

"Driving? No, I'm sorry, you're pushing him way too fast, Mark."

"I'm not pushing him. It was his idea today to take some further steps."

She spun back to Mark. "Oh, and so you just thought why not get your car out, Evan, and go driving around for the heck of it, Evan."

"It wasn't like that."

"Then what was it like? You think you know exactly what to do with Evan, don't you? Well, you've made a really big mistake here, let me tell you."

"Evan and I both agreed he wasn't ready for driving yet."

"But nevertheless he's out there doing it right now, isn't he?"

"We don't know that for sure. But okay...probably...I mean, yeah it looks that way."

Tracy shook her head and sighed. "My brother is out there somewhere in this dark, cold night, on slippery roads, a victim of agoraphobia, with his life at stake because of your playing doctor to him. Do you realize that?"

"I never assumed to be a doctor."

"Oh, but you have. Dr. Mark Rydell, reader of three library books."

"You liked the progress Evan was making."

"This is too much, too fast."

"Maybe things have just been too slow for too long."

"I'm worried about my brother, okay?"

"So am I," Mark said. "So why are we fighting about it?"

"Just when I finally started trusting your judgment, you—"

"He'll be all right. I'm sure he will." Mark tried to put his arms around her. But Tracy brushed him off. "You can't be sure. Don't tell me that you are."

"I know what I see, Tracy. I think I see a lot more strength in Evan than you do. And that's what I go by."

"What I'm going by more and more is how you and I have such different viewpoints about things."

"Only over Evan."

"Only? Don't say only, Mark. He's pretty important to me."

"To me, too."

She gave him a dubious look.

"It's just that maybe my common sense, where Evan is concerned, is a little more common than yours," Mark responded.

"Thanks," she huffed.

"I'm not putting you down, I'm just trying to reason."

"Thanks," she said again.

"Tracy, listen, I'm just saying that sometimes it's easier to have a better perspective of someone when you're not quite so close to him. Don't go flying off so easily."

"Flying off?" she shrieked. "If ever there was a reason for a person to fly off it would be now. I'm worried sick about Evan."

"Maybe we should look at this as a good sign, rather than a bad sign, about him," Mark suggested.

"And maybe we should consider it to be a bad sign, rather than a good sign, about us." She marched past him, heading for the living room.

Mark didn't follow. He stayed in the kitchen. Tracy didn't care. There was nothing more for them to discuss, nothing more to do but wait. And maybe it was best they do it in separate rooms.

Chapter 61

As with the Timmons' house, Evan had never been to the Howell estate before either, but he knew where to find it by the address. When he got there, he drove through the open gate and pulled over to a lights-out stop along the first part of the long driveway. About eighty yards ahead stood the mansion. It was wide, two stories high, tall windows, and a steepled roof over the front entrance. The place was dark, except for the pale moon glow upon it.

Sitting there gazing through the car windshield, Evan was struck with the realness of what he was doing. This wasn't a dream he'd simply wake up from to find himself back home. This was a real situation he'd gotten himself into and was committed to following through.

"Evan," Laurel, beside him, whispered.

He heard her but didn't answer. He was too busy breathing in, breathing out.

"This place looks very secure," she said. "How are we getting in?"

"Not we. Me. And I already told you how."

"Instead of breaking in, couldn't we just ring the doorbell, talk to Howell and ask him for the letter?"

"No."

"Why not?"

"His seeing that letter would cost Richard his job."

"The letter was that bad?"

"Evidently."

"This is Richard's problem. How did it become yours?"

"He's my friend." Evan turned his gaze from the house to Laurel and leaned over to give her a kiss. "You stay here. I won't be long." He opened his door and got out.

"I'm going with you," she said, opening her own door.

"No. This is as far as you go."

She was already coming around the car to him, insisting, "I'm with you all the way."

Evan never intended for her to do anything more than wait in the Mustang. "No, Laurel, I mean it, get back inside and stay here."

"I'm going where you go," she said.

"No."

She slipped her gloved hand into his gloved hand and started kissing him. Supposing he would worry just as much about leaving her behind in the car as he would bringing her with him, Evan gave in with, "Okay."

Holding hands, the two of them started up the driveway together. Long, dark tree shadows stretched across the snow. There was no wind, but it was bitterly cold.

"I'm not a criminal," he told her, just in case she was starting to wonder.

"I know."

"I've never done anything like this before in my life."

"I don't think it's criminal, helping a friend in need."

She walked fast for a girl. Evan's breathing problem made him wish she'd slow down. "Richard...he's in need all right. You should have heard him on the phone."

"How about you? Are you all right? Your phobia?"

"Sort of," he said.

"Only sort of?"

They reached the house and followed the cleared sidewalk around to the back. "I think it's always safest to break into the back of a house rather than the front," Evan said.

"Right," Laurel agreed.

They passed a patio door on the side of the house but kept going until they got completely around to what was likely the door to the kitchen. Evan tried it. "It's locked."

"You didn't think it would be?" Laurel asked.

"Yeah. I was just checking. You know...in case. Looks like I'll have to break the window."

"Okay," she said all too easily.

"Okay," he said, facing it, staring at it, but feeling a strong moral resistance holding him back.

Laurel stepped aside, giving him room, the full go-ahead.

But Evan didn't move. Couldn't. Wasn't ready yet. Needed more time. Needed more air. Took a deep breath. Then another. And another. Another. Suddenly he was gasping from having too much air in his lungs.

Laurel was bouncing up and down and hugging herself. "It's freezing out here. We've got to do something. Do you want *me* to break the window?"

"No. I'll do it." He clenched his gloved, right fist and punched it through a lower windowpane. The noise of glass breaking and falling, both inside and outside of the door, was loud and shrill but over in seconds. It wasn't until then that it occurred to Evan that there might be an alarm system. He waited. Listened. Was relieved at the silence. He reached through the opening, found the lock and turned it.

The two of them, moving together as one, proceeded cautiously into the dark kitchen. Despite their committing a felony, it felt good getting in out of the cold. They inched their way along a side cabinet, listening for any sounds. But the house was dead quiet.

"Come on," Evan whispered, starting into the next room. "We've got to find his office."

There was enough snow luminescence coming through the dining room sheers to prevent him and Laurel from bumping into the large center table or each other.

"Do you think his office is on this floor?" Laurel whispered.

"I'm thinking so, yes," Evan said.

Beyond the dining room was a hallway. It was much darker there. No windows, no snow glow. Evan looked both directions, and for what little he could see, he chose to go left.

He found a door, turned the knob, and opened it slowly. Dark shadowy shapes loomed in the faint window light therein.

"It's a bedroom," Laurel, closely behind him, made of it.

Evan could see the bed was empty. "It's okay. There's no one here." He flicked the light switch. "Must be a live-in servant's room. Guess we're lucky he's out."

Evan turned out the light and led Laurel down the hall the other way, toward the front of the house. They found the living room. The bluish-white moonlight coming through the bare windows revealed the generous size of the room. There was a long sofa, a loveseat, several big easy chairs. The carpeting felt thick and plush to the step.

Laurel bent down to touch it with her hands. "I *love* this house."

"Come on," Evan said, urging her along. "Let's try that doorway across the room."

"Are you all right?" she asked, following him.

He swallowed hard. "I just want to get this done and get out of here."

They were back in the hall. Evan tried another door. It was a closet. Laurel giggled softly.

The next door they came to was open some. Evan peered in. For sure it wasn't a closet. They slowly entered. Very dark. No moonlight or snow glow. If there were windows, they were covered.

Evan found something with his out-stretched hand. "File cabinets."

"The office!" Laurel cheered in a whisper.

"Desk. Where's the desk?" Evan continued his blind search, with Laurel close at his heels. When he bumped into something, she bumped into him.

"Desk," Evan identified the obstacle. "Lamp," he found it and turned it on.

A yellow splash of light brought the room alive. The two of them squinted at each other and smiled. And there was Richard's letter, lying in plain view. The ultimate reward to this whole risky operation. Evan picked it up, folded it, and stuck it into his jacket pocket. "That's it. Let's get out of here."

He turned out the light and they started out of the room.

"You're not going anywhere," said the voice of someone in the dark hallway.

Evan stopped sharply and Laurel bumped hard into him. Someone switched on a light. Someone was a white-haired old guy in silk pajamas, holding a gun on them.

Laurel grasped the back of Evan's jacket. Evan started to raise his hands in surrender.

But the man with the gun ordered, "Don't move!"

Evan put his hands back at his sides.

The man, undoubtedly Howard Howell, wanted answers. "Who are you? What's going on here? What the hell are you doing in my house? How'd you get in?"

Evan had nothing to say. No explanation. No defense. Certainly no name.

"You must be watchers," Howell decided. Even though his gun wavered in his hand, it nevertheless stayed aligned with Evan.

Evan wondered…if Howell shot him would the bullet go clear through him and into Laurel? Kind of like killing two birds with…

"Watchers?" Laurel asked Howell, peering over Evan's shoulder so closely he felt her breath on his neck.

"Watchers of my house," the man in the pj's explained, gesturing the entirety of his place with the wave of his gun. "To have picked the one night Webber should be away. Clever, very clever. But not clever enough to know that I'm perfectly capable of protecting myself." He flicked his gun up and down a couple times as proof. "Mmm...but you know, I just can't believe that girls, as well as boys, are into this sort of thing now days."

"W-what thing?" Evan asked, keeping a close eye on the moving gun barrel.

"Burglary," Howell said.

The man was notably inexperienced with a gun, which meant it could just as likely go off accidentally as on purpose. Dead was dead. Evan didn't want to die. He was just now starting to get his life back.

"We didn't take anything of yours," Laurel told Howell, as if she expected him to believe her and let them go just like that.

"And I'm suppose to say, oh, all right, thank you, good-bye, come again?" He motioned with the gun for the two of them to back up. "Into the office. I'm going to call the police. And if either of you makes a wrong move, it will be your last, believe me."

The three of them entered the office. Evan and Laurel exchanged nervous looks as they came to a stand in the center of the room, and Howell went straight to the desk. At least there was no angry letter from Richard lying there for him to find.

Evan was glad the letter was safe inside his jacket pocket. But he hated that he and Laurel got caught when just a few more minutes would have earned them their escape. He should never have brought her into this. What kind of guy was he, having done this to his girlfriend? What kind of guy was he, having done this at all? He regretted having charged off into this crazy feat like some sort of movie hero, having thought he could survive for this long outside of his own house. His body was trembling, reminding him of his phobia. *God, no...not now.* He had to stay in control. Had to. Or Howell might mistake such strangeness as his being up to something and shoot him. Only...the more Evan tried to calm himself, the more he shook and wavered. He was breathing through his mouth now.

Laurel knew what was happening and clutched his arm. "We've got to get you home."

"Get away from him!" Howell ordered her, taking the phone with his left hand while his right hand kept the gun directed at them.

"Wait!" Laurel pleaded. "He's sick. My boyfriend's sick."

"You think I'm falling for that?" Howard held the phone against his ear with his shoulder, freeing his hand to dial.

"Wait!" Laurel cried out again, so loud it surprisingly made the man do just that, wait. "He's really sick. Really. And he has to get out of here right now."

"I'd probably feel a little sick too if someone were holding a gun on me." Howell sympathized sarcastically.

Evan's chest was tight, legs weak, breathing shallow. So maybe he'd saved Richard's job, but what about himself and Laurel? What was going to happen to them?

"Wait!" Laurel shouted again, still managing to keep Howell from dialing. "He really is sick. We've got to help him. He might die. Do you want his life on your conscience?"

There were tears in her eyes. Evan hated that she was so scared and that he was to blame. Yet...this could very well have a beneficial impact on Howell. There was nothing like a girl's tears to break a guy.

Howard Howell still hadn't dialed 911. He almost seemed more interested in arguing. "A sick thief and a crying accomplice...sorry, won't work."

"Please," Laurel said, "he's got to get home. Let us go and we won't hurt you."

"Hurt me?" Howell said with a crude laugh. "Girl, I'm the one with the gun." His finger went to the nine button on the phone.

"No!" she screamed in desperation. "Don't call the police. Just listen, please listen to me."

"You couldn't possibly have anything I'd be interested in hearing."

"How do you know till you listen?"

Evan closed his eyes as a momentary escape from what was happening. But it was hardly enough since he couldn't close his ears. The arguing between Howell and Laurel was starting to blend together into one steady ringing sound. He felt hot, light headed, close to fainting. He tried to fight it, because if he passed out that would leave Laurel to fend for herself. Even though she actually seemed to be fending just fine for the both of them right now, he worried about her and wanted to stay conscious for her.

He opened his eyes, saying, "Drink...I...I just need a drink of water."

"Yes! He does!" Laurel begged Howell. "Look at him. He's going to be hitting the floor soon, and if he dies it will be your fault. Please...can I go get him some water from the kitchen?"

Low and behold, a kinder, softer look came over the face of the pajamaed rich guy who, as of yet, still hadn't dialed the police. "Okay, okay, we'll all go to the kitchen together." He motioned with the gun for his captives to go ahead of him.

"Thanks," Laurel took Evan by the arm as they started off.

"No touching!" Howell ordered.

She let go of Evan and went ahead of him down the hall.

"We'll get him a glass of water," Howell said from behind them, "and then I'll phone the police from there. This better not be a trick. My gun is ready to pop at your slightest mistake, believe me."

In addition to all the panic symptoms he was enduring, Evan felt a precise point on his back where he was sure Howell's gun was aimed.

The three of them entered the kitchen…Laurel, Evan, Howard Howell. Evan's mouth was dry, his swallowing difficult. He was starting to cough some now. But more than a drink of water, he needed to leave. Get Laurel safe, get himself home.

Howell flicked the light switch, immediately seeing the broken glass by the door. "That's how you got in."

"Sorry about the window," Evan apologized.

"Sorry?" Howell said. "Yeah, I'll bet you are. Sorry you got caught, you mean."

"This isn't at all what it looks like," Laurel told him.

"You mean it's not a break in?" Howell asked.

Evan coughed a couple times, held his chest and leaned against a cupboard.

Shaking his head with disbelief, Howell nevertheless opened a cupboard to get Evan a glass. "You're a strange pair of thieves, I'll say that for you."

As horrible as Evan felt, he watched for opportunity. It came as the opened cupboard door momentarily blocked Howell's vision of him. In that very instant Evan ducked out of Howell's gun point and wacked a sharp karate chop to his right wrist. The man let out a bellow of pain, the gun flew from his hand, hit the floor and scuttled across the linoleum to the door.

Howell stood frozen in place. Stunned at what had just happened, at having lost control so quickly, so foolishly. His toughness regressed to an old man with no gun up against two young people who had only to pick up the gun and blast him. He stood there. Looking at them. Then looking over at the gun. Back at them.

"How's your wrist?" Evan asked him.

"How do you think it is?" Howell snarled, rubbing it.

"I didn't mean to hurt you."

"I'm fine," Howell said, but hardly sounded it. He was staring across the floor at the gun, as if it might very well be the death of him.

But Evan didn't want anything to do with the gun. He only wanted to leave. "Come on," he said to Laurel.

They went to the door, stepping carefully around the broken glass, observing the gun lying amidst it.

Pausing with his gloved hand on the doorknob, Evan looked back at Howell. "I'm sorry about all this. I'm really sorry."

"So now what?" Howell asked. "You going to pick up that gun and shoot me?"

Evan had no intention of shooting him. "Come on," he urged Laurel, opening the door.

In spite of his weakness, once he was outside Evan's legs shifted into fast gear. He kept a tight hold of Laurel's hand as they ran off into the wintery, moonlit night. He hoped they wouldn't hear gun shots being fired at their backs. So far they didn't. Each moment bettered their chance of escape.

They reached the front of the house. The driveway. The sight of the Mustang.

Evan was glad he'd left his car down by the gate. They fled toward it. If Howell were chasing after them, at least as of yet there were no gun shots. But given his age, and the cold and his bare feet, it seemed unlikely he would've left the house.

When they reached the car, Evan leaned against a fender and bent over in gasps.

"Evan!" Laurel cried. "Get in! We've got to get out of here!"

"I know," he said, breathing, breathing.

"It won't take us long to get home, then you'll be fine. Come on!"

"I...didn't get my...drink of water..."

"You can drink all the water you want at home."

"I need...I can't...I..."

"Snow! Take a handful of snow!" she suggested.

Good idea. He scooped some up and smashed it into his mouth, licking and chomping at it like a ravenous animal. It was icy and tingly against his tongue, his teeth, his nose. Some of it bit into his eyes, blinding him for a moment But the amount going down his throat seemed to be helping.

"Come on, Evan!" Laurel pleaded frantically. "Howell's probably called the cops by now. We don't have much time. Give me the keys, I'll drive."

"No." He brushed the remaining snow off his face and directed her to the passenger side. "I'm okay now. Let's go." He got in behind the wheel.

The driveway was just wide enough for Evan to make a tight turn, then he drove through the gateway and onto the road. At last they were headed for home, security, solidity. How he needed to be back in his small, okay world.

"You've got the letter, haven't you?" Laurel asked. Her voice was softer and calmer now, and it touched him like an endearing reminder of how very special she was to him.

Evan's throat was dry again. He needed more snow but couldn't stop for it. He had to keep driving. He took one hand off the steering wheel to feel his jacket pocket. Richard's letter rustled through the fabric, insuring it was still there. He gave Laurel a nod. And he guessed amidst his harrowing panic he felt some reason and pride for saving Richard's ass.

"Mission accomplished," Laurel cheered.

"Yeah," Evan sighed with relief. Then asked with concern, "You okay?"

She was nodding and smiling in that cute little way of hers. "I'm always okay when I'm with you, Evan. How about you?"

"Yeah, fine," he said, speeding down the dark snow-lined country road, fighting his agoraphobia, fleeing from a crime. "I'm fine."

Chapter 62

▼

Tracy and Mark sat in living room chairs across from one another, waiting for Evan to come home. They didn't speak. Time dragged. Tracy was stressed out. Mark, *damn him*, seemed okay. Everything might have been a lot better if Evan was still a secret from Mark, and Mark from Evan. Thinking it made her feel guilty.

Finally the sound of a car pulling into the driveway gave her and Mark reason to at least look at one another again, both of them sharing the hope that it was Evan.

Tracy met her brother in the kitchen, expressing more anger than relief. "Where've you been? How on earth did you manage driving your car?"

"I've…been out," he said.

Besides his surprise of finding her and Mark waiting for him, Tracy saw trouble written on his face. "Something happened!" she insisted. "Evan, what? You owe me an explanation."

Evan exchanged a look with Mark, as if they had some sort of silent code between them.

It infuriated Tracy all the more. "All right," she said to the both of them, "what's going on?"

Evan shrugged and gave her a tight smile. "I took my car out for a drive, that's all."

"You have agoraphobia. You don't just go driving off like that after five years of staying in the house."

"I went to Wiley's last night," he reminded her.

"I know. That was a good beginning. But this, with your car, was a little too much, don't you think?"

Evan was eyeing Mark again.

As if Mark were responding to a signal, he tried to assure Tracy, "I, uh, think he's making some real progress on his road to recovery."

Tracy laughed. "Oh, right…he really looks good for all this progress, doesn't he? Look at him. I don't know whether to call the paramedics or the police."

"Don't call the police," Evan was quick to say.

"You've pushed him way too far here," she held Mark responsible. "And actually I'm beginning to feel really pushed in all of this, too."

"Sometimes that's all any of us need is a good push," Mark claimed. "Evan's okay."

Tracy shook her head. "Look at him. Just look at him. At what you've done to him. This is the worst panic attack I've seen him have in five years. He doesn't—"

"I'll be okay," Evan said, holding his hand against his chest. "I'm going up to bed. See you guys in the morning." Still wearing his jacket, he went for the steps.

Tracy grabbed his sleeve. "No, you don't. You're staying right here till we settle this."

"A nice alternative to pushing," Mark said of her technique.

"Stay out of this!" she told him.

"Settle what?" Evan asked, paused with one foot on the bottom step.

"Driving," Tracy said. "I want to know how you decided you were ready to go driving all of a sudden."

He looked beyond her, as though he were again seeking Mark's help.

"Quit looking at Mark!" she ordered him.

"Sorry." Evan returned his look to her.

"If you're truly getting that much better, that's great," she commended him, "but I just—"

"—don't want him doing it without your knowing about it," Mark smugly finished the sentence.

"Stop it!" Tracy demanded of whatever little game was going on between the guys. But then in the silence that befell the kitchen, she realized that she herself had nothing more to say anyway. She let go of Evan's jacket sleeve.

"It's not a good time to talk right now," Evan reasoned. "I…need to get to bed. You look pretty beat yourself, Tracy. Why don't you go to bed, too. The car's okay. I put it back in the garage. Good-night."

As he disappeared up the stairs, Tracy admitted to Mark, "I guess I'm not sure what to think."

"He's doing better, not worse," Mark said. "Why don't you think that?"

She frowned. "He looked better to you?"

"Well…"

"Something happened," she insisted, worrying more, not less, since Evan got home. "I could just tell by looking at him that something did. His condition, it's complicated. It's not something you all of a sudden cure by browsing through a couple library books."

"Three," Mark corrected her. "Look, Tracy, what's happening is that Evan is getting out of this house and that's good."

"Oh, like it doesn't matter where he goes or what he does, as long as he gets out."

"It matters, yeah. It also matters that he gets a lot of support and trust. Which you're not giving him. Don't you see that, realize that?"

"I supported his coming to the bar with you last night, didn't I?"

"Sure, because you were there to oversee him and what went on. But tonight," Mark said with a crude little laugh, "he managed to get away from his big sister."

Tracy stuck her hands onto her hips and raised her chin. "So what you're saying here is that I'm trying to keep Evan under my control."

"I don't know. Yeah, maybe. You treat him like a child, a small child that you don't want to grow up."

"That's sick."

"Exactly," Mark agreed.

Tears pooled into Tracy's eyes.

"Evan's getting better," Mark said. "You've just got to let it happen. Come here…I think you need a hug."

When he started to put his arms around her, she twisted away, saying, "I don't need anything."

"Evan is getting better. You should be happy about that. Why can't you just let him have his own life?"

When Mark tried again to embrace her, she hit him hard against his left shoulder. "Oooh…tough," he said, so astutely that it antagonized her into slapping his face.

Tracy couldn't believe what she'd done.

"Feel better?" Mark asked. "Because if hitting me makes you feel better then go ahead, by all means, take another shot. Take ten shots. Fifty."

"I'm sorry. You didn't deserve that. I guess I…I just don't like seeing some of the stuff you make me see. And it makes me a little crazy."

With his own eyes watering now, Mark gave a knowing nod.

Tracy tried to explain. "I never realized, until lately, how much my whole life has been centered around Evan in one way or another. I mean, at first he was naturally my little brother, right? Look out for Evan, take care of Evan, I'll help you, Evan, it's okay, Evan. Then he goes off on his own to become a man and his life literally falls apart. Then Mom and Dad are suddenly gone, and Evan gets agoraphobia. And so my life revolves around him. Because it has to. Has to."

Mark gave another nod.

She brushed her fingers delicately over his reddened cheek. "I'm sorry. I guess this was only bound to happen eventually, my coming unglued. Unfortunately you just happened to be in the way at the time."

"I'd like to try gluing you back together," he offered. "If you'll allow me."

As hopeful as she was amused, she asked, "You can *do* that?"

"I think so. Come on." He took her by the hand. "Your room or mine?"

She resisted the stairs. "Evan's up there."

"In that case, may I suggest the couch." Mark took her into the dark living room.

"It's been a while," Tracy said.

"You're telling me," Mark agreed.

Standing before the couch, they shared a long, deep kiss amidst a flurry of unbuttoning and unzipping.

Remington meowed from some dark corner of the room.

Chapter 63

▼

Evan awakened to someone shaking him and saying his name. He moaned. Blinked. Squinted. Found Tracy standing over him, haloed by the hall light coming through the opened door behind her. He wondered what time it was, morning or night, and what could be so important.

"I'm leaving for work soon," she said, "but I wanted to talk to you first."

"What time is it?"

"Seven-thirty."

"Seven-thirty?" Evan sprung up, feeling as though he'd missed half the day. "I never sleep this late. I—"

"It's okay." Tracy laughed and pushed him back down. "You probably needed some extra sleep. You were obviously very exhausted when you came home last night from wherever or whatever you'd been doing."

She was fishing for answers. She woke him out of a sound sleep to fish for answers. Evan closed his eyes, hoping she'd leave.

She stayed. But she was far sweeter than she'd been last night. Certainly a manner he had to be even more leery of. The kind that was apt to persuade him, before he realized it, into saying stuff he didn't want to say.

"How are you feeling?" she asked. "Better this morning?"

He opened his eyes halfway. "I'm okay."

"Evan?"

"What?"

"Are you really getting better?"

"I'm...feeling a little panicked right now."

"Because whatever you did last night must have—"

"I feel panicked for having slept so late. I usually have my step routine and the laundry done by now."

Tracy sat down on the edge of his bed. "I need to say something to you, Evan, that can't wait until tonight."

Say? She had something to say rather than ask? Maybe that was a good sign. Maybe bad. "Okay," he responded skeptically.

"It's kind of a confession."

"Okay." He could only be relieved that it should be hers and not his, though he couldn't imagine what hers could possibly be.

"I haven't been fair to you," she began uneasily, looking away from him for a moment, then back.

"What do you mean?" Evan asked.

"This phobia problem of yours. I...well...besides it being so hard for you, it's been hard for me too all along."

"I know."

"It's been the hardest for you, of course, Evan, in all respects. But for me...it's...well, I've had a difficult time being open about it to some people."

"I know," he said again.

"I withheld telling certain people about you."

"Such as Richard."

"Yes. And Howard. And Mark, at first. Stupid, really stupid." Tracy looked deeply into Evan's eyes. "It wasn't that I was ashamed of you, it was more that I, well...it just got so hard to explain and...and people, they—"

"I'm sorry I've been such a burden on you," Evan said.

"No, Evan, no...I've been my own burden. Me, myself. Mark's done a good job of making me see that. He's made me see that I never actually tried helping myself in the right way, let alone you. I never meant to hold you back from getting better, Evan. If I did, I didn't mean to. I am so sorry."

"I'm sorry I've caused so much arguing between you two."

"I want you to get your life back. I really do, Evan."

"I know."

"I guess rather than having gotten so upset with you last night, I should've said congratulations."

Evan's eyebrows rose. "For?"

"Going out with your car."

Evan moaned beneath his breath.

"I doubt that could've been easy for you," she went on saying from the extent of what she thought she knew, "but I guess you were making a brave step toward getting your life back."

"Yeah, brave," he agreed.

"Maybe a little too brave for starters."

"Yeah, you could say that."

"Your driver's license has obviously expired. Plus night driving isn't the best for you, having been away from it as long as you have. Plus you probably should—"

"Tracy, why are we having this conversation now?"

"Because something happened last night."

"H-happened?" Evan felt found out. Sort of. Maybe. Well, maybe not. No, the look on his sister's face didn't seem to depict a crime.

"I think we, you and I, we're both coming around in our lives. I think it's helped, your having Laurel and me having Mark. We're lucky, Evan, to have them. They've given us new insights, which I guess we've both needed. Before going to work today, I just had to come in here and tell you how sorry I am for acting like I did last night. I was scared. Worried about you. I've got to learn not to worry so much about you."

"Maybe you should pay more attention to Mark," Evan suggested.

With a whimsical look on her face, Tray told him, "Mark and I are back on track again."

"Track?" Evan squinted at her. Then he got it and smiled. "Ahhh...track, right."

Tracy stood up, with a sense of peace and contentment that Evan hadn't seen in her for a long time. "I have to leave for work," she said. "Go back to sleep. Or do your step thing. Or whatever. But have a good day, okay? See you later."

She left, and soon Evan heard her car start in the driveway. He would get up in a few minutes, because there was no more sleep in him now. He was wide awake and mulling over what he'd done last night. Wide awake but feeling like this was a bad dream.

After showering and dressing Evan went downstairs. He didn't want breakfast but put some fresh food and water into Remington's bowls. Then he wandered aimlessly about the kitchen, the living room, back to the kitchen. Mark was still asleep up in his room, which was good, because Evan needed some alone time to sort things out.

He relived last night's events in his mind. His talk with Richard. His decision to help him. Taking his car out of the garage and driving to Laurel's. Confronting her father at the door. Driving dark, slippery roads. Breaking into Howell's house to retrieve Richard's letter. Facing a gun. Getting sick. Hating himself for what he'd gotten involved in. Escaping from Howell. Getting Laurel back home. Getting himself back home, only to run smack into Tracy and Mark. Facing questions he couldn't answer. Lying awake for hours before he could sleep. And then Tracy's waking him to tell him stuff and ask him stuff.

It wasn't smart, what he'd done last night. Nor brave. He'd forced himself out of his phobia only to go out and commit a crime. He'd put his and Laurel's lives on the line for Richard's job. The scenario kept playing over and over in his head. He couldn't make it stop. He raked his fingers through his hair. Moaned. Felt hung over without having drunk.

Remington followed him about, looking quizzically at him, seeming to sense his disturbance. Evan bent down to give the cat some strokes, then he resumed his walk. It was nicely quiet, though hardly peaceful.

Maybe he'd saved Richard's job, but he hadn't been able to save Sam five years ago. It had been his idea, *his*, that he and Sam go out for a few drinks at that particular Minneapolis bar, located in a high crime area of town. Sam had been reluctant to go. In fact he'd said no, over and over, to the idea. But having heard some good reviews of the band playing there, Evan managed to talk him into going. And Sam wound up getting killed. How could that happen? They'd only been out for a fun evening. The fact that it did happen weighed heavily thereafter as Evan's fault. Then his parents' fatal car accident on their way to come get him. And he took that, too, as his fault.

He had to quit killing people and start saving them instead. Like with Richard. Maybe Richard's dropping into his life and almost immediately needing his help had been a sign. From God. Right, like God would really make him do burglary and put Laurel's life in danger? No, more like the devil. Now, worse than having agoraphobia, he had the devil on his back.

Evan pulled the slip of paper out of his pocket with Richard's number on it and went to the phone.

"Yeah," Richard answered.

"Hi. It's Evan."

"Hey, Evan. I'm just on my way out the door for work. Though I'm not really sure I still have a job. Kind of in a rush. Plus I've got a hellova headache. Sorry about last night, calling you, bugging you, dumping my problem on you like that."

"No, it's okay, I'm glad you did. We're friends. You helped me the other night. I wanted to help you back."

"Yeah, guess it helps to talk. But right now I—"

"I've got the letter."

"What?" Richard shrieked.

"The letter. You wanted it removed from Howell's desk, didn't you?"

"W-well, yeah, but—"

"I went over there. Retrieved it. Saved your job for you, Richard."

"Y-you're kidding."

"I'm not kidding." Evan crinkled the paper by the phone. "Hear that? It's your letter, right here in my hand."

"I don't believe it."

"Believe it."

"But how'd you even get there? How'd you—"

"Me. I took my car from the garage."

"You have a car?"

"Yeah."

"And you actually—"

"I don't want to keep you if you have to get to work," Evan said. "I know your job's important, now that you still have it. I just wanted to let you know that I have the letter, that's all. So you don't have to worry about facing Howell."

The line went silent.

Evan asked, "Richard, you still there?"

Richard's voice returned with hesitance, "I...I can't imagine how you—"

"I did. It's done. So go to work now, okay, before you get fired from the job I just saved you."

"Evan?" Richard no longer seemed in such a hurry to leave. "How did you actually get the letter?"

"I found it lying on the desk and took it."

"But how? Like you rang the doorbell, Howard answered and you waltzed on in past him saying, excuse me, I have to go get something off your desk?"

"It wasn't exactly like that."

"How exactly was it?"

"I broke in."

"Broke in? Evan, are you crazy?"

"No, I have agoraphobia."

"I mean, that's criminal."

"I know. But it's okay. I got the job done. I had to do that for you, Richard. Just don't say anything to anyone about it, okay?"

"No, of course not. Why would I? Man, I can't believe you did that."

"I know, neither can I."

"You really got my letter?"

Evan crinkled it by the phone again. "I'll hang onto it for you."

"I really owe you," Richard said, as if he were more thankful than shocked now.

"No, Richard, I owed you. For the other night. Now we're even. Okay?"

"It's just...I hate thinking that I helped you through one problem and into another."

"Just don't go writing any more vile letters you don't honestly mean, okay?" Evan jokingly advised him.

"Okay." Richard laughed.

"I'll let you go. Have a good day."

"You too, Evan. And thanks. You saved my life, man."

Evan hung up, feeling much better about last night, hearing Richard say that he'd saved his life. In a very small, but significant, way it almost seemed kind of like a make up for Sam. And if so, surely that had to be God, not the devil, working.

Evan next phoned Laurel, hoping to find that she was all right.

"Hello," her father answered.

Evan immediately considered hanging up.

"Hello!" Parker repeated.

"I'd like to talk to Laurel, please," Evan spoke carefully.

"Evan Lawton," Parker guessed the voice. "You've got your nerve, calling here today after what you pulled last night."

Though Evan was sure Laurel's dad didn't know what really happened last night, something sure had him riled. "Please, can I talk to her?"

"Why?" Parker snarled. "After last night, why?"

"I'm sorry I worried you, taking her off like that last night."

"Then why did you? As if it wasn't enough for me to contend with, seeing my daughter leave with you, but your driving at night in the dead of winter when you hadn't even been out of your house in five years?"

"I've...been out a little lately," Evan credited himself.

"Are you crazy? Is that what you are?"

"No, I have agoraphobia."

"I don't know what else, besides that foolish car ride, that you did to my little girl last night, but whatever it was she came home crying."

"Crying?" Evan realized that last night had had a worse effect on Laurel than he'd thought.

"Wouldn't talk to me about it, she just went straight up to her room. Maybe *you'd* like to talk to me about it."

"I'd rather talk to her, please," Evan said.

Parker didn't say yes, didn't say no. But some shuffling sounds indicated that Laurel was coming to the phone.

Following an exchange of argumentative words between the father and daughter, Laurel came onto the line. "Hi, Evan."

Hearing her voice immediately brightened his world again. "I love you," Evan told her, like suddenly nothing else mattered.

"Me too," she said, no doubt limited to what she could say if her father was still there. "Are you okay?"

"Yeah. I was just calling to see if you were. Are you? Your dad said you were crying last night."

"I'm fine. It meant a lot, your leaving your house like that."

"I only wish it had been to a better occasion."

"What you did was wonderful."

Evan shook his head. "I'm not so sure about that. At least I shouldn't have involved you in it."

"It's okay. I'm glad you did."

"I talked to Richard a minute ago, told him I got his letter. He was happy about it. I think we're safe, Laurel. I mean, Howell doesn't know us and I don't think he saw my car. I think we're okay."

"I know we are," she said with the sound of a smile in her voice.

He smiled back to her over the line. "I'll let you go. Maybe we can talk later when your dad's not around. I think we've got more than ever to talk about now."

"Yeah, we do. Okay. Bye, Evan."

He had just hung up the phone when Mark came down the steps into the kitchen. They said hi to one another and Evan went about making the coffee.

"You're running a bit behind schedule this morning, aren't you?" Mark observed.

At least it wasn't a question about last night, Evan thought. "Yeah, I guess." He headed for the living room, pulling his pack of Marlboros from his shirt pocket.

Mark followed him. "It's not nine o'clock either."

"I'm not thinking about routine today." Evan sat on the desk chair and lit a cigarette.

"Oh yeah? What are you thinking about?" Mark sat on the couch, waiting to hear.

"And so therapy time begins," Evan said smartly.

Mark was already studying him in that psychiatrist manner of his. "Maybe. Yeah. Do you want it to? You look rather filled up with something. I'm here for you, Evan. We can sure talk if you'd like."

"And you have questions, right?" Evan supposed.

"A few, yeah."

"I don't want to talk about last night."

"Who said anything about last night?"

"It's not your business what I did last night," Evan said defensively.

"You mentioned it, not me. Anyway," Mark said, "I think I really understand about last night."

Evan swallowed hard. "You do?"

"Since you've been progressing so well in your phobia recovery, and had helped shovel out the garage, you got the urge to take your car out and see just how much farther you could progress in the outside world. That was very brave of you, Evan, what you did last night. But maybe you really ought to take it a little slower."

Evan nodded, relieved at what Mark thought the extent of last night to be. "Slower, yeah, I know. You're right, last night was a little too much for me to have handled."

"You did look sick when you came home. It scared the hell out of Tracy and me."

"Sorry."

Mark grinned. "Anyway, it's a good sign, that you're working so hard at this. Just be careful, okay?"

"Careful," Evan agreed.

"You're going to make it, Evan. I know that now. I'm very proud of you."

Proud. The word struck Evan hard. Like a knife in his gut. Making him want to confess everything, exactly how it'd been last night, to clear his conscience. But he couldn't. Because Mark certainly wouldn't be proud of him if he knew he'd committed a crime. And it had become very important to Evan what Mark thought of him. Having agoraphobia was one thing, being a criminal another.

Chapter 64

Lyle Thacher, the fix-it man from Scherman's Hardware, worked at replacing the broken window in Howard's back door while Tracy worked across the kitchen from him, cooking bacon and eggs. How shocking it had been when she'd arrived and learned there'd been a break-in the night before. Though Howard insisted he was all right, he was notably shaken. And though there was a bruise on his wrist where the burglar had hit the gun out of his hand, he refused to let Tracy take him to a doctor. All he wanted of her, after telling her of last night's incident, was for her to make him some breakfast.

Crime was a rare occurrence in Drendal. Lyle Thacher, a family man in his forties, ordinarily sweet and gentle by nature, was angered by it. "I think Mr. Howell should have shot the sonovabitch first off when he had the chance. That's what I'd have done. Wouldn't have asked no questions. Wouldn't have waited around for him to plan his escape, that's for sure. Not me."

As disturbed as Tracy herself felt over what happened, she couldn't get past the fact that Howard kept a gun in the house, let alone what he should or shouldn't have done with it. To her that seemed almost criminal in itself.

"The police dusted for prints last night," Lyle said, sounding like a detective on a case, "but Mr. Howell attested to the fact that the couple had on gloves. Smart, real smart of them."

"It's winter," Tracy reasoned. "People wear gloves in the winter."

"In the house? They knew what they were doing, keeping 'em on."

"I understand one of them was a girl." Tracy said, disturbed as much by that as by anything else in the matter.

Lyle measured and marked the new glass for cutting. "I'll tell you, none of our people from around here would've pulled something like this. I'm sure this Bonnie and Clyde pair were outsiders."

"Right," Tracy said with sarcasm, "like a couple of outsiders would choose our little town of Drendal to come do a robbery."

Lyle, on his knees by the door, shot her a sure look. "No, no...this wasn't just an accident. They came to the house of the richest man in town, didn't they?"

"Howard said they didn't take anything."

"Only because they got caught first."

Tracy was beginning to sense that there was a lot more to this than met the eye, but hadn't a clue as to what it could be.

"I'll tell you," Lyle continued mightily, "if a crime wave starts up in Drendal, I'm out of here. I'll move away."

"Crime is everywhere these days," Tracy stated. "No place is totally free of it."

"Then I'll have my gun ready, I'll tell you. Good and ready."

"You have one?" she asked, amazed at this whole different side of Lyle.

"Uh, well, no," he admitted, "but I'll be getting one after this and I won't hesitate using it, like Mr. Howell did, if anyone breaks into my place."

Tracy was glad when Lyle finally stopped ranting and raving and turned his full concentration back to his task. She, too, needed to concentrate more on her cooking.

She'd just barely begun to appreciate the quiet lull when Richard came bounding into the kitchen.

"Hey, I just got here and heard what happened. Man! Can you believe it?" He checked out Lyle's project first, then came over to the stove.

Tracy moaned. "You've *got* to find Howard a cook."

"Yeah," he said, frowning at her pan of sorry-looking eggs. Then he turned back to Lyle with greater urgency. "So I guess they didn't get away with anything last night. At least not as Howard could tell."

Lyle scowled, "They broke this window, entered illegally, hit Mr. Howell and fled his attempt to hold them. I'd say that's plenty to have gotten away with."

"Yeah, I guess," Richard agreed. "So Howard must have given the police a description of them. What was it?"

"A guy and a girl," Tracy said.

Richard pressed for more. "Right. But what else? Ages? Appearances?"

She frowned at the eggs that weren't doing too well, turned the heat down, flipped them over, frowned even more. "Howard was pretty nervous when I got here. Beyond what he told me, I didn't throw a lot of extra questions at him."

"The couple was young," Lyle offered. "And the guy, he was sick, or at least acted sick."

"Huh…weird…" Richard made of it.

"Very weird," Lyle agreed.

When Tracy moaned again at how awful Howard's breakfast was turning out, Richard came closer, took a fork and poked at the rubbery eggs in the pan. "Not good."

"Window's done," Lyle announced and started cleaning up the after mess of his job.

"Great," Tracy said, envying his accomplishment over her own. "Thanks. Leave your bill and Howard will send you a check."

Lyle Thacher jotted something on a paper and handed it to her. Then he picked up his tool case. "Oh, by the way, Tracy, how's that poor brother of yours doing? Shame, just a shame how he's got that god-awful problem."

Tracy received a harsh look from Richard. He no doubt resented the fact that while he'd only recently learned about Evan and his problem, the fix-it man from the hardware store had evidently known all along.

"Evan's doing all right," she told Lyle, not making it into any more or any less than that.

"Good, glad to hear it," Lyle responded sincerely. Then, upon leaving, he paused at the coffee maker on the end of the counter and picked up the lax cord. "Did you mean for this to be plugged in?"

*The coffee…*she'd filled the pot then forgot to plug it in.

Lyle laughed and took care of it for her.

Tracy turned to Richard, expressing a silent cry for help.

"Okay, okay," he said to her pitiful need. He took off his sport coat, hung it over the back of a chair, and snatched the spatula out of her hand. "You've sure made a mess of this, haven't you."

Tracy pecked a kiss on his cheek. "Thanks."

"Whoa…you mean this is all I ever had to do to win you?"

"You haven't won me," she said on her way out of the kitchen, "only my appreciation."

"Nothing like an appreciative woman," he affirmed. "Okay, I'm starting completely over with this breakfast. Tell Howard fifteen minutes."

Tracy found Howard sitting slumped at his desk, still obviously upset.

"Richard sort of took over the cooking," she said. "It'll be about fifteen more minutes."

Massaging his sore wrist, Howard gave a nod. "It was pretty scary last night."

She took a chair before his desk. "Please can't I call a doctor for you?"

"No."

"You really should be checked over."

"Except for my wrist, and my pride, I'm fine."

"Pride? Howard, pride's got nothing to do with this."

"I let them get away," he said, with a bad case of self-reproach. "I had them captive, then fell for their scam and allowed them to escape."

"I'm sure you didn't exactly *allow* them," Tracy made of it.

"Oh, but I did," Howard said stubbornly.

"Maybe you should see about having a home security system installed."

"Webber's usually here. He's my security. So's my gun."

"Webber wasn't home last night. And the gun was—"

"I took my eyes off them for just a minute." Howard's shoulders straightened and his voice hardened. "A minute. I'd know better next time."

It bothered Tracy, hearing him speak with as much fortification as Lyle had. "Like next time you'd shoot them right off?" she verified disapprovingly.

"I don't know. Maybe." Howard's temperament softened. "No, I surely hope I wouldn't need to. I mean…well, I hope there won't be a next time."

"There won't," Tracy said.

"Those two, they weren't like common criminals. That's what's so baffling. There was something…almost…likeable about them." Howard actually seemed more caught up with the thieves' personalities now than their crime.

"Likeable?" Tracy found that oddly interesting.

Howard smiled. "I guess it would have been hard for me to shoot them. Either of them. No matter what. I…I guess I'm saying that I'm glad they got away before I actually came to that point of decision. I guess I'm not as tough as I'd like to think I am."

"You said they were a guy and a girl," Tracy verified.

Howard nodded. "Can you belive it? I sure never knew girls were into this sort of stuff now days."

Tracy laughed. "Well, I guess girls are free to choose the same professions as men these days."

Howard laughed as well. Then went on analyzing, "Somehow I got the feeling it…it really wasn't a profession to them. More like a…a mistake. And the guy…he seemed to be very sick. Unless that was honestly just part of their scam. I don't know…I'm not sure what was real and what wasn't. Either they were very sincere or very good liars. Whichever…I…I honestly don't understand the whole thing."

"Nobody understands crime," Tracy said.

"No, I guess not." Rubbing his stomach now, rather than his wrist, he said, "Well, in spite of it all, I sure am hungry."

"Good."

"Don't know how I'm going to manage without Anthony. Webber will be back later today, but I'm afraid he doesn't cook."

An idea suddenly zapped Tracy like a bolt of lightning, causing her to jump out of her chair. "Howard! I think I may have found you your new cook."

"Yes, you told me, Richard."

"No, not him." She flapped her hands in the air excitedly. But she had to be careful. This was too important to babble off like some joke. She drew a deep breath, calmed her hands, smiled assuredly at her boss. "What would you say if I told you I know someone who can do gourmet cooking, or regular cooking, or whip up just about anything you could possibly request. And…who lives right here in Drendal."

At first Howard grinned, as if she *were* merely leading him into a joke. Then he turned serious and hopeful. "Who? Tell me who?"

"There's just this problem," she had to say.

"Can't be money," Howard sputtered. "You're certainly not going to tell me he charges more than I can afford. Are you? Does he?"

"The problem is…" Tracy sat back down in her chair, nervous and hesitant.

"Tracy, come on," Howard urged her, "just say it."

"The problem is," she continued, "my recommending this person to you could—"

"Could what?"

"Cost me my job."

"Tracy, Tracy…what on earth are you getting at here?"

"Howard, I know how you feel about honesty. And…and I've always been very honest with you in every way. Except for—"

"Whatever it is, girl, just say it."

She stood up again, feeling braver on her feet. She strolled over to the window, gazed out, turned, came back to face Howard. "I've worked for you for some time now and I've always felt very respectful and close to you."

"So what's this got to do with your recommending a cook?"

She rolled her eyes toward the ceiling. "Howard…I've got this brother.

"Brother?" he asked.

"I never told you about Evan."

"Evan," Howard said the name with puzzlement.

"I can explain. I really do have an explanation as to why I never told you about this brother who lives with me."

"Lives with you?" Howard seemed to stumble even harder on that.

She nodded. "The fact is, Evan is a terrific cook. And he—"

"Whoa! Back up!" Howard also got to his feet now. Not a good sign. "Let's take one thing at a time here. How many times, Tracy, have I said I wished you weren't so alone and had family around here? And how many times have you told me you had none? Now you're saying you do. Why, in heaven's name, have you kept this brother a secret from me?"

"That's a whole 'nother story."

"I'd like to hear it."

She didn't want to tell Howard the whole Evan story right now. She only wanted to get to the point of her ingenious idea before she lost her nerve. "My brother, Evan, he knows how to cook every single dish on your hotel menus. I've been collecting recipes for him from the Howell Hotel chefs."

"He steals my hotel recipes?"

"No, I do."

Howard was rubbing his head now rather than his wrist. "Tracy, I don't understand this. You suddenly seem like a whole different person from who I thought you were."

"I know. I'm sorry. My personal life's been difficult. Complicated. And I know that's not an excuse, but maybe, at least, it's a reason. "Evan...he's got agoraphobia."

"Fear of open places," Howard said.

Tracy was impressed that he knew the meaning.

"How long has he had it?" Howard asked compassionately.

"Five years. He hasn't left the house much at all in that time. I know I should have told you about him right off when I first came to work here. But besides this problem being hard on Evan, it...it's been stressful for me, too. And I just felt like I wanted, needed, an escape from it part of the time." She paused to breathe.

Studying her, Howard waited for her to go on.

"I wanted to be able to come to work each day and not have anyone questioning me," she continued, "on how Evan was, or how I was, or if his phobia was getting better or worse, and if it never got better what were we going to do. The problem, the problem, the problem...that I couldn't do anything about. It was difficult enough for me to face, without having to face up to it through other people all the time. I needed an escape from it. I...I..."

"Tracy...dear, Tracy," Howard spoke from his grandfatherly heart, "don't you know that talking about a problem can help free you from it? I thought you and I were close enough to share everything, anything, with one another."

"My way of dealing with this has been so wrong," she admitted.

The smile Howard gave her was full of forgiveness and new interest. "So now, this secret brother of yours, he's quite a master chef, is he?"

"He's wonderful, yes. It's kind of been his mainstay in coping with his situation. He also does food orders for people around town who pay him."

"Ahh, so there *are* other people here who know about Evan. And Richard? What about Richard?"

"I've managed to keep Evan a secret from him, too, until just lately."

Howard shook his head sympathetically. "What a hardship you've had, dealing with all of this."

"Not me. Evan."

"Both of you, I'm sure. And I'm so sorry that I didn't know, couldn't help. But now I must ask the inevitable question, what's the outlook for him?"

She didn't mind Howard's asking. In fact, she didn't think she would ever again mind anyone's asking. And she wondered if this new attitude of hers was because Evan was getting better or because *she* was getting better? She happily told Howard, "He's making progress lately. I think he's finally starting to work his way out of his phobia."

Howard nodded, smiled and fingered his mustache. "And you're suggesting to me now that he may very well be the new cook I'm looking for?"

"Yes," she said proudly. "Evan's been getting out of the house a bit lately. He's acquired some real determination, thanks to Mark. And I'm thinking that Evan's having a job to go to each day, something that he really loved doing, would be a great incentive for him. Could you give him a chance? Just a chance, Howard?"

Howard's look of consideration seemed like an almost yes.

"How about if you come to dinner at my house tomorrow night," Tracy suggested. "Evan could cook something special and you could rate him on it."

"You've already suggested this to Evan?"

"No."

"Don't you think you should ask him first?"

"I'll tell Evan someone, but not who, is coming to dinner. If he knew it was you, the prominent hotel man that you are, he might feel a little nervous. Only after the meal is cooked and ready to serve and you actually arrived, would he know it was you."

"And this brother, he'd be okay with the surprise you sprung on him?"

"Yes. Once the cooking is done, he'll be fine with it."

Howard was as amused as he was intrigued. "Well…okay…let's give this brother of yours a try. Richard certainly hasn't come up with a cook for me yet."

Richard soon came in carrying a breakfast tray. When he placed it on the desk, Tracy didn't think the food looked any more appealing than what she'd failed at earlier.

"Whoops," Richard said from his own closer observance, "I forgot the silverware." He took off back to the kitchen.

Howard was more interested in Tracy's dinner invitation than Richard's breakfast. "What time tomorrow night?" he asked her.

"Seven."

"Fine. I'll have Webber drive me."

"Good." Tracy decided that since he was so acceptant toward that, it might also be a good time for her to bring up another idea she had. "I have another suggestion, Howard. I'd really like to speak out to you on behalf of Richard's job here and—"

"No!" Richard returned in time to stop her. "It's okay, Tracy. Everything's cool, really."

She knew from their recent talks that it wasn't. And if he wasn't ever going to try and promote himself seriously to Howard, then it was up to her, as his friend, to initiate it. "Howard, whether you realize it or not, Richard's a very devoted—"

"It's okay!" Richard stopped her again.

She grinned at his concern. "You don't even know what I'm going to say."

"Don't say anything, okay? Please, Tracy, I mean it."

She wasn't going to say anything bad, if that's what he was worried about. Thus she continued to Howard, "How would you feel about Richard and me switching jobs?"

"Switching?" he questioned.

"Switching?" Richard echoed.

"Yes," she said, proud of her second brilliant idea of the day. "I've been thinking that maybe Richard would enjoy traveling and getting away for a change. And that maybe I might enjoy staying here in Drendal more. Why not let him be the field manager and me be…well, not your right hand man, but how about your girl Friday? What do you think?"

Surprised, amused, considering, Howard looked back and forth between his two employees. "You kids are both okay with switching?"

Though the plan was only moments new to Richard, he was already smiling and giving it a thumbs up. "Sounds good to me."

"Me too," Tracy said.

"Well, all right then," Howard gave his approval, "let's give it a whirl." He shook hands with each of them.

"Better eat your breakfast before it gets cold," Richard advised, motioning to the tray.

"Oh...yes..." Howard gave it another look, deciding, "You know, I'm afraid that with all that's been going on here this morning, the excitement's made me...well, I...I do believe I've lost my appetite. Sorry, Richard."

"That's okay," he said, staring dismally at the food he'd put so much effort into. "Can't say as I blame you. I admit I'm no cook. But I'll be a good field manager, Howard, I promise you that."

When Richard left the room, Howard told Tracy, "I'm very anxious to meet your brother, the cook. I can't wait for tomorrow night."

Chapter 65

▼

Mark looked out the window the next morning, finding that a measurable amount of new snow had fallen over night. With a rush of excitement, he threw on his jacket and hurried out the back door to grab a shovel.

It was cold and silent, and dark but for the soft throw of light from the kitchen window. It was nice. Who would've ever thought that some day he'd be shoveling so much snow. In Drendal, Minnesota. And enjoying it so much.

He shoveled just enough so that Tracy would be able to get her car out. Then he went back inside to have breakfast with her and Evan. *Damn*, he felt good. Invigorated from the fresh air workout and happily mesmerized from having finally spent an entire night together with Tracy. In her room. Her bed.

Mark was glad to see that Evan was making French toast. He was *so* in the mood for French toast. He exchanged a special smile with Tracy behind her brother's back. Then as they sat across from one another to eat, their stocking feet played footsie beneath the table. He felt as lighthearted as a kid. As sexually aroused as a twenty-year-old. More in love with Tracy in Drendal than he'd ever been with her in New York.

After she'd left for work, and he'd helped Evan clean up the kitchen, it surprised Mark that Evan offered to go out and help with the rest of the shoveling. "Great. But only if you really feel like it."

"I do," Evan assured him.

The guys worked side by side, scooping and heaving. Mark couldn't believe how one little town could continually get so much snow dumped on it. Maybe it snowed equally as much in New York but was so instantly plowed up and hauled away that you didn't notice. Here, in Drendal country, with a wide-span view in every direction you looked, it was much more discernible. Also, here in the Midwest, he was convinced that the snow and the air were by far more pure than anywhere else in the world.

Mark took special notice of Evan, his doing good with the shoveling, his managing his agoraphobia. "I'm proud of you," he told him.

Evan laughed. "You're probably just glad to have someone help you with the shoveling."

Mark also laughed. "Hey, I've done this whole driveway by myself, you know."

"Too much for one person."

Mark took an extra deep breath of the invigorating air. "I feel so good today, I think I could do ten driveways."

"Any particular reason as to why you're feeling especially good today?"

"Lots of reasons. Biggest one is that Tracy and I are okay again. Another one is the way you're starting to fight this phobia, Evan. And another is that here in this snow country I feel like I've really found my niche." He rammed his shovel hard into the snow, brought it out loaded, and tossed it off to the side.

"I thought your niche was writing books in New York," Evan said, drawing out his own shovelful of snow and throwing it aside.

"Maybe it's time to switch my niche," Mark stated.

Evan laughed, but warned, "I wouldn't want to see your life diminish to what mine has. Be careful of that, Mark. Sometimes, all of a sudden before you know it, a person's world can get too small and comfy for his own good."

"Yeah…I guess," Mark took him seriously.

"I have to admit…" Evan continued amidst his shoveling, "I really resented you at first. But now…I'm grateful for…for all the motivation you've given me."

"What about the other night, Evan?" Mark thought it was a sort of good time to ask.

"What about it?" Evan sounded defensive.

"Weren't you a little overly motivated?"

"W-what do you mean?" Evan kept answering questions with questions.

Mark threw another scoop of snow to the side. "I'm just not sure you were ready for doing what you did."

"I didn't…I mean…" Evan's words didn't go anywhere.

"That was quite a risk you took the other night," Mark said.

"Risk?" Evan was acting like a frightened child over this.

Mark hadn't meant to bring the guy down over taking his car out. "Evan, I'm just saying that maybe you need to work your way through recovery a bit more gradually, you know? Take things a little easier, okay?"

"Gradually, yeah, okay," Evan agreed.

"You shouldn't go doing what you did the other night until you're really ready."

"Right," Evan said, with a connotation Mark didn't get.

Laurel's car, with the pizza sign on it's roof, came off the road and up into the portion of driveway that was cleared.

"Kind of early for pizza, isn't it?" Mark commented to her as she got out and came stepping through the unshoveled area of snow toward them.

"No pizza," she said, looking more at Evan than at Mark, as though she couldn't believe seeing him out there shoveling.

"Therapy," Evan explained it to her.

Though she reacted happily, there seemed to be something of greater importance to her right then. "Can we go inside to talk?" she asked him.

"Sure." Evan dropped his shovel in exchange for her arm, signaling to Mark that he was taking a break. "This is weird," he said, "someone asking me to go inside rather than outside for a change."

"I'll save some snow for you," Mark called after him.

Chapter 66

▼

Evan and Laurel stomped their boots on the rug as they entered the kitchen, and Remington came to lick the brought in snow.

"Everything seems so different since the other night," Evan said.

"I know," Laurel said, as though their night of crime was just as heavily on her mind.

After several minutes of staring at one another in quiet confusion, they became involved in some passionate kissing.

"Nobody has to know about what we did," Laurel assured him.

"Now that the secret is out about our relationship, we have a new one to keep about our crime." Evan took a step back from her, feeling miserably irresponsible. "I should never have involved you in it, Laurel."

"Yes, you should have. It's okay." She closed up to him again and laid her head against his chest. "We're okay. You did a good thing for Richard."

"For Richard, yeah, but not for you. It was really dumb of me to take you with like that."

"No, Evan, no. I was glad you did. I was glad you came for me. I was glad to be there for you. It was kind of exciting."

He gave a helpless laugh. "You handled it well, I gotta admit."

"So did you. Do you realize how free you were that night, Evan? Do you?"

"What kind of freedom is that, putting both of us at the risk of being sent to prison?"

"It turned out okay."

"I don't like what I did, Laurel."

"Okay, so you don't like it, the break-in part," she said, "but you've also got to think of the good part."

"Good part?"

"Your proving that you can be free if you really work at it. Because you were that night. You were out there in the world, Evan. Oh, I know that you got sick in the process, but you survived it. You did, Evan. And hopefully next time you won't get sick at all."

"Next time?"

She smiled her cute little smile at him. "Your next outing won't be driven by a crime, of course."

"Well, there goes my motivation," he quipped.

"I think I might be able to supply you with some motivation."

Evan liked the seductive sound of her voice and the look in her eyes that went with it. "Okay," he said, tightening his arms around her.

She put up a playful struggle. "But not right now."

"Come on," he coaxed, "motivate me." He held her face tenderly between his hands, kissed her forehead of brown bangs, then her cheek, then her nose, then her...

"Evan," she sighed, giving in to him as his lips touched hers.

It didn't matter that they were standing in the kitchen with their jackets on, with Mark practically right outside the door and Remington brushing against their ankles, they wanted each other and claimed all they could from their brief moment alone.

"This...this isn't why I came over here this morning," Laurel eventually got around to telling Evan.

"Could've fooled me," he said with a laugh.

She giggled. Then shared another kiss with him before saying, "I wanted to tell you that what you did the other night made a good impression on my dad."

"The burglary?" Evan asked uneasily.

She giggled again. "No, you're coming over to our house and standing up to him the way you did. It's made him see you a lot differently."

"Like a normal person?"

"I think so, yes."

Evan shook his head. "I don't know, Laurel...your dad, he still seemed pretty riled to me on the phone yesterday morning."

"Your phone call threw him some, yes. But everything's been working on him since then for the better. Because later I could tell he was starting to seem a lot more accepting of you, of us. Really."

"But he doesn't know where we went that night or what we did, does he?"

"No, of course not. And he doesn't need to know. The main thing is how his attitude about you is changing."

Evan nodded. "I want your dad's acceptance."

"And mine?" she cooed.

"Especially yours," he said ahead of kissing her.

The blast of a car horn startled them and caused them to jump apart.

Evan opened the back door to see what was going on.

It was Mark, with his hand through his open car window, pressing the horn repeatedly. Seeing that he'd obtained Evan's attention, he let up and called to him instead. "Hey! Am I going to get any more help with this driveway or what?"

"Got to get back to work," Evan told Laurel, rather liking the sound of himself saying that.

"And I've got to get back to Dave's." She zipped her jacket and grabbed her gloves off the table.

They left the house together.

"Laurel," Evan called after her as she started toward her car.

She stopped and looked back.

"Do you want to come to supper tonight?" he asked. "I'm cooking a special meal. Tracy invited a surprise guest and told me I could ask you."

"A surprise guest? Who?"

Evan laughed. "I told you, it's a surprise. Even to me. I haven't a clue."

Laurel looked at Mark, standing there with a sly grin on his face. "I suppose you know."

His grin widened. "Yeah, but I'm not telling."

"Sounds very mysterious," she said back to Evan. "Okay. Sure. I'll come. What time?"

"Seven," he said.

She started walking again, then stopped and turned once more to tell him, "I'll wear a dress."

"A dress? Wow." Evan had never seen her in a dress before and the thought excited him. He watched her get into her car and leave, feeling totally mesmerized.

"Evan," Mark's voice came from somewhere outside of his dream world. "Earth to Evan."

Evan blinked and brought himself back to the here and now. He picked up his shovel and resumed working.

"Nice girl," Mark said of Laurel.

"Yeah. I've never seen her in a dress."

"Serious step, when a girl wears a dress," Mark warned him.

"Yeah." Evan was almost as scared as he was excited. Things were moving fast for him these days. He had a lot of new stuff to contend with. Though he wasn't getting a shortness of breath now, like he usually did at a time of panic, there was a strange whirling sensation going on his stomach and he…"Hey!" he said to the burst of snow that suddenly hit him in the face.

Mark had thrown it. Evan got even by scooping up his own handful of snow and throwing it back at him. In addition to Mark's laughter, Evan heard someone else's laughter in his head. It was Sam's laugh. And it was nice. It was kind of like maybe Sam was finally okay, at peace, and was happy that Evan was happy.

Chapter 67

▼

After Tracy returned from work that night and had freshened up, she set the kitchen table with a brown-checked tablecloth, everyday dishes, and paper napkins. A casual setting on which would be served an elegant meal.

"There," she said to Evan of her finished task. "You, me, Mark, Laurel, the surprise guest and...I also asked Richard."

A strange look came over Evan. "Richard? Why Richard?"

"I thought you guys were buddies now," Tracy said, confused at his reaction.

He shook some curry powder into the pot on the stove. "We are. I just don't see how he fits in with...with this mystery you've got going."

"He doesn't. I just asked him as a friend. There will be enough food, won't there?"

Before Evan could answer Mark came from the living room, pleasantly noting, "Hey, smells good out here."

Evan opened the oven door to check the chicken. "Hope it will taste as good."

"Anything that smells this good will undoubtedly taste as good," Mark assured him, taking a peek into the pot on the stove.

Richard was the first guest to arrive. Coming in the back door, he commended, "Nice shoveling job on the driveway."

"Evan and I thank you," Mark shared the credit with the cook.

"But," Richard laughed, "I'm sorry to have to tell you that it's snowing like crazy again."

"Oh no!" Mark and Evan said together in moans that quickened into laughs.

Tracy went to the door window to check it out. "It wasn't snowing when I came home a little while ago...but wow, look at it now!"

"So Richard," Evan began, "do you know who the surprise guest for dinner is going to be?"

"No," Richard had to say. "I was kind of hoping for Meg Ryan, but I suppose that's beyond the possible."

"Way beyond." Tracy maintained the mystery behind her smile.

"Anyway," Richard said, taking off his jacket, "I feel honored, having been invited to a dinner with a surprise guest, whoever it might be."

Tracy decided that okay, maybe she'd offer something to the suspense. Passing a look around at the guys, she began, "Actually, this is kind of a combination celebration tonight. And I guess I can tell you the first part now."

Evan, Mark and Richard stood waiting curiously.

"It's about Richard and me," she said. Before Mark could take it wrong, she clarified, "About our jobs. Something happened that—"

Evan dropped a spoon and it clamored against the linoleum floor. He picked it up, put it in the sink and shot a worried look at Richard.

Richard gave him some sort of little hand signal. To which Evan nodded and made some sort of signal back to him.

Tracy caught them sending messages, but had no idea what they meant. All she knew was that something was going on. Something. Distracted as she was, she continued with her news, "Anyway...Richard and I have, uh, switched jobs."

"Switched?" Mark questioned.

"Switched?" Evan echoed.

She nodded to the both of them, as well as to the already knowing Richard. "Howard's approved it. Richard's going to be the field manager from now on and I'm going to stay here in Drendal as Howard's assistant."

"You won't be visiting New York anymore?" Mark verified.

It disturbed Tracy that he was seeing this backwards.

Then with a mysterious grin he added, "We'll talk later."

Besides the strangeness of Mark, Tracy continued catching more strange behavior between Evan and Richard. Like Evan's pulling a folded paper out of his pocket and passing it to Richard. Then without even reading it Richard crumpled it and tossed it into the corner wastebasket.

She was almost to the point of demanding what was going on when Laurel arrived. And then everyone's attention turned to her and to the way Evan eagerly opened the door and swooped her into his arms before she even took her coat off.

"How's the snow?" Tracy asked her.

"It just started up out of nowhere," Laurel said, extending her look beyond Evan to the others. "Hopefully it'll stop soon. Hi, everybody."

The pizza girl took her coat off, gave it to Evan and he hung it on one of the wall hooks. Then as his eyes fully took in her loveliness, in a blue-print dress with a fitted bodice and flowing skirt, an adoring, awestruck smile lit his face.

When Evan and Laurel were through checking each other over, Tracy noticed how the both of them seemed to fixate on Richard. What *was* it about Richard tonight? This was definitely a night of more than one mystery. Not just Howard's coming to dinner, but something involving Evan, Richard and Laurel…the three of them. And there was definitely something with Mark.

Remington came prowling into the kitchen. He checked everyone out, then went upstairs.

Soon came the sound of another car pulling into the driveway. Evan was the first one over to the back-door window. "A limo! There's a limo out there!"

"No way!" Richard exclaimed, shouldering against him to also get a look.

Evan turned from the window, blinking his eyes with wonderment. "Jeez, Tracy, just who did you invite?"

"I know who," Richard said, leaving the window with notable alarm.

"Howard Howell," Tracy told Evan.

She watched Evan, Richard and Laurel exchange nervous looks between them. It was almost as if Howard's arrival had some connection to whatever it was they'd already been acting so elusive about.

"Come on, you guys," Tracy fretted, wishing she understood what was going on. "Why the faces? Can you please just act a little happier over this and—"

A knock at the door cut her words. Evan and Laurel slipped farther back into the room, while Richard froze in place beside the table. Tracy went to open the door.

Webber stood there in his straight, professional manner. "Mr. Howell is here, Miss Tracy."

He assisted Howard up the steps and onto the stoop. "I'll be waiting for your pick-up call, Sir."

"Thank you, yes, Webber." Howard entered the kitchen, removed his camel-hair coat, and wiped his shoes on the rug.

It wasn't the kind of coat you hung on a hook. Tracy put it on a hanger first and then onto the wall hook. "Howard," she began introductions, "this is my friend Mark."

The two shook hands.

"It's so nice to finally meet you," Howard told Mark.

"A pleasure meeting you, as well," Mark said.

"And you know Richard," Tracy needlessly motioned him out to Howard.

Howard smiled and gave Richard a handshake also.

Tracy motioned at Evan and Laurel, who stood partially in the alcove. "And these are—"

"You two!" Howard blurted before she could say their names. For some unbeknownst reason he seemed to know them and was infuriated by them. "No! I don't believe this! What's this all about? What's going on here?"

"Maybe you should tell *me*," Tracy suggested.

"They're the ones!" he said, pointing at the couple.

"What ones?" she asked, starting to feel a little sick. "Evan?" she zeroed in on him for the answer.

Evan had nothing to say. Nor did his girlfriend. The couple just stood there holding hands and looking scared.

"They're the ones," Howard repeated, more surely than shocked now. "The ones I caught in my house the other night."

"What?" Tracy shrieked.

"The ones I held my gun on," he said, "until he knocked it out of my hand and got away."

Tracy shook her head at the impossibility. "Howard, that's absurd. This is my brother Evan and his friend Laurel and—"

"I don't care who they are, they're the ones. The criminals. My criminals. And I come here to dinner tonight, finding them standing right here in your kitchen like some sort of bad joke."

"Whatever are you talking about?" Tracy said nervously. "This isn't a joke." She looked to her brother. "Evan?"

Evan swallowed hard, dropped hands with Laurel, and stepped over to the stove. "Just a minute, I have to turn my white sauce down."

Tracy wasn't feeling well at all. "Explain this to me!" she ordered him.

He picked up his wooden spoon, stirred the pot, and lowered the heat.

"Evan!" she screeched.

"I don't get any of this," Howard sputtered. "You say this is your brother, Tracy?"

"We didn't take anything, Mr. Howell," Laurel told him. Then scrinching her face, she added, "Of yours."

Getting no consolation from that, Howard again looked to Tracy for answers.

Having none, she turned her own questioning look on Mark.

Mark shrugged and shook his head, claiming, "This is the first I've heard of it. I don't know anything more about this than you do, Tracy."

When she next looked at Richard, his eyes shifted off in the opposite direction so fast it was like immediate proof of his involvement.

"What's going on?" she demanded of him, of anyone. "I want answers. Now!"

All she got was silence. A long stretch of awkward silence.

Until Evan, still stirring his white sauce at the stove, eventually volunteered, "There's only one."

"One what?" Tracy snapped.

"Answer." His look went from her to Howard and back to her again. "Laurel and I, we did break into his house the other night, but—"

"How could you?" Tracy exploded. "Why on earth would you do such a thing? I don't get it how you—

"Let him speak," Mark shushed her.

"It's like Laurel said," Evan continued, "we didn't take anything of his."

Howard asked, "Do I have the right to know what it was that you may have been *intending* to take?"

Evan lowered his eyes, as though he'd gone his limit and that was all they were going to get out of him.

"Tell us the rest of this, Evan!" Tracy said.

Evan gave her a look, but no words.

Richard surprisingly offered, "He was there because of me."

Howard, Tracy and Mark all shifted their looks to him.

"You're involved in this, Richard?" Howard exclaimed.

Willing but tense, Richard began like an accused on the stand. "I had this really bad day the other day. Tracy, you and Howard surely know the day. Before I went home that night I wrote out a brutal letter to you, Howard, about how unfair I thought you were to me and how I hated, really hated, my job. In the letter I so much as told you that you could just take my job and...well, you get the picture. I was blowing off steam. But after getting home and thinking about it for a while, I decided things really weren't as drastic as all that. I regretted having left that letter there for you to find when you came downstairs in the morning. Though I was feeling really dissatisfied with my job, I...I didn't want you to fire me, Howard, and I really didn't want to quit. I guess I wasn't quite sure what I wanted. Except that I did realize I didn't mean the stuff I said to you in that letter. Upset as I was, I phoned Evan and —"

"I went to retrieve it," Evan said.

"And I went with," Laurel added proudly.

"Oh, Evan, how *could* you?" Tracy wailed.

"It's my fault," Richard insisted.

"No, it's not," Evan said, drawing everyone's attention back to him. "He didn't ask me to go get the letter, he just phoned to tell me about it. He didn't know I went for it until the next morning when I told him."

"But I was the one who wrote it, left it there," Richard said.

As Howard's look switched from Evan to Richard, he became surprisingly calm. "You couldn't have talked to me, Richard? You had to write me a letter?"

Richard's eyes glimmered. "I'm sorry. It's just the way I felt at the time. But then I got over it, Howard, and I was truly sorry."

"And therefore he no longer wanted you to read it," Evan said. "So I went to retrieve it."

Howard's look returned to him.

"I'm sorry about that night, Mr. Howell," Evan apologized, "but it was something I...I just had to do. To help a friend, you know?"

A silence befell the kitchen. Until, in spite of everything, Howard gave Evan a fond smile and said, "I suppose I have to admire such an act of friendship."

"No," Evan said seriously, "you don't have to."

Howard turned to Richard. "You know I also admire honesty."

Richard nodded. "I know."

"If you'd have only been honest with me in the first place, in regards to your job dissatisfaction, none of this would have come about."

Richard lowered his eyes in shame.

Back to Evan, Howard continued, "And you..."

"I'm sorry about my brother," Tracy cut in, dreading what might be coming next, hoping to prevent it.

Howard held up a stop hand to her in order to finish saying to Evan, "You're the most unusual thief I've ever heard of. Somehow you made me care about you, despite the circumstances."

"Thank you," Evan said meekly, as if it were a legitimate compliment.

Howard rubbed his chin and smiled, hardly seeming angry with Evan anymore. "I...I wasn't exactly sure, at the time, if you were really that sick or I was really that dumb. Now that I know who you are, Evan, Tracy's brother, I realize it was your phobia."

"She told you about me?" Evan was surprised.

"Only recently," Howard said. "Before that, I'm afraid she was another one who'd been putting off the truth to me. Both she and Richard know how I feel about the truth, yet they both chose to keep if from me. That disappoints me."

"Yes, I did keep Evan and his phobia problem from you," Tracy admitted, "but I honestly knew nothing about his breaking in to your house the other night. Nothing, Howard."

"I'm sure," he said, giving her that much.

"I wouldn't blame you now, after what happened, if you changed your mind about considering him for that job."

"Job?" Evan looked back and forth between the two of them. "What job?"

Howard told Tracy, "Oh, I think I still might be interested in him."

"What job?" Evan repeated.

"You're not serious!" Tracy exclaimed to Howard. "I mean, surely you don't still want Evan to work for you after he broke into your house. Do you? I…I mean, you surely don't *have* to hire him now."

"What job?" Evan continued to ask.

"He certainly isn't a hardened criminal, by any means," Howard reasoned. "He's your brother. And that's pretty good substance to me. Also…mmm…if the way this kitchen smells is any indication of how good dinner is going to taste…" He stopped mid sentence to specifically address Evan, "How would you like to work for me?"

Evan took a deep breath, more stunned than happy. He looked to Tracy, then back at Howard. "Job? Like repairing your back door window?"

"No, no." Howard laughed at Evan's unsuspecting nature. "I mean like becoming my new cook."

"Cook?" Evan questioned, as though the word were foreign.

"I hear you're very good at it. I lost my cook and I desperately need a replacement. What do you say, Evan?"

A slow smile came over Evan's face. "I guess I do need a job."

"That's a yes?" Howard asked.

"Maybe you should have dinner first before considering me," Evan suggested.

Howard laughed. "Yes, all right, I suppose that would be the proper procedure. We'll discuss it further after dinner then, okay?"

"Okay," Evan agreed.

"He might have to sort of ease into all of this," Mark, in his doctoral manner, tried to prepare Howard. "He probably shouldn't take on too much too fast."

"I'll give him complete control of that," Howell promised. "He can ease into it on his very own comfort range. I'll not pressure him. And, whichever way he prefers, he can either live at my place or stay here and drive out to my place on his workdays. His choice."

As happy as Tracy was for her brother, she had some concern. Going over to him, where he was continually fussing at his white sauce on the stove, she asked, "Evan, do you really think you're ready for something like this?"

He gave her one of his irksome grins. "Guess I won't know till I try. All I can say is that I'm ready to try."

All of a sudden Remington came lickety-split down the stairs and into the kitchen on one of his wild-notioned sprints. It startled Howard, and as he took a fast step backwards out of the cat's way, he accidentally bumped over the wastebasket.

The crumpled piece of paper, that Evan had earlier given Richard and Richard had tossed into the trash, tumbled out across the floor. Remington eagerly pounced on it, like the start of a game, and took to batting it across the linoleum.

Richard made a frantic move to take it away from the cat. They tangled a bit before he succeeded.

"That wouldn't just happen to be the letter you wrote to me, would it?" Howard asked as if he already knew.

Richard squeezed the paper into a tighter ball as Howard started toward him. He looked scared, as if he thought Howard was going to snatch it away from him, read it and kill him on the spot.

Evan put his hands in the air as a signal for Richard to toss him the ball. Richard shot it across the room to him. Evan missed the catch and the ball went into the pot of white sauce. Howard burst into a fit of laughter, which got everyone else to laughing as well.

Evan dipped his long-handled spoon into the sauce and lifted out the gooey wad of paper. He offered it forth to Howard, as if he might still want it.

"No, thanks," Howard said. "That's okay. I had no intention of reading it anyway. The letter was evidently a mistake on Richard's part. Only a mistake. People are allowed mistakes. We've since rectified his job situation anyway. Haven't we, Richard?"

"Yes, thanks, Howard," Richard replied gratefully.

"Quite some cat, quite some cat," Howard said, observing a quieter Remington now. "Maybe I ought to get me one." He bent down to pet him.

The gray tabby rubbed against his ankles affectionately. "Mir-oww."

Getting back to the dinner preparations, Tracy took the water pitcher to the sink to fill it. As she stood there running cold water into it she leaned forth over the faucet to have a look out the window. She smiled, seeing that it was snowing even harder now than it was fifteen minutes ago. She turned to the others announcing, "I just want you to know that should this become a blizzard we've got plenty of blankets and, well, you're all welcome to spend the night here if necessary."

"I don't know when I've had so much fun," Howell said, laughing again. "I guess I've been such a recluse up there in the hills I've forgotten what the outside world can be like. Maybe I've had a touch of agoraphobia myself." He gave Evan a special look.

Evan cautioned him, "It's not a good thing, shutting yourself away."

Howard agreed with a nod.

Feeling a draft, Tracy turned to find that the back door was open a crack. She went to close it but saw that Mark was standing just outside, on the stoop, in the falling snow. She left the kitchen and stepped out beside him.

"What are you doing?" she asked, slipping her arms around him. He was wearing his heather gray sweater. How she loved him in that sweater. How she loved him in the snow. How romantic a spot this was right now.

Smiling that charismatic Costner smile of his, and putting his arms around her as well, he answered, "Just standing here. Enjoying the weather. And…sort of waiting for you to come out and join me."

"Like you knew I eventually would?"

"I knew, yeah. And I kind of thought…maybe…"

"Maybe what?" A fluttery feeling danced inside Tracy.

"It would be a good place for…"

"For what?" she prompted him.

"For telling you that I'm going back to New York."

"Oh." Tracy's heart sank fast and hard. For having totally, stupidly, misjudged this moment. "New York," she verified bravely.

Mark gave a long sigh ahead of saying, "I want to give notice on my apartment. Pack up all my stuff. Mainly my computer. And bring it back here. I mean, if you'll allow me."

"Back here? Allow?" Tracy had the flutters again.

"I like Drendal," he declared, as if with his own sense of surprise. "A lot more than I ever expected to. I think it could be a very inspirational place for me to write."

"To write," she said with a nod.

"And while I'm writing book three, I thought I'd get a job, some sort of job, in the area."

"A job," she said with another nod.

"And while I'm busy writing, and working God only knows where, and shoveling snow to no end…"

"Yes?" She blinked at the snowflakes catching in her eyelashes.

"I thought I could be a good husband to you, and a good brother-in-law to Evan, and a really good back-scratcher to Remington. Tracy…will you marry me?" He pulled her intended diamond ring out of his pocket and slipped it onto her finger.

Tracy looked at the ring. And then at him. Nothing stood in the way this time. With her heart as free as the falling snow, she smiled and told him, "Yes."

They held each other. And kissed. With snow falling upon them and around them. And when they opened their eyes again, they found Evan, Laurel, Richard and Howard all watching them through the back door window.

Correspondence to the author should be addressed to:
Marilyn DeMars
P.O. Box 28234
Crystal, MN 55428

0-595-32561-0

Printed in the United States
21753LVS00002B/91-162